UPSIDE DOWN
KINGDOM

UPSIDE DOWN
KINGDOM

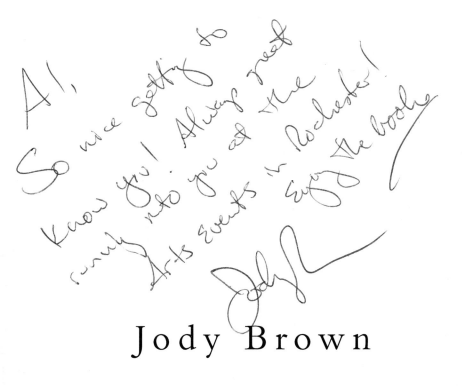

Jody Brown

To order additional copies of this book, contact:
Xlibris Corporation
1-888-795-4274
www.Xlibris.com
Orders@Xlibris.com
108992

For Verrick O. French,
the inspiration behind Mr. Watters,
& the most understanding and encouraging boss
any daydreamer could ask for

"In this, our upside down kingdom, just when you think you couldn't be further from God, there He is."

—Cliff Young, Caedmon's Call
Minneapolis, 2003

ONE

D rumbeats pounded out from the Circle. The sound went unheard in the restaurant but was unmistakable once I stepped outside. The alley was still puddled with yesterday's rain, and I crossed it unconcerned about the dirty pools and arrived at the next sidewalk having missed every puddle. I passed the corner beauty shop and walked up the next staircase, where I found bouncers Dante and Dennis sitting outside Tumult's doorway.

"Hey, Amy, I saw you walking up," Dante said. His dark Italian features did him justice even under the street lights. "Did they let you out?"

"Nope," I answered. "Today I let myself out."

They both looked impressed. "Congratulations."

"Good for you," said Dennis, who was built more like a blonde bear.

"Want a beer?" Dante tilted his head toward the doors behind him.

"Actually I came to tell you I'd be in the Circle. But now that you mention it, yeah, I could really use a beer."

Dante held the door open for me just as Shaggy's "It Wasn't Me" began to play inside. "Frank's at the front bar."

I made my way through the crowd, past the dartboards and pool cues, and sat down at the corner of the front bar. This spot got a lot of the wait-staff traffic so there was usually an unoccupied chair. Frank saw me, and I waited as he finished pouring a few drinks. Frank was one of those people who could be any age, from twenty-eight to forty-eight. He was quick-witted with a boyish face and his blue eyes showed happiness rather than life's pressures. But his light brown graying hair, slight potbelly, and the fact that he could make any drink, even the most obscure, from memory, made you think he'd been at this for thirty years.

"Hey, Blondie, did you just get out?" he asked me, thinking it's quitting time already. Frank didn't live by the clock, so time had lost all meaning to him.

"No, I left early. And for good," I declared.

"That's a call for celebration. What'll ya have?"

"Beer." I smiled. "Any kind. Surprise me."

He poured me something dark from the far tap and awaited my reaction. "Wow. Now this makes everything worth it. Frank, what is it about a cold beer?"

"Bubbles," he said, glad that I liked his choice. "This is the prize for making it through the workday. Even for those who refused to take one more step in a bad situation," he winked and started to walk away.

"Woo! What's a girl got to do to get a drink around here?" A woman stepped up to the bar beside my chair. "Two cosmos, please." She fished in her purse for a mirror and glanced toward me. Her dark skin was covered in silver sparkles and J.Lo perfume. "Amy! Well, look at that. How you doing girl?"

"Hey, Michaela." I smiled at the thin, six-foot brunette wearing a tight white blouse and pink miniskirt. *Michael by day, Michaela by night* she told me months ago when I met her, saying the first part in her original voice and the second in her more natural, feminine voice. "I'm just fine. What about you, got the night off?"

"Don't you know it," she opened the mirror and checked her appearance. "Ugh, I am so glad they finally caught that sniper. Can you believe it? All those people, my God," she shook her head. "I hadn't slept in weeks and it's causing these dark circles under my eyes."

"Everybody's got those. You'll blend in."

"Honey, bite your tongue! My makeup lady works all the way out in Tyson's and I was too afraid until yesterday to go out there and get more concealer. With those open parking lots? I don't think so." She lightly touched the skin under her eyes and closed the mirror. "And none too soon, either. See that man in the corner getting us a table?" She pointed to the right behind me. "That's Wayne. Isn't he delicious?"

I leaned my chair back to look. "Whoa," I said, seeing the tall, dark skinned and built man she pointed a pink nail at. "He looks athletic."

"I hope so." She smiled. "I saw Dante on the way in. He looks good."

"Yeah," I agreed, slowly becoming aware that I smelled like coffee. My tight outfit was cute, but my ratty ponytail coupled with the coffee smell weren't working for me.

"Well, just so you know, Juan over at DIK has his eye on Dante."

"So I've seen." I rolled my eyes. "Last time we were there Juan all but threw himself at him."

"Shameless, I know," she presented a folded bill to Frank. "Thanks, babe," she winked at him and reached for her cosmos. "Listen, Amy, you and Dante should come by the club again. We're doing bingo Sundays and Thursdays now."

I nodded and watched her cross the floor toward her date. "You look good, Michaela!"

"Don't I know," she said, accenting each syllable.

At the restaurant two doors down, the customers were getting restless. I'm probably on a smoke break, flirting with a busboy in a corner somewhere, goofing off by some and all means. *"This is coming out of the tip,"* they'll say. Of course it will.

They'll push cold coffee cups to the edges of the tables, toss napkins onto their plates, look around some more, bewildered, agitated. *"This is certainly coming out of the tip."*

They'll shake their soda glasses to clang the ice, grown up babies with rattles vying for attention. By now fingers will wave in the air, *"Miss! Over here, we're ready,"* they'll say to anyone carrying a tray or just walking by. *"Sir! Over here."*

"Wait 'til I tell my coworkers about this place tomorrow."

"Wait 'til I tell the folks at home the lousy service they have in the nation's capital."

They're going to miss movies, the beginnings of favorite TV shows, they won't finish the work they brought home from the office.

"Wait 'til I speak to the manager, that waitress won't know what hit her."

A breeze blew in from the door and woke me from my daydream. Frank was at the other end of the bar, pouring martinis. I finished my beer and left him a ten, knowing he hadn't charged me for anything.

"I'm gonna head up to the Circle," I told Dante as I stepped outside.

"Feel better?" he asked. "Are you sure?"

I nodded. "This is just what I needed."

A wave of people reached the top landing and Dennis started checking ID's. "Well, you're out of there," Dennis said. "Can't go back now."

Dante and I exchanged a look. "Of course she can go back," Dante laughed. He looked at me, "They probably don't even know you're gone."

"You could go back in and they wouldn't know you were gone?" Dennis asked, handing the last girl in his line her ID.

I laughed. "That's kinda the way that place works," I said. "Oh," I looked at Dante, "Michaela says they're doing bingo twice a week now. She wanted me to tell you."

"Cool. Who's the new guy she's with?" A commotion stirred from the alley and we looked to the right of Tumult where a guy was pushing his way through the crowd.

"Huh? Oh, his name's Wayne," I said, distracted by the movement. "I don't know where she met him. Maybe at the club."

Two police officers came running from the alley behind the pushy man, the lead officer shouting at their prey and plodding through the puddles as he continued the chase. A girl screamed as the cold water from yesterday's rain hit her legs.

The second officer stopped chase and leaned on Tumult's railing to catch his breath. Doubled over, he shouted into a hand radio, took a few deep breaths and started chasing again. The girl was wiping her legs and skirt with tissues that her friends handed her. "What a jerk!" she said, and her friends agreed.

The man being chased ran toward the movie theater's alley that led to the equally crowded Connecticut Avenue and probable freedom, but instead ran past the theater to what looked like a dark alleyway on the other side.

"What's he doing?" I asked. "Oh, he's done."

"Yeah, that was stupid," Dante said.

"That's no escape, buddy! It's a brick wall!" Dennis yelled. Laughter echoed up from the sidewalk below as everyone was watching the scene unfold. The police caught up to the runner, pinned him on the ground, cuffed and searched him. The drumbeats from the Circle started up again.

"Yeah . . . " I said as things wrapped up. "I'll be in the Circle if you need me."

Dante kissed my hand. "I'm done in two hours, but I get a break before that," he said. "I'll come find you."

Two guys and their dates ascended the stairs toward us. "What's going on over there?" one of the girls asked.

The three of us looked at each other, deciding which of us cared to say anything. Dennis said one word, "Drugs," in monotone, already bored with the scene. I descended the stairs, heading toward P Street and the drumbeats.

The air was filled with perfume and cigarette smoke, and even the wide sidewalk couldn't accommodate the night crowd. Many people just walked in the street alongside the traffic. I was in no hurry, so I meandered the sidewalk. The night air was chilly, but I was still so warm from work that it felt refreshing.

The sidewalk was lined with trees, each tree with a two-foot high wall of light-colored stone built around it. During the day people sat or lounged on the walls reading or talking on the phone. At night, the walls served as resting places for people out bar hopping. Tonight was no exception. Teenagers with skateboards sat on the long wall encircling three trees outside Tumult. Across the alley, the 20's and 30's crowd had taken over the walls surrounding single trees, all the way up to P Street. The sidewalk and alley were filled with groups of friends, from black-clad guys and girls with pink and purple hair to slightly older men and women both with chests bulging, dressed in their skimpiest or tightest clothes, to even older friends in jeans with tight and low-cut shirts, all the way up to the silver-haired couples elegantly dressed for expensive dinners. Here and there were a few suits, a few frumpy dresses, and the occasional man dressed as a woman. There were groups of friends, couples, male couples, female couples, pretty much everyone but children. I was a little surprised, this being the day before Halloween, that no one was in costume yet.

I passed the Upscale, watching the manager try to deal with the angry people I left behind. "Alright sir, what did you order?" I heard through the open door, and then the commotion started as the entire section realized someone was being helped. Some of them called the manager to them; others rushed toward him to get his attention. This being the first time I ever walked out on a job, I stopped to watch. The manager hadn't heard "Mr. Red Shirt's" order and asked him to repeat it. At the same time two more malcontents approached from his left flank and started yelling their version. Somebody dropped a tray of glasses in the back of the restaurant, an hourly event met with cheering at the Upscale, and the confusion was only getting started. Part of me, the responsible part, wanted to go back in there and finish the job I'd started. That part even felt bad for the people I'd left behind.

But then I spotted my tray, still on the coffee girls' table where I'd left it. I was finally on the outside looking in again. I'd come full circle, and going back in there was the last thing on earth that I would do. I willed my feet to keep moving. I heard, "Has anyone seen Amy!?!" just before walking out of earshot.

The drumbeats were getting louder as I approached the Circle and I found the drum guy at the Metro entrance banging away on his buckets. He worked up a distinct rhythm using buckets of various sizes that he wheeled around from corner to corner in a liquor store cart. You could recognize his sound from blocks away, especially when he worked in his signature blasts from a lifeguard whistle tied around his neck. I stopped and watched for a little bit, bouncing to the beat with the rest of the crowd. A few drunken people stepped up to dance and the drum guy paced his beat to their movement. When they started falling on each other, I decided to move on.

I crossed into the park, which was easy this time of night because the circle traffic was nearly at a standstill with bar hoppers and cabs bumper-to-bumper. Dupont Circle boasted a park in the circle's center, with a fountain and trees, benches and grassy spaces. It was a gathering place for all types of people, for good or ill, twenty-four hours a day while the traffic circled around. The neighborhood surrounding the park was also known as Dupont Circle, gay capital of Washington D.C., and a sort of happenings hot spot. There were plenty of tourists by day, but the nightlife was full of people who went out to see and be seen.

When I first debated living in Washington, D.C., I was given specific and strange warnings about Dupont Circle. Specifically: "Stay out of the park, especially at night. You'll probably get shot." And strangely, rumors warned of cross-dressers wandering the Dupont streets, and of drag races on certain holidays. That was men dressed as women running toward a finish line, not car races. These things were in addition to the usual crime, corruption, and prostitution of typical cities. Dupont Circle was a crazy place, with its own set of rules that would defy logic if it were anywhere else. But here it worked. It was Washington, D.C. like no one outside this town had seen.

I found an empty space on the west side of the fountain where I sat down to consider my options. It had been two years since I'd moved to the nation's capital. It was in my first year that, thankfully, my life went to shit. That's when things started getting good.

That's just about the time I'd heard of the Upscale.

TWO

T he person responsible for my arrival in Washington was the lobbyist Norm Watters, widely known and respected in his field, as much for his successful track record as for his kind demeanor. Watters & Company represented a number of clients, the biggest of which was a trade association made up of department stores—anybody with something to sell and employees to pay. Department stores still had money to burn at the turn of the new Millennium, and that definitely got the attention of Congress.

"We handle all the finances for the association," my new coworker Chad instructed. "Anything from membership dues to office overhead to the lobbyists' payroll."

"When do the lobbyists come in?" I asked.

Chad laughed. "They don't. They have their own office, on the Hill. I've been sent over here as Watters' right hand man, to assist his own clientele separate from the association. It's a big step for me, for my career. And I don't intend for anything to screw it up. Got that?" he stared up at me. Chad was in his late twenties, portly, and about eight inches shorter than me.

"I'll do my best," I said, trying not to be so tall.

The office was beautiful. The building itself was a historic landmark, a few blocks from the White House. The lobby was wide and filled with white marble. We entered our office space through a grand cherry door that locked behind us automatically. All of the office spaces were located in the corners of the building, so we had plenty of windows and lots of light, antique cherry and mahogany desks, and spotless, plush carpets in cream and forest green. It was a magnificent place to call my workplace.

Chad continued talking, "It is also our job to deal directly with the association's membership to gauge their company needs. We relay those needs to the Hill office, so that the lobbyists can do their thing with Congress. They relay their progress back to us, and we translate it out of Hill-speak and into regular human English in our monthly newsletters to the association. Ms. Ashe, why do you have that look on your face?"

"Oh, I'm just not sure why the two offices."

He sighed. "*You* work for Watters and Company, first and foremost; the association has their own office. Besides that, the lobbyists spend most of their days and evenings away from their office, 'showing the flag.' This way, retailers can call over to us and always reach someone. Make sense? Good, now let's get to the newsletters. You did say you had a job before this, right?"

"Yes. I worked for the University while I finished my degree."

"Well then, this should be no problem for you. Open this link, and . . . Here, from this page hit the toolbar, right click, bring in data from the main page, bop, bop, bop, and save it with the other docs, got it?"

"I think so . . . Wait, what did you hit to pop the data in?"

"Come on! Weren't you listening at all? Fine, we'll go through it again . . . Toolbar, click the arrow, then bring in the data," he banged the mouse and keyboard. "Got it this time, Ms. Ashe? You know, there's a lot that I need to teach you today and this is just the first thing on the list. I was here late last night *making* the list so we'd start with the easy stuff first. If you can't get this *child's play* then maybe you're not the right person for this job."

"No, I think I got it now. I missed a step because I was writing notes."

"So you're an expert then? I don't know why I bother teaching you. *You* know everything. You worked in an *office* before, right? I mean, you weren't working at a college bar?"

Thankfully, Chad wasn't my boss. Mr. Watters was a pleasant man in his early sixties who had been at this lobbying business long enough that virtually nothing got him down.

"When does Mr. Watters come in?"

Chad laughed. "It's August," was all he said.

Despite Chad, the job really was a nice way to make a living. I had a parking space downtown, a gym in the building that was open twenty-four hours a day, and an excellent health plan.

My first Friday in the office, Chad invited me to lunch at Capitol City Brewery. This being the first nice gesture Chad had made, I didn't want to pass it up.

We walked a few blocks in the heat and the sunshine to Cap City, which was buzzing with the downtown lunch crowd. They brew their own beer there, but we stuck to cokes—mine regular and Chad's diet.

Surrounded by stainless steel beer vats and chalkboard beer lists suspended from the high ceiling, Chad and I settled in for our industrial business lunch. "So how do you think you're doing in the office?" he asked after we'd ordered our sandwiches.

Ah, the dreaded question. What does anybody think? What he really meant was, "What do you think my opinion of you is?"

"Well, I get more and more comfortable every day," I lied. "And I've been thinking of ways to alter the newsletters a bit." Chad suddenly gave me a sharp look and I knew I'd said something wrong. I quickly explained myself, and tried not to use the word "uh."

"I don't think we need to change anything." Chad dismissed.

"Yes, but the feedback I'm getting seems to support a couple changes."

"What feedback are you talking about? Have you been talking to the members?" Chad and I had agreed to let him handle the calls from members while I handled the paperwork aspects of the office. He did "lobbyist duties," whatever those were, and I did the "grunt work," the bill paying, filing, and typing.

"Well, yes. Yesterday when you were out at lunch the phone rang a couple times."

"You were supposed to transfer everyone to my voicemail. Can I not trust you in the office by yourself while I'm out at lunch?"

Chad went for two-hour lunches every day. "I did transfer everyone, but some people talked to me. Nothing major—I guess you'd sent out a memo that there was a new person on board? They just wanted to put a voice with the memo."

Chad freaked. "You are not supposed to be talking to the members! I'll be sure to bring this up with your boss." Our food arrived at that moment and I thanked the waitress, happy to have a distraction. Chad kept going anyway, his voice getting louder by the sentence. "You may think I was at lunch with my girlfriend, but I was getting the Senate's opinion about our new bill. And here I find that while I was gone you are 'chatting it up' with the members."

"Did you need anything else? No? Okay," the waitress said without pausing for any response. She put her hand on my shoulder briefly and walked away.

"What's her problem?" Chad asked.

I needed a change of topic. "So, um, did the Senate have anything good to say?"

Chad sighed. "It's really none of your business. Connie's information is between me and the Hill office. *We're* the lobbyists here."

Right. I concentrated on my sandwich for a while. "So, how's Connie?"

He immediately brightened. Chad loved to talk about Connie. "She's doing well. You know, if you would have told me two years ago that I'd meet this smart, beautiful, and funny woman I wouldn't have believed you. I'm thinking about proposing . . . "

"Well that's really great," I said.

"Yes, but we're both so committed to our jobs that there hasn't been a good time to plan it out."

If it would help him mellow out, I was all for it. "Well, don't keep her waiting or she might not know you're serious."

"So now you're the dating expert?" He actually said it nicely, but his word choice made it sound worse than it was. He was a real piece of work, but I was getting used to him. After a while, he dropped the condescending "Ms. Ashe" tone with me and just started calling me Amy.

Chad wasn't my only major adjustment. My commute into the city every day wasn't the best, but at least it was time outside the office. Route 1 was bumper-to-bumper and had stoplights every block of the way into D.C. During the hour-long trip into the city, I never once used the gas pedal since simply letting my foot off the brake here and there would drift me into the city with the other traffic. But the trip ate up gas anyway and I'd be at the gas station every three days. This was not an affordable way to spend my time or my money, so I tried taking 201, more of a highway-like drive. I could cruise along for nearly fifteen minutes, giggling to myself at how early I was going to get to work when without warning, roadwork where 201 becomes D.C.'s New York Ave made the traffic utterly stop. The road was not quite as wide as two lanes at this point, though it was painted to look like two lanes and cars sped along trying to pass one another anyway. The road was enclosed by jersey walls—concrete half-wall barriers where the white lines should be—so any false move and it was bye-bye paint job. As an added degree of difficulty, the road surface tilted from left to right and back again at odd intervals. Cars would lean right and suddenly shift to lean left while drivers tried to guide the vehicles straight to avoid the barriers. After that obstacle was a straight stretch where the flow of traffic would speed up to fifty miles per hour and then stop without warning at a stoplight hidden on the other side of an underpass. If the brakes held, I had nearly a half-hour left of bumper-to-bumper driving to reach my office fifteen blocks away. I usually arrived sweating through my blouse, so I started wearing a T-shirt and changing into my blouse when I got to work. But it would still take another half-hour before my hands would stop shaking.

I would drive Route 1 on Monday, cursing at myself as I sat in traffic going nowhere and would vow to take 201 on Tuesday, which would leave me cursing and shaking back to Route 1 again on Wednesday. I alternated like this for a couple weeks, each day believing my course would suddenly prove clear and smooth and fast. But soon I started to get good at the drive, believe it or not. Route 1 was never less than frustrating, but it was clockwork: after an hour of coasting and braking I'd be at work. And though I never drove 201 without experiencing at least one moment of sheer terror behind the wheel, I usually managed to get those moments down to one per trip.

But the daily grind proved too much for my old car, which grunted and groaned and threatened to give out on me.

The Metro at College Park was only five minutes from my temporary apartment, but the train ride into the city took nearly as long as driving because the track wasn't yet finished. Each train line is color coded, but while construction ensued on the Green line, Green trains shared the Red line. It allowed for Maryland commuters northeast of D.C. to ride the Metro into work nearly two years before the completion of the Green line. The down side was that the shared track meant Green trains would stop in a long tunnel and wait their turn between Red trains. It was normal but spooky, and people would start freaking out. But the hour and a half daily round trip in high heels on a stuffy and overcrowded train car that swayed back and forth and stopped in tunnels, this was actually not the worst part of my day. That part was still reserved by Chad.

The Metro delivered me to the mercy of Chad every morning, who yelled most of the day—about the morning traffic he'd encountered, about the lady in his building who hogged the dryer, about some minute flaw in my work, and about the other applicants he wished would have been hired instead of me—until finally the Metro would haul my sorry self back to the apartment at night. Everything set Chad off. One day it was the Polar Water man that did it.

Chad started to rant that if D.C. would take better care of their pipes we wouldn't have to buy bottled water. "The pipelines are the originals put in when the city was first built."

"You don't say? I didn't know that," the water man said cheerfully.

"Of course not," Chad started.

"Well, thank you for the water!" I jumped out of my chair to escort the water guy to the door. "We'll see you next month at this time, right?"

"Yeah," he nodded to me, but it was too late, Chad was coming up fast behind us.

"I went to GW, that's why I'm so educated about these things. I guess they don't teach you that in delivery school. Just a bunch of crack-heads teaching other crack-heads how to drive, isn't that right?" Chad's new word was *crack-head*, and everyone was one, from the water man to the clients who called and even Mr. Watters was a crack-head at times.

"Well, thanks again! I don't want to keep you from your deliveries," and I let the man out the door. He looked back at me as he walked down the hall and I mouthed, *I'm sorry* to him.

"Amazing how they let such people into offices," Chad remarked. I wasn't sure which of us he was talking about. "I'll be in my office," he sang as he walked away.

THREE

I scrutinized my map. "These state streets that don't seem to have any rhyme or reason to their directions. The numbered streets go north and south, that's easy enough, and the letters go horizontally . . . "

"East and west," Chad corrected. We were on stake-out in his car one sunny afternoon instead of sitting in the office.

"Right, east and west."

"D.C.'s got four quadrants, based on where you are from the Capitol Building."

"The quadrants make a lot of sense to me, actually. And some of the states go on diagonals from the Capitol, I think I've got those, but what's with these circles?"

"Once you drive around for a couple months you should figure it out. It only took me about a week, but that's me," Chad said. Chad had driven us through "Embassy Row" on Massachusetts, along the business-lined K Street, and up Connecticut Avenue as I traced our route on my map. I saw brownstone buildings, rows of townhouses, and gothic apartment buildings with green courtyards lining wide Connecticut. We'd crossed a large bridge and passed the zoo before Chad took a right on a random side street and stopped the car in front of a small, white house. "That's Connie's house," he'd said.

"Yep, I spend a lot of my nights here, for five years now."

I frowned. "I thought you dated Connie for two years."

"No. I think I would know my own relationship. It's been *five*. Someone else's car was here the other day. Probably the other guy she's seeing, which fucking sucks!" he raged. "She must think I'm stupid!"

"You don't know whose car that was," I reasoned. I was getting good at calming his tantrums.

"No, I don't. But I will. I know someone who works at the DMV from back at my GW days. We used to get drunk and smoke up together. She said she'd look it up."

"I don't think they're allowed to give out that information," I said.

"People aren't allowed to do a lot of things that they do," he scoffed. "She'll help. I have friends all over this town," he laughed. "Nobody does anything that I don't know about." He stepped on the gas and kept to the side streets and I could no longer follow our location on the map. After a few blocks of laughing to himself, Chad slowed down again and seemed to calm down. "Watters has agreed to our changes for the newsletter," he said matter-of-factly.

"My idea? You told him?"

He cleared his throat. "You mean 'our' idea, remember both of us brainstormed your suggestion and came up with this better idea."

I shook my head. "No I talked to the members and they told me specifically . . . "

"Yes, I was sure not to mention to the boss that you were talking directly to the membership. I don't think he would like to hear that the office poet was chatting it up with the membership. You're not politically minded, Amy. This is Adam's Morgan," Chad said on a random residential street where he stopped the car. "I live here."

"That's your house?" I asked, seeing the three-story house.

"Yeah. It's broken up into apartments of course, but it's the best neighborhood in D.C.—if you want to party. But it's pretty expensive to live here. You would do better on your salary to live in a less sought-after neighborhood. What's your timeframe?"

"Hopefully soon. I'm staying with my friend's cousin at the moment. I got the job here and it was all a bit last-minute. But the sooner I get my own place the sooner the poor girl gets her couch back."

We went in so Chad could check on his cat. "See the bars on the windows? Every place here has them; it's required."

I decided to stay close to the door. It wasn't too hard; the front door opened to his bedroom. The door cleared the edge of his bed by inches. "This is what you get for $800 a month. Everywhere in D.C. is expensive unless you live in a really bad neighborhood." Off to the right was a hallway-size kitchen that led to the closet-size bathroom. We didn't stay there long.

We took 17ᵗʰ Street south, passing more bars and restaurants, and eventually made a right onto P Street. "This is Dupont Circle," he said as we drove past rows of old townhouses with front steps lined with plants.

"It's beautiful," I said. I was trying to ignore Chad at this point, but Dupont Circle really was beautiful. "Wow, I would love to live here."

"Well, everybody in Dupont is gay," Chad said. "And see that park in the middle of the circle? Stay out of there, especially at night. You'll probably get shot."

Apartment searching was taking its toll. Because of my commute, I ruled out getting another place in Maryland. Everywhere was expensive, be it D.C. or Virginia, and single bedrooms were at the top of the price list. For a week, I entertained the thought of renting a two-bedroom, and finding someone to rent the second room from me. If I could share office space with someone like Chad, I could get along with anyone. But then I got an offer from a girl named Beth—a friend of a friend of my current roommate—to live in a house with three or four other girls. August was winding down, and Chad assured me the days of stakeouts at Connie's place and lunches at Cap City were coming to an end. Once Congress returned in September, it would be work, work, work. I really needed to get my living situation settled. I decided to call Beth as soon as we got back to the office.

"I'm so glad you called! Patty said you might!" Beth said. She had a light, breathy voice, and did most of the talking. "There will be five of us now, including you. I've been talking to the other girls and I let it slip that you might be interested in living with us. Everyone's excited to meet you! I'm so glad this is going to work out. Okay, there are these housing guides near the Metro that should help us a lot. I'll meet you at Ruby Tuesday tonight, at Pentagon City Mall, around seven? I've got shoulder-length dark hair, and uh, a George Mason T-shirt. See you then!"

She sounded nice enough. And just as she'd said, outside the Metro entrance I found housing booklets stacked in a newspaper rack right next to the Spanish papers, and they were free. I'd never noticed them before. With one phone call, I'd found roommates and two *TV Guide*-size directories to housing in the nation's capital. Things were looking up.

Even Chad found a way to be in a good mood for a change. He'd found the owner of the car parked in Connie's driveway, some Jennifer-something. He spent the rest of the week alternately bursting into song and dance numbers—voice straining to hit all the notes—and marveling that he could be a detective if he wanted to be.

"I could, you know," he said. All day he'd been interrupting my daydreams of finding a new place to live with new and fun friends. "I could be a great detective, if I weren't already a great lobbyist. Did you know we have new neighbors next door?" He didn't wait for a response. "I saw this odd man in the hall yesterday so I asked him what his business was. We don't need vagrants and crack-heads wandering in our building for crying out loud. Turns out he's one of the employees of the travel agency that's moving in next door." Chad spouted off facts like he was on *Dragnet*. "Travel Mania. They have four employees, and you can't miss this guy. He has this wild silver hair, and get this, he's gay. But I'm cool about these things. Next trip I take, he'll book it for me. A gay travel agent? How chic."

I soon ran into our new neighbor on my way to the mailbox. "You look tired, darling," the man said as I pressed the elevator button for the main floor.

"Oh . . . yes," I snapped out of my daydream and looked up at the silver-haired man beside me. "I'm house-hunting and it's taking its toll."

"That it does, in this town," he said. He put his right hand to his chest, "I'm Beau," he said and extended the hand to me.

"Amy." I smiled, shaking his hand. "You're in the office next door to me, the travel agency, right?"

"Word gets around. Yes, that's me. We're expanding from our Virginia office." He put the back of his hand beside his mouth and said in a low voice, "I almost liked it better over there. The commute was so much easier than getting into the city every day."

"You get used to it," I offered, wondering what seemed out-of-place about this guy.

"Honey, it's nothing I want to get used to," he laughed. "I have enough drama already without dealing with maniacs in suits on the road." Then it hit me: he wasn't wearing a suit. He was at work, looking as relaxed as though he'd just stepped off a beach. Beau had on a floral short-sleeved button down and wrinkled khaki shorts, with flip-flops, no less. And he was tan.

I thought back to my first few days in the office and how it had been fun for me to get dressed up for work. But I quickly tired of ironing my clothes, buying new stockings every other day, and my feet seemed to cringe getting into my dress shoes. Some days I got the feeling that I was a little kid at Thanksgiving suddenly sitting at the grown-up table. But I was getting used to it, especially since everybody else was dressed like me.

And some days a sharp outfit was the only armor I'd had against Chad's negativity.

"Where are you moving to?" Beau asked. He leaned forward and pressed the button for the parking garage.

Still moving things in . . . That explained his clothes. "Oh, uh, Virginia. If we can find a place."

"Virginia's fabulous," he said. "I moved there fifteen years ago and I love it." The elevator doors opened to the lobby and I stepped out. "Good luck with your search," he said.

I turned back to him, "Thank you. It was nice meeting you."

He tilted his head to the side and winked at me, "Likewise," and the elevator doors closed. For a gay man, he seemed to be flirting with me. The thought quickly passed as my mind went back to my housing dilemma.

Beth and I had had seen every smelly, rat-infested apartment and house that was advertised. Just when I wanted to give up, she'd get a burst of energy, and vice versa. Finally, we found a house off King Street that could accommodate all of us, and it was well within budget when we divided the rent five ways.

Beth called the other girls to tell them we found a place, and they all agreed to move in, sight unseen. The landlord allowed Beth and me to sign the lease and move in over Labor Day weekend, and the others could sign the lease when they got into town.

The new house in Virginia was deceptively small from the outside. Inside, though, the main floor boasted a large living room/dining room combo, decent kitchen but without a dishwasher, two bedrooms, and a bathroom. The basement was a maze of hallways and rooms. The stairs led down from the kitchen into an area nearly as large as the upstairs living/dining room. We came to call this the Rec Room, even though we never put any furniture in it, and eventually used it as storage. Off to the right was a winding hallway that opened to a common area that stood between three bedrooms and a basement bathroom.

To the left of the Rec Room was the laundry room, which led to the back door on one side, while the other side housed an oil tank to supply our heat. Behind the oil tank was a dank, unused space, about the size of a small bedroom. There was no lighting back there, and the walls were unfinished. On the first cold day of the year we would run out of heating oil, and I would crawl back there. Flashlight in hand, all I really saw were shadows of spiders moving in their webs.

There were closets at every turn in the basement, and a hallway that led nowhere, from the back door away from the laundry room, around a bend, and into nothing. I'd seen my share of secret passageways on TV, and always thought them interesting. But this house was downright spooky.

"Hi, I'm Tracy," said a voice behind me, causing me to just about jump out of my skin. A girl with frizzy, dark hair and freckles had followed me into the hallway to nowhere.

"Oh, hi . . . "

"You're Amy, right? You and Beth have the bedrooms on the main floor, right? Are you going to come to our worship center with us? That would be a lot of fun. Everyone's already excited to meet you. Have you met Tiffany yet? Tiffany, come out here and meet Amy! She's trying to hang posters on her wall. I told her I'd help . . . There you are. Tiffany, this is Amy." A taller, quieter version of Tracy appeared in the hallway. "I told you I'd help you with those posters," Tracy told her and then looked back at me, "Amy, we always have lots of activities going on at the Center. Don't we?" she paused for Tiffany to agree. "And since we're all just getting back into town again—Tiffany and I just got back from the *extended* leadership program—I'm sure Beth told you all about it. But if you want to hear more, I can certainly pop up to your room and fill you in and help you unpack and everything. Right, Tiff?"

"Oh, thanks, but don't worry about me, I can handle it. There's not much to unpack."

"What's going on over here?" A tall, athletic girl with red hair appeared with a box in her hands.

Tracy spoke up. "Oh, hey, Karen, come and meet Amy. Do you need help bringing things in or unpacking?" Tracy offered.

"Oh, thanks, I brought most of it in already," Karen said. "This stuff is just lesson plans and other work junk. I'm not even going to take it out of the box."

"Karen's a teacher," Tracy informed me. "We all met at the leadership program."

"Well, I can't teach in Virginia yet," Karen said. "I'm not certified. But while I'm waiting, I thought I'd check out some admin jobs over at the university."

"Oh, we can help you with that. Tiffany and I go to school there."

"That would be great, thanks," she said. "Amy, is that your SUV in the driveway?"

"Yes, I'm sorry, am I blocking you?"

"No, you're fine. It's very nice. Shiny—is it new?"

"Yes! Thank you. I just got it. Now I know I shouldn't break down as I ride in to the city every day."

"Very cool. Well, nice meeting you. I've got to get my room situated," Karen said.

"Come on, Tiff, let's get your posters up," Tracy said. "See you later, Amy."

From this initial meeting, I mentally nicknamed Tiff and Tracy Tweedle Dum and Tweedle Dee. Karen seemed alright.

FOUR

I n September, Mr. Watters was coming in to the office more and more often. He would come in, praise all the work I'd done for him, point out any changes he wanted to make, and would leave it up to me how to fix them. I made fewer formatting mistakes when the boss was around, not because he signed my paychecks but because he let me think for myself, and that put me at ease.

"Amy, I'm going downstairs for some coffee. Would you like anything?" Mr. Watters asked one afternoon.

"Oh, coffee sounds good actually. I can make another pot," I started to get up from my desk but Mr. Watters held up a hand to stop me.

"Not necessary. I'll go downstairs. Be right back."

Mr. Watters was certainly not the stereotypical boss. Chad was definitely more demanding and griping. But when the three of us were in the office together, even Chad was much nicer to be around.

Mr. Watters had daily lunch meetings set up with Ted Harvey, a friend of his from way back, when the two had gotten their start working for a Presidential campaign. Now the owners of Watters and Company and Harvey & Graham, respectively, they shared information, threw business each other's way, and helped each other out whenever possible. This being the new Millennium, the phrase on everyone's lips was, "It's not what you know, it's who you know."

These Harvey-Watters lunch meetings had Chad in an uproar. He was sure Mr. Watters was up to something big with the retail bill, and was furious to be left out of it.

"I'm his chief lobbyist. I don't understand why I'm being left out of their 'boys club.' This is fucking absurd! Amy, where did they go this time?"

"Mr. Watters didn't tell me."

"You mean he set up his own lunch?"

"Yes, he does that sometimes. I'm sure he has his cell phone if you need him."

"Ha! Shows how much you know. I can't call to interrupt his lunch to ask where he is so I can join him. This is why he sets up his own lunches, because you're too incompetent. You just don't get it." Chad stalked off into his office and got on the phone. He emerged a minute later with a look of triumph on his face. "He's at the Carlyle Club. It's Ted's favorite place," Chad bragged. "Everybody knows that." Chad put on his suit jacket.

"What are you doing?" I asked.

"Hold my calls. If anyone needs me I'll be at the Carlyle Club," he said. "Better yet, don't hold my calls. If anyone needs me, they can reach me on my cell."

"I don't think you should crash a business meeting, Chad."

"Oh? And who put you in charge? If something is going on, as this company's chief lobbyist, I have a right to know." He took a folded piece of paper out of his jacket and tossed on my desk. "Type this up, will you," he said, and walked out the door. I dialed Mr. Watters' cell phone.

"Watters here," he answered after a few rings.

"Mr. Watters, it's Amy. I'm sorry to interrupt your lunch, but I thought you should know that Chad is on his way there to join you."

"Delightful, we were just talking about him," Mr. Watters laughed. "Thanks for the tip," he said, and hung up.

"Delightful?" I hung up the phone and looked at the paper Chad left. It was his "To Do" list, including things like "Pick up Dry Cleaning" and "Get Cake for Connie's Birthday."

Mr. Watters was clear on this when he hired me: he'd rarely ask me to run any personal errands for him and even then I had the option to decline. And those parameters went double for Chad. "You've got to be kidding me," I got up and tossed the paper back on Chad's desk.

Chad and Mr. Watters returned together a few hours later and announced Chad was being sent to Brussels on business.

"I have so many arrangements to make, Amy, that I'm going to need your help," Chad commanded.

"Okay . . . " I said, waiting for the punch line, but there wasn't one.

"I've got to be off now," Mr. Watters said. "My wife has tickets to something at the Shakespeare Theatre, so I'd best get home and pick her up."

Chad went into his office and called his parents. "Amy, get in here," he commanded. I found him with his feet up on his desk, phone to his ear, toying with a pen in his right hand. He put the pen down. "Hold for a moment, Mom," he said, "the assistant is here. Amy, what's this?" he picked up the To Do list. "I asked you to type this up."

"It's not work-related."

"Well, Watters assigned you to help me prepare for Brussels. I need this list typed so I can focus on other details of my trip."

"That's your grocery list. But if you insist, I'll ask Mr. Watters if that falls under my jurisdiction."

"You know what? Forget it. I'll do it myself," he said. I left his office and went back to my desk. "Oh, but Amy . . . " he called and I was right back in there again. "I do need you to trot next door and see if you can get initial prices on flights to Brussels for me. Flights leaving next Monday-ish. That's work related, right?"

I left his office for the second time.

"Ugh, it's hard to find good help these days," I heard him say to his mother. "That's what we get for hiring a hippie. Well, Liberal Arts major, same thing . . . Yes, it is, Mom. Anyway, about Brussels . . . "

I left the office and went next door. I returned a minute later. "They're closed. There's a sign on the door that says they'll re-open tomorrow morning."

"Am I the only one working?" he huffed. "You'll just have to try back in the morning."

"It's getting late, so I'm going home."

"Fine Amy, I have nothing else for you."

It was raining, which delayed my drive home nearly forty-five minutes. Why rain brought traffic to a standstill I would never understand. And the city had begun roadwork on Pennsylvania Avenue, a main east-west thoroughfare that everyone traveling south to Virginia had to cross. At least I-395 from D.C. to Virginia was a smooth road, unlike the Maryland roads I used to drive. But with construction on Pennsylvania backlogging and confusing motorists, accidents abounded. All I wanted to do was get home, kick my shoes off, and finish settling in. A cold beer was starting to sound perfect.

I finally got to the house and found about twenty people in the living room, sitting in a large circle singing worship songs. A number of songbooks were lying on the floor. They didn't seem to notice that I walked in, but I didn't want to disturb them so I went back outside. I walked around to the back door and let myself into the kitchen. But to my surprise and frustration, there was no beer in the fridge. The bottle of wine that I'd put on top of the fridge was also gone.

"Excuse me? People in the living room, has anyone seen my roommates? Oh, there you are," I saw One through Four look up at me from the corner.

"Amy! Everyone this is Amy, our roommate. She lives in the first bedroom we showed you. Amy, these are some friends from the Center."

"Hi, everybody. Beth, uh, where's the beer?"

"Oh, Amy, we dumped it out. Beer doesn't lead to a sublime existence." I saw nods around the room. "Amy, don't get mad. Did you have a bad day at work?"

"What? You did what?"

Beth was whispering to the girl beside her. "Amy, we'd really like it if you joined us. Come on, we're just about to sing . . . "

"Maybe later," I said. "Right now I have to go on a beer run." I walked through the center of the living room this time, accidentally kicking one of their hymnals as I did. It spun a few feet and stopped in front of the crossed knees of a young, blonde girl.

I drove to the grocery store and bought a 12-pack of beer and a bottle of red wine. You've got to love a state that lets you do that. When I got back to the house I found the creepy group waiting for me.

"Amy, we really would like you to join us," they said.

"No, thanks. But listen, this is my beer," I held up the blue and yellow box so they all could see. "And this is my wine. If you dump it out, that's *stealing* since I paid for it. Stealing is wrong. Enjoy your séance." They moved out of my way as I went to the kitchen. I twisted the top off a beer, and poured it into a glass I had in the freezer. I put the rest in the fridge, and then walked back through the living room toward my room. When I reached the hallway I could hear them whispering, so I closed my door and locked it.

I kicked off my shoes and took off my suit jacket. My roommates' insanity would have to wait. I went over the day's events to see what sense I could make of my afternoon at work. Chad wasn't Mr. Watters' right hand *anything*. He was an office assistant under the delusion that he was a lobbyist, barging in on a meeting and not getting fired for it. On top of that, he had the nerve to come back and treat me like a hired hand.

I switched on the TV and set to work unpacking the last of my boxes, the whole time questioning whether I shouldn't just pack up and leave. What was with my roommates? A dozen or more people at the house every night singing and praying, and now, shunning alcohol? What kind of religious sect was this? And what were they doing in my room earlier?

My mood focused my work, and I quickly finished getting organized. Everything had a place, and there were shelves already on the wall with plenty of space for my candles and knickknacks. And my closet was amazing. Finally, I could stop ironing my work clothes every night because they weren't smashed in a box.

I emerged from my room starving, and found the house empty. I ate a few cookies and decided to make some spaghetti, but by the time it was done I was hardly hungry anymore so I packed it up for lunch instead.

Bored, I decided to just go to bed. I popped in a movie in my room, but barely got past the opening credits. I opened my eyes to sunlight and my alarm going off. Time for work again.

I seemed to have the house to myself in the mornings. My roommates' fall schedule was nice for that, at least. Two roommates would get up and leave early, and the other two would sleep in because they had afternoon classes. As to be expected, though, my spaghetti was gone. Whoever ate it didn't even bother to cover her tracks; I found the empty container in the sink. But all eleven beers were still in the fridge, and the wine bottle was sitting on the shelf where I left it. A note on the message board read, "House Meeting Tonight, 7 p.m." Great.

I arrived at work before Chad and started turning on lights. He showed up soon enough, though, talking loudly on his cell phone. He wasn't in the door two steps before he started with me. "Amy, did you get over to Travel Mania to find flights to Brussels yet?" he put his hand over the mouthpiece of his phone.

"No, I just got here."

"Well, I need you to do that." He went back to his phone conversation, "Sorry about that. I had to talk to the *assistant*. So you were saying you've never been to Brussels?" and he wandered into his office.

I sighed. I grabbed a notepad and a pen and wandered over to Travel Mania. I was surprised to find their office full and buzzing. The reception area was crowded, and the two other desks I could see had colorful knick-knacks and picture frames. Posters of distant lands covered the walls, phones were ringing, and people were chatting. Further back I could see the office had been divided into cubicles with the occasional office door here and there. The space seemed designed to hold a dozen, easily. But then our own office space could probably hold close to that, and there were only the three of us.

"Welcome to Travel Mania. I'm Peggy," said the fortyish redhead at the reception desk. "Have we booked a trip for you before?"

"Hi, Peggy. No, this is my first visit," I told her. "I'd like to talk with Beau about a flight for next week."

"Well, Beau handles his own clientele," she said cheerfully. "Let me just see if he's available. May I have your name please?"

"I'm Amy, from Watters and Company next door."

Peggy went into the office behind her desk and appeared a moment later. "You can go in, Amy, Beau will see you now," she said, not realizing Beau was directly behind her.

"Yes, he will see you now," Beau said in a girly voice.

"Would you stop doing that?" Peggy laughed.

"Right this way," Beau gestured toward his office like one of Bob's Beauties. Amazingly, Beau was wearing another floral button-down, this time with blue shorts. The flip-flops were the same as the day I met him in the elevator.

"Aren't your feet cold?" I asked. It was still sunny and warm outside for September, which is also why the air conditioning was still on.

"I'm warm-blooded," Beau scoffed.

Beau's office was much the same as the reception area: same mauve carpeting, beige walls filled with posters, colorful pens in a cup on the desk. Beau had lizard Beanie Babies on top of his computer monitor, and numerous photos of himself standing in front of famous monuments from around the globe.

"Wow, you've traveled a lot," I said, getting caught up with all the photos.

"But of course," he teased. "Comes with the territory. Come in, sit down. It's nice to see you again."

"Are you sure I'm not cutting in the line? There's a bunch of people waiting . . . "

"No, I handle my own clients. Mostly law offices and some corporate-types for their business travel, and my family and a few friends for their vacations. I'm part owner here so I get to decide what projects I take on. Those folks out there are mostly walk-ins; they're usually the messiest travelers so I don't handle those too often. They change their minds too much, make my life a living hell." He laughed. "So, where do you want to go?"

"Oh, it's not for me, it's for my coworker, Chad. He's going to Brussels for a week and needs to leave this Monday. I'm pretty sure our office is paying for it."

"Okay, leaving this Monday," Beau started typing. "And when's he returning?"

"Hopefully never," I said, and caught myself. "I'm sorry, that was mean."

"Only to the people in Brussels."

I looked up at Beau to see he had complete delight on his face. "I met that uppity SOB and in my opinion, he's a jackass," he said with a smile.

Now I laughed. This was refreshing.

"I don't know how you put up with him," Beau said.

"You know, I don't either."

We found Chad a couple flight options. Each was a little more expensive than the last, but all in all, they weren't bad prices for the last minute, I thought. Beau printed out the different options and handed the paper to me. "See what he thinks about these, and let me know."

"Thanks."

"Don't be a stranger, Amy. Drop by anytime you like." Beau did his signature wink and head tilt with a laugh.

FIVE

With as many times as Chad changed his mind about his flight, I was no stranger to Travel Mania. By the end of the day I'd been to their multi-colored office enough to know most of the staff by first name. But I wouldn't send Chad there to make his own changes; I liked Beau too much for that.

As usual, I got home late that night. I found my roommates sitting around the dining table that someone in their Center had donated to our house. There were no more chairs, so I pulled over the yellow easy chair that matched the yellow couch, both of which were donated and hideous to look at, but they were remarkably comfortable.

"Sorry I'm late," I said. "It took forever to get out of there today."

"That's okay. My class ran late so I just got here, too," Beth said. "Okay, this house meeting comes to order."

We opened what was to be a three-hour meeting with a prayer. Next the girls congratulated each other on a successful move. When that was done they announced that I could have beer in the house, so long as I talked to their friend Kimberly who would be coming over at some point. They refused to let any boys in the house after midnight, because it was a bad example to the neighbors. But boys from the Center could stay since church boys had good purposes for being there. Then we had to vote on what nights we would cook for the house.

"There are five of us, so each weeknight is covered," Beth said. "And if we could have a volunteer for Saturday . . . "

"I object," I said. "Every night there's at least a dozen extra people running around the house, and now you want me to cook for them?

Don't these people have homes to go to, or homework they should be doing?"

"We're not forcing you, Amy," Beth said. "But you should be able to make dinner once a week for us. I don't think that's a lot to ask. Our friends don't care what you make."

"Yeah, they'll eat anything. Remember when Billy ate that leftover sausage like a week after the pancake breakfast?"

"Oh, yeah. When was that?"

"It was right when we first got here."

"Yeah, that's right. He just picked it up and ate it. That was so funny!"

This went on for a while. "Guys, where is the money going to come from for all these dinners?" I interrupted.

"Don't your parents send you money?" Beth asked. "Oh, you're not a student. But you have your job."

"But I'm not working to feed your friends," I told them. "Speaking of which, if I buy something, I want to come to the kitchen and find it there. Not like my spaghetti that disappeared sometime between eleven last night and eight this morning."

"Oh, that was me," Tweedle Dum said. "Billy and I stayed to finish painting the Center last night and by the time we left, everywhere was closed. What's the big deal?"

"How about, 'it wasn't yours'?" I said.

"As sisters in faith, we're a family," Beth said. "We share everything. It doesn't matter who bought it."

"I think we should eat only what we buy, not just anything we find in the fridge," I said.

"That brings up a good point," Tweedle Dum said. "House food shopping. We need volunteers to buy groceries each week. These will be for our house dinners. And this way, anybody can eat anything they find in the kitchen. That makes it much simpler."

"We should have a well-stocked kitchen," Beth said. "Just like at the Center. So we'll have to get a jar and everybody pays in. We'll need our essentials first, like cookies, potato chips, juice boxes, ground meat . . . " This was met with, "Right, right," from the others.

"Here, let me get some paper and I'll make a list. Oh, I'll need a pencil, too. I'll be right back."

"Guys, I think we should waste a bunch of money on all that stuff," I interrupted. "I think we're better off buying our own food."

"But if we each contribute seventy-five or a hundred dollars we could have a well-stocked kitchen," Beth said. "Then when the youth group comes over, we'll have plenty."

"That's a lot of money," I said. "Okay, look, if you guys want to do that, cool, go for it. But leave me out of it. I'll buy my own groceries, okay?"

"Then how do we divide house dinner?"

"I'm at work all day long. I get home late. The last thing I want to do is cook the evening away to feed an army."

"We can help you. We can do cooking lessons!"

"Ooh, it'll be fun!"

"We'll all come up with recipes and get together in the evenings to buy the food and make it together. Then our friends can come over and try what we made!"

"It will be a great house project!"

What little life I had left outside of work was quickly being spoken for. "I'm sorry, guys. You can do whatever you want, but just don't worry about me, okay?"

"It's okay," red-haired Karen finally spoke up. "I mean, not everyone likes to cook. I love cooking. I'll take Amy's night."

"That's very gracious of you," Beth said.

This was taking a long time, so I decided to compromise. Any food I bought for myself I would write my name on. I agreed to contribute to the house fund for cleaning supplies and dinners they were making for their friends. With the tough stuff out of the way, I moved on to what I thought was a no-brainer.

"We need to start locking the front door," I said. "As women I think we need to be more careful. Also, if it's evening and you're the last one out of the house, I think we need to turn on a light or get little nightlights so that the next person to come home doesn't walk into a dark house."

"Oh, Amy, you're being silly," Beth said.

"Actually, I talked to the neighbors already and they're keeping an eye on the house for us," one of the Tweedles said.

"You did?" I asked.

"Of course," she said. "I told them we were a houseful of girls and we don't always lock the door so could they keep an eye out for us. I told them we could be kind of helpless, you know, being girls, and the neighbors said they'd watch things here."

"Did you tell them we also have valuables and where we keep our jewelry?" I asked.

"Amy, don't be ridiculous," she said.

"Tracy, I rebuke you for calling Amy ridiculous," Beth said.

"I acknowledge the rebuke," the Tweedle said. "I apologize, Amy."

This was insane. "Okay, since the neighborhood knows that we're just girls and that we're not too bright, can we please start locking the door?" I asked. "And can we leave a small light on at night for safety? I don't want to walk in here and interrupt one of the neighbors stealing our things and have them attack me."

"Amy, you could see them coming at you and get out of the way," Beth said.

"If someone's in here, in the dark, they can see us coming in, but we can't see them until our eyes adjust to the darkness."

"Why do you have to be so spooky, Amy?"

"I'm not trying to be spooky. Let's lock the door at night, and leave on a small light, for our own safety."

"How about we leave on the porch light?" Beth asked.

"Because," I said, hating to point it out, "the porch light is outside. We need to leave on an *inside* light. Why is this so hard?"

"Okay, guys, let's leave on a light—*for Amy*," Beth said, "That reminds me, we got the electric bill today. We owe eight cents, so I'll just pay it myself."

"What do you mean, eight cents?" Karen asked. "That doesn't sound right."

"Where did you put the bill?" I asked.

"It's in my room," she said, like it was a done deal. "Oh, I'll go get it." She returned a few minutes later. I was starting to get a headache. "Okay, here it is. And here at the top, it says eight cents, see?" she handed it to Karen.

"That's eight cents per kilowatt hour," Karen corrected her. "What we owe is over here, sixty-five dollars. It looks like . . . a hook-up fee of forty dollars and about twelve dollars a week for two weeks. That's not so bad. Okay, guys, let me show you how to read this," Karen said to the others. I let her handle it and went to the kitchen for some Tylenol. How could they not know how to read a bill? Beth wanted to call her dad for help—and she was 28. I went back in sat down again, just as Karen was wrapping things up.

"Okay, guys, next thing," Beth took charged of the meeting again. "Amy, have you checked the answering machine?"

"No, why?" I saw everyone exchange glances.

"Uh, well, Pastor Jeff has left a couple messages for you and said you haven't returned his calls."

"Every time I checked the machine, it was completely full," I said. "We need to do something about it."

"We're looking into getting voicemail, that way we each of us will listen to messages that come in for us individually," Karen said. Karen was fast becoming the most logical of the roommates. "The phone company offers a four-person plan, a six-person, and an eight. I say we go with the six and then we have an extra box for anyone wanting to leave a message for our whole house. It's close to $10 more each month," Karen said. "Everybody in?" We all agreed. It was the quickest thing we accomplished thus far.

"Amy, what are you going to do about Pastor Jeff?" Tweedle Dum asked.

"I don't know. What does he want?"

"If you'd listened to the machine . . . " she sounded annoyed.

"Okay, okay guys, let's listen to this machine," I said, going to the end table and hitting the button.

Their friend Betsy called. "Hi everyone! Blessed be for this beautiful day. I'm here at the Center and I just wanted to let you know what a beautiful job you all did painting. It's lovely! I woke up this morning and even before I got out of bed I asked that this be a good day, and indeed it is! What a glorious . . . "

I pressed the "Skip" button. Next we had a message from their friend Kevin. "Good morning everyone! It's Kevin, Kevin King, from youth group. This message is for everyone, and a special hello to you, Amy, our newest recruit! Amy, I know we haven't met yet, but I hope to see you at services this Sunday. Oh, pray for me today, everyone, as I am ordering the new song books for the Elders Group . . . " I pressed the skip button again.

"Hello, it's Kevin again, Kevin King from the youth group. Your machine cut me off. Hello again to everyone. Uh, I need to know the number of people you expect for the retreat this weekend. I'm bringing a surprise for everyone. So, give me a call here, oh, where is the number . . . " Next.

"Beth, it's Sarah Jo from the Center! Don't you just love all this sunshine! I am in need of the cookie list for the ladies' group. Beth, I know you put it here in the office somewhere, but it's not on the shelf. It's not in the box, not near the table, or did you put it in the front office? Let me get the cordless phone and go to the other office. Glory be! Where is the cordless? It's not on the desk, not on the table . . . "

I stopped the machine. "How much space does the voicemail system give us?"

"I think it's unlimited," Karen said.

"Let's hope so." My roommates looked confused and I sighed. "Okay, what does your Pastor Jeff want?"

"Amy, he's concerned about you skipping services last Sunday. Not to mention . . . "

"I'm not a member of your church, center, thing," I said. "Not to mention what?"

"Well, the drinking. Amy, you have a problem. Kimberly's been leaving messages for you, too, if you would listen."

"I had a beer after a tough day at work. You guys agreed that I could keep beer and wine in the house. Remember?"

"Yes—until you talk to Kimberly about your problem. Then, together, you can dump it out."

"I don't have a problem," I said.

"What about the other day?" Beth said. "Yelling at everybody like that? Amy, faith is the answer, not beer."

"Amen," the Tweedles said. I was staring at a sea of very caring and very blank faces.

"Okay, but Amy," it was Beth talking this time, "Kimberly's on her way. Her mom was an alcoholic and she knows a lot about this. We're praying for you, Amy. Kimberly will be able to help." She smiled at me sadly, as though there really were no reason to hope.

There was a knock at the door, and, speak of the devil, Kimberly entered.

"I suggest we all think about things to discuss at the next house meeting," Beth said.

"Another house meeting?" I asked.

"Yeah, I think we should do these weekly, don't you guys?" Beth asked, and everyone nodded. We adjourned the meeting in prayer.

"I'm sorry my roommates made you come over here," I said to Kimberly, the teenage blonde girl my roommates sanctioned to talk to me. "The house meeting lasted pretty long, my head hurts, and I still need to write my name on my food before I go to bed."

"It's worse than I thought," Kimberly said gravely to the girls. "Amy," she gave me a full compassionate look, "Amy, my mother drank for many years and I'm pretty sure I can read the signs. What you're going through right now is withdrawal." She pronounced the word carefully. "Withdrawal is when you stop drinking, but your body has come to rely on the alcohol in your system. That's why you have the headache."

"No, I have a headache from the house meeting. I'm pretty sure."

"Were you drinking during the house meeting?"

"Nope. So obviously I don't need to drink all the time, right?"

"That's why your body is going through withdrawal. Amy, we need to talk. How much do you drink daily?"

"I don't drink daily," I put the yellow chair back in its place.

"She's in denial," Kimberly said to the others.

"Kim, honey, I can hear you," I said. "And I'm not in denial. Is the intervention over? 'Cause I'm going to bed." I heard them whispering behind me but I kept going anyway. My home life had turned into an after school special—and somehow *I* was the bad kid.

CHAPTER SIX

I woke up exhausted. I hated to go to work, but there was no way I was staying home. All of my roommates were at home packing for their retreat. But by five o'clock, they'd be on their way to wherever they were going, and wouldn't be back until Tuesday or Wednesday. I couldn't wait.

Work had become Brussels Central. Chad had called everyone he knew to remind them he'd be in Brussels, wrote "Chad in Brussels" on every calendar in the office, "copied" me on his Brussels itinerary twice and then emailed it to me just in case, reminded me that his cell phone wouldn't work in Brussels, re-recorded his phone message to say he was in Brussels, told the chairman of the trade association he was going to Brussels, drove home at lunchtime to start his laundry for his trip to Brussels . . . I hoped Brussels would keep him, but they probably had better sense.

The end of the day finally arrived and I was glad to have the weekend to myself. I was sure Chad would call me Monday before he left his apartment, then once on the drive to the airport, and then twice while waiting for his flight to board. Four more phone calls, and less than that if I happened to go to the ladies' room.

Monday came and Chad actually called five times because I was in the ladies' room once so he left a long message and then called right back. Mr. Watters didn't come in on Monday, so I had the office to myself to get a jump on the newsletter.

On Tuesday, Mr. Watters came in bright and early, and asked me to get a cup of coffee with him. We went downstairs to the aptly named Little Shop in the building. It was busy—as it always was—in there, but we waited a moment and managed to get a small table near the windows.

The sunlight streaming in felt nice at first. I figured I'd be sweating if we sat there long, though.

"Amy, I think you're doing a fine job for us," Mr. Watters opened the discussion. "And I've been noticing some things about your work."

"Okay . . . " I said. I couldn't tell from his tone if these were good or bad things. I braced myself for the worst. If he didn't like the work I was doing, he'd fire me. Then I'd be free of my contract and of dealing with Chad for the next year, but I'd be broke. I hadn't even made the first payment on my car and now I'd have to return it. *Why did I buy that car?*

"Amy, I don't think you're living up to your potential."

"Okay . . . " I nodded, and waited.

"I want you to start doing the newsletters on your own from now on. I think Chad's input is getting in the way. And the company is prepared to compensate you for this extra work."

"Really?" I was braced for the worst and maybe this was it. I wasn't being fired after all, not being set free, forced to abandon my lease, rid of hearing Chad complain about me every day. I was being given a raise.

"Thank you. I've already got a jump start on the newsletter," I assured him.

"I figured as much. Chad has been reporting to me how difficult it is to work with you on the newsletters. But when I ask you to draft letters or anything of the kind for me, it's always top-notch. Then Chad comes to me with some changes, and I could tell these changes had 'Amy' written all over them. I let him play his game. But taking credit for someone else's ideas, that's a no-no. *That's* why he's in Brussels right now."

"What do you mean?"

He laughed. "It's a little ploy Harvey and I invented. This week as you know, the House is set to vote on the retail legislation. There are two key Members that we have to sway our way. Harvey and his team have one, and I'm working with the Hill office on the other. But with Chad following my every step, calling the Hill office every hour for updates, wanting to talk about the upcoming election predictions, it's a nuisance and a distraction. The kid needed a vacation, so I sent him to one of Harvey's cousins in Brussels for a ruse."

"A ruse?"

"He's going to pitch Watters and Company to Larson Jones, Ted Harvey's second cousin, and get a week out of my sight in the process."

"You just paid for him to have a vacation?" This was ludicrous and I couldn't help it, "Send me on vacation!"

"I can't do that. You'd enjoy yourself. Chad's not going to have any fun—it's not his way."

"This plan of yours . . . I'm sorry, what happens when the next big bill comes up for a vote?"

"The Harvey family has many cousins," Mr. Watters laughed again.

"That's a lot of money to spend on nothing."

"Not when you have plenty, and have retail legislation on the table."

"So why are you telling me this?"

"Because I know Chad can be overbearing. But you've got strength of character, I knew it when I hired you, and I saw a lot of it with the newsletter situation. You didn't need credit for your idea, you only needed to see that it was put into action. I want you to know I'm paying attention. Chad, God help him, is a workhorse. And his budgeting skills are impeccable. Before he came along I had the Hill office crunching their own numbers." He drank the last of his espresso. "The Board dictates that we do an audit every year for the trade association to make sure that we're on budget. It's a good 'checks and balances' system: keeps us accountable for our decisions, and lets the membership know exactly where their money's going. But I tell you, those audits were a real headache before Chad came along. Everything was in the wrong categories. Don't let lobbyists handle your finances."

"I'll keep that in mind," I said. So, despite his attitude, Chad had complete job security. "But Chad thinks you're going to let him lobby with you."

"Chad also thinks the front door has his name on it. He's doing just fine with his research and the annual budget work. He's a good kid, and if he deals with his anger problem, in the future he could be a valuable part of the lobby team. I've told him as much. But until then, I can't have him throwing tantrums in front of Congress." He looked at his watch. "I'd better be off to the Hill. Keep up the good work."

This was the weirdest thing to happen to me yet. Mr. Watters was right, though, Chad might have enjoyed bragging about his trip, but while he was there, he'd hate every minute of it. And he could brag all he wanted; I now understood that Mr. Watters had been on to Chad all along. His behavior wasn't going unnoticed. All this time I'd been worried that Chad was feeding lies to Mr. Watters about my work, and that at any moment I could be fired. Chad could give whatever impression he wanted; things would be different when he got back.

The House passed the retail bill Thursday afternoon. I got calls from each of the lobbyists who were in touch with staff members on the floor of the vote, and Mr. Watters called from the chamber outside the voting room itself. He asked me to draft an announcement for the membership, and then called back half an hour later instructing me to broadcast my announcement to our members. He was celebrating with the lobbyists and wouldn't be back to edit my draft. Complete writing autonomy—this was a day indeed.

I got home that night still feeling the enthusiasm of the day's activities. The Senate bill still needed to be passed, but Mr. Watters and his friend Harvey were pretty confident about it. Though, Mr. Watters said, you never could tell, which is why he loved his work so much.

"Damn!" I said out loud when I got home and found my roommates' luggage and sleeping bags all over the living room. Instantly my good mood was sucked out of me. Life in the group home was definitely taking its toll.

My roommates and their friends watched me whenever I was around, and whispered to each other as I left the room. It was enough to make me *want* to drink. But any time I drank anything, be it wine or Kool-aid, I saw them give each other sad looks and heard them say they'd pray harder for me. I thought about buying a little refrigerator for my room, but why should I have to spend more money just to hide something I thought was normal?

While they were away on their trip, I'd been living it up: painting my nails red, watching PG-13 movies in the living room, drinking a glass or two of wine, all without feeling like a criminal. But tonight was different. Knowing they could show up at any minute, I just couldn't get comfortable. Within an hour I saw headlights in the driveway. It was Beth. She walked in smiling, but changed her demeanor when she saw the wine glass on the coffee table.

"Hi, Amy," she said, sounding consoling. "Where is everybody?"

"Note on the fridge says they're at the Center. I thought you were with them."

"No, I had to fix my class schedule at the school. I should call the Center, though, and find out what's up." She left me to go into her room, and emerged again within minutes. "Amy, is this a good time for us to talk?"

I dreaded what was coming next, so I braced myself. "Uh, okay." I put down my book and turned to face her. "You're not going out to join the others?"

"No, something more important came up." She sat down beside me on the yellow couch. "Amy, it seems to me that you're not happy," she said. She took a deep breath. "Is it something I did?"

I shook my head. "No, Beth, it's not you. It's just the house in general. I had no idea that I was moving into a, well, a commune." I tried to say it as politely as possible.

"Amy, we'd like for you to let your guard down and open up to us. Everyone would like you to start attending services with us, including Pastor Jeff." As she talked, she nervously tucked her dark hair behind her ears, let it fall, then tucked it again.

"I thought," I said, "that living with a bunch of girls, we'd have squabbles over the bathroom, but that, on the good side, we'd go out together, we'd go drinking, dancing, have dinner together for a night on the town, borrow each other's things . . . But this is more, I buy food and everyone eats it. I buy shampoo and it gets all used up. It's hard enough for me to deal with work every day without knowing that I'm working for nothing. I'm slowly going into debt living here," I hated to think about it. "I hate having weekly house meetings where we discuss rebuking each other and how we can pressure Amy into joining the Center, joining the youth group, making dinners for the house. I hate that your friends come over thinking I have a drinking problem, I hate that your pastor calls me. I hate that the machine is filled with your friends who couldn't tie their shoes each morning without calling here to tell us about it." Once I got going, it was hard to stop.

Beth's voice remained as calm and even as ever. "Amy, first of all, we're not about to go drinking with you. And if you would sit in with us one night, you'd see that our friends have nothing but the best intentions. We told them all about you and they're looking forward to your joining us. They're just looking out for you."

"I don't want to *join* anything. I feel like I'm your newest recruit, to fill a quota or something. If you guys would just leave me alone, I might want to come with you at some point. But pressuring me isn't going to get me there."

She nodded. "Amy, before I had religious favor in my life, I felt just the same way."

"No, that's just what I'm talking about. This 'I have favor and you don't' thing. Who says I don't have religion? Did you ever ask me? I'm not new-wave or anything the way you guys are, but I'm Lutheran. That still counts. How come the whole time we were house-hunting you never said a word about any of this?"

She hid her face in her hands for a moment, then emerged with tears in her eyes. "I don't know. I'm not as strong as the others with my faith yet. I'll get there. For right now, I do better when I'm around everyone else. It's like a feeling that I get caught up in. But my challenge point is showing my faith when I'm on my own."

"I'm sure you'll get to where you're meant to be."

"I know," she nodded and gave me a hug. "I'm glad we talked, Amy."

"I am, too," I said. Aside from trying really hard to fit in with her friends, Beth really was a nice person.

"I'll pray for you, Amy," she said, getting up and walking toward her room.

That phrase was thrown around a lot when I was nearby, and never with any compassion. It made me feel like I was beyond all earthly hope. I picked up my book and decided to call and old college friend for some advice. But when I picked up the phone Beth was already on it.

"Did you try crying?" a male voice said.

"Yes, I did the crying, but she still wouldn't budge," Beth said. My mouth dropped open and I forgot about hanging up. Beth kept whispering, "I did everything by the book, just like in the practice sessions. But I think she's warming up to the idea of joining us. She trusts me, in any case." A noise escaped from my throat.

"Is someone else on the line?" the man asked.

"No, I don't think so," Beth said. I realized myself and hung up as quietly as I could. Robotically, I got up and locked the bedroom door. I sat down on the bed and stared at the wall, for how long I don't know. To say I was horrified would be, well, hitting the nail square on the head. Who *were* these people? Devising practice sessions to convince me to join their Center religious thing? What kind of organization *was* this? And how soon could I get out of the lease?

Realizing that I was paranoid and that it was justifiable, I got more than just scared. I got angry. For weeks they'd been making me uncomfortable in my own home. I'd instinctively had reservations about joining their activities, but they made me feel like something was wrong with me for not being more open and willing. I'd been following my instincts, and I wasn't about to feel guilty any longer.

I had to figure out what to do. I really didn't know anybody in town. How could I not have any options? I didn't have any other friends, and I had no money. I'd spent my savings on the down payment for my car. Besides, it had taken weeks for Beth and me, working together, to find this place. How long would I have to look to find something that I could afford on my own? On top of it all, I'd signed a lease.

I carefully picked up the phone again to see if Beth were still on it. I got the dial tone, so I dug through my day planner and found the number for our landlord.

Mr. Fringe told me that if I could get someone to pay my part of the lease that I could go. I was sure I could find one of my roommates' friends willing to take my room. But if that person didn't pay for some reason, I'd be held accountable. Unless, of course, I wanted to break the lease; in which case, he'd charge me a fee and re-write the lease for the rest of the girls. He favored this option since he hadn't charged us for some of the house's last-minute repairs and was looking to nearly double the rent for the next tenants.

"What kind of lease-breaking fee are we talking about?"

"Oh, well, I'd have to check on that," Mr. Fringe said in his slow, even tone. "But I believe I can charge half a year's rent."

"My rent, or the whole house rent?"

"Whole house."

"Well, could you check on that for me?" I asked, my heart sinking. "And even if you could charge me that much, would you cut me a break since you'll be able to rewrite the lease for more money anyway?"

"Miss Ashe," he said, "I'm out the money for the new water heater, the window blinds, and the carpet cleaning. Yeah," he chuckled, "I sure would like to see some of that money back. I'm afraid I'd have to charge you."

"What carpet cleaning?"

"Are you questioning my business practice?"

"I'm just saying I spent days scrubbing spots off the carpets when I moved in."

"I'm afraid I don't like your tone, Missy. I had those carpets cleaned. I even have the receipt."

"Well, they weren't clean when I moved in."

"I had extra work done before you moved in."

"Right . . . " I said. "Well, thank you for your time."

Someone knocked on my door and I about jumped out of my skin. Karen's voice was on the other side. "Amy, emergency house meeting."

I wasn't ready. I needed time to regroup before I faced my roommates again, if ever. But I needed one of their friends to take over my part of the lease. And I couldn't very well hide in my room. They knew where I was.

I pulled myself together as best I could, and took a deep breath. I grabbed a pad and pen and, sweating, walked ominously out of my room.

I sat down stiffly and we prayed for the salvation of the sinners. Then Tweedle started talking. "Okay, guys, remember that electric bill we paid last week? Well, I found it in my car today."

"It's a miracle you found anything in that car of yours."

"Yeah, I know," Tweedle said.

"I thought we were going to clean out our cars together!" Beth complained.

"Oh, I didn't clean it," Tweedle told her. "I just happened to find the bill. We'll still clean cars together."

"Okay, so where's the bill now?" I interrupted the banter.

"Oh, it's still in the car," she said. "It's right on the front seat so I'll remember to send it next time I'm at the post office."

"Why didn't you just put it in the mailbox?" Karen asked.

"Because I go past the post office every day. I thought this would be faster."

"What's the due date on the bill?" I asked.

"I think it's probably late," Karen said.

"Is that bad?" Tweedle looked at the other Tweedle.

"They could turn us right back off again," Karen told her. "They *probably* won't, but paying the bill late doesn't look good for us. We should call the company and let them know the money's on the way."

Everyone looked at me. "What? You want *me* to call?"

"Well, Amy," Tweedle said, "You *are* the meanest."

"Yeah, Amy, you can fix it for us," the other Tweedle said.

I rolled my eyes. "Okay," I said. "Since I'm the *house troll*, I'll call them. But next time, can we just put the bills in the mailbox and send them on time? Rent is due pretty soon for next month, so let's try to pay that on time."

"Rent's not due yet," the other Tweedle said. "We have until the 10th. I read the lease."

"The lease said *up to* the 10th, we really should get the money there sooner," I said.

"What if it's postmarked on the 10th?"

"Let's do that," Beth said. "If it's postmarked then we're fine."

There was no way, dealing with these people, that I would find someone responsible enough to take my place in the house. I'd be held accountable every time the rent was late and we had to pay fees for turning utilities back on again. I'd have to stay in the house until we managed to get ourselves kicked out. Eviction was the shining light at the end of the tunnel.

The girls kept talking, but I started plotting my situation. I broke it down like this: The house was costing me a small fortune in groceries and other house "necessities." I was using my credit cards more often than I liked. I nodded here and there, and looked up once in a while so the girls would think I was paying attention. Karen had done this at the last meeting, and it seemed to work for her.

Brainstorming away, I realized that no matter how little of a life I allowed myself, without extra income I was looking at nearly a year of packed lunches and staying in every night with the girls in order to pay off one minor school loan and three major credit cards. The girls were still going on and on about Center things and what hilarious new thing Billy did, so I went back to my paper.

Next thing: Chad. As of Monday, he'd be back from Brussels. Every day that Chad was in a bad mood was another long day knowing that my job was all I had. I depended wholly on my paychecks. My life was spiraling out of control. It seemed Washington, D.C. was a huge mouth about to swallow me up.

I looked over my scratch paper and organized my plan of action like any good office assistant would: I made a "To Do" list.

1. Get out of debt. The only thing hanging over my head worse than weird Chad every day was the fact that I owed Visa, MasterCard, and AMEX a bundle.
2. Meet some new people. I needed a new scene, one with friends I could trust.
3. Get the hell out of the house. The less time I spent in Cult-ville the better. If I couldn't get out of the lease, then I'd at least get out of the house.

My solution for all three: a waitress job. I'd waited tables in college while taking classes; I could do it a couple nights a week on top of my office job. Why not? It met all three goals at once. But where?

I wanted something fun, something that wasn't stuffy but paid well. A new restaurant just opened close to the house, down along the waterfront. I'd passed it on one of my drives in the new car. But they probably had a full staff by now. Then again, it couldn't hurt to fill out an application. It was getting late. If I left now I could be there by 9. I looked down at my dress. Not the most conservative thing I owned, and even slightly fun for office wear. It would have to do.

I stood up. "I gotta go."

"Uh, okay," Beth said. "What's so important?"

"Something I have to do," I said, heading toward the door. I left them to their meeting and drove to the waterfront. The night air still held some of the day's warmth, so I drove with the window down and enjoyed the smell of leaves. It amazed me that I lived just outside of Washington, D.C. and yet could smell trees and leaves as if I were driving in the country.

The Upscale had been open for business for at least a month already. Now that my mind was made up, I dreaded to think that they had all the staff they needed by now.

"We just went through our first round of servers," the manager told me. "We're a fast-paced restaurant, and many people can't handle that." He scrutinized my application, "Looks like you already have waitress experience."

"Yes," I said. "Two years in college at different restaurants near the campus."

"Do you have transportation?" he asked. "We're near the Metro, but we close *after* the Metro closes, so you'll need a way home."

"I have a car," I assured him.

"A reliable car?"

"Yes, it's brand new. I just bought it." I realized I'd just said the same thing twice.

Just then a tall girl approached us. "Mark, you have a phone call," she said.

"Thanks, Jenny. Excuse me for a moment," Mark said, and left me at the table.

Jenny smiled at me. "Are you applying to waitress?" she asked me. "Don't worry about Mark," she said, fixing her long, brown ponytail. "He's a softy. Don't let him try to scare you. It's a fun place to work and the money's awesome."

"Jenny, pizza's up!" one of the cooks called to her. She smiled at me again and left.

Mark was still on the phone, so I used the opportunity to glance around at my surroundings. The entire restaurant was one big, open space. The smoking section was near the bar, and non-smoking took up the rest of the place. The restaurant was bustling when I'd arrived, but now people were really starting to pack in. The two hostesses had their hands full at the door. I saw Jenny turn a dial on the wall, and the lights went low, and a moment later, the music got a bit louder.

Behind a Plexiglas counter, the cooks were talking to each other. Everything was out in the open. I could see a separate dessert area and the obvious coffee and bar areas—nothing behind closed doors.

The wait staff stood together behind a counter near the bar, goofing around and laughing. They were all probably about my age—three girls and one guy—and they seemed to be having a great time. They all looked so cool. Suddenly I was longing to be hired, and I hoped no one would realize how uncool I really was. Just then Mark hung up the phone and walked back over to me.

"Amy," he held out his hand to shake mine. I stood up. "Can you start Tuesday?"

"Really? Yeah, I can start then," I said. I tried to contain my excitement.

"Great, come back Tuesday at seven and we'll do your paperwork and start your training."

"Great, okay, thank you," I said. I reached for my purse and turned to walk away. "Oh, what do I wear?"

"Uh, black or blue, you choose," he said. "And good shoes."

"What about my hair?"

"Your hair looks great," he said, disinterested, and walked away.

"Okay!" I said. *My God, I'm so not cool.* But I had a waitress job at a fun restaurant, just like that. No waiting period, no major interview process, no references to check ahead of time. Just show up Tuesday and hope to not make an ass of myself.

This moment would propel my life in an entirely new direction. I was no longer Amy Ashe, boring secretary. I was Amy Ashe, secretary and waitress.

CHAPTER
SEVEN

"I had no idea you were looking for a second job," Beth said. The house meeting had ended but Beth and the Tweedles were still sitting at the table. "Why won't your parents give you money?"

"Because I'm not going to ask them," I said. "I can do it. It's only a couple of months," I said, trying to sound nonchalant. A little encouragement was all I needed.

Instead I got, "We'll pray for you, Amy," from Tweedle.

And Beth said, "I'll pray you get forgiven for wasting your time making money instead of helping out at the Center." The others were nodding.

"Well, I think it's a great idea," said Karen, who was standing behind the girls in the kitchen. "I think paying off your debt is a great goal, Amy, and I hope this job helps you accomplish it." She winked, grabbed her sandwich, smiled at the girls, and went downstairs. Karen had a mind of her own. I wondered how long the girls would let that last.

Over the weekend, I went through my closet for any black or blue clothing, and made a pile of properly colored party clothes that I wouldn't mind possibly ruining at the restaurant. I dug my gym shoes out of the closet, only then realizing that I hadn't been to the gym since I started house hunting with Beth. And last, and most importantly in my restaurant preparation, I made up a ground rule: The office comes first, for many reasons including salary, benefits, parking, not to mention the fact that it was steady. I'd promised Watters and Co. a full year and I owed it to them to do a good job. If I started to slip up at all, I'd drop the waitress gig.

On Monday, Chad showed up at the office, almost straight from the plane, and tried to work through the jet lag. Luckily Mr. Watters was in and told him to go home and rest up.

But Tuesday he'd shown up and wasn't his haughty self. In fact, once the bulldog attitude was stripped away, Chad was very human.

"Amy," he said, emerging from his office. "I'm going for some coffee. Would you like any?"

"Yeah," I said, more than a little amazed. "That'd be great, thanks."

"No problem. I'll be right back."

Maybe Mr. Watters knew what he was doing after all. I didn't know how long the change would last, but the timing couldn't have been better. Between tension at home and tension at work, I didn't know how much more I could take.

Leaving the office on Tuesday, I was thrilled to not be going home. I drove past the house, toward the waterfront and the Upscale. I wasn't disappointed: the place was fun, just as Jenny had said. Specializing in coffee and homemade desserts but offering a whole menu of entrees, appetizers, and beers, the Upscale had something for everyone. The menu was pricey, but the atmosphere was very relaxed and informal, which drew in businesspeople and students alike. There were smaller tables along the walls that could hold two people, with laptops, complete with outlets every few feet. It was at one of these tables that I sat for my interview with Mark. There were larger free-standing tables next to the "two-tops" that could hold four to six people each, and at the center of the restaurant were long picnic-looking tables that could hold parties of eight to twelve, depending on the placement of the chairs. There were padded benches that could seat four people on one side of the big tables, while individual chairs sat on the other side. The long bar stood to the right of the front door, with the smoking section directly in front of it.

The music was loud and upbeat. Upscale's corporate offices had a whole department dedicated to obtaining rights to popular songs for use in their restaurants. The end result was a trendy place to hang out or get work done, talk to friends, eat, drink, even dance, and everyone could get in regardless of age or dress. Customers flocked to the place, and there was a wait list for tables every night. Upscale's concept was all about fun, and we were encouraged to carry on and have a good time.

Behind the scenes, Upscale had a full staff of people to help the wait staff. Prep people took care of all the side work that normally would belong to the wait staff. The cooks prepared all the soups and salads, a pastry chef was on hand to ready the desserts, someone was in charge of the dessert display for takeout orders and also to fill coffee and tea orders for the servers, and busboys cleared the tables for the dishperson who sorted and stacked the dishes into a hefty machine that washed, sanitized, and dried the dishes, and then everything from plates to glasses was restocked out on the floor for server use. Basically, all the wait staff had to do was serve.

I'd worked in restaurants before where it was the waitress' responsibility to do some or all of these things, and the service was lousy and the wait staff was exhausted. You ran all night and made very little in tips because everyone was waiting for you to prepare salads or finish the dishes before you greeted their table. Upscale had all of that beat. The computer system operated on a touch screen, and when the order was entered, the computer would automatically send the food orders to the kitchen printer, the dessert orders to the printer at the counter, alcohol to the bar, and the specialty coffees to the espresso bar. The alcohols and coffees were ready first, and we'd bring them to the table freshly poured and coffee steaming. Appetizers would be ready next, followed by the entrees in due time, and right when you needed them, the desserts would appear on the countertop, complete with clean forks and raspberry syrup swirled on the plate.

It was an amazing set-up, and one that allowed each server to handle twice the number of tables than at any other restaurant. Depending on a restaurant's elegance, a server would normally be given four to six tables, and even fewer at a very nice place. But those restaurants specialized in excellent dining, and the servers needed to dress up, pull their hair back, train for a whole afternoon on the proper presentation of a wine bottle, etc. There was no uniform at Upscale, which was why Mark was so nonchalant about whatever I wanted to wear for my first day. We were free to wear pants or shorts, any style or fabric, and girls could wear skirts or dresses if we liked; length didn't matter. And because we wore our own clothes, we were comfortable and felt good. We could kid around with our customers, sit down with them, let our hair down, and we could present the wine bottles any way we pleased. Each of us was given anywhere from seven to ten tables, depending on the number of people each table held, and since the restaurant was helping us with our workload we had time to spare.

The wait staff was made up of guys and girls alike, so we called ourselves *servers* rather than waiters or waitresses. Gretchen, Haley, and Jason were students trying to make spending money; Jenny, Quinn, Sharon, and I worked day jobs in the city and were each looking to get out of debt or build savings accounts. As for Sam, Upscale was his only source of income and the work seemed to wear on him the most. It took five to seven servers to run the floor, depending on what night of the week it was, so from the start I was able to get three and four shifts a week without having to work my way up for more hours.

Upscale opened daily at 4 p.m., and usually the students were scheduled on the four o'clock shift. The majority of us didn't get out of D.C. traffic until closer to six or seven, and so there were staggered start times for everyone. Regardless of your start time, everybody left at the same time, which was whenever the work was done—usually half an hour after the kitchen stopped serving. Weekdays the kitchen stopped at midnight, but Friday and Saturday it stopped at 2 a.m. My day job started at nine, so being home by 1 a.m. on weeknights, I still got plenty of sleep before I had to get up and fight rush hour traffic.

"Long sleeves?" Sharon asked me. "You're going to be sweating." Sharon was in her upper twenties, was tall, with shoulder-length red hair and green eyes, and she gave off an air of confidence. By day she worked at the Pentagon. At first she was a little critical of me, but I assumed that came with the territory.

"It's thin material," I assured her. "I'll be fine. I'll keep up."

"First thing, I'll take you on a tour of the whole restaurant, show you where we keep anything in case you run out mid-shift and need to restock. Let's get to it."

Over the next few days, I managed to keep up with Sharon—barely. The pace was pretty fast. But it wasn't until I passed the menu tests on Friday that she dropped her skepticism.

"You did really well, Amy," she said as she finished checking my last menu test. "Is there anything you want to review before we hit the floor?"

"Well, I'm still having trouble recognizing the dishes by sight," I confessed.

"That'll come with time, don't worry about it. So you really think you want to work here?"

"Yeah," I said. "I need to, well, pay off some debts, and I'd like to get out of the house more."

"Well, this is the place for that. I'm hoping to pay off my car early, that's why I'm here," she said. "And I'm sorry about earlier this week. I've gone through the whole training procedure with four people already this month, and none of them made it. Three never passed the menu tests, and the fourth guy just had a rotten attitude with the customers." She narrowed her eyes, "It's a little tiring for me," she confided. "But I'm sorry if I got bitchy. I think you're doing a good job. So, are you ready to get out there?" Seeing me nod, she said, "Now, this is *Friday*, it's going to get really busy." She put on her black apron and took a deep breath. "Alright, grab your tray, let's go."

Sharon wasn't kidding about the pace. We had seven tables in our section, two of the large middle tables and five smaller tables near the windows. The five smaller tables alone were a lot of work once everyone ordered appetizers then soup and salad, then entrees. The weekday crowd we'd been serving to this point usually only ordered drinks and entrees. We had to step up our pace from the days before, and it seemed that we no sooner delivered an appetizer that another was ready to be delivered to the next table, without delay or their entree would be ready and would have to wait. The movement was constant between greeting tables, delivering food and drinks, and refilling sodas. Just when I felt I'd found a good rhythm, the hostess sat our two larger tables, and I had to start the process all over again, and time the drinks and appetizers of the new tables with the entrees of the smaller tables.

Sharon and I were so busy that we split up to handle all the work. She took orders and ran food, and I delivered and refilled drinks and restocked everything from napkins to ice to water pitchers for the servers, because we kept running out of everything. I spent most of the night doing this necessary and mindless work, but the music was pumping, my clothes were hugging my body, and I was moving through the crowded restaurant without missing a beat. In the end I realized that I could keep up with a tray full of drinks as fast as everyone else, and Jenny, Quinn, and Jason thanked me for all the restocking I'd done to help them. Sharon was grateful for all the work I did, and told me that Gretchen and Haley told her she'd done an awesome job training me. I went home that night, still unable to recognize some of the foods, but I'd earned the respect of the wait staff, and I felt more alive than I had in months.

On Saturday my roommates had all gone out "missioning" by the time I woke up. I knew they'd be home by dark, though, and I was glad to have the Upscale to fill up my evening hours. I spent most of the day resting my sore feet and aching body. But by "show time," I was ready.

"Amy! Glad to see you!" Jenny said as I clocked in.

"Hey, Amy! Thanks for all your help last night," Gretchen said, pointing at me as she passed.

"Sure, no problem."

"Oh, great you're here!" Sharon walked up to me. "Okay, since tonight's your last night of training, I'm giving you a small section of tables that you'll handle on your own. We're in the front of the restaurant tonight, with a lot of smaller tables, so they've given us two five-table sections. You can take the tables against the windows, and I'll take the rest. And if you need anything just ask me. Okay? As long as you're able to hold your own, I'm going to let you keep your own tips. I know technically you're still training, but since I won't be following you around, I think it's only fair. Oh, and they scheduled Boy Wonder tonight—even though it's a Saturday, so watch out." Sharon watched me raise my eyebrows, so she continued, "Sam. You'll see. Come out on the floor with me and I'll show you."

"Here," she said, pointing to a group of small tables between the bar, the windows, and the host stand. "These are your tables along the western windows. People like to linger when they sit there, so those tables don't get as much turnover. You should do fine, especially after the rush we got last night. Now these other tables are mine, here, and my section borders Sam's, right there," she pointed to a section that was in the center of the restaurant. "Gretchen's in the section we had last night, and Quinn and Jenny are in the back. You and Gretchen and I are stuck with Sam. He likes to disappear and whoever works beside him gets stuck helping his tables. It really sucks. I don't know why management hasn't figured out *not* to give him a big section on the busiest night of the week."

Just then Mark emerged from the office. "Okay everyone, get ready. I'm unlocking the doors."

My first table of the night was pretty easy. I was nervous and kept checking back on the man because he was my only table for a while, and each time he wasn't ready to order yet. Eventually a woman joined him and they ordered a light dinner. By the time I brought them their food I had two new tables, and my little section was nearly full. I ran around for a while, bringing drinks and appetizers out, intermittently checking on my first table. The last window table filled up, and I was off and running. When I finally brought the check to my first table, the man stopped me from leaving right away. Table Three needed drink refills, and Four's appetizer was ready, and I didn't really want to stop and chat.

"What is your name again?" the man asked.

"Amy."

"Amy, you are a great waitress," he said. The woman with him was nodding in agreement. "How long have you been here?" he asked me.

"At Upscale?" I asked. "Tonight's my first night." The man looked surprised, so I explained that I'd been training all week long, and that my section was kind-of small.

"Well, Amy, let me give you my card. My name is Brian, and this is my sister, Heather," he said. I shook their hands. "We manage a restaurant in the city, and we'd like it if you'd consider working for us," he said.

"The service was excellent," the woman said.

The man continued, "You checked back with us to make sure we didn't need anything, every time I looked down my coffee was refilled."

"You don't belong at this place," the woman said. "You really should be someplace a little fancier where you can make amazing money."

"Please consider it."

I thanked them, and accepted the man's card. He and the woman tipped me well, and I was thrilled by their compliment, though I didn't give their offer much thought. I had the impression their restaurant was one of those places where I'd have to "sir" and "ma'am" all the customers, wear a starched shirt, and not do anything out of line. I had enough repression with my day job and the cult house.

Things continued at a hectic pace, and then turned downright frantic at one point when all of my tables were leaving at the same time and I was given all new ones, one after the other.

Suddenly Sam was MIA and every time I crossed his section on my way to pick up drinks or food for my own people, his customers would stop me and start asking for things. I was in a hurry as it was, but knew how lousy it was to try to eat dinner when my drink was empty, or I needed another napkin, or my food was cold to begin with. I helped them as much as I could, as my own tables started to wonder where I was. Sharon took over babysitting Sam's section so I could get back to my own tables, and I really had to hustle because entrees were nearly ready and my folks didn't have their appetizers yet.

"Where the hell is Sam, anyway?" the bartender asked. "His drinks are up here melting."

"The jackass is either smoking up in the bathroom again, or he's out back," Sharon said, and then she looked at me. "Not that we have time to go get him anyway. Now you see what I'm talking about," she loaded her tray of drinks. "Sandy, you got that last Guinness for me?"

"Right here," the bartender said.

Sharon went on. "They want to be known for their excellent service, yet they keep putting that idiot on the weekend schedule. Thanks, babe," she said as Sandy placed the beer on her tray.

When Sharon moved out of the way, I set down my tray and started grabbing my drinks. "You're new, right?" the bartender asked me.

"Yes," I said. "Hi, I'm Amy," I held out my hand to the petite and very tan girl behind the bar. Her short hair was twisted in all directions, each twist held in place by a small white clip and ending in a little fan of blonde hair. It looked impressive, like something you could only accomplish in a salon.

"I'm Sandy, nice to meet you," she said, shaking my hand. "Good to have you here. Are you having fun?" she asked.

"Yeah, definitely." I counted the drinks on my tray, and realizing something was missing. "Oh, shit," I said, and looked back over my scribbled lists. "Sandy, I need a Chianti, I forgot to ring it in."

"The good stuff or the crap?" she asked, grabbing a glass from the shelf without looking.

"Good stuff," I said.

"Got it, here you go."

"Awesome. I'll ring it in in a second. Thank you."

"Wow, politeness! We don't get much of that around here. You're welcome."

Sharon was yelling at Sam as I passed with my drink tray.

"Disappear again and I will shove your head in the pizza oven . . . " she was saying. It was funny, except that her tone showed she obviously meant business. The tall, dark-haired Sam even apologized to her.

"Bullshit!" Sharon cut him off. "We both know you're not sorry. Cut the shit, okay? I'm not watching your section anymore. You're on your own." Sharon walked off.

The pace kept up for hours. I never had less than five things to try to do at one time. My shirt was sticking to me and my feet were really starting to hurt, but I had to keep moving. Despite all that, I found myself having a good time. The last table of the night was sat in Sam's section, but he offered it to me.

"I'm too fucking tired to deal with any more people tonight. Will you just take them for me?" he asked.

"Yeah, sure," I said. I was starting to see all my customers as little dollar signs at this point. One last table meant more money—and I had credit cards to pay off. His last table ended up leaving me five bucks, but it was five more than I'd had before. After putting everything away and sweeping the floor, I got out around 3 a.m. The girls and I left the restaurant together, and walked through the cool night air to our cars. I enjoyed the chill in the air as I listened to them complain about Sam.

Jenny lit a cigarette. "I don't care what he's up to. Tonight he disappeared for twenty minutes just when half his section was about to leave. I passed by *right then*, and got stuck running his credit cards for him. How am I supposed to separate someone else's check? I don't know what they ate. It took forever and my section suffered for it. Do you smoke?" she offered me her pack.

"No," I said.

"You will, working here," Sharon said.

"Sam might be the world's worst waiter," Gretchen said, smiling, "but you have to admit, he's cute as hell. Tall, dark, and yummy."

Jenny laughed and nodded. "Cute, yeah," Sharon agreed. "But fuckin' dumb."

I did quite a bit of running for Sam as well, but, as the new girl, I kept quiet. Instead, I thought about the near $160 in my pocket.

"Hey, guys, I've got some wine at my place," Sandy said.

"Nice!" Gretchen said. "I'll be over."

"I'm in," Jenny said.

"How about you, Amy?" Sandy asked me.

The girls were inviting me over? It was late, but then, I didn't have any plans. "Yeah, okay."

"Good! My place is a couple blocks away. You can follow us," Sandy said.

We rounded the corner to a side street where we'd parked our cars. Sandy's Jeep was right in front of my car, so I followed her. We drove a few blocks east and then made a right and drove south for another two blocks when Sandy slowed down and I could see she was looking for parking. She stopped at one space and leaned out her window to tell me to take it. I managed the best parallel park job of my life to this point and hopped out. Driving in the city was really sharpening my skills. Sandy had parked further up the street, so I walked toward her Jeep. The other girls were coming from differing locations, converging in the middle of the street, chatting away like it was the middle of the afternoon.

Sandy's apartment was a small townhouse that she shared with two others, who were both out of town for the weekend. She invited us to sit down in the living room, which was a nautical-looking blue and white room, while she went into the kitchen for wine glasses.

Sharon ran upstairs to the bathroom, obviously familiar with Sandy's apartment. Sandy brought wine glasses for everyone, turned on some music, and went to the corner of the dining room to a tall wine rack.

"Are these all yours?" Gretchen asked, coming up behind Sandy and grabbing at bottles on the rack.

"Most of them," Sandy said. "Some belong to my roommates. *This* is my favorite," Sandy said. "It's really smooth, you're going to like it. The stock boys at the grocery store always save me a few bottles."

"Hey, Sandy, can we light these candles?" Jenny was standing near the stereo.

"Yeah, go for it. There's some matches on the stairs."

"Oh, here they are," Sharon said as she descended the stairs.

"I've got my lighter," Jenny said.

Sandy opened the bottle with a pop and poured for each of us. Jenny and I sat forward on the couch to pick up our glasses. Sandy sat down on the armchair, and Sharon and Gretchen crawled closer to the coffee table from their floor locations. "Okay, everybody," Sandy held up her glass. "To friendship, old and new, to waitresses fast and pretty, and to bartenders who pour heavily."

"Here, here!"

"Cheers!"

We drank and complimented Sandy on the wine. "Oh, you guys, I waited on the most disgusting couple tonight," Jenny said. "They were all over each other. They were in one of those oversized chairs in the back," she rolled her eyes. "Both of them were sitting on one chair together."

"The captain's chairs aren't wide enough for two people," Sharon said.

"Tell me about it!" Jenny said.

"Well, I had to wait on all the kids tonight," Sharon said. "Table after table of high schoolers."

"At least they weren't the college kids," Sharon said. "They can't tip for shit."

"Hey!" Gretchen protested.

"I didn't mean you," Sharon said. "You know what I'm talking about. They come in with their Banana Republic shopping bags, pig out, and leave ten percent if you're lucky."

"I hear you," Gretchen agreed. "They're spending their parents' money anyway, why not leave a decent tip? I doubt they realize we get paid two bucks an hour without tips."

"Thanks for getting my back tonight," Jenny said to me. "They double sat me while I was stuck in Sam's section fixing the mess he made with those stupid separate checks. But thanks for getting everybody started on their drinks for me. That was a huge help."

"No problem," I said. "I wasn't all that busy right then."

"Why does that clown still have a job?" Sandy asked.

"Because he's cute," Gretchen said.

"Okay, Gretchen, we get it!" Sharon said. "If you're after Sam, you can have him! None of us is going to fight you for him, dear."

"No way," Jenny agreed.

"Oh, come on, though. You have to admit he's damn good-looking," Gretchen said. She stretched out on her back and crossed her arms behind her head. "Ah . . . " she said.

"Knock it off!" Sandy poked at her with her foot.

"I admit he's cute, but there's no way in hell I'd go out with him again," Jenny said. "He's a pothead and a player. You can have him."

"How was your night, Amy?" Jenny asked.

"Not too bad," I said. "My people were all pretty nice. Oh, but this one lady brought in her little boy and he wanted McNuggets. I told her we didn't serve them and she looked at me like I'd grown a second head."

"Hello! McDonald's is down the street!" Gretchen said. "Our menu's even posted outside! People can see what they're getting into before they walk in the door."

I sat back in the couch in complete awe. I was in Sandy's living room, drinking a glass of wine in the open, listening to the girls laugh and swear and carry on in complete freedom. This was so different from my own house. This was comfortable, and inviting.

"Sandy, I didn't know you had this," Sharon pulled a CD from the stack next to the stereo.

Sandy eyed it, "Blondie?" She nodded.

"Can I borrow it?"

"Yeah, take her. But bring her back."

"Don't I always?"

Sandy laughed. "Yeah, actually you are pretty good about it. Some people take shit and I never see my stuff again."

"Wow, is it really four o'clock?" Sharon asked.

"Yeah," somebody else said.

"I've got to get going," Sharon said. "Mark talked me into doing the prep work tomorrow. I have to be back there in a couple hours."

"Sucks to be you," Sandy said.

"Yeah, tell me about it. But it's ten bucks an hour." Sharon placed her empty wine glass on the coffee table and stood up. Everyone else followed suit. We thanked Sandy, grabbed our purses and keys, and headed for the door.

"Do you work tomorrow?" Jenny asked me as we stepped outside.

"No, Monday," I said.

"I'll see you Monday," Gretchen told me.

"How about Thursday?" Jenny asked, stopping at her car. I nodded. "Okay, I'll see you Thursday," she said.

Sharon pushed a button on her keys and her Nissan squawked. "I'll see you guys on Thursday, too," she said. "Goodnight!"

"Goodnight!" I called out and hopped into my own car. I couldn't wait to get home, rub my sore feet, and fall into bed.

EIGHT

On Sunday I slept late, and then drove around looking for a place to be other than at home. It was a beautiful fall day, but a little too cool to wander outside on the National Mall. The Upscale wasn't open for a few hours yet, but then again I didn't really want to hang out there on my first day off. I just needed somewhere to go, other than work and home. I settled on Barnes and Noble, thinking I could spend the afternoon looking for something to read. I got a coffee in the packed café area, and wandered through the store sipping my cup and browsing the shelves. The bookstore was nearly as crowded as the café area. I passed people carrying coffee cups in almost every aisle, some of them sitting cross-legged on the floor, flipping through books. This was definitely the place to be.

I gathered a small stack of new fiction and old poetry, and sat down in a corner on the floor to look through the pile. Soon two others joined me, and then a third, each with their own stack of books. No one talked, but we shifted here and there to make more space for the others. I looked through all my book choices and eventually read a good deal of one of them. I bought that one and put the others back; though I'd watched other people read for a while and then put their books back on the shelves without buying anything.

On my way out of the store a man stopped me. "Hey, you work at the Upscale, right?"

"Yeah," I said, looking at the tall, dark-skinned man in front of me.

"You were our waitress yesterday when I came in with my girlfriend."

I looked at the man for a moment and then suddenly remembered him. "Yeah!" I said. "You got a pizza, extra sauce, I remember."

"Yeah, that was us. Your pizza's awesome. What's your name again?"

"Amy," I said. "Yeah, yesterday was pretty crazy. It was my first day working on my own."

"Really? Well, you seemed like you knew what you were doing." He introduced himself and we shook hands. "Thanks for taking good care of us."

"No problem," I said. "Come back in again."

"We will," the man said.

This was the first time I'd been recognized by anyone since I moved to D.C. And okay, so I didn't know this man. But I suddenly felt noticed, like the dust was blown off me and I was visible.

There were other changes as well. One morning as I got coffees for Chad and me, the man ahead of me in line dropped his cup, spilling it on the condiment table, the floor, and even some on his suit. "Oh, let me help you," I said, and had the whole mess cleaned up and another coffee ordered for him before he knew what happened. Others had stepped out of the way, the same as I used to do, and even some decided they didn't need sugar for their coffee if it meant dealing with a mess in order to get it. The man thanked me and I went on my way, realizing after the fact that this was out of character for me.

Chad, of course, was back to his usual self. "Amy, I noticed you didn't check the fax machine again. I did it for you."

"Great," I said cheerfully. "Are you sure you don't want to just check the machine every day?"

"That's *your* job!" he screamed. "I'm a *lobbyist!*" and ran into his office. I smiled.

Mr. Watters came in shortly after that. "Amy, I've got a project for you," he said. "The trade association would like us to throw a party to celebrate the Senate passage of the retail bill. We put a lot of man hours in on that one, for well over a year. It's time to celebrate. Would you call around and see what kind of cost we're looking at? Find a nice meeting space, or small ballroom . . . catered . . . And let's do it in November—but after the elections. The association's picking up the tab for all of it, so find someplace good."

"Sure thing," I said.

"What's this about a party?" Chad emerged from his hiding place.

"Association wants to celebrate the retail bill," Mr. Watters said. "I'll need you both to be there."

I called around to the convention centers and different hotels and got prices on space and menus faxed to the office. By lunchtime I was going through everything at my desk, eyeing the decadent menus and wishing I had more than my canned soup to eat for lunch.

"Amy, did you bring two lunches today?" Chad asked as he rifled through the little fridge.

"Oh, that's my dinner."

"Dinner?"

"Yeah, I, uh . . . I started waiting tables in the evenings, and I'm leaving straight from here to go to the restaurant."

"Waiting tables?" Chad came around the corner to look at me. "*Moonlighting?* Where at?"

"The Upscale, in Virginia."

Chad looked slightly impressed. "Oh, really?" he said. "That's a very hip place. I've been there, of course. Didn't they just open up?"

"Yeah, pretty recently. And it's not going to interfere with my work here. This job is definitely my priority. I just need to get a grip on my spending."

"Sounds very responsible. You know, I waited tables while in grad school at GW. Oh, but waiters everywhere just spend their money on alcohol and cigarettes. Something about restaurants makes you spend more than you'll ever make. That, and overwork yourself."

"I'll take my chances," I said, fully confident. Going from one job to the other *was* a bit much at first, but I was handling it.

I was eating dinner and changing clothes at the office, then driving straight to the restaurant. I had just enough time to go home between jobs, but absolutely didn't want to. Soon enough I'd made friends with the cooks, who managed to "mess up" foods here and there and would offer them to me.

"That's my girl, Amy," Big Charlie would say daily. "Nobody better mess with my Amy. I slave away over here making pizzas from scratch, and when they're ready you guys just leave 'em sittin' here to get cold. But not my Amy," he'd flash a white smile that looked brighter next to his dark skin, and he'd try to get his ex-Marine bulk to look coy and demure. "My Amy picks up her food right away so all my work doesn't go to waste. You want me to make you a pizza?"

"No, Charlie, but thanks. I already ate the sandwich you gave me and the fries Sharon didn't finish."

"You want me to make you another sandwich?"

"No, Charlie," I'd laugh. "I'm fine!"

"Girl, you look skinny. We need to fatten you up. You got any fifties?"
Big Charlie buried fifty-dollar bills in his backyard. His first wife had
divorced him and took him for all he had. After that, he decided to hide
his money from his second wife rather than bank it. "That woman ever
leaves me she gets nothin'."

"I hear ya, Charlie," I'd say. "Sock it to her."

"Look at that Amy, she's the only one working around here," he'd say
to Theresa who worked beside him.

"Um-hmm . . . " Theresa would ignore him. This scene played out at
least three times a week.

My roommates kept up their nightly séances and sing-alongs, but
they stopped bringing their friends into my room—at least while I was
home. Wherever I went in the house, tension was sure to follow, and after
a while I just got used to it—as much as any person can, anyway. Even
their all-hours singing didn't bother me. I was so tired from working two
jobs that I found I could sleep through anything. Only on my rare days
off did I really have to interact with them.

"Amy, Pastor Jeff left you a message," Beth told me on one of my
nights off as I was getting home from the office.

"Beth, ever since I moved in here it seems no one approves of anything
I do. I know I'm outnumbered here, but what if it's not *me*?"

"Huh?" Tweedle asked from the table.

"What if we could all just drop the pretenses, say what we mean, and
be okay with each other no matter what came out?"

"What do you mean?" Beth asked.

"Pastor Jeff says that we don't have to . . . "

"Pastor Jeff again? I'm not worried about what Pastor Jeff thinks. I've
never even met the man. What do *you guys* think, honestly, your own
opinions?" I stunned them. It was like watching robots malfunction, they
blurted out syllables and didn't really understand what I was asking of
them. These girls didn't have an ounce of common sense among them.
People think you have live someplace remote and worship some bizarre
god, or even the devil, to be in a cult. But here I was, living with cultists,
right in the suburbs of our nation's capital. "This is what I'm talking
about," I said, looking into their blank eyes. "This is *exactly* what I'm
talking about."

The next day with Chad wasn't much better. "Amy, get in here," he
yelled from his office. "Read this email and tell me if it sounds nonchalant.
Here's what she wrote me, and my response is on top."

"Okay," I said, sitting down in his chair. "Are you going to hover over me like that?" I asked.

"No," he caught himself. "No, uh . . . I'm going to sit over here." He took a chair on the other side of his desk.

I read the email Connie had sent first. "Chad—We should talk. Meet me at the Club today at lunch. This has gone on long enough.—Connie."

Chad's response was, "Hey Connie, what's up? Hope things are kosher with you. Meeting at the Club sounds great. Can't wait to see you. Love, Chad."

"Do you think I sound casual?" Chad asked. "Because I'm going for 'cas,' you know, not too excited or anything. What do you think?"

"Well, um . . . Yeah, I guess it sounds casual. Maybe you can cut out the 'can't wait to see you' part."

"Do you think that's too much?"

"Yeah. And maybe ending it with 'Love, Chad' is too much. I'd cut out the love part."

"But she sounds like she wants to see me, right?"

"Oh, yeah, she definitely sounds like she . . . needs to see you."

"I knew it," he said. "See, I've been sending her these daily emails. Nothing major. Just jokes and then a few poems that I wrote to her. And it's taken her a couple weeks, but I think she's coming around. Don't you think so?"

"Uh, I really don't know Connie," I said.

"Well I do," he said. "And she's coming around. My persistence is paying off. She even got a new email address, but I looked her up on the Senator's website and found it." I just looked at him. "Don't just sit there. Fix that stuff and send it back to her."

"Chad, are you sure that you want to . . . "

"Amy, will you send the fucking thing? I don't have all day. I have to get a haircut, and I want to stop across the street and pick up a new tie before my lunch today. Send that thing so I can get out the door."

"Okay," I said. "There, it's gone."

"Great," he said. "I'll be back later. Or should I wait for a response from her? No . . . " he thought out loud, "I have to get my hair cut. Okay, watch my computer and if she writes back, call me on my cell. I'll be at Shear Heaven."

Chad returned hours later, after his lunch with Connie. He rushed in and went straight to his office and called his parents. "No, I don't fucking understand it," I heard him say. "She said she doesn't want to see me. So why ask me to lunch to tell me that? What kind of mind game is she playing?" He closed his office door after that. When he emerged he came over to my desk and sat down on the corner of it. "Can I ask you something? If a woman says she threw away the birthday cake you left on her porch, does that mean she's just a cold bitch and I should come to accept that?"

"Huh? You left cake on someone's porch?"

"For Connie's birthday a few weeks ago. She wasn't home so I waited for her, and it got dark so I just left it. I left her a note with it so she knew it was from me. What? What's that look for?"

"You left a cake on her porch. Isn't that weird?"

"No, it was her birthday."

"Why didn't she have plans *with you* on her birthday?"

"She was busy. So what?"

"So you got her a cake anyway, even after she told you she had plans already?" this wasn't working. I tried another angle, "Before today, when's the last time you saw her?"

"A while ago," he shook his head. "I don't know. What are you getting at?"

"I'm sorry, Chad, but I think you guys are, well, broken up," I leaned back in my chair and braced myself for an explosion. None came. "Chad?" he was looking right through me.

"A weekend getaway," he said, nodding. "We need something to spark the romance back into our lives," he hopped off my desk and went toward the door. "I'll be at that travel agency next door to set it up." Between Chad and home, I found comfort in the fact that I had a second job to keep me sane.

That night at Upscale, I had the front section, which included the small window tables again, and the hostess filled them with couple after couple. The couples whispered and giggled, stared into each other's eyes, held hands across the table. I felt like I was intruding every time I approached. They didn't want me to be there; I didn't want to be there. I wanted to sit at the table, be with a great guy, whisper and hold hands. It seemed I was so far from having something like that in my own life.

For hours I had all couples come in, until finally, one guy showed up by himself. He sat drinking a coffee and drawing in a stencil book. As I refilled his coffee I looked over his drawings of dragons and various monsters. He caught me looking and smiled. Pretty soon I caught him watching me no matter where I was in my section.

"Derek!" Jenny ran over from her section and sat down with the guy. They talked for a moment and Jenny called me over. "Amy, this is my friend Derek," she introduced. "Derek, this is Amy." We shook hands. "Amy came with us to Sandy's the other night for an impromptu wine party," Jenny went on. "Where do you work during the day again?"

"I work downtown for a lobbying firm. We represent the retail industry," I said.

"Sounds impressive," Derek said.

"It does sound that way," I said. Really, most office staff in D.C. did something similar. But at the restaurant I had to be careful not to sound like I was bragging.

"Derek is applying to work here as a waiter," Jenny explained to me. "Amy just started here." I nodded.

"Yeah, I could use a job at a place like this," Derek said. "My other job is a little different."

"Amy!" I heard Big Charlie yell from the ovens.

"Oh, I'll be back," I said and rushed off to explain the half-cheese-half-pepperoni pizza I'd just rung in. When I returned Jenny was back in her section again, and Derek was sitting alone. The couple next to Derek saw me approaching, and motioned me over.

"Excuse me, but my sandwich doesn't have enough mayonnaise. Can I have some more?" the female half of the couple asked.

"Sure, right away," I said. Derek looked up at me and I smiled. He looked over at the mayonnaise girl and rolled his eyes, then looked back at me again.

I got the mayo, and Derek called me over. "Amy, I hate to bother you, but I don't seem to have any mayonnaise either," he said.

I laughed. "Would you like that in your coffee?" I asked.

"Uh, no," he grinned. "But I would like another cup, if you don't mind."

I got the coffee pot and stopped to grab a handful of creamers, remembering that he'd gone through a bunch of them already, and walked back to his table in time to find him standing to greet a girl who'd just come in. He kissed her as she approached the table and they sat across from one another, still holding hands. Of course he hadn't been flirting with me. I knew that.

"Just a water for me," the girl sitting with him said to me.

"Sure, I'll be right back," I said, a little too cheerfully.

Sam was using the water pitcher when I approached. "Where are the other pitchers?" I asked.

"Not sure," he said, eyeing me strangely. "How many do you need?"

"Just one."

"You can take this one," he said, taking a full glass from his tray and handing it to me.

"Thanks," I said.

"You're the new girl," he said, and didn't let go of the glass. "Amy, right? You're more mysterious than these other girls. I don't know anything about you. I'm Sam."

"Nice to meet you, Sam," I said. "But I'm not mysterious," I said, taking the glass from him. "Thanks."

I turned my back on Sam and returned to my section, though I could feel Sam's eyes on me as I did. I delivered the water and checked back with mayonnaise girl to see that she had enough, and then cleared away the extra dishes from her table.

"So what do you think of my friend Derek?" Jenny asked me as she brought a stack of plates back to the dish room. "He seems to like you," she gushed.

"Jenny, he's with that girl," I said, dismissing the subject as politely as I could. Sam walked in just at that moment.

"Girlfriends are speed bumps, honey," Jenny said. "Not roadblocks."

My mouth dropped open. "Jenny!"

"Trust me, Sweetie, he likes you," she said, oblivious that Sam was listening.

"Uh-huh," I rolled my eyes at her and left the dish room. I finished up my tables, cleaned my section, and did my best to avoid both Sam and Derek. Sam was easy: I just had to keep cleaning knowing that he avoided situations where work was involved. Once everything else was clean and I had nothing left to do, I dropped the check at Derek's table.

"Thanks," his girlfriend said to me. Derek said nothing but reached for the check. His girlfriend grabbed it first and I left them to their who-should-pay argument. In the end, the girl won, took some cash from her purse and left it on the table. I stood at the bar and helped Sandy clean up until they were gone. Thankfully, Sam was nowhere around. I turned in my credit card slips, put my percentage in the tip-out jar for the kitchen staff, and left for the night.

As I walked to my car, I thought of the lousy ten percent tip I got from Derek's girlfriend. I also thought of the predatory way Sam had been looking at me. If Mr. Right were out there, he'd never find me here. Look what I'd become.

I didn't want this to be my entire life. Spending my days stuck in the office, spending my nights waiting on nice couples, feeling completely alone all of the time. I dreaded waking up in the morning, knowing that I had to find the energy to work a double before I could go back to sleep again. I got to the first stoplight on my way home and suddenly fell apart.

I cried, knowing it would take months of this to pay off my debts, months of pouring coffee and serving pizzas to couples that had each other, while I had only my work. I cried because I needed this job. I needed it to save me from my debt, to save me from my roommates, from my weird officemate, and from my life that seemed to be going nowhere. I cried for the dread I felt every time I had a day off when I'd have to go home. I liked to think I could handle the tension of the house, but it was a lie. I was cracking.

Most of all, I cried because I needed the companionship of my coworkers more than I liked to admit. I was lonely. I didn't realize how much until just this moment. I was on my own, and everything was up to me. I didn't even know where to begin.

I was exhausted, mentally and physically. I felt hollow, like I'd been searching for something that I just wasn't finding. It was all too much for one person. My life had to be better than this. It just had to.

NINE

My Upscale schedule was getting hectic. I could do four or five shifts in a row, but any more than that and I just got clumsy. One such night I dropped a glass that exploded strawberry milkshake all over my legs and the floor.

"Honey, are you alright?" Sandy asked me, leaning over her bar to survey the mess. "I'll get the floor, you clean yourself up. Go."

"Jason, I need another strawberry milkshake. I'm sorry. Thank you!" I said as I ran past his counter on my way to the dish room where I could clean up away from my customers. I hadn't worked much with Jason and I knew milkshakes were a pain in the ass to make. But he didn't say a word once he saw the cold, sticky milkshake running down my legs. Once in the dish room, I surveyed the mess. Thankfully, very little of it had hit my skirt. I poured water on some paper towels and tried to clean myself up.

"This is the most excitement my thighs have had in months," I mumbled to myself. I heard a laugh and looked up to find Jason standing in the doorway watching me.

"Be glad none of the other guys came in just now," he said, "because this is probably a turn-on."

"How is *this* a turn-on?"

He shrugged and smiled, "Straight men find the strangest things attractive."

"Jason, I'm gonna be sticky for the rest of the night," I complained.

"Amy, just stop!"

"I meant my legs, weirdo!"

Jason composed himself, barely. "Machine's running. Your milkshake will be done in a second. I'd give you a hug, Sweetie, but I don't want to be sticky . . . " He laughed again.

"You jerk," I gave an embarrassed smile. "And my whole section watched me drop it, so they're going to be jumpy every time I walk by with another drink. This sucks . . . "

"Come get your milkshake . . . " he sang as he went back to the drink area. I followed him out. "I'm sure nobody noticed," he said.

"Ha!" I said.

Jason stopped the blender and poured the new milkshake. "Well, Derek wasn't here to see it. He doesn't start for a couple days yet." He handed me the glass and read the look of surprise on my face. "Honey, I'm in the middle of the restaurant. I hear everything. Jenny's on a mission to get you two together."

"I don't know why. I don't think he's interested in me."

"He's not your type anyway. That reminds me, Sam has his eye on you."

"Sam? The pothead player?"

"That's the one," he nodded.

"Great." I sighed. "Do I look alright?"

"Fabulous, if a little sticky. But hey, at least you didn't spill it on anybody else. You took one for the team, Amy."

I delivered the shake and went to thank Sandy for cleaning up my mess. The girls were all congregated at the bar.

"Amy, are you coming out with us after work?" Sandy asked.

"Oh, I don't know, guys," I said. "I need a shower. And I'm just so beat."

"I know what you mean," Sandy said. "I can't wait 'til we get another bartender trained. I could use some time away from this place."

"I'm about ready to set up a cot in the basement and just sleep here," I said.

"It's not a bad idea," she said. "There's food down there, and even alcohol so long as you have the key." She twirled the bartender's keys on her finger and smiled triumphantly.

"You're coming out, right?" Jenny approached us.

"I'm in," Sandy said. "But Amy's on the fence."

"Amy, you have to come! It's my birthday! And Derek is working his last night at his other job—we're going to see him. It'll be a blast. You're coming, okay?" she said. "You're coming."

I nodded. "Okay, okay," I said. "I can postpone sleep a little longer. And I can sleep in tomorrow anyway." Mr. Watters had closed our office in the morning so we could go vote.

After work we piled into two cars—Gretchen and Jenny went with Sandy, and I had Haley and Sharon with me. We followed Sandy's car into D.C.

"Why isn't Jason coming?" I asked.

"His boyfriend won't let him," Sharon said. "He thinks we're a bad influence on him."

"How long have you guys worked at Upscale?" I asked.

"Forever," Sharon said. "I worked at another one in the city for about eight months and then transferred to this one when it opened."

"I started about two weeks before you did," Haley told me.

"And you're a student?" I asked her.

"Yeah, Georgetown. I'm still trying to figure out what I want to do," she seemed to dismiss the subject, but then added, "Actually, it's not so bad. I take all these strange classes, just to try things out. Anything from chemistry to snowboarding. I've tried all sorts of stuff. Currently, though, I'm an English major. As of this semester."

"They offer snowboarding?" Sharon didn't believe her.

"Yep, I took it last spring. Once a week they bussed us out to the slopes and we had lessons," Haley fussed with her hair. "We go snowboarding and get gym credits for it. It was a hell of a lot more fun than chemistry, I can tell you that."

Sharon turned to face Haley, who was in the backseat. "I don't think that's going to help you get in," she said as Haley pulled her straight dark hair into two low pigtails. "Now you look twelve."

"Not twelve, *sassy*," Haley corrected. "And they'll let me in, don't worry."

"Why don't you just get a fake ID?" Sharon asked.

"Why bother? I'm 21 in six months. And would you stop worrying? I'll get in I'm telling you."

We drove into southeast D.C. "Are you sure our cars are going to be okay?" I asked when we had parked in a run-down neighborhood and met up with the other girls.

"The cars will be fine," Jenny dismissed. "But listen, none of us walks alone for any reason. If we're in groups of three or more, we'll be alright. If you walk alone, you run the risk of being dragged off into an alley and never heard from again."

"I'm from New York," Gretchen said. "I can handle this."

"No," Jenny warned her. "Let's be safe tonight. Nobody walks alone, you got me?" Gretchen agreed but when Jenny turned Gretchen rolled her eyes at Sharon.

"Stop that," Sharon elbowed her.

Wet was in a downright nasty part of town, and night's darkness couldn't hide enough of it. The hair on the back of my neck was standing up.

"My spidey sense is kicking in," Haley said in a low voice.

"Mine, too," I said in all seriousness. We were all quiet at this point, listening to our own footsteps and a siren in the distance.

"Your what sense?" Gretchen asked.

"Duh, Spider Man," Haley laughed, breaking the tension around us.

"Hey, guys, try to avoid the puddles, okay?" I said.

"Ugh, it hasn't rained in over a week," Sandy said.

Trash was piled on the sidewalks and men were lurking in the darkness around the abandoned-looking buildings. They called out to us as we passed, but Jenny said something that shut off our spidey sense altogether.

"So it's a strip club, just so you're prepared," she informed us.

"You brought us to a strip club?" Gretchen asked. "Nice!"

"This is exactly what Martin was talking about," Sharon said.

I shot Haley a look. "Jason's boyfriend," she whispered.

"*Wet* is a gay strip club," Jenny said. "And Derek is dancing tonight."

"Derek is a stripper?" Sandy asked.

"Yeah, for gay men," Jenny said.

"But he's . . . " Gretchen started.

"No," Jenny laughed. "He's not gay. But he *is* broke."

We walked up the cement stairs into the club, and surprised the bouncer—either because we were all clad in black or because we were women. Haley led the charge.

She smiled at the bouncer who was sitting behind a dirty countertop. She turned and slowly lifted herself up to sit next to the cash register, then turned her head so that she faced the bouncer. "Hi," she breathed. "We want in."

We each paid five bucks and got our hands stamped, except for Haley who got in free. TV monitors mounted at the ceiling around the room were showing porn videos. I stared for a moment, shocked that we were still only in the front room and I was already getting an eyeful. I looked from screen to screen, and realized there were no women in the videos. Then I realized I was staring. I quickly looked down.

The music from the next room poured in through the curtained doorway and Jenny and Gretchen were bouncing along to the beat. "Amateur night is still going on in there," the bouncer informed us. "It'll last another half hour and then we'll have our dancers come out. You ladies enjoy."

We stepped through the curtains and into the club.

"Haley, how did you do that?" I asked. "You're underage with no ID *and* you got in free."

She shrugged. "I don't know. It doesn't always work on gay men. Today it did."

The club was a wide and dark room filled with silhouetted people and in the center was a rectangular bar with naked men dancing on it. I quickly looked away and hoped we'd find a corner to settle into. The club air was warm and the whole place had a sticky feel to it. I mentally warned myself not to touch anything.

"Oh my God!" Gretchen said, lighting a cigarette. "Check these guys out!"

"I'm trying not to," I said.

"Amy, look! That guy looks like he's never been naked in his life. What's he *doing* up there?"

"Amateur night," Jenny reminded us. "These guys don't seem to understand how to look sensual."

I braved another look and sure enough, Jenny's impression seemed right. There were five guys dancing on the bar, and all of them looked awkward in their nakedness. I was trying not to stare, but it was like looking at a traffic accident. The five were of various ages and sizes, and all of them were writhing, in a halted fashion, to the music. It all seemed unnatural, like watching birds try to be snakes.

"What did we get ourselves into?" Sharon asked.

"Can you imagine seeing that guy do that in the bedroom for you?" Gretchen asked.

"No," I said. "Oh, but now I'm picturing it!" I covered my eyes. "Ew!"

"My eyes! My eyes!" Haley laughed.

"That guy needs a comb for his back," I heard Sandy mumble to Gretchen. The two of them were staring at the men with amused looks on their faces.

"Hey, you two," Haley interrupted. She lit a cigarette. "Drinks?"

"That looks like the only bar," Sharon nodded to the one the "dancers" were on. "I don't want to get any closer than this."

"Fine, I'll go," Haley said. "Sandy, come with me. What do you guys want? Nah, forget it. You're getting what I bring you."

As my eyes adjusted to the darkness I started to see the people around us. We seemed to be the only women in the building, except for the two bartenders who both seemed to be male underneath the wigs and all the makeup. There was a circle of guys next to us, one of which stood out to me for some reason. He was a really attractive guy, but if I blinked and thought of him as a girl, he was just as beautiful. His skin was a smooth brown; he was thin but muscular; his eyelashes were better than any girl's I'd ever seen. He saw me staring, so I smiled.

"Girlfriend!" he said and walked up to me. "What's your name?"

"Amy," I said.

"Amy, you have a beautiful smile," he said in a voice that, male or female, was musical.

"Thank you. What's your name?"

"I'm *Latte*," he said, pronouncing it as though it were a title, not just a name. "And these are my friends." He introduced the group he was with and I said hello to each of the guys. None of them were as over-the-top as Latte with his pink feather boa and tight t-shirt with the word *naughty* printed on it. The shirt was cropped to show his stomach, and his jeans were equally as tight. "Do you need a drink?" he asked me.

"No, my friends are getting me one," I said, pointing to Haley and Sandy who were returning with their hands full of drinks. "But thank you," I said, and he smiled. At the same time, more people were joining his group.

"Latte, get your fine self over here and say hello," one of the new guys complained.

"Oh my, I have to go. Amy, I'll see you around." He smiled and gave me a quick hug as if we'd been friends forever.

"We just got a bunch of rail drinks, so who wants what?" Sandy asked. "There's a splash of tonic in each one. This is whiskey . . . "

"Ooh, mine!" Sharon said.

"This is either vodka or gin," Haley held out a glass.

Jenny drank from it. "Ugh, gin," she said.

"Mine!" I said.

"Then this must be the vodka . . . "

"I'll take that," Jenny said.

In the meantime, the amateurs were leaving the bar/stage and one of the bartenders was talking over a loudspeaker. The music changed and got louder, and the bartender started announcing the club's regular dancers as they came out. "Ken, Rico, Terence, Derek!"

Derek came strutting out when called, stark naked except for socks, which Jenny explained held his tip money. The girls and I shrieked, adding to the noise level in the room.

"Oh my God!" Gretchen said to Jenny. "He's *your* friend, how come you didn't tell us he looks like *that*?"

"I didn't know!" Jenny said, just as shocked.

Derek looked like he spent his days in the gym, muscle rippled from his shoulders to his calves. His chest was broad and built, his stomach was a six-pack leading down to his rather impressive manhood, and all of it was held up by tree-like legs. His back was defined, and below that was absolutely grab-able. Gretchen and Haley did squeezing motions with their hands to accentuate this. I tried to pretend I wasn't looking, but Derek exuded sex.

Sharon, Sandy, and I were embarrassed but making the best of it by talking about work between glances, Gretchen and Haley danced around and smoked cigarettes as comfortable as ever about their surroundings, and Jenny celebrated her birthday like a pro. She drank, she danced with Derek when he pulled her onto the bar, and when he planted a giant kiss on her, she grabbed the back of his neck and kissed back.

Derek wasn't the least bit shy. Completely naked in front of strangers and even with his new and old friends watching, he seemed as comfortable dancing on a bar as anyone else would be taking a stroll through the park. Song after song, the dancing went on, fast, slow, rhythmic. And then we discovered why the club was named *Wet*.

At the corner of the bar were mirrors with showers mounted to them. For the show's finale, Derek and two others turned the showers on and lathered up with body soap. The music pumping, water splashing everywhere, we watched Derek take a shower.

After the finale, the girls wanted to wait for Derek and then go to another after-hours club, but I was getting pretty tired so I figured it was time for me to go. I waved goodbye to Derek who was finishing his shower, hugged the girls, and enlisted Sharon and Gretchen to walk me to my car.

"Goodbye, Amy!" called a familiar voice as we crossed the room toward the door. I turned to see Latte with his friends waving at me.

"Bye, Latte!" I called back as Sharon and Gretchen gave me strange looks.

"Amy, you know people here?" Sharon raised her eyebrows.

"I do now," I said.

It was somewhere in the wee hours when I arrived at the house to find all the lights on and the house full of people.

Beth was giving a tour of my room to a group of people. "Oh, Amy!" she said. "I hope you don't mind that I use your stereo. Everyone, this is Amy. This is her room." I watched the group stare at my photos and pick up the knick-knacks and stuffed animals from the shelves.

"Hey, this is nice," one girl was touching one of my silk suits. The guy behind her was staring at the underwear in my laundry basket.

"Everybody out!" I shut off the stereo.

Beth stammered, "Oh, uh, come on, guys, there are more rooms to see."

"Take my room off the tour," I told her.

"Amy, why are you being so rude? And . . . Why do you smell like smoke?"

"I was at a strip club."

"A *what*? I thought you went to work."

"I did. The restaurant closed four hours ago. Thanks for noticing."

"Well, I think we need to have an emergency house meeting tomorrow night."

"Count me out. I'm done with those stupid meetings. Did I mention it was a gay strip club? In Southeast. G'night." I closed the door on them and locked it. Alone at last, I felt free.

I slept in the next day, which was wonderful. And voting for a new President didn't take as long as I thought it might, so I had time to enjoy a cup of coffee at the Little Shop before heading up to the office.

Chad was at my desk, messing around with my computer. "Nice to sleep in today, right?" he asked. "Did you go to a last-minute election rally? I did."

"No. No rallies for me. Nothing at all to do with the elections, actually. What's wrong with my computer?"

"New virus software. Should only take a couple hours."

"Hi, Amy, Chad," Mr. Watters walked in and set his briefcase on my desk. "Amy, can you type this for me?" he handed me a stack of notes from the briefcase. "Doesn't have to be done right away if you're having computer trouble," he looked at Chad.

"Just new virus software," Chad said.

"Well, tomorrow's fine. I'm only here to make a few phone calls and them I'm off to the Club to watch the election tallies." True to his word, Mr. Watters was gone within the hour.

Chad tied up my computer for most of the afternoon. He simultaneously did his own and Mr. Watters' computers, so I couldn't really get any of my work done. Finally, I decided to use the old typewriter in the copy room for Mr. Watters' notes. At least they'd be typed, and I could re-type them into my computer the next day.

Finally, the "end" of the day rolled around, and it was time for me to leave the office and go back to the Upscale. As luck would have it, the restaurant was practically empty due to the election. It seemed people were at home watching the tallies or out at political parties. With little work to do, I hit the coffee pretty hard to keep myself going. For some odd reason, standing around in a restaurant is downright draining. I'd much rather have been overworked than under.

"Oh man, when Derek came out wearing nothing but what God gave him I thought I would die!" Haley said.

"That was awesome!" Gretchen said. "One hell of a night." We stood around giggling about it.

"I'm so glad he's not here tonight," I said. "I'd be so embarrassed."

"Why?" Gretchen asked.

"Yeah, what are you talking about?" Haley asked.

"Oh, come on, you guys. You know what I mean," I said.

"What's the big deal?" Haley asked.

"Girls, leave Amy alone," Jenny teased as she approached us. "Amy has her *reasons*."

"I do not," I said, as honestly as I could. Even when Derek kissed Jenny at the strip club, I hadn't felt the slightest hint of jealousy. Obviously it was a passing thing. "Seriously," I assured her. "I just don't want it to be awkward now that we've all seen Derek's goods. The poor guy works with a bunch of women who've all seen him naked."

"Derek isn't that shy," Jenny assured us.

"Well, I am," I said.

"Not me," Haley said.

"Me, either," said Gretchen, and the two of them walked away, giggling. I shook my head.

"So you *don't* like Derek?" Jenny lowered her voice so we wouldn't be overheard.

"Jenny!" I whined. "He has a girlfriend. And I hate to point out the obvious, but you did kiss him just last night." I wanted someone in my life, but I didn't want it like this.

"Okay," Jenny conceded. "I won't bug you."

Sandy emerged from the basement stairwell, talking with Jason. Both of them had their arms full of beer bottles. "The idiot bartender yesterday never bothered to restock," Sandy said as they approached. "Oh, wait, that was me," she laughed. "Hey, everyone! Check it out, Jason's our new bartender-in-training!"

"Awesome!" Gretchen and Haley hugged Jason.

"Thanks, girls," Jason beamed. "I figured since they've got me making drinks anyway, I might as well learn the alcoholic ones. I'm a little nervous, so go easy on me, okay? Drinks might be a little stronger than usual."

"No one will complain," Jenny said. "That is, if we get any people in here tonight."

"At this rate I'm liable to fall asleep," I said. "I was fine right up until an hour ago. How is it that all of you are so awake?" Sharon was off for the night, but Jenny, Gretchen, and Haley all seemed fine. Sandy was the only one who mentioned being tired, but she looked as vibrant as ever.

"You know why that is, don't you?" Sam the predator asked me as I refilled my coffee cup. It seemed he overheard my conversation with the girls.

"No, why?"

"Because they're not like us," he said. He leaned his tall, lanky self on the counter next to the coffee machines and looked at me.

"What are you talking about?" I asked, trying not to look at him.

"They're all 20 and 21. Why do you think you get along with Sharon the best—because she's 32," he answered his own question.

"She is not," I said. "She's mid-twenties, like me," I defended, though I really didn't know that.

He shook his head. "She's 32. And you're an old soul."

"Right," I said, recognizing a line when I heard one.

He laughed. "I'll bet you get along with people three times your age better than with your peers."

"Doesn't everybody?" I sounded as disinterested as I felt.

He shook his head. "No, you're an old soul, Amy. And that means something. I've been watching you. I pay attention."

"Amy, get out of here," Manager Mark said as he walked by. "You too, Sam. You're cut. Let's see, who else can we send home?"

"Really?" I asked.

Mark looked at me. "Well, we've got practically no customers, we're making no money, and Corporate will ream my ass if I pay six employees all night. Go on, go home. You got the rest of the night off."

"Oh, thank you!" I said, relieved. I turned toward the employee room to get my purse. I couldn't wait to fall into bed. It was 9 p.m. and I could be home and asleep in twenty minutes and didn't have to get up again until eight . . .

"So, Amy . . . " it was Sam's voice behind me. "Want to get a drink with me?"

I stopped and looked at him. "No," I shook my head. Sam looked impressed for some reason. "But thank you. I'm really tired. I'm going home."

TEN

The phone rang early Wednesday morning, well before my alarm clock summoned me. It was Mr. Watters.

"Amy, the office will be closed this morning. It seems all of D.C. was up late last night with the election frenzy, so no one's working yet. We'll open again at noon, so you can go back to sleep."

I'd forgotten all about the election. What day was it, anyway? "Do we have a President yet?" I asked.

"No, not yet," he chuckled. What did that mean? I switched on the news and found out what the rest of Washington already knew.

When I got in, Chad was complaining about the electoral process over the phone to someone. Mr. Watters arrived shortly after that, and Chad quickly ended his phone call.

"Should we postpone the office party until the election gets sorted out?" he asked.

"Well, that's a possibility," Mr. Watters considered. "But then the party is really to celebrate the passage of the retail bill, regardless of the Presidential situation. And this recount could go on for a while."

"A while?" I asked.

"I imagine until Inauguration at the very worst," Mr. Watters said.

"That's two months away!" I said, realizing how much longer the construction on Pennsylvania Avenue was going to last.

"Yeah, well, it's not just about two people vying for the Presidency, it's about all those people under them as well: all those supporters, the backers, the money, all the jobs promised . . . A lot of people are in the balance over this, not just the President and Congressional majority. This could take some time to sort out."

Chad spoke up, "I guess there's no real sense in delaying the party for that long."

"So it's settled," Mr. Watters nodded. "The party happens Friday, as scheduled. Well, I've got a few calls to make before I head up to the Hill. What a puzzle this election is proving to be. Congressional majority hanging in the balance . . . Ah, what a day, huh?" Mr. Watters smiled and his eyes sparkled with amusement.

Chad followed him to his office, but Mr. Watters, true to his word, made a few calls and ignored Chad. Eventually, Chad gave up the eavesdropping and went back to his own office. Mr. Watters hung up the phone and approached my desk wearing his coat and hat and carrying his briefcase. I handed him the notes I'd typed for him. "Thanks, Amy. I'll be on the Hill," he said, exiting the office with a spring in his step.

"By the way, Amy," Chad said. "You might want to call caterer and tell them the party's back on. She called this morning and I told her everything was in flux."

"Yeah, okay," I dismissed. The caterers were under contract to work with me, exclusively. Just as I congratulated myself on having set it up that way, I noticed Mr. Watters' handwritten notes in my trash can. "Chad, did you throw these away?"

"Coffee got spilled on those. But you already typed them, right?"

"But I did them on the typewriter. I need to have a copy in my computer."

"Then should have done them on the computer."

"You were on it all day."

"Then you should have made a copy of what you typed."

"I didn't need one. I had the notes."

"This is why you never get anything done." He closed himself in his office and started watching the TV he'd insisted to Mr. Watters that he needed. "A lobbyist needs to know what's happening on the Congressional channels," he'd said. I'd never watched the Congressional channels myself, but I was sure *Oprah* wasn't on them.

I separated the pages as best I could, and typed as much of the writing as I could make out. The penciled notes seemed to dissolve, so I did what I could from memory. Before the end of the day, I called the caterer who assured me all was on par for the party. Chad had snuck out of the office at some point when I wasn't looking. This is what we'd become.

I arrived at the restaurant that night and found myself stationed next to Sam's section. I had a headache already. This was the last thing that I needed.

"Amy, you look stressed," Sam said as I emerged from the employee room.

"I am stressed," I said. "And listen, we have to try something different for a change. I need you to take care of your own section tonight, because I just can't do it. Okay?"

"Did you have a bad day?" he asked with what sounded like sincerity.

"Uh, yeah I did! So can you . . . "

"What happened?" he sounded concerned. "Do you go to school during the day, or do you have another job? I have no idea what you do all day, Amy."

"I have another job," I said, wondering how long his new "care for Amy" crap would last. "And an evil coworker who is just maddening. You don't have to give me that impressed look, okay? Lots of people have two jobs."

"Lots of people . . . " he repeated. "I don't."

"Yeah, well, that's why I need you to . . . "

"You *need* me . . . "

"Sam, cut it out!"

"Fine, Amy. Let's say I manage my own section for a change, will you let me buy you a drink tonight?"

"You know what, if you can handle your own section, you can buy me two drinks. Now take care of your customers." I doubted that Sam would actually lift a finger, which meant I was off the hook. On the other hand, he was the only guy in a fifty-mile radius paying any attention to me.

But, true to his word, Sam did all his own work. A couple times I caught him looking over at me. He'd mouth, "See?" and gesture to his happy tables and smile at me. Okay, so he was attractive.

At the end of the night he caught up to me as I cashed out. "So, where would you like to go?" he asked. "Oh come on! I held up my end of the deal. I did all my own work tonight. Did you have to do anything for my tables?"

"No," I admitted. "But why can't you do that every night?"

"Ah," he stopped me. "Let's discuss this over that drink. Where can I take you? How about Galifty's? We can walk there."

I sighed. "Fine." He was buying, after all.

"Are you always this hostile when someone asks you out?" he asked as we stepped outside together.

"No. I just don't trust you, that's all."

"Ah," he said, as if the pieces were falling into place. "Are you always this direct?"

"Try to be," I said, keeping my eyes focused in front of me and shoving my hands in my coat pockets.

"You've been hurt," he said, as if the pieces were falling into place.

I looked at him. "Who hasn't?" I trumped.

It was chilly outside and we stepped up our pace. A car stopped in the middle of the street and the driver's window rolled down. Jason popped his head out. "Hey, guys! Need a ride?"

"No, we're fine!" I yelled back. "Thanks anyway!"

"Okay, then! Goodnight!" Jason drove off.

"That was nice of him!" I commented.

"Yeah, it was," Sam agreed.

"I just love Jason!" I marveled.

Sam shook his head. "Girls always love gay men. They're safe or something."

"Think what you want, but Jason is honest. He's real," I said, taking the time to look Sam in the eyes. "If he's nice to you, it's because he likes you. If he ignores you, it's because he doesn't care for you. That's very different for this town. And like that, just now: He offered us a ride because he was concerned. I mean, sometimes you just don't know what your friends want from you, and you don't know if your customers are being nice because they're nice or because they want to date you. With Jason, the lines are drawn. He doesn't want to date me, has no interest in hitting on me. If he's nice to me it's out of friendship. That's refreshing."

Sam nodded and looked at me sideways. I wasn't sure if I'd offended him or not, and I didn't much care. Gretchen adored Sam, why not ask her out instead? Why me, when I was, as he said, hostile toward him?

We reached Galifty's and Sam held the door open for me. We found a table inside and ordered two beers. Sam lit a cigarette, then realized himself and offered me one.

"No, thank you," I said.

"You don't smoke?" he raised his eyebrows. I shook my head. Sam looked impressed. "So what do you do, Amy?"

"What do you mean, 'what do I do?' I work. What do you do?"

"I don't *work*," he said.

I smiled. "Yeah, I know that. So what do you do all day?" Our drinks came and I took a big sip.

"I read," he said. "I take walks. I enjoy life. Why, what is it you do?"

"None of that," I said. "I work in an office by day, a glorified secretary, if you will. I wear suits, fight rush hour traffic, and deal with a coworker who's decided that since he's not happy in life, nobody else should be," I paused to take another sip. Sam seemed to be waiting, so I went on. "Okay, so . . . Then I come to Upscale, to make extra money and really, to get out of my house. I'm currently living with some cultists, who make me feel like I'm a convicted and practicing sinner."

"You articulate yourself very well. I would guess that you have an English degree." I nodded. "Let me guess," he said. "Journalism?"

I had him there. "Poetry."

"Really?" Sam looked intrigued. "I never would have guessed that you were so impractical. I'm sorry, I'm not trying to be rude."

"No, I understand," I said. "It's not an extremely useful degree."

"And you seem so level-headed to me. Who knew that beneath this 'got-it-all-together' exterior that you're a dreamer. Now I understand why I'm so drawn to you. Let me explain . . . "

Sam talked about books, about travel, and the countries he'd seen. He could relate any subject to something he'd read in a book, could articulate the nuances of Hemingway and Goethe, he could bring it all full-circle with an anecdote from one of his travels. He'd seen Spain, Italy, France, Germany, China, and India. Sam was a lover of people, places. He worked dead-end jobs, lived simply, and always saved his money toward his next big travel adventure. He was everything I wanted to be, and had never known.

"I don't read as much as I should," I admitted.

"How can you not? If you want to write well, you have to read a lot. You need to know what's out there," he said.

He finished his beer and asked me if I wanted another. I needed to get home, so I thanked him but shook my head.

Sam paid the check walked me back to my car. I knew from our conversation that he didn't have a car, so I offered to drive him home. He was staying at his brother's apartment, a few blocks south of the Upscale. When we arrived, he invited me in.

"Well, I really have to get up early tomorrow," I said. "I'll come in, but just for a minute."

We entered the small kitchen, and even with the lights off I could see it was clean and modern. He reached for my hand and led me through the dark dining and living rooms to a door off to the side of the couch. He opened the door and switched on a table lamp that was on the floor.

"This is my room," he whispered. We entered the near-empty room and he closed the door behind us. "My brother," Sam was no longer whispering, "works in an office in the city like you do, so I try to be quiet at night."

I nodded, looking around the large room and the few things in it. Sam had a chair and folding table in the corner, a blanket and pillow in another corner, and books all over the place. I couldn't believe this room was attached to the well-furnished and spotless apartment. "I don't have much furniture," Sam said, reading the look on my face. "But this works for me." He rolled out the blankets from the corner and kicked off his shoes. "Want to tuck me in?" he asked.

Sam layed down on the blanket and pulled the sheet up to his waist. He reached behind his neck and pulled his shirt over his head, tossing it through the open closet door into a pile. "Looks like you tucked yourself in," I said.

"So I have," he said. "Sorry, force of habit. But you can lay down here with me if you like." He moved slightly sideways and patted the sheet next to him.

"What exactly do you think is going on here?" I asked him, sitting down on the floor cross-legged.

"I'm not trying to make a move on you, Amy."

"Aren't you?"

"No," he yawned. "Man, I'm tired. No, no moves." He shifted the pillow under his head and closed his eyes. "I'm not making any moves on you tonight. I think you and I like each other, but we don't know what to do about it."

I sat quietly for a few minutes, thinking about this and listening to his breathing. Soon I realized he was asleep. Beside me was the pile of change and other pocket items he'd emptied before settling down on his blankets. I picked up his passport that he was using as an ID in lieu of a driver's license, and flipped through the pages. Corsi, Samuel Robert, birthplace: California. Birthdate: Oct 3 Year: 1972. The picture wasn't all that bad, either. Kind of made him look a little devilish, but I think that was his eyebrows. And sure enough, there were stamps from France, China, Greece, Spain, and multiple stamps from Italy and Germany. Envious, I closed the passport and put it back on the pile. I looked over at Sam and wanted to kiss him. But like he said, I didn't know what would happen if I did. I sat there for a moment thinking about it, and then I got to my feet. I switched off his lamp, and let myself out.

The next day at the office I tried my best to finish the newsletter, but kept catching myself mid-daydream about Sam. The daydreams were a lot more interesting than the African trade bill's effect on the retail industry, although, deep down, I found that interesting as well. Realizing I was getting nothing done, I headed out for a candy bar to perk me up.

"Hey, Miss Thing!" I heard behind me at the corner newsstand.

"Hey, Beau," I said, turning to see my office neighbor behind me. "How's the travel business?"

"Oh, it's work," he said, as if that were true. "You look a little down and out, what's wrong? As if I can't guess."

"Well, Chad's behaving himself today, which is more than I can say for yesterday. I'm just happy to get out of the office for a change."

"Well, I don't think that candy bar is going to cut it," he said, seeing my reason for walking to the newsstand. "Chocolate is amazing, but what you need is alcohol. No, really," he went on. "Peter and I are having a few friends over next week. A small dinner get-together. He'd love to meet you."

"That's really nice, thank you!" I said.

"A week from tonight," Beau said.

"I'll be there," I said, making a mental list of servers who would switch with me if I happened to work that night.

Back at the office, Chad was sitting at my desk with a smirk on his face. "Oh, Amy, back so soon? I was just writing you a note. Sam called."

"Sam called? Oh, I gave him my business card," I nodded.

"I'd assume he's your new boyfriend, but, have you seen yourself lately? He left a number, but you walked in in the middle of my writing it down. I'm not sure what the last four numbers were. Sorry."

"Oh, really? Gosh, I hope Mr. Watters didn't need that number." I shook my head. "Of course not, he'd obviously *have* the number of his chief lobbyist, right?"

"What?" Chad snapped.

"Well, you know about Sam, right? They're like this," I crossed my fingers and held them for him to see.

"Then why was he calling here for you?"

"He does that sometimes so I can get messages to Mr. Watters. Well, I'm sure he'll call back. It's not your fault, Chad." The lie was getting under Chad's skin, which made me feel less disappointed about missing Sam's call. Yes, this is what we'd become.

That night I got to the restaurant hoping, for a change, that Sam was working, but found he'd had the night off. Derek was working in the section next to mine, and I wasn't the slightest bit nervous. In fact, I hardly noticed him. My section was up front, near the bar where Jason was working his first night solo. Everything went fine until an hour before closing, when Sam arrived for a drink sporting a pretty blonde on his arm. The two of them sat at the bar, mere feet from my section, holding hands and kissing.

I felt like the wind was knocked out of me. I shot Sam a look but he didn't notice. Why bring this girl to the restaurant where we work? I was about to march up to the bar and slap Sam when I caught Jason's eye. But he just smiled and went about making drinks. If Jason didn't think this was strange . . .

It occurred to me that Sam never kissed me; in fact, he never laid a hand on me. Did he even like me in the first place? If he did, why hadn't he made a move? He said we liked each other, right? I'd had two beers and I was very tired, but he did say something like that, didn't he?

If I made a scene in front of the whole restaurant, Sam would know that he'd got to me. I couldn't give him the satisfaction. I knew better than to start liking a player. I went to the dish room to calm down. I got a drink of water and wiped my face with a cold towel. But when I emerged and saw Sam nuzzling the blonde at the bar I was sure my face was red again. I turned my back to them and set about cleaning my tables.

"I'm going to go to the ladies' room," I heard the blonde girl say.

"Okay, I'll settle up here and meet you outside," Sam's voice said. Suddenly his voice was behind me. "I'd like to talk to you," he said. "I'd like to explain . . . "

I looked at him and willed my face to look emotionless. "No, you don't have to explain anything to me. In fact, you never have to talk to me again. Please, go on and ignore me." I went back to cleaning my tables. My face was burning. I felt like a complete moron. He stood there for a moment watching me, so I proceeded to the next table and turned my back on him.

"Alright," I heard him say, and then I heard the unmistakable sound of him shuffling away. Was I this easy to walk away from? I squeezed my eyes shut. I should have slapped him when I had the chance.

I cashed out and left the restaurant, ashamed that I didn't stick up for myself. I couldn't cry or scream or anything I imagined I'd do once I was alone. Regret weighed on me heavily. Other than that, I just felt cold.

Nobody was at the house when I arrived, and on the one day I was looking for a fight, too. I fell into bed and turned on the TV, hoping to drown out my thoughts. Did I just have poor judgment? How could it be that, I dressed nicely and took care of myself, and still no one paid any attention? My thoughts kept coming; the TV was no help at all. I lay awake half the night.

In the morning I awoke surprisingly refreshed. In the light of day, the whole situation with Sam didn't really seem that important. Nothing had really happened between us. I hadn't made a scene, and hopefully that showed him that he hadn't made that much impact. Nobody else seemed to notice, and even if they had, it was minute enough to be forgotten by my next shift, which wasn't until tomorrow. Tonight I was off from the restaurant. The day of the retail party had finally arrived.

I spent most of the day out of the office, double checking the last of the party arrangements and catching cabs all over town. I was glad I brought my party clothes separately after all of the running around I'd done. I had a new, navy pinstriped suit I'd bought especially for the party. The jacket pulled in a little at my waist, and the straight skirt ended right at my knees. Add in high navy heels and a tussled bun of curls and I felt I was the picture of success, with style.

The party was held at the Phoenix Park Hotel, which boasts elegance, attention to detail, and fine Irish hospitality. We held the party in the upstairs bar and restaurant, which is long and narrow in shape, and full of polished dark wood and paintings of the Irish countryside in large gold frames. It was elegant yet cozy, and seemed the perfect place for a gathering, especially since they gave us the whole place to ourselves.

"I'm Archie, I'm your bartender," the Anthony Hopkins–looking man said to me.

"Hello, I'm Amy. Nice to meet you, Archie."

"Archie, I'm Chad Scrouchoff," Chad edged me out of the way. "I'm a lobbyist for Watters and Company and I'll be keeping an eye on you. I'll have a glass of white wine."

"Certainly." Archie smiled warmly and without hesitation. This guy was good. He poured a glass for Chad.

"Ignore him," I whispered to Archie when Chad wandered off. "It's really the best way to deal with him."

Archie gave a polite nod, "What can I get you?"

"A glass of red, please. Anything."

"Right away . . . This is a cabernet," he said, setting the glass on the bar.

"Thank you," I said.

Archie lowered his chin and made eye contact with me. "No, thank *you*," he blinked purposefully. He glanced in Chad's direction and back to me again. He gave another slight nod and then greeted Mr. Watters, who had just arrived.

"Nice party, Amy," Mr. Watters said to me as Archie poured him a glass of red wine as well. "Great job."

"Thank you," I said. "So what happens now?"

"Well, we mingle," he said.

"The schmoozing stuff, right?" I said with a slightly disapproving tone.

"Yes, Amy," he said and chuckled. "The schmoozing stuff. Give it a shot. Maybe you'll make a friend."

I raised my eyebrows at him as we were barraged with guests. It was your typical, dressed up political crowd, and I didn't particularly want to talk to anybody. I stood with my drink, looking for a corner to slink into, and wishing my girls from Upscale were there. All around me, top executives from major retail companies greeted and talked with one another like old acquaintances. I tried my best to fit in, but it all seemed so phony to me. I drifted through the party, wishing to be alone with my thoughts, but guests kept coming up to me. I should have worn a more wallflower suit.

"Oh, you work with Chad, right? He's such a hard worker."

"You're the one who works downtown? We've talked on the phone."

"How is it working with Chad? He's always so pleasant."

I pasted a smile to my face and just kept nodded. Were these people kidding?

"Delightful young man."

"Here, here."

The polite-talk was all getting to me. I excused myself to get my third glass of wine. The only other twenty-something in the room approached me and started talking. His light brown hair was perfectly disheveled, like a Hollywood actor, and his gray suit was the sharpest in the room—next to mine, of course. His nails had a clear, shiny polish on them. We talked about money, of all things, and I told him I'd been working at Upscale in the evenings.

"I'd like to bartend," he said, "but to make the good money you have to tend bar topless and I'd rather spend a month in the gym first."

"You? No, you look good," I said. And because I'd had some wine and he was being candid with me in a room full of pretend conversations, I kept talking. "I went to this club called '*Wet*' the other night with my friends from Upscale, and let me tell you, it was amateur night. Some of those guys, ugh."

"I've been there!" he said, and I was relieved that I hadn't crossed a bad line with my conversation. In fact, this seemed to solidify our friendship. "Never on amateur night," he said, "but I can imagine. That's not the best neighborhood."

"Tell me about it."

"I'm Andy."

"Amy," I shook his hand. "I like your bracelet."

"My ex gave it to me. What a drama queen," Andy rolled his eyes. "I dumped him but kept the bracelet. Goes great with the suit, doesn't it?"

"It really does. Can I try it on?"

"Absolutely. You know we should get together for dinner. How is next week for you?"

"I'll just have to check with Upscale to see what nights I have off." I admired the bracelet on my wrist and then gave it back.

"Here's my card. Email me when you get your schedule."

"I will," I said. Andy hugged me and we parted ways. *That was easy.* In all of Washington and in the middle of this schmoozy party, I managed to make a friend.

"I hear you have a degree in writing," said a gruff voice behind me. It was Ted Harvey, Mr. Watters' friend, who approached me. "Well, how do you find Washington?"

"Oh, I don't know that this is the town for my kind of writing," I said to the silver-haired cowboy-looking Ted Harvey. "I'm not a journalist. I prefer poetry and fiction."

Mr. Harvey laughed. "No wonder you ended up in D.C. Look around you," he said. "This *is* fiction."

His honesty was so refreshing that, for a moment, I became Archie: suddenly allowed to drop the politeness and I found myself to be whole again. A smile came to me slowly.

"By the way, that Chad fellow you work with, he's a delight." Mr. Harvey winked at me.

"Fiction, you say?" I stepped back and surveyed the room with new eyes.

"Now you're getting the picture. Have a good evening, Amy," he said, and walked away.

Eventually we did get a new President and the construction finally stopped on Pennsylvania Avenue. And I had a revelation.

ELEVEN

O ver the next few months I dedicated myself to trying out everything
I could. I'd been looking at Washington all wrong. It was a town
all about appearances and connections, but its saving grace was that it
could laugh at itself despite the image. I made connections of my own in
Andy, Beau, Quinn from Upscale, and the least likely of sources, my own
house.

Andy soon became my dinner and a movie date, which made me
appreciate sitting down to eat for a change. On my nights off, we started
meeting up at Union Station for pizza, and after dinner we'd hit the
theater.

Andy and I talked about relationships, and we'd complain about men
together. And even though we worked for opposite ends of the same
trade association, we rarely talked about work. Obviously Chad was a
topic of conversation, but I wasn't the one to bring him up. Andy let it
slip one day that he thought Chad was a "pompous loser." That paved the
way for me to vent about Chad's newest antics.

"Chad has started cardio kickboxing classes as a New Year's resolution.
He's even named it 'Resolution 2001.' But these activities aren't limited
to just the gym."

"Let me guess," Andy said. "Every day he tells you what he's eaten,
how many calories it contained, how many glasses of water he's imbibed,
and how much he weighs . . . I can't stand people who go on diets."

"Oh, yeah. He brought in a bathroom scale for his office. And
apparently the best way to stay in shape is to kick and punch the office
plants every time he walks by. He has a personal vendetta against the
fichus. I let a laugh slip once, which sent Chad into a new form of rage:

karate chopping the air while shouting obscenities. So now when he assaults the plants, I go out for coffee or a candy bar. Usually I run into Beau in the hallway."

"How was that dinner party with Beau? I don't think you told me about it," he said as our pizza arrived.

"It was a blast," I admitted as Andy dished slices for us. "You should come with me to the next one. Beau's partner, Peter, is a great cook. He's a lot shorter than Beau, kind of a portly fella, and he talks really fast. They're quite a match. And all their friends are just as colorful and silly as they are. Peter's a florist, and their house is filled with fresh flowers and photos of important people—from Presidents to Kings to Ambassadors—who've come to Washington and attended big banquets. Peter did the flowers for the banquets." Peter was in his forties, with dark hair and a short beard, and a constant smile. He loved to talk about the witticisms his aging mother would tell him in their frequent phone conversations.

I'd been to a number of their dinner parties. Beau poured drinks for everyone and told stories about living in the '60's in San Diego and the riotous parties that went on. Their friends were an eclectic mix of gay and straight couples, all of whom talked about anything from parties to recipes, books they were reading, to who had recently died. No one talked about work, or the President, or the fact that we were living just outside the heart of the world. This was Arlington, which considered itself part of the South, and the laid-back lifestyle reflected it.

I soon joined a book circle formed by some of my customers, and a writing group that got together once a week to read one another's stories. And as for Sam, rumor had it he and the blonde high-tailed it to Italy where someone's family owned a castle. Whether the story was true or not didn't matter, all that mattered was that I never ran into him again.

Andy shook his head as I mentioned Sam and Italy. "I'm telling you, I also just got dumped for Italy. There is something in the water. I wasn't going to bring it up, but when you said that . . . You and I are in the same boat. Barry ran off and called me from Rome. The least he could have done is taken me with him. Well, that's it, no more bartenders for me."

"And no more waiters for me," I declared.

"So no Quinn?"

I'd made friends with Quinn, a mild-mannered and straight-laced waiter who answered phones for a Congressman by day. "Quinn and I are strictly friends. He's happy to have someone to hang out with at all his political functions. I'm happy to have a place to go. Besides that, he's way to perfect."

"Oh, you mean that he's tall, dark, handsome . . . "

"No, not that. I mean perfect pedigree, a perfect wardrobe, perfect connections. His dad worked for one of the Presidents back in the day, wrote speeches or something. They could certainly afford to give him a stipend larger than my year's salary if they wanted. He's damn good-looking, but he never stops talking about politics."

Quinn only took me to Republican parties. I was sure there must be Democratic counterparts, but no one ever invited me to any. Each party had a name and a theme, but Sin Tax Night was probably the most famous of the parties Quinn and I attended. Held on April 15 at the Republican-run Capitol Hill Club, Sin Tax was a party devoted to smoking and drinking. Clouds of smoke hovered in the air so thick it was difficult to see. Ancient men in suits preyed upon the twenty-something interns. Tuxedoed bartenders poured three-finger drinks and lit cigarettes for the smoking clientele. Quinn smoked and drank, and I stuck mostly to drinking since smoking gracefully seemed beyond my capabilities. We mingled, ate finger foods, and mingled some more.

Quinn introduced me to some of his officemates, who seemed to have more personality than most. We joined their circle for a little while and listened as they told stories.

" . . . Okay," one girl says, "so I'm in Dupont Circle one afternoon waiting to cross the street and I see all these TV cameras across the street pointed at all of us waiting to cross. I was new to D.C. then so I'm looking around for the president or someone like that to be standing there when I realize the woman next to me is Monica Lewinsky herself!"

"No way!" one person says in awe.

"Yeah, she's standing right beside me and she sees me staring at her. And I'm going, 'You, you're, you're . . . ' and the Walk sign pops up and Monica starts to cross the street. I'm standing there like a dope, and all I can think to say is, 'You go, girl!'"

"Get out!"

"No, I'm serious. But anyway, here's the best part. Monica hears me yell 'You go, girl!' and cracks up—just starts laughing in the middle of the street. She comes running back over to me and gives me a big hug and then keeps going on her way. Do you believe that . . . "

I ran into a few of the lobbyists who'd been at our office party, but mostly it was the same crowd of Congressional interns in pearls and sweater sets and smart glasses who were in attendance at every party. I was the only one in silk—a green and white dress that was very classy but a great bit more feminine than the boxy suits and sweater sets around me. The ancient suited men weren't sure what to do with me. A few tried to hit on me and I politely declined, and the rest just stared.

"What are you drinking, my dear?" asked a puffy, sweaty man probably three times my age. I sighed inwardly, but pasted a pained smile to my face.

"It's wine," I said.

"Let me get you another one," he offered.

"Thank you, but my friend went to get one."

"Have I seen you before?" he walked closer, looking me up and down. "Here, let me introduce you to my colleagues," and he put his hand on my back to lead the way, breathing alcohol on me.

So I met his friends, though I already knew some of them from our Hill office. I smiled and talked for a minute, and then excused myself and found Quinn again. I'd been to enough of these to know the drill.

First thing, don't make eye contact with anyone staring at you. Somehow it's construed as an invitation for a pick-up. If thrust into a situation, don't show any weakness, or any dubious strength. For instance, don't fidget, twirl your hair, or let them steer the conversation. At the same time, don't flirt or laugh, and don't be caught drinking scotch, whiskey, or anything masculine because two percent of the time you can handle it and ninety-eight percent of the time you can't and everyone knows it. Beer is also hard to pull off in ladylike fashion. It's tough to belch in polite conversation, and it says "college" when you're not in a bar. Above all, don't use any sexual innuendoes or anything remotely close or Old Sweaty will tell you his rendition of a good time. It's difficult, but possible, to politely get away. But now, here's the clincher: don't be afraid to be impolite, or even downright rude. Yes, rude. Etiquette says "never," but the drunk Hill types know the Hill ladies were brought up to be charming. So when the charm drops and you embarrass them in front of their friends, they'll generally leave you alone.

I was learning a lot and having fun with my new lifestyle, but to truly fit in I would have to dress the part in those dime-a-dozen pearls and sweaters, and there was just no way. I'd have to talk politics, take a stand on every issue, and argue my point as if it were the only correct one. But with all the other voices arguing their points, why bother? It seemed to me that the Hill crowd all majored in debate. The Hill crowd reminded me of hothead teenagers who thought they knew more than their parents. Countless twenty-somethings forever stuck in that adolescent realm of "I know everything." There would always be work for them on Capitol Hill. Having outgrown that stage myself, I could only have fun at the parties for so long.

But my busy work and play schedule afforded me less time at the house with my roommates. I'd spent the entire spring out on the town. By summer when all of Washington was talking about the search for Chandra Levy, I found I had a friend in the house, a sympathizer who stopped attending the cultists' church. I overheard the other roommates whispering about Karen and what they were going to do about her wayward soul, and it dawned on me that somebody else in the house was getting the rebuke treatment. Karen and I realized our shared mistrust of the others and became confidantes. We started having our own guarded conversations about the cultists when they were out "missioning" to people. We'd sit in the dining room over a few contraband beers, discussing our inevitable escape. At first it was a way to vent our anger and frustration. But after a while, our conversations were more therapeutic and constructive.

"Sometimes you have to do exactly what you're afraid of, because it will teach you the most about yourself," she told me one night. "The fact that I'm here shows me that God's looking out for me."

"Even after this place?" I asked. "You don't think you read the signs wrong, that maybe you're not quite where you're supposed to be? I mean, our whole living situation is pretty messed up."

"I agree," she said, playing with her beer label. "I think I'm supposed to be here, I just don't agree with what their Center is teaching. So I'm setting out to find another church. I've thought a lot about it, prayed a lot about it, and this is what I need to do." Karen suddenly sighed, the first evidence that this was a tough decision for her. "But it's scandal as far as the girls are concerned."

"What isn't?" I asked.

"Good point," she conceded.

"You were there at the house meetings, you know how frustrating it is to get them to change their minds or open up to a new idea outside their own realm of 'We can be stupid, someone else will do the work for us.'"

"And do you know why they think that?" she asked. "When I went to their Center, I found it to be a dictatorship. The Center was built twenty years ago, and Pastor Jeff has been its only pastor since it opened its doors. They believe what he says, to the letter, and they don't ask questions."

"But how do you get past all the guilt trips and the fear of eternal damnation for thinking differently than they do?" I asked. "For months now I've been questioning my own sanity, almost daily. But, if they're right, then God would have to be rather close-minded, wouldn't He?"

"But you have to understand that Pastor Jeff has been their only example as to how to live. He decides everything for them, from who their friends should be, how they should pressure others into coming to their way of thinking, and even who's allowed to date whom in the congregation."

"That's ridiculous!" I said.

"Yeah, but they're following, aren't they?" she stated.

"But that's exactly my point!" I said. "They make everyone feel guilty unless we join them. I mean, how could God let them . . . " I stopped, seeing that Karen had raised her hand in protest and was shaking her head.

"Don't blame God," she said. "Blame people. God doesn't make mistakes. I agree with you. But it hasn't occurred to them to think for themselves yet. That doesn't make them bad people. They believe 'religion' is a title, not a way of life. And they have good intentions."

"But *you're* not like that."

Karen breathed a laugh. "Pressure only keeps people suppressed for so long. You're a prime example. You seem more outspoken, more aware of who you are than when we first moved in here. I think it's this waitress job that has been the big change in you, and I think it scares our roommates. So, tell me about it. What is this job doing for you?"

"Well, I guess waiting tables for a living is a bit degrading—it's a humble job. But I guess humble is good, it keeps you real. I think to be really good, you have to be willing to get inside the customers' heads . . . enough to bring them the little things they forgot to mention. And it's good for people-watching. And unlike other jobs, if you're having a bad day as a waitress, you only have to wait a half hour or so until your customers clear out and you get some new ones that might make it all worthwhile. The best days are when you're taken to the emotional limits of nearly walking out and leaving it all behind you . . . "

"That's a good thing?" Karen interrupted.

I smiled. "When you're pushed so far you find the *readiness* to leave it all behind? Yeah, that's the best. When you're in it up to your eyeballs and you can look around at all the chaos with a smile on your face, then you know you've broken through. Something inside you smiles out from the inside."

Karen smiled. "I think you've found God in your own work."

I smiled, feeling embarrassed for the way I was carrying on. "I just think that so many people walk around brain dead to the world, drones who do their job and go home at night to watch TV and waste their time, but waiting tables gives you a different perspective, because there are no guarantees when you're putting yourself out there for your own take-home pay.

"There's a moment right when you approach a table and introduce yourself, half a moment really, when they accept you and you accept them. It doesn't always happen, but when it does, you know you'd trade half your lifetime just to have another one. Somehow in all that, it makes you feel alive."

Karen was smiling. "Amy, you're not lost. You may not have your way planned out right now, but you're far from lost."

Karen was my moral support for the house, and she was helping me see my life in a deeper way. She believed everything had a meaning, and by putting the meanings together, we could point to an answer.

When the lease finally expired we quickly packed our things, and we were the only two to leave the cult house. The others found replacements for us and renewed the lease. And I guess because of the painful year we'd spent living there, Karen and I never kept in touch. But our conversations had given me a lot of hope.

My friends were tremendous comfort, each in different ways. Andy and I shared our emotional problems with relationships, and usually found ways to laugh about them. Beau got me through the workday. He got the biggest kick out of my demented life, and showed me how to laugh at it, too. And I had my girls at Upscale for impromptu get-togethers. Quinn's parties made me feel like a part of the Washington scene, though it couldn't keep up forever. I was "in," but I needed a sanctuary. I hardly slept, and I ate only when I was on the move, because I was always on the move. So when Beau invited me to dinner at his house one particular night and he and Peter announced that I could live in their guest room, I took it without a second thought.

CHAPTER
TWELVE

Late that summer, I put most of my things in storage and moved in to Beau and Peter's guest room. Their townhouse sat in a quiet Arlington neighborhood seven miles from our office in the city, but since Beau and I didn't share the same office hours, we rarely traveled in together.

"I prefer not to stay late at work," he told me. "That just makes them think I'll do it all the time."

Beau and Peter had lived in the townhouse for nearly twenty years, a milestone by any relationship standards. They knew everyone in the neighborhood, and though this was the suburb of the nation's capital, most everyone left their front doors open in the evenings to encourage one another to drop by. Beau filled me in on the neighbors. "Ours is the place for dinner," he said, "And next door is good for blended margaritas. On the other side, Paulette makes excellent cookies, and two doors down on the right, Hank'll open a bottle of wine and would play guitar for anyone who drops in. Paulette even has her own wine glass that always sits on Hank's coffee table."

Beau and Peter's townhouse had three levels, including a finished basement with a laundry area and a second bathroom. On the main floor was the kitchen, dining room—site of the dinner parties—and living room, and upstairs was the main bathroom and two bedrooms. The front door opened to the tree-lined street, and out the back door was a private patio decorated with lush and exotic plants that Peter had found. A patio table under the lilac tree was the setting for many of their dinner parties. To me, the place was paradise.

Beau and Peter were very easy-going. I paid rent and did my part to keep the house clean, but I could talk about any subject with them and I was free to use any kind of language. I could drink anything I wanted, and instead of making me feel like a criminal for it, Beau would usually join me. For months I'd imagined I'd become a vulgar alcoholic atheist the first chance I got outside the cult house. But when left to my own devices, I did the unthinkable: I relaxed . . . That is, when I wasn't working.

My summer had been extremely busy. Office work had finally slowed down in August when Congress was out of session, but the restaurant was busier than ever. I was making a good amount of money, and my debts had all been paid, so everything I made went into my savings. Just knowing that I was debt-free and had enough to live on for one month, then two, then three, really made me feel free. Mr. Watters postponed our conversation about my expiring contract until after his August vacation. I didn't mind; it gave me a few more weeks to make money before I broke it to him that I didn't want to renew.

It would be hard for me to say goodbye to Mr. Watters. What little I knew of him I liked. He loved his work and got a kick out of the jokes he'd play on Chad. But it was the thought of not having to deal with Chad anymore that I loved. Even when he was spreading his misery as only Chad could, all summer I was able to look him in the eye and smile, thinking of my savings and how I was out the door the first chance I got.

My social life slowed down considerably. Not only was it something that didn't seem so interesting to me anymore, but I also didn't have the time. I'd been doing the two-job thing for nearly a year, and really, I was good at it. Other than a few small quirks, I was nearly normal by all standards. My schedule was the biggest giveaway that I was a little different.

I ate at odd hours, slept at odd hours, and timing was paramount. From laundry, the grocery store, gas station, post office, making phone calls when others were awake, getting personal work done, etc., all had to be scheduled to be completed in the shortest, most efficient time possible. Days and even whole weeks were mapped out according to tasks, work obligations, and one setback would mess up the entire week. What I needed was my own personal assistant, but that wasn't going to happen. So, organization became essential, different foods became staples because of their quick prep time or their mobility, i.e. they could be eaten while driving or while sitting at my desk at work. Calories and fat content were the last things on my mind, and really didn't matter because of all the constant movement I was doing.

Being single meant I didn't need to keep normal hours for someone else's sake. I hated to admit it, but it was actually easier to be on my own. Not that that was much comfort.

"There's nothing wrong with you, Sweetie," Peter tried to convince me one night.

"I know," I said, pretending I did. "It's just that everyone seems to have someone, except for me. Even Chad's been dating somebody."

"Oh yes, that weasel who makes Beau crazy," Peter nodded. "Please, if somebody like that could find a relationship . . . "

"Exactly! What's wrong with me?"

"Nothing! You're looking at this wrong. If someone like *Chad* can find someone then you're *certain* to."

"I guess so."

"I mean, where did Chad meet this girl?"

"All I know is that she works nights at the Pentagon and she lives in Chad's new housing complex." Chad had finally taken the plunge and moved "across the bridge" into Virginia. It was all he'd talked about until he found Marcy. "He spotted her while she was jogging one day, and soon had followed her and memorized her jogging route. He also found out which condo was hers, which car, parking space. She rented a single bedroom place, and no men had come or gone while she was under Chad's surveillance."

"What a desperate attempt to find somebody. Normal people don't act like that."

"Then he makes these kissing noises into the phone all afternoon when he calls her."

"Gross! I hope your boss gets back from Texas soon and puts a stop to all that. How inappropriate. But listen, Amy, the thing with you right now is that you work too much. You don't have time to give to anyone. I don't want to get into your business, but I haven't seen you in days."

Peter did have a point. Lately I always felt tired, sometimes to the point of walking around in a daze. I couldn't remember things; I couldn't always see straight. My life felt like when you wake up from a dream and try to remember it, only you could barely piece together scenes that didn't make sense. Sleep did no good. I woke up after a couple hours with my mind racing again. Racing around what, I didn't know.

Just then Beau came in with ice cream. "Mmm-mmm!" He shook his head. "I love Baskin Robbins! Here, Peter, I got you a sundae. Amy! I didn't know you'd be home. Let me get another spoon. You can share mine," he went into the kitchen and emerged a moment later and handed me the spoon. "Not at the restaurant tonight?" He sat down beside me.

"Nope. Tonight's my night off for the week, at least until Saturday."

"At the rate your Saturdays have been going, you'll get called in to work anyway," Peter said. "Next time they do that you should just say no." He was devouring his sundae and his words came out all garbled.

"Yeah but that's $150," I defended. "Hopefully more. But I'm totally off this Sunday, too."

"Big whoop," Peter said.

"Get some more caramel sauce on yours," Beau instructed me. "That's the best part."

"I was saving it for you."

"It's every man for himself," Beau said. "Go for the caramel. It's so good it'll change your life."

"Oop! It's seven o'clock!" Peter said and picked up the remote. "Wheel of Fortune is on."

"I can't believe the crap you watch," Beau said as he got himself comfortable for TV-watching.

"I love it because these people are so stupid," Peter told him.

Beau rolled his eyes and kept watching TV, and I laughed. My life was good. Sure, it was my day off and I had mountains of laundry to try to get done, and I hadn't been to the grocery store in over a week. But then again I wouldn't be home again until the weekend, so who needed fridge food? Anyway, my life was a whole lot better than it had been.

By Sunday I forced myself to the gas station, the grocery store, car wash, and a host of other silly errands I'd been putting off. In any normal town these things would have taken two hours. In D.C.'s suburbs, they took most of the afternoon because of traffic and the lines of people everywhere I needed to be.

"Back, Amy?" Beau asked me when I walked in.

"Yeah. What a nightmare. I swear more people are out on the roads on Sundays than during rush hour. But I don't think I have to go anywhere else today. Phew!" I sat down on the couch.

"Good! Want a drink?"

"Yeah."

"I'm making dinner. Peter should be back soon, too, so we can all eat together."

"Sounds really good. Thanks," I took the glass he handed me. "What is it?"

"Gin and tonic surprise," he winked.

I took a sip. "Whoa, is there any tonic in it?"

"Surprise!" Beau said. "I'm gonna make myself another one. So how was work last night? You got in pretty late."

"Yeah. Did I wake you up?"

"Oh heavens no. My sleeping pill wore off around three so I got up for another one. 'Round then I heard you come in."

"Yesterday was bizarre and awful," I said. "I made awesome money, but I don't know . . . "

Beau raised his eyebrows, stirred his drink and sat down ready for a story.

"Don't tell Peter," I said. "I don't want him to worry. But lately if the smallest things happen to mess me up or throw me off course for the day, I get really . . . confused and upset."

"Oh?"

"It's weird. Take yesterday. They fired Derek from the Upscale, and he started crying. He's been going through some really tough things lately, and I guess it's been affecting his waiter skills. I guess he disappeared on one shift for about thirty minutes and no one could find him," I sighed, realizing I'd have to really explain the situation for Beau to understand my point. "What happened was, a couple weeks ago, on his way to his car from his other job, he was attacked."

"Oh dear God."

I nodded. "He's okay. But he was pretty beat up, had his money stolen, all that. He was off from work for a while, so Jenny told us what happened."

"Did they catch the guy?" Beau asked, his drink sweating onto his lap.

"Not yet," I said. "But he came back to work a few days ago, and we've all tried to be there for him, and we took up a collection to help pay his Emergency Room bill. But since he came back he's been 'off.' He just needs time. But I guess the restaurant can't afford to have a server mess up a food allergy or something, not with all the lawyers in this town. But even the manager, Mark, said it would have been better to wait to tell Derek. I don't see why they couldn't have given him counter shifts for a while, or just laid him off for a couple weeks until he got it together. But Corporate stepped in because of all the complaints filed. Derek was pretty upset, because it's one more thing for him to handle right now, and because Upscale is his family at the moment . . . It's silly, but true. Mark knows my personal life better than my own mother because he schedules me around it. He knows my finances like the back of his hand and knows when I needed extra shifts. My coworkers have become my best friends because we share this experience together. Now Derek's out."

"That's why they called you in yesterday," Beau pieced together. "Oh, honey, I'm sorry."

I nodded. "Derek was out on the smoking deck when I got there. He was a mess, so Quinn was watching him. I relieved Quinn so he could go in and check his tables. Jason saw that I was gone and waited on one of my tables for me, my tables that really were Derek's to begin with. So we all kept taking turns watching him, and then at one point I went out to find him and he wasn't there. No one knew where he ran off to in his state, and what he would do, but then someone found him in the men's room just fine. Eventually, Derek was okay enough to sit at the bar with Jason until Jenny could come to take him home.

"And while all this was going on, the restaurant was full of customers and business was booming. There were hungry people everywhere and none of them had any idea what was really happening. We had more important things to do than refill Cokes and bring another sugar packet for some dumb iced tea. Who the hell cares? One petty demand after another—did they really need all that stuff to be happy? Does the extra plate that they'll never use anyway somehow make them feel better about themselves? And why did they need their desserts cut in half? Share it, or cut it in half, I don't care, just don't make me do it."

"You tell 'em!" Beau cheered.

"It's not like I asked them to eat it with the same fork. And for that matter, what's with splitting the check? If you couldn't go out with a friend and pick up the tab, tax included, then don't fucking go out. I can't tell you how many petty people will parse a check down to the nickel, and refuse to pay for even an ounce of their friend's food. It's your friend! It's only money!

"So I'm sitting in traffic today and I had plenty of time to let this all sink in and found it was really getting to me. Overwork, stress, emotional exhaustion, memory lapses, confusion . . . You'd think I had all these things going for me, but so far I have nil to show for it. From laundry to traffic, grocery shopping vs. not eating, work, work, work . . . I have no time for anything or anyone. I grind my teeth at night; I have nightmares that leave me exhausted in the morning. And the slightest thing will have me in tears lately. Sometimes they're happy tears, but man, I'm losing it."

"I won't tell Peter," Beau said. "He'll only worry more than he does. I'll make you another drink," he got up and went over to the liquor cabinet. "The bright side is you only have a few weeks left and then you can have that talk with your boss and tell him you're not gonna renew your contract."

"I have no idea what to do with myself after that, though. I've thought about writing for a newspaper, but those jobs just don't pay enough to live on. And I don't think I can keep waiting tables forever. I'm sick of it."

"Don't worry. A few good nights of sleep should help you a lot. And if not, there's always gin."

I managed to smile at his joke. I sat for a little while, staring at my ice cubes. Then Peter came in, all in a rush. "Turn on the news! They've got an update about the Chandra Levy case. Hurry! I heard about it on the radio in the car and thought I was going to miss it."

Peter was soon engrossed in the newscast, Beau went into the kitchen to get started on dinner, and I went back to staring at my ice cubes.

"Can you believe that?" Peter asked.

I snapped my head up. "What? Did they find her?"

"No. Just another bulletin on the questioning and more allusions that the interrogations were illegally done." Peter always talked quickly I noticed.

Beau emerged from the kitchen, wiping his hands on a towel to stare at the TV for a moment. "Can you imagine what her poor family must think?"

"All we hear is the rumor-mongering, and it seems like everyone's forgotten to be discrete. She was a person."

"People are saying the most awful things," Peter said. "And the police don't have any new clues."

"Back in May everyone was so concerned for Chandra," Beau pointed out. "And when they didn't find her right away the rumor started: Was she killed? Was she pregnant? Did she sleep around? Now the poor girl's reputation is dragged through the mud as they continue to search for her. That's all anyone's talking about."

"We get tourists in to the restaurant who ask me my opinion about it," I said. "And I tell them if it were me, after a few days people would say, 'I wonder what happened to that little yellow-haired girl?' But after a few months they'd say, 'Oh, that girl? She cut me off in traffic once . . . Oh, Amy brought me lukewarm coffee one day, the idiot . . . She flipped me off one day, that bitch . . . '" I did different voices for each complaint.

"Really, now. If that were me, what lousy things would people be saying? As if anyone has any room to talk."

"As far as I can tell, after any amount of time, you are only known for the worst things you've done . . . " Peter said. "Sometimes your legacy is to be misunderstood for the choices you've made in life, even if those choices made the best sense at the time. Now where did I put that damn remote? Turn on CNN, Beau. I haven't watched it since this morning. Let's find out what else is happening in the world."

We had no idea that the day was coming when Washington would stop talking about Chandra Levy.

THIRTEEN

I got up as usual one bright and sunny morning, and got myself ready for work. As I filled my travel mug with coffee, I considered staying home from the office. I just didn't feel like spending a whole day at work. The 8:45 military planes buzzed the house like clockwork, reminding me to get moving.

"Morning!" Beau walked in, dressed and ready.

"Hey, I thought you were off today. What's with the fancy duds?'

Beau twirled so I could admire his collared shirt and black dress pants. I'd never seen him in anything that wasn't floral. "I'm helping Peter with a banquet on the Hill today."

"Well, you look great."

"Why, thank you," he said, bowing slightly. "You better shake your tail feathers if you're going to get to work today."

"Here I go," I said, hurrying so that he wouldn't know how lazy I felt.

I got in the car and started off. Before the Pentagon, I heard the announcer on the radio say something about "a jet, no, two jets," that had struck the World Trade Center in New York. The announcer himself didn't believe the report, and said he'd set to work finding what it was all about. The radio went to commercial. I figured it was a fluke, or an accident, or a joke, and tried to dismiss it. But, with a sinking feeling, it occurred to me that a radio announcer in Washington, D.C., the town of lawyers, couldn't say what he'd just said without major repercussions, which meant that what he said was true.

The announcer came back after the short commercial and again made the announcement, though he sounded completely confounded by the report. In an effort to explain his confusion, he said maybe it was a hoax, but that it couldn't be. It must have been a mistake, then, that one, no, *two* planes carrying passengers crashed into the World Trade Center. "How awful . . . How did they get so off course? But you just don't have that kind of accident, not with two planes . . . " And he mentioned "suicide missions," and though I wanted him to stop talking, I didn't turn the radio off.

Just after nine, I was still sitting on the highway outside the Pentagon, stuck in traffic as usual. I knew I wouldn't make it to work by 9:30 at this rate, so I thanked my stars that I'd found a new shortcut the day before, and I managed to exit and take Jefferson Davis Highway instead. Still listening to the radio reports, which were constant as they'd stopped playing music now, I continued driving with tears in my eyes.

I got to work at nine-thirty, and went straight to Chad's office not knowing if he'd heard yet or not. I wanted to turn on his TV to see what the news channels were saying. None of it seemed real, like when you walk in a dream and people tell you the most absurd things and you just nod and events keep happening, though you don't really believe them. Chad saw me coming and told me he was already watching the TV coverage of New York, though I hadn't yet said a word. The TV showed one plane smoldering in one tower as a second plane full of people came in closer and closer and then exploded in a ball of fire. And I couldn't watch, knowing that at one moment, all those people were alive, and then suddenly weren't. I went back to my desk and sat down, feeling how unreal this was and waiting to wake up.

I started an email to my parents, noting the time and what was happening. It was very confusing. And I can't remember what happened next, if Chad screamed because the first tower fell, or because the Pentagon was hit. Soon, though, I ran back to see the footage of the Pentagon. Who hits the Pentagon? And how did they get here? Here in our city, that I was sure was being protected by guards. Back to my desk, I typed away at the email as I heard the State Department had been hit, that there were fires on the Mall, and that we were under siege. I closed the email with the time, hoping that if someone read it they would have confirmation of the last time I was accounted for, and maybe that would help them find me.

Treasury was evacuating, which was only three blocks away. Mr. Watters called and told us to go home if we could. Chad and I debated whether evacuating or hiding out in the building would be safer. We couldn't decide, and Chad kept crying out Marcy's name. "Marcy works nights!" I said. "She's not at the Pentagon now. She's not there. What are we doing?"

I called our courier service and told them to cancel our pickup that day. Minutes later Chad and I agreed to evacuate, and I knew I had to make the call to my parents or they would worry. I couldn't call from the road because I never got a cell phone signal downtown. I had to call now. I dialed my mom's work, but the phone kept going dead. I thought they'd need to know where to look for my body, so I wrote another email including the route I was planning to take out of the city. I tried my dad's work number. Nothing.

Beau called in. Somehow local calls were coming in just fine. "Amy! Are you okay?"

"I'm alright," I said without emotion. "You're okay?"

"Yes, but the radio said the National Mall's on fire, the Metro's closed . . . I'm on the Hill now and everyone's evacuating and I can't find Peter." There was a lot of commotion in the background.

Oh, God, I thought. "Have you heard about the Pentagon?"

"No."

"It's been hit."

In a voice not his own, Beau said, "What?" And then suddenly, "I found him! I see Peter!" And it seemed he started thinking clearly again. "Amy, listen! If the Pentagon's been hit, they'll close the highways. You'll have to take 66. They'll close it all, roads, bridges, everything near the Pentagon. Head toward 66 and we'll see you at home. Good luck."

The phone rang again as soon as I hung up. It was Quinn. He'd taken the Metro to a meeting downtown and now he had no way to get back. He was a block from my building. I told him to meet me outside and I'd take him home. For some reason, I asked him what to do about his car.

"Forget my car," he said. "We should get out of here."

I cleaned out all my drawers of candy and goodies that I keep, and got a couple bottles of juice so that we'd have rations for the ride, in case we didn't get out of the city and needed something to eat. I wondered if I should take band-aids from the first aid kit. But then I asked myself what good band-aids were going to do.

I went to the bathroom, waiting all the while for the building to shake and tear open. My skin felt tingly, my senses were alert and listening to a noise I could not hear. I was serious, clear-headed, heavy-hearted.

I found the back stairwell that I'd never used, and walked downstairs and out onto the street. It was like nothing I'd ever seen before. People were everywhere, and all seemed to be just standing or moving in slow motion. It was sunny. Cars filled the streets, not moving, and no one was running red lights or honking like they usually do. Everything was quiet. I recognized the building personnel standing on the sidewalk with me. We were all wide-eyed, looking one another in the eye, searching for some reaction to tell us this was all a dream, but all we got was the same searching look mirrored back.

There was a slight wind, more of a tiny breeze that was enough to lift your hair and gently set it back down again. I didn't feel it but I could see it moving the hair of the man next to me. There was still no sound. Then I heard distant sirens, and I braced myself, waiting to see an airplane through the blue sky come over the top of a building and crash into something, breaking the waiting. Someone grabbed my shoulder, and I turned. It was Quinn, and we were ready to go.

We got my car from the garage and set out onto the streets of D.C. I told him about the number of driving routes discussed in my office just before we left, that I figured driving past the White House and getting onto Constitution Ave would put us on the highway pretty easily. It would be harrowing getting past the White House, but beyond that, smooth sailing. He agreed, and we proceeded to drive half a block closer to the White House over the next fifteen minutes. That's when the radio announced that an airplane that wasn't responding to signals, headed straight toward D.C.

The radio announced rogue planes all over the place, one within ten miles of D.C., heading straight for us. Quinn and I were closing in on the White House, knowing the plane coming toward us would either hit there or the Capitol Building.

"Quinn, if you were a suicide terrorist, which building would you hit?" I asked urgently. "I'd aim for the White House," I said. "To kill the President. They're coming right where we are."

"No," Quinn said. "They'll hit the Capitol. It's the symbol of our government."

"The White House is our government."

"No, the Capitol makes our laws."

"The White House signs the laws!"

"They sign on the lawn! There's nothing there today. The President's probably not even in the building."

"Do the terrorists even know that?"

"Look," Quinn said, "if the President's wiped out, we have backup. If Congress is obliterated, the government structure is gone." We looked at each other. "Turn around," Quinn changed his mind.

"Are you sure?" I asked, trying not to panic.

"Amy, we're too close. It's going to hit something and we're too close."

We did a U-turn despite the traffic and drove away from the White House. Once back at my building, the parking officials refused to let us back in to the garage, where we thought we'd be safe for a while. So we kept driving, avoiding government buildings and churches, and looking for the first place we could leave my car that it wouldn't be sitting in the middle of the roadway. All the while, we watched the sky, listening and waiting. And we weren't the only ones. The people around us, stuck in the same massive traffic jam, were all doing the same thing with the same looks on their faces. There was so much traffic that we were literally inches from oncoming drivers and could look each other in the eye. Finding no comfort there, we'd look up to the skies again.

"Anything explodes around us," Quinn said, "We ditch the car and run."

"Okay," I nodded.

Crowds on foot moved through the city, weaving in and out of the cars, and no one yelled about it. When buses ran the red lights and blocked intersections, no one honked. When we did move, we merged, changed lanes, and merged back again. By now, we'd heard nothing from the direction of the White House. No crashes, nothing. The plane would have been here by now. *Where was it?*

We were driving toward K Street, my back up plan, that ran through the center of the city and had nothing but businesses on it. No churches, and no infamous government buildings. Yet when we turned onto K Street, Quinn spoke up.

"The FBI has office space here."

"The FBI?"

"I think so. Somebody does. It's temporary office space, but it's on K Street."

"Why didn't you say something earlier?"

"I forgot until just now."

"Okay, but if you forgot, and I never even knew about it, maybe the terrorists don't know about it, either."

"That sounds good."

"Yeah?" I asked, nodding. "Okay."

It was 11 a.m., and we'd managed to get four blocks from my building. On the plus side, we were about six blocks from the White House.

We tried calling from our cell phones, to no avail. Once in a while we got enough of a signal that the phone would start to ring when dialed, only to produce a recording telling us the circuits were busy and to try the call later. I was deeply regretting the email I'd written, now thinking it cryptic, and wishing I'd got through to at least one of my parents, or anyone on the outside for that matter, who could get a message to my family that I was alive at the moment.

Quinn and I were glad to be in the car together, at least. He could have been trapped on the Metro with strangers, waiting underground for the stopped train to let him out, and I could have been battling the traffic by myself. We counted our blessings that we were together. We had the radio, and its constant updates. Even though they were confusing and they weren't giving us very good news, at least it was something, some outside link beyond the confused and surreal streets of Washington.

No one was in a hurry. We didn't see any accidents. We complained that D.C. didn't have a better evacuation plan. The government workers all came in at staggered times, and left at staggered times, so the streets were always full but never took on full capacity at once. This was full capacity. And we kept looking to the skies.

The radio announced Virginia schools were evacuating, for parents to pick up their children.

"No!" I protested. That was the last thing we needed, for all the traffic-jammed parents to suddenly have to be somewhere.

We weren't really scared. Concerned, maybe. Concerned for our safety as a whole, the safety of our city, country. No one's needs or safety was put above our own, as evidenced when no one wrecked or ran red lights (except the Metro buses) and no one drove in a panic. There was a feeling of community, of togetherness in this awful day. We were suddenly all a family, all hoping, rather than trying, to get somewhere to safety. Maybe we doubted that safety existed at that moment, but fear was just not something that crossed our minds. I passed car after car heading in the opposite direction. We stared at the skies together, offered directions when asked, even asked how each other was, as we inched along the streets of D.C.

There were no religious ramblers shouting from street corners, no elephants running through the streets, no women screaming and fainting, no glass breaking, in fact no sirens at this point . . . There was no panic, no real noise. Nothing. Just a traffic jam and a lot of very calm drivers. And a feeling of clarity in a surreal world—a feeling like you were only alive so long as you kept your wits about you.

K Street was jammed. But K Street also has service roads on either side of it that no one was on for some reason. "Do you see that?" I asked Quinn. "Why do you think that is?"

"I don't know. That doesn't make any sense."

"Think we should try it?"

"It can't hurt," he said. "But stay in this lane until we pass Connecticut, then move over. Connecticut has that curb and you have to turn. It won't let you go straight."

We waited it out, got passed Connecticut and onto the service road. It worked. We sped past five blocks of sitting traffic in about three minutes' time. We were nearing the end of K Street, and looking at another traffic nightmare as everyone was waiting to get onto 66. "We're running low on gas," I said. "Not too low, but we can't sit in traffic anymore."

"Go to Georgetown. *Those* people aren't moving," he said, referring to the highway traffic. "Let's see how bad Georgetown is."

It was a ghost town. The usually bustling college atmosphere had been replaced with eerie silence. Streets that were usually filled with traffic—the only section of D.C. to have rush hour twenty-four hours a day—were completely empty. This was very wrong.

Much as we wanted to get out of there, the absence of people made Georgetown appear almost safe. Who knew what lay beyond the Key Bridge for us? We decided it was better not to know yet. We could get out of the car, stretch our legs, press our luck at remaining in the city for another hour, maybe even be doing ourselves a favor by waiting out some of the traffic, anything—anything except cross the Key Bridge and see what was happening on the outside.

We turned down toward the waterfront and easily found parking, which was another bad sign. We found a restaurant that let us in, and we sat down with all the other bewildered customers to force down some food. The pub atmosphere was subdued, but music was playing in the background behind whispered conversations, which gave me comfort and I'm not sure why.

A couple came in wearing suits and sat down next to us. I wondered how many others escaped downtown and took the same route we did into Georgetown. To my surprise, the woman started talking—loudly. At first it looked like they were conducting a business meeting, because she took out a notebook and jotted a few notes to herself. But then she switched the subject.

"So he said that it was her fault and we all knew he was just saying it because his wife is on the Board," the woman said loud enough that the whole pub stopped what they were doing and looked over at her. She didn't notice and kept on talking. "But Susan said the whole thing got started when John picked up the memo in the first place, even though it was addressed to the office staff and he qualifies under that, but why Melvin wrote a memo to the department head complaining about the mess between Susan and Alfred in the first place I'll never know. And you know what he said to me . . . "

Our sandwiches arrived and I noticed the comforting music was gone. I strained over the voice of the woman beside me to hear it, but it had been turned off. A TV set on the other side of the room had been turned on in its place. A man on the TV was trying to explain something. It looked like a press conference. The whole restaurant leaned in close to hear an explanation. All except the woman beside me. She went right on talking. I looked at her lunch date, a normal-looking man in his thirties who was intently listening to her gossip. I shot her a dirty look and watched her ignore it, as she ignored the various "Shhh!" warnings given to her from around the room.

"So Harriet told Susan just to forget about it, but you know Susan's kids aren't going to be happy about that . . . "

Didn't these people have any idea what was going on? How oblivious could they be? In D.C. it is your *job* to know what's going on around the world, whether you're important or not. Not only did they have no idea what was happening outside of the pub, but they didn't even notice the nasty glares and shushing from everyone around them. *Would you shut the fuck up?* I wanted to say, but I wondered if that very sentiment was the spirit behind the day's events so far. The news conference ended and Quinn and I didn't know what was said. People were whispering the news to one another so that everyone in the room eventually answered everyone's questions. The TV was turned off and the music turned back on and the woman just kept talking. "*What* did they say?" she asked the table beside her.

A lady passed on the message that had come from the other side of the room. "They said they were sorry about the attacks of this morning but that they didn't do it."

"Oh, okay, thanks!" said the woman beside me, and she went continued her conversation again.

"Let's just get out of here," I said.

"Yeah," Quinn said.

Quinn called his parents for the umteenth time and finally got through. "Hey, have them write down my parents' number and call them. Let them know I'm alright," I said.

"Amy, we have a signal now. You can call them in a minute."

"No, Quinn! It'll go out again. Please!"

"Alright," he said and dictated my parents' phone number to his. When he hung up I immediately dialed my parents but the signal was gone. "Damn it!"

"My mom wrote it down. Maybe she'll be able to get through," he said.

I nodded. We got back in my car and headed for the Key Bridge, which was as empty as Georgetown. Halfway across the Potomac, away from the buildings of Georgetown, we saw a large black cloud of smoke curling up into the sky from our left.

"Oh my God," I said.

Quinn's mouth dropped open. A smell hit us that wasn't like anything I'd ever known.

When I was little, we used to go camping. And one day, actually on our way back from camp, we'd smelled a fire and my mom said, "Somebody's got a nice fire going. Makes you want to get some sticks and roast some marshmallows, doesn't it, Amy?" And when we got home and turned on the news that night, we found out it was a house fire two miles away that we'd smelled. That family had lost everything, and my mom felt bad for saying what she did about the marshmallows.

But this smell was nothing like that. Nothing at all. It smelled like metal. And if concrete could burn, it would have smelled like that, too.

Once across the bridge, police were directing us to turn right and go through Rosslyn. My cell phone suddenly rang. It was Beau. "We just got home. Are you alright?"

"Yes," I said. "I have Quinn with me. We detoured through Georgetown and are in Rosslyn now."

"Good. Paulette's here. She wants to go to the hospital to donate blood, but her car is back at her office. She walked from downtown to Georgetown and then hitched a ride back here. Little Paulette! So if we're not here when you get home that's where we'll be."

"Okay," I said and hung up. I dialed my parents again and still didn't get through. But at least we were in Virginia now. Though I dreaded it, my next priority was to find a gas station. I only knew of two gas stations in D.C. itself, and both were on the opposite side of town from where we'd been driving. But Virginia has tons of them, and we really could stop at any time. I glanced again and again at the gauge, and so far we were alright, so long as we stayed out of bumper-to-bumper traffic. The thing of it was, I didn't want to stop. What would people think? Gasoline was an explosive, would I even be allowed to get any? No one else was stopping at the stations. I comforted myself with the notion that now I *could* stop for gas if the situation got absolutely desperate.

We zigzagged across Arlington and around road closings. Around 2 p.m. with an increasingly nervous eye to my gas gauge, I dropped Quinn at his house, and then went to the closest hospital to donate blood. But the line at the hospital was three hours' long, and I hated myself for it, but I just couldn't wait. I promised myself I'd return the next day after work. But for now, I just wanted to be home again.

I reached the house around 3 p.m., still on the same tank of gas, and Beau and Peter said they'd only just arrived back themselves. Paulette got our other neighbor, Hank, to wait with her at the hospital, apparently, so we were all home for the night. I called my parents from the house phone, finally able to get through, and told my mom I was alright.

"I'm so glad to hear from you, Amy!" my mom cried. "Are you alright?"

"I'm okay. It just took a long time to get out of the city. And back at the office before I left, I tried calling but couldn't get through."

"I know, we're hearing on the news that phones aren't getting signals all over the place, on account of . . . on account of . . . well, New York . . . "

"I know, Mom."

"Are you sure you're alright?"

"I'm fine."

"I hadn't heard right away. I mean, our lab is in the basement and it could be storming outside or a hundred degrees and sunny, we just don't know. We have no real contact with the outside world, no TV's, no radio . . . All I knew was that a plane had crashed close to here and we were bracing ourselves to take on whatever patients the city hospitals couldn't take. Nobody said anything about anything else. I was in the basement!" she lamented. "We were waiting for victims when Lori approached me in the hallway and asked if I'd heard from you. I told her you were fine, that I'd spoken to you just the other day, and she turned pale. She was like, 'So you don't know?' and I said, 'Know what?' and that's when she told me . . . I just, and I called your father to see if he'd heard from you. Our phones were working fine by this point, and he said you were fine. 'So you heard from her?' I asked and he said, 'She's fine,' 'How do you know? Did you hear from her?' I asked and he said, 'No, but she's *fine.*' He kept saying it, like saying it meant it was real. Oh, God . . . "

"It's okay, Mom. I am fine. Beau and Peter are both home, too, and they're fine. We're alright."

"Okay, well I'm so glad to hear it. I'm going to call Grandma and let everyone know. But I'll call you back as soon as your dad gets home so he can hear your voice, alright? I love you, Amy."

"I love you, too, Mom."

I hung up, relieved that they could stop worrying about me. Then I broke down and cried. It hit me from out of nowhere, and once I started I just couldn't stop. Beau and Peter sat quietly and let me, as if I were getting the emotion out for all three of us. Nothing had happened to me directly, and I felt like I had no real right to be crying, but couldn't stop anyway.

Beau and Peter relayed their story of how they'd gotten separated during the evacuation. I kept wiping my eyes and sniffling through the entire story, and they didn't seem to mind. Beau's car had been valet parked behind a zillion other cars, so they took Peter's car and sat in traffic on Independence Avenue all the way to the highway instead of hitting downtown and K Street like I did, but they only got home before me because they hadn't stopped to eat.

That night after Beau and Peter had gone to bed, I sat up watching the late-late news by myself. I saw people jumping from the towers in New York, and found myself reaching up to the TV screen, cupping my hands under the falling people, hoping to catch them, with tears streaming down my face. Eventually I found an old Three's Company rerun on an obscure channel to watch instead. I was exhausted, but hated the thought of laying in my bed crying, so I sat there through a few more shows.

On September 12, I woke up and for a few seconds, I was fine. Then the events of the day before hit me, and I wished it weren't true. Mr. Watters had called the night before, during Three's Company, to tell me the office would be closed for a day. The government was asked to report, to show the country that their elected officials were still doing their jobs, but Mr. Watters said there was no reason for us to go in, being that none of us would get any real work done anyway.

I dragged myself out of bed and decided to drive to the hospital to donate blood. On the radio I heard about a bomb threat at the Pentagon that was tying up traffic. So I drove south, away from the city to three different hospitals and two Red Cross's in order to donate blood. I put myself on the waiting list at the hospitals, because their lists were full of donors for a solid week. This gave me some heart; people were lining up however they could to help. But at the last Red Cross I went to, the organizer told me that blood wasn't necessary because they weren't pulling out a lot of survivors. His lack of compassion made me angry, and I insisted that he could send blood to New York.

"They aren't pulling out a lot of survivors up there, either," the man told me, calm as ever. I refused to look reality in the eye like this man did, so, angry, I left.

FOURTEEN

I had work to do. And like everyone else, I didn't know why I bothered. I was back to questioning why I went to the office every morning. I had no corporate career goals, or any real career goals for that matter, so why spend five days a week of my own time sitting in an office building? I had to be at the restaurant nearly every evening, ready and happy to serve, and where was that getting me in life? Sure, I made extra money, but what good was money when I didn't have anything to spend it on? I didn't own a house, didn't have a significant other in my life to share it with. Why was I doing any of it?

These thoughts swam through my head as I sat in traffic in the morning, staring at the scorched Pentagon building with a large hole in the side of it, as Chad moped into the office and yelled at me for not telling him the root beer in the fridge had caffeine because he was up all night again, as Chad grabbed another root beer hours later and yelled at me that he'd drink what he damn well pleased, as I sat in traffic on my way home, glad that my homeward view of the Pentagon was of the intact sides, and I heard these thoughts loud and clear as I walked into the Upscale at night to start my shift.

"Amy! How's your evil coworker?" Jason asked as I walked by.

"Evil!" I said without missing a beat. This had become our new routine. I'd told so many Chad stories that the whole staff now looked forward to the daily Chad installments. "Today he brought his kickboxing trophies in to the office as a deterrent against terrorists."

"Kickboxing trophies?" Jason asked. "Don't tell me beating up the office plants is actually making him better at it?"

"Not exactly. Oh, the fichus is definitely worse for the wear, but I think it could still take him. No, Chad went out and *bought* these trophies." Jason and his bar customers cracked up, so I continued. "So today he brings them in and tells me that any terrorists that get in the building will see these and will know their place. He's getting more paranoid by the day." I shook my head. "And don't get me started about the root beer."

"What about the root beer?" Jenny asked, new to this week's saga since she'd been off all week.

"Chad claims he can't have caffeine past noon or else he'll be up all night," Jason informed her.

"But he drinks it anyway and yells at Amy that it's her fault," Haley said, setting her tray down and leaning on the bar.

"How is that your fault?" Jenny asked me.

"Oh, we're getting there," I said. "Today he tells me he's severely allergic to caffeine—in the afternoons, of course. This has nothing to do with the three-cup minimum that he has going for coffee in the morning. That doesn't count. But this new allergy of his causes him to *crave* caffeine, you know, because allergies make you crave the stuff that could hurt you, right?"

Jason shook his head. "An afternoon allergy!"

I nodded, acting casual, though, at the time Chad had been screaming at me and punching the air with such a vengeance that there was nothing casual about it. But that part of the story wasn't funny, so I left it out. "So it's my fault that he drinks it," I said, "because I'm the one who orders the sodas for the office and I'm *obviously* doing it on purpose."

"Of course," Jason said.

"Today he had three of them and then decided to see the building manager about putting his trophies in the lobby to help protect our building. It's part of his new Kick-Ass Gargoyles plan."

"Where is your boss when all this is going on?" Jenny asked.

"Texas," Jason answered for me.

I nodded. "An access control company down there wants government funding. I don't know how long he'll be gone. Technically, I'm working without a contract right now."

Sandy walked up to us and tossed her purse behind the bar. "Hey, I didn't know you were working tonight," Jason said.

"Hey! No, they called me in to waitress tonight for some reason," she said.

"Why'd they call now? It's the middle of the shift."

"Oh, no, they called me a couple hours ago. But I figured since they didn't bother to call until ten minutes before they wanted me here, they could wait. My time is valuable."

Jason smiled. "You're unbelievable," he said.

"Hey man, don't let the job *own* you," she said.

Here I stood, at the mercy of my own two jobs, face-to-face with someone for whom that was not an option. Sandy's way of thinking didn't work in the corporate world and wouldn't get her an Employee of the Month award, but somehow she did have a point. Work continued, and the earth continued to rotate on its axis, though none of it had anything to do with my own personal will. If it had been up to me, or anyone I knew at the time for that matter, life as we knew it would have stopped altogether and nothing but the fun stuff would have been left. No more work, no more day in and day out of doing things other people said we should do. And just like that, I decided to take a month off from the restaurant.

As the weeks dragged on, hearings were held on the Hill to find which agency was responsible for letting September 11 happen. There was a lot of name-calling and finger-pointing, and few government agencies denied leaks. It seemed everyone was ready to take the indirect blame. And when the Majority Leader was delivered a letter tainted with anthrax, the headaches continued. The sky over D.C. remained a no-fly zone, but now large military planes flew over the city every few hours. We cringed and looked up to make sure all was well. We were on edge.

Most things tended to make the news outside the D.C. Beltway more often than within it. My parents and relatives would call from out-of-state to get an insider opinion on the city itself, but most times their information would be news to me. Some things just weren't important. Within the parameters of D.C. itself, nothing was noteworthy except for cleanup efforts, care of the victims and their families, and the possibility of war.

Our heroes were our own President Bush, Mayor Giuliani, and Donald Rumsfeld. The President for his patriotic address to the nation after the attacks, Giuliani for all the obvious reasons, and Donald Rumsfeld for reportedly running into the burning Pentagon again and again to save people as he found them. One report said that a fireman had to tear Mr.

Rumsfeld away from the building, insisting that, "Sir, we need you alive. We'll rescue the others, but *stop going back in there.*"

A drug called Cipro was handed out at will. Instructions were handed out in buildings all over D.C. telling us what to do if a suspicious package were to be delivered. The post offices had signs up identifying what suspicious packages looked like. According to the signs, they looked like four-year-olds had packed them.

"The building is passing out our anthrax instructions," I told Chad. "Here's your copy." I went back to my desk and read my own instruction sheet. "If you have something suspicious in the mail, cover it immediately with the garbage can or some similar object. Wash your hands with soap. Alert your office, call 911, and tell the building. When the health department arrives, they will ask you for your clothes, but they will give you a jumpsuit to wear instead. They'll swab your nose to see if you've been infected. They'll start you on Cipro."

And even more secret office space had to be found. That fall, most of the government employees were diverted to buildings all over town to continue their work in unmarked office space. Some Senators were working from vans parked outside the Hart Senate Office Building while their offices were being decontaminated.

But none of these things kept business from functioning. It may not have been business as usual, but nothing was usual anymore. So business, unusual, continued.

I decided there was no need to panic. For a little while, mail service stopped altogether. Finally when we did start getting mail again, it was all discolored to a yellow-brown because it had all been sent to Ohio for irradiation.

I saw others going to the mailbox every day wearing gloves and surgical masks, even though our building was across town from the Hill. And we had no White House offices that the public knew about, and really only housed lawyers, lobbyists, and one travel agency. Who would want to send us anthrax? We just weren't important enough.

Bills needed to be paid, but I just didn't have the energy to track everybody down. Since mail service had been stopped for a while, our office wasn't receiving bills, either.

It took a few weeks, but eventually I either received the bills in the yellow mail with previous balances owed printed on them that I happily paid, or I fielded colorful phone calls from bored collection clerks.

"Hello, Ms. Ashe? You are delinquent on your payments to us at Yet-Another-Company America, and we are going to prosecute you if you do not pay."

"Hello, Yet-Another-Company," I'd say brightly. "Okay, let's see, I haven't paid you for probably a month, right?"

"That's correct, ma'am. You owe us and you're late in your payments. We sent the bill out weeks ago."

"Right," I'd say happily. "I'm sure you did."

Here they'd get testy. "Well, ma'am, you do understand that you are supposed to pay those bills when you get them in the mail." (Never mind that I'd been paying them on time up to now and obviously had figured out how the "we send you the statement then you pay it" system worked. Obviously all of this good behavior meant nothing the split second one payment was late.)

"Oh, yes, I'm well aware. But tell me, did you *mail* those statements?"

Angrier now, "Yes, of course we did. Now about the payment . . . "

"Right, well see, we're in Washington, D.C., and we have anthrax here. So our mail service has been stopped until they can send everything to Ohio for irradiation, and then we should get that mail back sometime in the spring if we're lucky."

"Oh, ma'am, I'm sorry. I . . . I didn't know. We didn't realize . . . "

"It's okay. I'm sorry I didn't pay it on time.

"No, ma'am, it's our fault. I, uh . . .

"Well, can you fax the bill to me?" I'd ask.

"Uh, sure we can! We can do that!"

"That's great," I'd say. "Just go ahead and fax it from now on and I'll send you a check today."

"Take your time! Really! I'm going to waive this late fee as well, let me just put a note in the system here."

"That's nice of you," I'd say, sweet as pie and never intending to pay any late fee in the first place.

"So, uh . . . " they'd say, "how are things going in Washington?"

And I'd tell them. We were going day to day with the surprises, bomb threats, color-coded terror warnings, mail stoppages, random road closings . . . Each day was some new, frustrating thing, and we just had to keep going through the motions. But we dealt with the surprises and we refused to panic.

"We're not New York," the people of D.C. seemed to agree. "We don't know how they're coping." We had all the sympathy, and all the respect in the world, for New York and for the pregnant Mrs. Beamer, the woman with all the strength. And anything handed to us was easier to deal with when put into that perspective.

Andy and I met up one night for dinner and a movie, and though we tried, we couldn't avoid talking about it all.

"How are you doing?" he asked me.

"Oh, the usual," I said. "I still cry myself to sleep every night and question what the hell I'm doing with my life, but other than that I seem to be alright." I felt no qualms about discussing such a personal matter. For one thing, everyone I knew was pretty open about crying themselves to sleep now.

"Me too," he said. "What the hell are we doing with our lives?"

I shrugged. "Just trying to get by, I guess. Maybe one day it will hit me what I should be doing instead. But you like your job at least."

"Yeah I do, but lately I've been wondering if working eighty hours a week is really all that good for me. I used to love the game, loved staying late at the Club pressing Members for opinions, loved coming in on the weekends to research possible leads and new projects. I even loved reading legislative language. Some people like romance novels or suspense thrillers. Me? Give me a Senate Resolution any day and I'm a happy camper."

"Ugh!" I made a face. "I'd rather read stereo instruction."

"I just eat it up," he said. "But lately I've been wondering if this is really a good way to spend my life."

"I know!" I said. "Maybe we're not supposed to work so much. Maybe I should be taking time off to smell the roses and travel the world or something. I want what you have: I want to love what I do."

"That's what I'm going on right now," Andy said. "If I didn't have such a love of my job and what I do, I don't know. I don't know where that would lead me."

"That would make you me," I said.

Andy was quiet for a moment. He was about to say something when our waiter approached.

"Sorry for the delay, I'm T.J." said our thin, blonde waiter. "What can I get for you?"

"Two cokes," I said.

"Can you make mine with rum?" Andy asked.

"Yeah, mine too," I said and watched T.J. nod. "And we'll share a margherita pizza."

T.J. looked pained. "Okay, well, we're out of plates right now, so is it okay if I give you a bunch of napkins instead?"

Andy shrugged so I said, "Yeah, that's cool."

"So long as there's rum, I don't think we'll care," Andy told him.

"Okay, I'll be back. Thanks, guys," T.J. said.

"He was cute," Andy said.

"Yeah he was."

"Thin, but not too thin, blonde, big brown eyes . . . " Andy went over our waiter's features. "Why can't I meet more men like that?"

"What I want to know is: what's the deal on the plates? If that were me, I'd be back in the dish room doing the dishes myself to avoid running out." We happened to be eating at the Upscale. Not my Upscale, though, this one was in Dupont Circle. Andy wanted their pizza for a change from our regular Union Station deep dish.

"Yeah, that was odd, wasn't it?"

"You know, from the outside, Upscale seems to be so organized, but once you work there you find out what a mess it really is. I'm sure that's true of any place, though."

"But you're right, this place seems kinda lax about things," Andy said. "Maybe we should have gone to your restaurant."

"No way. Even a month out of that place was too short. And it's all the way down in Virginia, anyway. This one's closer to the movie theater . . . But you know, I've always thought of this location as 'The Big Time.' They do the most business of all the chain stores, and this neighborhood is just awesome. I love being up here."

Andy nodded. "How's office life treating you? How's Chad?"

"Oh, he's paranoid now."

"Didn't I hear he was seeing a Pentagon worker?"

"How did you hear that?"

"Chad called our office and happened to mention it."

"Of course. Well, actually he and Marcy have broken up."

"Because of September 11?"

I nodded. "After that, she decided she was still in love with her ex-boyfriend, so she went back to him to work things out. Chad didn't take it too well, but instead of being typical Chad and screaming about it, he just got more depressed."

"Join the club," Andy said. "It sucks being single right now. I know three couples that were on the verge of breakup just a couple months ago. Now they're engaged."

"Same thing happened with my friend Quinn. He went back to his old girlfriend and I haven't heard from him since. If I had a guy to go back to, I'd really prefer that to being alone right now. Lucky for me, no one's really interested in me," I said dryly. "But I've been calling home more often, just to hear a friendly voice."

"Me, too. It feels like the city is collectively gathering everyone in its arms. Everybody's reaching out to hug loved ones, even across the miles. People seem to be getting closer. Just don't be *too* happy or everyone will look at you weird. I think we're finally coming out of that. You saw Ellen on the Emmys, didn't you?"

"Yes! I remember *before* the Emmys, I once caught myself laughing out loud at something," I said, "and I felt ashamed . . . like I was a criminal just for laughing."

"Thank God for Ellen. It's okay to laugh again! Sometimes, anyway." Andy glanced out the window and something caught his attention. "Do you see that man in the orange jacket?"

"With the glasses?" I asked, pointing.

"Yeah. I'm sorry . . . It just reminded me that my mom told me she bought me a bionic suit."

"A what?"

"A bionic suit, so that I won't get anthrax."

"How much did that cost?"

"I don't know. A lot. But that's the thinking going on outside D.C. right now. She doesn't know why I live here, why anyone would want to. But I've told her there's still nowhere I'd rather live. Despite everything."

Andy was right. I'd been in D.C. a year, and I was starting to see it as home. It had its quirks: everyone was tuned in to current events, foreign affairs, and the impact of even small decisions on the world economy. CNN was the channel of choice, the place where we found out about suspicious packages, threats of terrorism, daily demonstrations, protests, and the like. We were alert in times of danger, we prepared for the traffic problems, road and bridge closings, marches, crowds. It all just came with the territory.

But if asked of September 11, our voices came out thinner, flatter. There was no "I lived through this" prize. There were only hard memories.

Andy broke my thoughts. "I saw something the other day that made me feel a little better."

"What?"

"Well, you know how everyone's been so polite lately, even on the roads? A couple days ago I saw a car cut off another one, and the guy who got cut off started swearing and flipped him off."

"Yes!" I cheered.

"It's the first time I've seen that in weeks, and it was such a relief," he said. "We're down, but we're coming back!"

FIFTEEN

B eau and Peter had taken a break from their dinner parties, but by mid-November were starting them up again. It seemed we all needed cheering up. I had less idea than ever what to do with myself. Beau was in a similar boat; the travel business was in trouble. He'd given out so many refunds in September when the FAA banned all flights for a few days that he was in the red for the month. October hadn't been much better, with fewer people traveling and airlines cutting commissions to the agencies.

"I don't see why they need to cut commissions, even if they are losing money," I said.

"Well, that's what they're doing," Beau said sullenly. "They can't fill the flights, so they're taking money from *our* pockets instead."

"If *I* were an airline, I'd remind agents that I was still giving out commissions, and maybe they'd be more inclined to recommend *my* flights to travelers. There are still people traveling. Business people can't get around it, and some folks just plain aren't scared. Airlines could fill up their flights like that," I snapped my fingers, "If they teamed up with the travel agents."

"It's too bad you're not running the show," Beau said appreciatively.

"Hey, you two!" Peter called us in from the patio. "Margaret's here, and I think Francesca and Paolo just pulled up."

"Francesca and Paolo?" I asked.

"Yeah, crazy isn't it? Just like Dante's, what, Second Circle of Hell?"

"I think that's the one," I said. "Francesca and Paolo, the Lovers."

"Wait 'til you meet them," Beau winked. "We better get in there."

Inside, a group of people were already laughing and carrying on. Beau said his hellos and introduced me to Margaret, a stout woman with red hair, Roger, a tall blonde man with freckles and a wide smile, Paolo, an equally tall silver-haired man with glasses, and Francesca, a tiny blonde woman with a booming voice.

One of Peter's quirks was that he felt dinner parties were best done with an odd number. "It keeps the conversation going. It's only sensible," he'd told me one night as we heckled contestants on Wheel of Fortune.

Beau poured drinks and invited everyone to sit outside. "Let's enjoy what's left of the sunlight."

"It is a marvelous day for November!" Margaret said, initiating our long conversation about the great weather. Almost all the leaves had fallen but the air had a warmth and sweetness to it, at least until the sun went down. By then we'd moved the party back inside for dinner and changed the subject.

Paolo and Francesca both spoke with slight accents, but only if you were listening very closely. During dinner I learned they were both born in Italy, met and were married when Paolo was twenty and Francesca nineteen, and then they moved to the U.S. Paolo then began his antique business and Francesca studied English so she could become a teacher.

"We barely spoke any English!" Francesca mused. "I don't know what made us move here without that skill, but we learned and we managed, didn't we?" her eyes met Paolo's and he smiled with pride.

"Were you scared?" I asked them.

Francesca looked at me, "A little intimidated, yes," she said. "But you must remember, in Europe it is customary to speak three or four languages, and between the two of us we already spoke Italian, German, French, and we do okay in Greek. English was not easy, but not impossible. Truthfully, it was easy to pick up, just not easy to learn *properly*. The rules kept changing. But that was twenty years ago."

"We've had practice since then," Paolo assured us, which brought a laugh. Just then a plane flew overhead and paused our conversation.

"Does that happen often?" Roger asked, trying not to look uneasy.

"Every couple of hours," I told him.

"Twenty-four hours a day, though," Beau said.

"We're putting our pharmacist's kids through college with the money we're spending on Beau's sleeping pills," Peter said. "It's because we live so close to the Pentagon. These stupid military planes buzz the house constantly."

"That one wasn't too bad," Beau said. "Sometimes they rattle the windows. You can't hear yourself think."

"It's a constant reminder that things aren't right," Peter said.

Roger sneezed. "Oh, I'm sorry," he said, getting up from the table and sneezing again. "These allergies. Please excuse me."

"There's allergy pills in the medicine cabinet," Peter said. "Help yourself."

"Thank you," Roger said as he disappeared up the stairs. He returned shortly, red-faced, but said he felt better. "I've never had allergies until now."

"Lots of people suddenly have them," Margaret said. "I hear the debris from the Pentagon is what's causing it."

"You know, I heard the Pentagon might be completely fixed by Christmas," Beau said. "Now if that isn't amazing."

"Is that right?" Roger asked.

"I heard it, too," Margaret said. "I don't know, by the looks of it. But that's what's being reported on the news."

"Is it me, or is it just *exhausting* to live in this city lately?" Roger asked, and saw nods around the table. "There's nowhere else I'd rather be, and yet I'm tired of looking over my shoulder. Sometimes I'm at my wit's end."

"The end of the day is the worst," Margaret said. "It's like you collect negativity all day long and then just need a way of getting it out once you get home."

"For this place it's new," Francesca said. "But there are people who live this way all the time. Every day, looking over their shoulder."

We were dealing with the same tough emotions, and there was comfort in the idea that we were all going through it together. I was quiet through the conversation, just focusing on the kinship I felt.

The conversations became more light-hearted after dinner. I helped to clear the table and stacked the dishes into the dishwasher as Beau readied the ice cream bowls with mango sorbet and Peter's chocolate brownies. "So, Roger," we heard Peter's voice say, "Have you ever met our friend Kevin?"

"No, I don't think so . . . "

Beau stopped what he was doing and looked straight at the kitchen cabinets in front of him. "Peter, you knock that off," he called into the dining room.

"I was only asking, Beau," Peter defended innocently.

Beau shook his head and looked at me. "He needs to stop playing matchmaker." He put the back of his hand beside his mouth and whispered, "The last one turned out disastrous. Ugh!" He rolled his eyes and I laughed with him.

"Shh!" I said, "They're gonna hear us."

"Too late!" Peter said, continuing their lighthearted banter. "Beau you're just so loud. And it was not disastrous. Roger, I think you'd like Kevin."

"Oh, please!" Beau snorted.

"Beau you knock that off!"

"*We* were introduced to one another by friends," Francesca said. "My sister was dating a man in Paolo's circle of friends. So they introduced us to each other, and we've been together since."

"Did you hear that, Beau?" Peter said as Beau and I came back in with dessert and coffee for everyone.

"Oh, I heard it. But I know your track record," Beau said.

"One time! And that's not my fault. Those two were incompatible for anyone," he dismissed. Beau and Peter could carry on like this for hours, and never seemed to notice that everyone around them was giggling.

Halfway through dessert Francesca asked me how long I'd lived with Beau and Peter.

"Almost three months," I said.

"Oh? Where were you before that?" Margaret asked.

Ah, the dreaded question. "I was living not too far from here with a bunch of girls. But group living got to be too much for me."

"So we took her in as our little sister." Peter beamed and I smiled at him.

"Yes, they were kind enough to take me in until I can figure out what I'm doing with myself."

"For as long as you need, Sweetie," Beau said.

"So what *are* you doing with yourself?" Francesca asked. She really knew how to get right to it, didn't she?

"Uh, well . . . I'm not too sure. My contract with the office expired a little bit ago, but my boss and I haven't sat down to discuss it because of everything that's happened. And now he's away on business a lot, so I don't know when we'll get to it. We agreed by phone just to keep going as is for now. I'm so used to it, I don't know what I'd do instead. But it would be nice to get away from my coworker."

"You can always pop in when you need a break," Beau said.

"Why, thank you," I said. And then I explained, "Beau's travel agency moved in next door to my office. That's how we met."

"Speaking of travel," Margaret said, "Paolo, I hear you two are off to Italy for a while."

"Yes!" Paolo said. "We've been dabbling with larger restorations lately. I combined my restoration skills with my passion for ships, and 'Cesca and I successfully restored a yacht last year."

"Really?" Roger asked. "That sounds fascinating! How did you get started in that?"

"Oh, we were at a dinner party much like this and one of the guests had just bought a yacht for himself," Paolo said. "He had it docked down in Virginia Beach and was thinking about restoring it back to its original condition. He and I talked ships for hours and I convinced him I could achieve his goal."

"Just like that?" I asked.

"Yes. But of course we were drinking most of the night. Chianti always helps," Paolo winked.

"Don't let him fool you," Francesca said. "It took a lot of research after the Chianti night. A lot of reading, photographs, visiting the old shipbuilding factories, talking to workers who retired years ago . . . It was a lot of work."

"But we hired a carpentry team and moved the boat to the shipyards for seven months while we did the restoration," Paolo said. "Really, ships are just large antiques, and antiques I can do."

"It turned out so beautifully that the owner recommended Paolo oversee another of his boat restorations about to start in Italy. This one should take a little longer. So, we are getting paid to go home."

"That's amazing!" Margaret said. "When do you leave?"

"As soon as 'Cesca defends her thesis," Paolo said. "December fifth?"

"Yes, December fifth is the defense," she repeated, the date obviously etched in her mind. "So after that we go."

We continued talking, and I learned that Margaret knew my friend Andy, and Roger worked at Treasury, just two blocks from my office building. Despite the things I had in common with Margaret and Roger, though, I couldn't help but get absorbed by Francesca and Paolo. Their lifestyle, the places they'd been, the things they'd done, all of it sounded fascinating to me. "Wait 'til you meet 'em," Beau had said. He was right.

Francesca called me at the office the next day. "I hope you don't mind my calling you at work," she said.

"No, not at all," I said. "It's nice to hear from you."

"Peter told me you work so much, and suggested I call you at the office rather than at home."

"It's fine, really."

"I'm wondering if you would like to have lunch at our house this Saturday. Really, Paolo won't be there, it will just be the two of us. I'd like to talk to you about something."

"Saturday? Sure, yeah, I can make it." I had to work all weekend, but really only at night. If I got less sleep Saturday, I could easily make it to lunch.

"That's great. Shall we say early afternoon then? Peter can tell you where the house is."

"Very good. I will be there."

"Wonderful. See you then. *Ciao*."

I arrived that Saturday relatively tired, but happy to have been invited. Peter had given me directions and I'd found the place easily. He also mentioned how unbelievable the house was, so I was excited to see this amazing place.

Francesca came to the door of the three-story townhouse and welcomed me in. "How are you?" the tiny blonde said in her loud voice.

"I'm fine, how are you?"

"I'm wonderful," she said. "But you look tired." She put on a look of concern.

"I am a little."

"You work too much," she said, pointing a finger at me.

"Okay," I said. She had the air of a petite, happy fortune teller. It seemed best not to argue. She was right anyway, I *was* tired. The glass front doors opened to a foyer where a second set of doors were open to a wide staircase. Francesca pointed out a wooden door on the right side of the foyer that was the apartment they rented out. We started up the staircase to the second floor.

"I'm sorry Paolo is not here. He's with the accountant. They need to file another tax paper for the shop."

"He still has the antique shop?" I asked. I don't know why I thought he hadn't.

"Oh, yes. He loves that little shop. Last year he had his apprentice run it for him while we made the trips to the restoration site. William will take care of the shop again while we're gone." We reached the landing to the second level. "Ah, here is where we live."

Straight ahead of us was the kitchen with a gray ceramic floor and tall red maple cabinets. It smelled of tomatoes and basil, and a myriad of other herbs she had cooking on the stove. On the opposite wall from the stove was a large dining table sitting impressively under the leaves and flowers of two enormous trees.

Francesca saw me eyeing the trees. "Ah," she said. "Oleander, from the Mediterranean. It's too cold for them in the winter, so they live here in the kitchen until summertime." The trees were skinny, but probably eleven feet tall. With the kitchen's high ceilings they still had room to grow before needing a larger space. Francesca had them planted in two large, decorative ceramic pots. She checked the food on the stove and then said, "Come, I'll show you the rest of the house."

Back out to the stair landing, we wound through a curved hallway lined with French doors. She opened the first set of doors to a living room lined with books on high shelves. To the left was a writing desk and computer. The far wall had a fireplace in the center with a TV to the left of it and a set of open French doors along the right wall. In fact the room was "L"-shaped, and we were in the shorter part of the "L." As we went through the doors into the adjoining room, the furniture changed from large leather couch and armchair to smaller, more formal and high-backed chairs set around a circular glass coffee table.

"This is the salon, and over here, the dining room," Francesca said. She and Paolo had a dark wooden dining table set for eight beside another fireplace. Everywhere were antique vases with flowers, photographs in shiny frames, and large paintings on the walls. Francesca opened another set of French doors and we were back in the hallway again. We traveled up another narrower flight of stairs, past more bookcases lining the upper landing, and found ourselves on the top floor of the house. From the windows I could see we were eye-level with the treetops. There were two bedrooms on this top level. The guest bedroom was dark blue in color with dark wood floors, while Francesca and Paolo's room was a Hunter green with plush pillows and a bay window.

There was also a large bathroom on the top level, with an enormous tub and two sinks.

The house was incredible by any standard. The most amazing thing to me was that, from the outside, it looked like just another townhouse. From the street no one would know the beautiful and ornate space that was on the inside.

"Your home is just beautiful," I said as we returned to the kitchen after the tour.

"Thank you," Francesca said with a slight nod. "It is a good home to us. Please, sit down. Lunch should be ready."

I sat at the kitchen table, under the trees. Francesca served penne pasta with a red wine tomato sauce, and gave me a glass of carbonated water. She sat with me and we grated parmesan over our pasta. When I was only half finished she insisted I have another bowl. And after that she made us espresso on the stove and brought out two small bowls of sorbet from the freezer.

"Now," she said over dessert, "The reason I have asked you here is to ask you a question," she paused ceremoniously and then continued. "Paolo and I are leaving next month for Italy, and we will be gone at least until summer, maybe later. He and I, and again I'm sorry that he could not be here to ask you, he and I would like it if you would take care of this house for us while we are gone."

Just then I'd been wondering how I was going to fit sorbet into my already-full stomach, and I didn't comprehend exactly what she was saying. Since the moment I'd walked in and saw the kitchen trees, I knew I'd love to live in a place exactly like this; but I wasn't sure if I'd really heard her right. "Um . . . Stay here?"

"Yes. Normally, we travel and William stays in the house."

"Oh," I said, wondering who William was. Then I remembered she'd said he took care of their antiques shop.

"But William is older and does not like all the staircases. Still, we need someone we can trust. This is our *home*."

We sat quietly for a moment and I looked around the kitchen from the painting on the wall to my left to the stove in front of us, the bookshelf next to the sink, the shiny black refrigerator, and finally to the leaves hanging over us.

Francesca sat patiently as I did this and since she hadn't heard a no (and she wouldn't; my mind was screaming *Of course!*), she said, "You can move into the guest bedroom right away, I will give my defense of my thesis, and Paolo and I will be off. But that should give you time to know the house. You will need to keep it lived in, keep lights on, things like that. The neighborhood is okay, but we don't want the house to be dark and empty, or it will become the target of vandals.

"It is a big house for one person. Collect the mail, and the rent from Gerry, who lives in the first floor apartment. And William will come to get all of that. We will pay the house bills online while we are away. All except the electricity. They are giving us problems about paying online. I don't know why. This is the new millennium."

"So, stay in your house?"

"Yes. But you need to pay the electric bill, which is usually around $130 or so, and any other incidentals that may arrive. We can have William reimburse you as you go, from the shop income, or we can pay you back when we return. Just keep your receipts. Whatever you need."

"You don't want me to pay rent?"

"My goodness, no!" she scoffed. "You're doing us a favor! But you need to keep the place up. William can help you if anything breaks. If I ask too much, please tell me. You are not the first person to say no. We asked Beau and Peter, but they have enough worries with the travel business. It was Peter who suggested you. It took a while for us to set up the dinner party so we could meet you, but we agree with Peter that you're exactly the person we're looking for. You are trustworthy."

With that, Francesca had just cleared away my one drawback. My living arrangement with Beau and Peter was temporary, though there really was no deadline. But I didn't want to agree to anything without discussing it with them first. "So Beau and Peter know you're asking me this?"

"Of course," she said with a smile.

"Well, I'd like to talk it over with them to be sure they're okay with it, but I think I'm going to do it. Yes, I'll do it."

"Great," she said, and it was settled, just like that. "I'll make us more espresso," she said in a tone that suggested the espresso made things final, and celebratory.

SIXTEEN

This new offer changed everything. I'd be living in the city itself for one thing. Francesca and Paolo's place was much closer to the office, and much further from the Upscale in Virginia. Why leave the city if I didn't have to? It was a long shot, but I thought perhaps I could work at the Dupont Circle Upscale.

The start of my next shift in Virginia seemed to solidify my decision. It was nine hours of running around with trays and dishes and checks, but for all the work I did, we weren't as busy as usual. At our busiest point, the host stand was only telling people there was a fifteen-minute wait. Back in the summer the typical wait time for a table was an hour, at least.

The first of three obnoxious tables showed up at the start of my night. The Kid Table were obviously tourists. I had the kitchen put a rush on their food, and brought the kids' food out right away. But the food didn't stop them from screaming, and neither did their parents. The monsters then proceeded to throw food all over the table and floor, and then their parents left about ten percent even though I had to clean up all that mess. Gone were the heydays of busboys at Upscale. This mess was entirely mine to deal with. The parents were drinking iced tea, a typical tourist drink since no one ever seems to order iced tea when out close to home, and unlike soda that can be refilled at stations all over the restaurant, iced tea is only brewed in one central location. Refills took extra time, which equates to a pain in the ass. By their fourth refill each, I admit to purposely making them wait for more. They racked up a forty-five dollar bill and left me five bucks. My efforts in giving them tea and extra napkins alone amounted to more than five dollars of work.

Jenny nodded when I complained about them in the dishroom. "Well, you know, parents go out to eat to let someone else worry about their kids for a change. They honestly don't care how much of a mess they make. You're their babysitter for the hour while they're here."

"That's crap!" I said. "First of all, it's irresponsible. Second, a babysitter gets paid more than five bucks an hour!"

"Maybe that's why they couldn't find one for the night," she said. "Actually . . . They paid you in cash?"

"Yeah."

"Go back and void off some of their food. Tell the computer you rang it in wrong. Get their bill down to like thirty-five dollars, and keep all the cash."

"You're kidding, right? That's stealing, Jenny."

"Amy, everyone here does it. How do you think we walk out of here at the end of the night with money in our pockets? If we settled for what we were given we'd never make the rent. People don't realize the prices when they sit down. And then they get the bill and figure they can take it out of the tip, which is taking it out on you. There's nothing right about that. Oh, and if you get a lousy credit card tip, let me show you what to do." She pulled a few receipts out of her apron. "Here, see this one? They left three dollars, so I wrote in a one and made it thirteen."

"Okay, *that's* a federal offense," I protested.

"Would you stop the goody-goody act? I'm not saying on every table. Just the really shitty ones. It's nice to get a little retribution. We work hard, damn it. And people don't check their credit statements that closely anyway. I mean, do you?"

"Not really."

"See?" She shook her head at me. "You got a lot to learn, Amy."

I stood there for a moment, just dumb-founded. Was I really that innocent?

"Amy, you have two new tables," Gretchen poked her head around the corner.

"Hey Gretchen, can I ask you something?"

"Yeah?

"Nah, never mind."

"You sure?"

"Yeah. Two tables, okay."

"Yeah, you just missed getting the McIntyres, so thank your lucky stars."

"Awesome! Who got stuck with them?"

She raised her hand. "That's right, yours truly."

"Ugh!" I groaned. "I'm sorry."

"Thanks," she said. The McIntyres were a thirty-something couple that came in weekly, and sent back everything at least once. It was annoying enough on weekdays, but if you got stuck with them on the weekend when things were, knock on wood, still busier, you had a hell of a time keeping up with the comings and goings of their food.

My next two tables made me question my faith in humanity. The Snooty Woman at table twelve looked down her nose at me for everything, ordered a water after I'd already brought it to her table, and reminded me three times—enunciating, mind you—that she wanted extra lemon with her fish sandwich. After I'd brought her everything to her liking on the first try, I said, "Okay, I'll be right back with some more water for you, is there anything else you would like?"

She had the nerve to scrutinize the table and tell me, "Yes, I need water," and she picked up the glass to show it to me, then set it back down again. I didn't expect she'd part with her money easily, and I was right.

My Dessert Camper Table was just plain obnoxious. Three girls who came in for dessert only, which was fine enough by me, except that they sat for three hours. They'd finished dessert within fifteen minutes, and the rest of the time kept ordering waters and wouldn't pay the check. When they finally left, they'd given me a three-dollar tip, which was twenty per cent of their dessert bill, but I could have made a lot more had they left in a timely fashion and made way for more guests.

I agree with you," Gretchen said. "There should be Table Rent. I'd say five dollars an hour every hour that you sit there, plus a tip on top of that. That way if you just want to be out for a while and have nowhere else to go, you can sit as long as you like but your waitress isn't going to come up short for it. That's happened to me a million times. Lucky for me, I now live in a dive where the rent is cheap."

"I don't mind them sitting around," I said, "but they needed to answer this question: Had I not sat here for seven zillion hours, and instead let this table rotate with paying customers, how much money would the server have made off this table alone? Then tip accordingly."

And as for Jenny's scam, I just couldn't bring myself to do it, even though it was extremely tempting. I could agree to issuing arrest warrants for lousy tippers, making them serve out their time as waitresses, but steal from them? What next, spitting in their food? No, the line had to be drawn somewhere. We already ate our weight in free food the cooks gave us. Jenny and the others could do what they wanted. I knew where I stood.

The only one of us having a decent night was Sandy. She only had one customer at the bar for nearly half the night, but she made the best of it and struck up a conversation with the lone man, helped him decide what to eat for dinner, and talked sports with him. He asked her what kind of a night she was having, and instead of saying she'd like to have more bar customers, Sandy talked about her day instead. A shop down the street just put a leather jacket in the front window, and she tried it on while on her way to work. It was a hundred dollars, but fit her perfectly and she was making a plan to pick up an extra shift or two so she could buy it before someone else did. The man drank two beers, demolished his pizza saying it was the best he'd ever tasted, and stayed to talk to Sandy for hours. When he did leave, he shook her hand, saying, "I'm a man of God myself, and I believe people should get what they want in life. I thank you for the company. You have a good night." With that, he left. His tab had come to seventeen dollars, and he'd paid it in cash exactly. And under the seventeen, he'd hidden a hundred dollar bill.

It was one of those unbelievable things you only hear about. Our manager agreed to watch the bar for a few minutes, and Sandy ran out the door. When she returned, she had the jacket. "I couldn't find the man to thank him!" she said. "He was completely gone. But this was still in the window and the shop was just about to close. Awesome, huh?"

I had to admit—and mind you, I was not in the best mood—but it really *was* awesome. Truly.

But after the night I'd had, I was starting to doubt that I had the right personality for this job. I usually monitored how good a server I was by the tips I got. There were times when tips didn't reflect the job done, and not just in a bad way. There were days when I felt plenty "off" but still managed to make good money somehow.

But when you got a lousy tip followed by another, followed by yet another, it made you question yourself. Three tables in a row must mean that I was lousy, that it wasn't just a fluke.

When the end of my shift finally arrived, I went home and collapsed into my bed. Sunday morning arrived a little too early for me, but my mind was racing the moment I woke up, and I couldn't get back to sleep.

I went downstairs and got a cup of coffee. "Hey, you're up early!" Peter said.

"I can't sleep anymore," I groaned.

"Want some breakfast?"

"Absolutely. It smells awesome," I said.

"Beau went out for orange juice. He's been gone an hour, so he should be back any minute and we'll be ready. Go sit down and have your coffee," he said.

"Okay," I yawned. Normally I'd offer to help with something, but this time I didn't protest. I went to the living room with my coffee and sat down to watch the steam rise from the cup. I was a good waitress, even if some of my tables didn't acknowledge it. I knew it. Of all the things I'd attempted and failed, here was something I was good at. I knew how to listen to people, how to give them what they wanted, make their time enjoyable. I was good at setting my problems aside so I could care for others and be cheerful about it. "I should be nominated for sainthood," I said dryly, and sipped at my coffee. Okay, maybe not. But I was a good waitress. Good enough to work in Dupont Circle. Certainly.

The door popped open and Beau walked in with a grocery bag. "Hey, little sunshine," he said to me. "I got the OJ, let's eat! Peter, it smells great. Are we ready?"

Peter emerged from the kitchen with two plates piled high with scrambled eggs, sausage, and toasted bagels that he handed to Beau and me.

"Yummy!" Beau said, setting his plate down to reach into the grocery bag. "I also got us some salmon cream cheese."

Peter rolled his eyes, and turned on the news.

"Sounds weird, Beau, but I'll try it," I said.

"You'll love it, Honey. It'll change your life," he declared. It wasn't half bad.

Peter talked during the commercials. "So you had lunch with Francesca yesterday, huh, Amy? How did that go?"

"You know how that went," I teased him and smiled. "She asked me to house-sit for them while they're gone. And she said the dinner party was my interview for the job."

"The party?" Peter smiled. "Of course. Had you known you might have been nervous, and then you wouldn't have been yourself. This way worked out pretty well, don't you think? So are you going to do it?"

"I told her I would."

"Wonderful!" Peter said.

"Oh how fun for you!" Beau said.

Then back to Peter again, "Oh you know we're not trying to get rid of you. We love having you here, Amy. But this sounded like such an opportunity, and you'll be able to live in Dupont Circle for nothing. How often does that happen in life?"

Beau now, "Isn't their place amazing?"

"Yeah! I couldn't believe it when she showed it to me. And then she asked me, and I thought, 'Wow, I really get to live here?' But now, of course, my mind is racing with all the stuff I have to do. Moving is easy, but I have to figure out what to do about my jobs."

"You're quitting one, right?" Peter asked.

"Well . . . "

"I think you should get away from Chad," Beau said.

"I think you should do what you want, Amy," Peter said, and gave Beau a look.

"Oh, I'd definitely like to get away from Chad, but I don't know when that will happen. And for now, it's steady income, whereas the restaurant isn't doing so hot lately. But I'm wondering if Upscales in the city are doing better . . . Maybe in Dupont Circle?"

"Ooh, that sounds like fun," Beau said. "And you'll be living right there. Sounds perfect!"

"The city is its own world, but you're not that far away," Peter said. "You know our door is always open."

"Thank you. I'm really gonna miss living here with you guys," I said. "You've done so many great things for me."

"Oh stop!" Beau said.

"We haven't done anything that friends wouldn't do," Peter said. "You're like a little sister to us, you know that."

"And since September, my God, I can't imagine if I'd been living on my own or in that cult house. I'd be a real wreck if I couldn't be myself right now."

Peter looked thoughtful. "It's easy to accept others when you've accepted yourself. Being gay, we've dealt with our own truth. It makes it easier to deal with everyone else's truth. Not that we've had to 'deal' with you, sweetie, you've been a peach to live with. And you can come back any time—you know that. But we have time; the news is back on."

But time was moving pretty fast. That night at Upscale, I asked the manager to stop scheduling me.

"What? You're leaving us?" Mark asked. "No, Amy . . . "

"Yep," I said. "I'm moving into the city."

"That's too bad," he said, but with the revolving door on servers he'd seen lately, he understood. "You're a great waitress. Are you really sure?"

"Yeah, I need a new scene for a while. I'm thinking to take December off, then apply at Dupont Circle."

"Well, I hate to lose you," he sighed. "But there's no real money here lately. Some of the Upscales in the city are booming, though, especially Dupont Circle, and you might make good money up there. But if you want to come back to us . . . "

"Thanks, I appreciate it."

But I was already thinking about the money to be had in Dupont Circle. I was on my way to the Big Time itself. Over the next two weeks, I'd moved my clothes and books into Francesca and Paolo's guest room, and was learning the household checklist.

Lights had to be turned on and off at particular times each day. The upstairs skylight needed to be checked nightly that it was shut tight and locked, as once Francesca had come home and found it open and a man on the roof with a crowbar trying to pry it off. The security alarm took me a few days to figure out. There were settings for when I was in the house and moving around versus not moving around, settings that differed per floor, and various beep sounds and signals that let me know whether it was on a time delay or whether it was set for immediate response.

I commuted back and forth to Virginia for my restaurant shifts before my last day at Upscale finally arrived. It was a Thursday night and the place was pretty empty. I made good money anyway, because I gave out a couple of free desserts, and told all my tables that it was my last day.

The girls were sorry to see me go, just as I'd been sorry to see Sharon go months before this. One memorable thing did happen: Jason told me he'd miss me. And he also mentioned that Sam had been asking about me.

"What are you talking about?" I asked.

"He admired you," Jason said. "Didn't you know?"

"Last I heard, he ran off to Italy," I said.

"Yeah, but he was back after a month. I run into him sometimes. And he always asks about you."

I frowned. "Maybe it was just small talk."

"No. I watched him date Jenny and break her heart, then move on to Gretchen and Haley, and then finally to you. And you seemed the least impressed by him, Amy, so I thought you'd never go out with him."

"We really didn't go out," I said. "We hung out maybe once and did a lot of talking—well, Sam did a lot of talking, but nothing ever really happened. It's kinda lousy, when even a player changes his mind about dating you."

Jason gave me an incredulous look. "You're looking at it all wrong," he said. "He has a great deal of respect for you. Maybe that's why nothing ever happened. But he thinks you're an amazing person." I just blinked at Jason, knowing that eventually, that line would sink in.

I expected a crescendo or something as I walked out the door for the last time, but there was only the noise of a utility truck idling as workers re-decorated a tree whose Christmas lights had fallen down onto the street. I watched them for a moment, and then walked to my car. The girls burst out of the door a few moments later. "Hey, Amy! Wanna have a drink down at Chadwick's for old times' sake?" Jenny shouted.

"No, you go on without me," I called back. "I'll see you girls!"

"Stop in on us sometime, Amy!" Gretchen said, and they headed down toward the waterfront. I looked back a few moments later when I could no longer hear their chatter, and they were already gone. I got to my car and started the drive home, thinking about what Jason had told me. Sam, for all his faults, had encouraged me to take an interest in myself.

Once I got past thinking that he was a jerk and that I was an idiot to like him, I realized he'd taught me a great deal. Sam was a player, yes, but a philosopher and an avid reader. And he lived life on his own terms, and didn't pretend to be anything he wasn't. He didn't pretend to like people. His behavior bordered on rude, but he didn't compromise what he thought for anyone or anything. For that, he was admirable.

Francesca was wide-awake when I walked in the door. "How was your defense?" I asked.

"Beautiful!" she said. "I graduated!"

"They told you already? I thought you wouldn't get the results back so soon!"

"'Cesca! *Cerco-la!*" Paolo burst into the kitchen with a bottle of wine in his hands. Seeing me, he switched to English. "Amy! You're home, too! Perfect! Grab some glasses in the cabinet. 'Cesca, I found the cabernet."

"Cabernet? Shouldn't you have champagne?" I asked, picking up three wine glasses from a six-foot tall cabinet built to hold only wine glasses.

"We finished that already," Francesca said as Paolo uncorked the bottle he'd found in their wine cellar. "Now we switch to wine."

"To my beautiful wife," Paolo raised his glass to toast, "who today has received her Doctorate!"

"*Salute*," Francesca said, and I followed. "Your accent is good," she said to me after drinking from her glass.

"Thank you," I said tentatively, hoping I hadn't insulted her somehow.

"No, I mean it!" she said, and Paolo agreed.

"You have never studied Italian?"

I shook my head. "I pay attention when *you* are speaking," I confessed. "Though I don't usually know what you're saying."

"Ah, but you have an ear for language," she said. "You have been here two weeks and sometimes I forget and ask you questions in Italian. You answer me in English without noticing."

I drank from my glass. The wine was big, and wonderful. "I'm sure I don't . . . "

"Yes," she said. "And sometimes you even have the right answers."

"I have heard it also," Paolo said, just as we heard shuffling at the door.

"Is Gerry home?" Francesca asked.

"I think so," Paolo said, looking through the kitchen doorway and down the stairs.

"Ask him to come up and have a drink with us," she said, and Paolo went out.

"It's about time that you meet Gerry. He lives in the apartment downstairs. He will give you the rent on the first of the month. He is always on time and shouldn't give you any trouble. Now, what I was saying? Yes, of course, have you ever thought about taking language classes?"

"I don't know. That sounds expensive."

She shook her head. "No, the government offers classes in the evenings, taught by native speakers. I even taught them for years until I went back for my Doctorate. They are very good classes for language, and they're not expensive. The next semester will start up in February. You should try it."

"Maybe I will," I said.

Paolo came back in, followed by a twenty-something young man. Francesca handed him a glass of wine and we toasted again. "Gerry, this is Amy. She will be looking after the house for us."

"Hello, nice to meet you," he extended his hand to me and looked me up and down. Gerry was very tall and black-skinned, with a mischievous-looking smile. "I'm in law school over at Georgetown. It's my first year. I graduated top of my class from Duke. What do you do?"

"I work for lobbyists," I said. "And I wait tables."

"You work in an office? That's great," he said. "That's going to be me someday. I can't wait. The easy life, making a hundred grand a year to start, working in a nice office all day long . . . Oh, but wait tables? Now that's something I'll never do," Gerry said. "It sounds like a lot of work. I'll have people waiting on *me*, thank you very much," he drained his wine glass.

"I thought today was your last day," Francesca said.

"It was," I said. "But I'm going to apply at the Dupont Circle location, since it's right here and all. They're *really* busy. I can't wait." Tonight was a turning point for me. I'd slowly gone from a person looking for a white-collar career and romance to someone who preferred blue-collar work and spending time with the people you shouldn't bring home to mom. Every time I made a safe choice, things turned out badly. But when I shot from the hip I enjoyed life a whole lot more.

"That sounds lovely, if you're into that sort of thing," Gerry said, cleaning his eyeglasses with the bottom of his sweater. "Francesca, thank you for the wine. And congratulations."

"Thank you," she said.

"Paolo," Gerry turned to face him, "Can you take a look at the tile under my bathroom sink? It seems to be chipping away."

"Sure," Paolo said. "But depending on the damage I may have William handle it." They walked out together.

"He's interesting," I said to Francesca.

"Yes," was all she said.

"So, what is your thesis about?"

She refreshed our wine and sat down at the table. "Basically, it is about how we set our goals and how we learn, or not, to achieve them, specifically in language acquisition, but it includes life goals as well." She gestured with her hands in front of her, as if presenting the information to me or trying to carry a tray, then she curled her fingers up, and swirled her hands around in circles. "You see, we are all created in the image of God. Therefore, we are all little gods." That brought a smile from me, but she kept talking. "Ah," first finger up in the air, "but let's admit it, we are blessed. And keeping with that, we have been given our own answers. Think about yourself, do you agree?"

"I suppose," I thought. "Well, for me," I said slowly, "Any time I've known what I need to do, the problem is the 'how to do it' part. It feels like I'm locked behind a door that I can't open."

At this, Francesca got very excited. She picked up a blue booklet on the table and leafed through it, turning to a page with a sketch of a man unlocking a door with a skeleton key, with words written in Italian above it: "It's not the key, it's the way you turn it in the lock," she translated. "Being little gods, I believe we already have our own key, and so we're wasting time searching for the keys to unlock the answers. Have faith. The key is right there, just . . . " she gestured this, "*Turn* it."

Live like little gods. Turn our own keys. I was pretty sure my own answers were hiding from me. But maybe Francesca's way was worth a shot.

CHAPTER
SEVENTEEN

At nine the morning of their flight, Paolo went to the antique shop for a last look around, and Francesca sat down to sort a mountain of paperwork into folders. She asked me to sit in with her during this process so she had someone to talk to. By ten, a friend of theirs stopped in so Francesca made the three of us espresso on the stove. By eleven, she asked me to defy the laws of physics and stuff a mountain of clothes into two suitcases while she took a shower. Somehow I got it all to fit. Paolo arrived back at noon, assuming his wife wouldn't be ready yet, and was floored when I told him she was.

"My 'Cesca? Are you sure?" he kept asking me until she came down the stairs and he saw for himself. Still, it was a mad dash, but they got out of the house and headed to the airport mostly on time.

My first night alone in the house was a long one. Someone's dog got out and decided to make Francesca and Paolo's back deck his new perch so he could bark for half the night. From my bed, all I heard was heavy footsteps on the back stairs and barking. I thought somebody was lurking around outside and trying to break in. I knew I'd set the house alarm, which hadn't gone off yet—not that that was much comfort. I crept to the window, waiting for the alarm to sound at any moment, and peeked out. That's when I saw the huge dog that could have been Cerberus straight from Hell. He barked like mad and then I saw him jump down and chase another dog back and forth along the back service road.

The next morning, I went to work early, because I was awake anyway, and took advantage of the extra time. As I promised Francesca I would, I searched online and found an Italian class offered through the government. It wasn't very expensive, just as she'd said. The class met twice a week, from 7-10 p.m., so as long as I was out of the office by six-thirty on those days, I could make it on time. Our typical workdays ended around six lately, so I had plenty of time. I called Mr. Watters on his cell phone to see if he had any objections.

"It sounds fine to me, Amy. You're good at getting your work done, so I don't foresee any reason for you to stay late. Doesn't sound like an interference to me."

"If I need to, I could always come in earlier," I assured him.

"Listen, Amy, I know we haven't discussed your contract," he said. "But, of course, I'd like you to stay on. How does a ten percent raise sound? Retroactive to last August, of course. And we won't mess with any contracts. You can work for Watters and Company like a regular employee."

"Sounds great to me," I said, which sounded like someone else's voice, even to me. "Thank you."

"Well, I think you're doing a great job, and I'm sorry you had to wait so long for that to get settled. Enjoy your class."

A raise? And the ability to give my notice whenever I liked? This was the next best thing to actually being fired.

"You're doing what?" Chad asked, monotone.

"I'm taking the Metro down to L'Enfant Plaza at lunch today. I need to pick up a book for a class I'm taking. I won't be gone long. Mr. Watters okayed it."

"What class?"

"It's an Italian class on Monday and Wednesday nights. It starts right after the holidays."

"Whatever, Amy. Have fun with your little class. I never had to take language courses. I've always had an ear for foreign languages. I can listen in for a few moments and pretty much tell you what someone's talking about."

He walked toward the door, "I'm going to an early lunch. If anyone needs me, they can find me on my cell."

Signing up for the class was only one of the things I needed to accomplish before the holiday break. Here it was, days before Christmas vacation, and I still needed to apply for a job at Dupont Circle's Upscale.

Rumor had this location was a lot more hip than mine in Virginia. I couldn't help but feel intimidated. But if I hoped to land a New Year's

Eve shift, I'd have to get myself hired. At the worst, they'd refuse to hire me, and at least then I'd know.

I found that the application process was easy enough: So long as I could speak some English and spell my name, I was granted an interview. This Upscale was smaller, but had a dramatic staircase near the bar that led to upper-level seating. Other than this impressive feature, the tables, chairs, and wall colors were the same as I'd known in Virginia.

I sat down at main-level table with Stuart, the short and squirrelly manager. "Just so you understand," he informed me in a way meant to put me in my place, "To get you in here and trained would take a couple weeks. If you don't hear from us by next month, stop in again just in case. Okay, let's see . . . " He turned my application over to see my work experience. Suddenly he looked interested, and I heard excitement in his voice. "You worked for Mark?" he asked.

I nodded, feeling like I suddenly had the upper hand in this interview.

"Mark's my golf buddy," he said. "Why didn't you say you had Upscale experience?"

"It's all right there," I pointed out.

"Hold on a second." Stuart went into the office, leaving me alone to survey the restaurant. It was busy, and boisterous, especially for a Tuesday night, but most of the servers were congregated at the corner of the bar, laughing and watching the TV that hung from the ceiling. Stuart emerged from the office a few minutes later.

"I just talked to Mark, and he had nothing but praise for your work."

"Really?" I asked.

Stuart assured me, "He said if he could, he'd hire three more just like you. When can you start?"

Yes! I was *in*. All I had to do was follow T.J. around for a shift to learn the layout of the restaurant. We set it up for the following night. And since I was new, they were willing to work around my Christmas vacation and my classes starting up in January.

"Would you mind working New Year's Eve?" Stuart asked.

"No, I'd love it," I said.

"Great, you're on."

Awesome. I showed up the next day and met T.J., who looked a little like a blonde Elvis. He was quick-witted and seemed familiar to me.

Then I remembered that he'd waited on Andy and me the one and only time I'd eaten there.

"We sat over by the window, and you were out of plates."

T.J. nodded. "I hate to say it, but that happens a little too often around here."

"We used to run out of plates, but they would make us take turns washing dishes," I said.

T.J. laughed. "So you *had* plates, right? When we run out of plates here, I mean we *run out*. We don't have enough, so usually by eight o'clock we have to get creative."

"You're kidding! Why don't you . . . "

"Ask Corporate for more?" He shook his head. "That's the way it's supposed to work, but around here . . . You'll see. This restaurant's a head case. Let me show you around."

The layout of the restaurant was very different from what I was used to. What the Virginia Upscale had in sprawling size the Dupont location made up for with its second floor. The main floor was only about six tables wide, and the length of the restaurant was around fifteen tables. The upper floor ran the perimeter of the restaurant and overlooked the main floor. The "P" as T.J. called the upper perimeter, held twenty tables, none of which held more than two people. The East side of the P was much wider, with a bar, small kitchen for soups and appetizers, a coffee station, a few four-person tables, and the entrance to the outdoor deck. The deck overlooked Connecticut Avenue, and was closed for the winter. When it opened again, T.J. explained to me that it would hold eight large and small tables that could be moved around to accommodate large parties.

"You have to be organized—especially if you work the upper deck," he said. "Drinks and appetizers you can get up here, but you still have to get entrees from the main kitchen downstairs. So it's worth your while to carry heavier trays loaded with food for multiple tables rather than make the trip five times with light trays."

"Got it," I said.

"The stairs suck at first, but you'll get the hang of them pretty quickly. You didn't have stairs at your Upscale, right?"

"No, we were all one level."

T.J. nodded. "I think we're the only one with an upper level. Okay, looks like we've got some customers, so let's get started," he said.

My old Upscale had been a walk in the park compared to Dupont Circle. Had I started working in the city first, I never would have made it past training. The pace on a Wednesday night in the city was as fast as any Saturday night in Virginia. Not only were there more customers, but Dupont also had fewer servers. Running with T.J. all night was exhausting. I don't know how he kept all the orders straight. I was a fan of writing things down, but T.J. memorized everything as he went from table to table. This guy—who'd given me napkins to eat on—was the best I'd ever seen.

"It'll come with time," he assured me. "Once you get comfortable with your surroundings you won't have to write anything down. You'll get good at it."

"I don't know, I always write things down," I considered. "But I guess I can . . . "

"This place will demand comfort out of you," he said. "It'll force you to relax and get in the zone, drop your pretenses, shake off any hesitation, and get into rhythm."

I nodded. "But what if that doesn't happen, though?"

T.J. furrowed his brow. "It'll kick your ass," he said. Then he raised an eyebrow and smiled at me.

I had no idea what New Year's Eve would be like, but I was sure I couldn't handle it. After a short trip home for Christmas, I was back in D.C., tray in hand, waiting with the other servers for the doors to open. Besides myself, there were three guys and three girls working the New Year's Eve shift.

"What are we waiting for?" asked a guy with a shaved head next to me.

"Um, I think the manager wants to speak to us," I whispered back.

"Okay, quiet down," Stuart said as he stepped out of the office and walked toward us. "Alright, this won't take long. We're well stocked on everything tonight, so sell like crazy. It's gonna get tough, gonna get busy, gonna get rough, so be prepared, be flexible, keep moving, and ask for help if you need it. Drunks: cut 'em off, get 'em out of here, hail 'em a cab. We brought up all the extra tables and chairs from the basement which should help you guys, but we're gonna be busy as shit tonight. And when we reach full capacity, hit the point of no return, make 'em wait. Alright. New guys Raul and Amy: you'll be downstairs here with T.J. and Charlotte. Jessica, Katie, Carlos, you're upstairs. Any questions? Ready to open the doors? Let's do it."

In Virginia, the most we ever got out of a manager before a shift were the occasional "we're out of something" talks. This was different;

nerve-wracking. It was the moment before the big show. And what a show it was. New Year's Eve wasn't just busy. *Mobbed* was more the term for it.

By five, every chair was filled, including the extras from the basement. It was hard to maneuver through the serving floor, and even harder to keep up with all the demands. I was moving as fast as I could, breaking a sweat, and still never less than three tables behind. And yet, I was having the time of my life. After Stuart had assigned us our locations, T.J. split the main floor into three sections. Raul and I were assigned fifteen tables each, while T.J. and Charlotte had a few more than that. We got so busy so fast I really only caught glimpses of my coworkers until closing time.

Unlike in Virginia, we didn't have a pastry chef for desserts or someone taking care of our soups or plain coffees and teas. We did all of that ourselves from a two-by-two countertop which was covered in mess within an hour. After that, we used any available space we could find, and by the end of the night we'd have things thrown and stuffed everywhere. We were creative about it: using the shelves of the refrigerator as counter space for slicing pies, lids of the soup well as drink holders, the ice bin as a tray stand, and everywhere served well as a garbage can.

There weren't busboys to help us out, so our priority was cleaning up the tables to make room for more customers, not cleaning up after ourselves.

By ten, most of our customers were in costume, from pixies to vampires to celebrity look-alikes, to Baby New Year—a grown man dressed in a diaper—to cats, strippers, and even a man in black with a lampshade on his head. The line waiting to get in was trailing out the door and along the sidewalk outside. "Standing Room Only" turned into "Stand Anywhere You Like."

For our sake, it was slightly faster to get drinks through a server rather than face the crowd at the bar, so most customers were remarkably polite.

"Honey, how about a drink?" the guy wearing the lampshade asked me.

"How about drinking slower?" I said. "Or order two at a time."

"I like your style," Lampshade said. "Bring me two. And a round for my friends here." A vampire had left the table closest to us in order to hit on a table of pixies nearby, and Lampshade sat down in his place. The table started to protest until he said, "Put it all on my tab." Handing me a fifty, he said, "And this is for you."

I was having a great time. I'd had no New Year's plans, and yet I was out in the thick of things, and making a small fortune instead of spending it.

About ten minutes before midnight, everyone's focus slowly turned toward the bar TVs and the ball about to be dropped. Things quieted down some, and our music became audible just as it was turned off.

"Amy, take these," Stuart came out of nowhere with a box of confetti, noisemakers, and silly hats. "Pass them out and go see Patrick."

I nodded, grabbing a crown for myself, and started dropping handfuls of goodies on each of my tables, much to everyone's delight. As they celebrated their new toys, I hoped no one would ask me for another drink. There was no way I could order anything and have it made in time before the ball dropped. To my credit, everyone was pretty well stocked. The few who weren't were given drinks by someone at their tables, and we were all set to ring in the New Year. I saw Patrick standing on top of his bar, pointing at me, so I made my way through everyone to him.

"New girl, here you go!" he said, handing me a plastic cup filled with champagne. "This is on the boss man tonight, so drink up."

"Five-four-three-two-one . . . Happy New Year!" Everyone cheered, confetti rained down, Patrick and Stuart alternated flickering the house and bar lights, and one of the vampires planted a kiss on me as he worked his way through the crowd. Welcome, 2002.

"Hey, there she is!" one of my customers called out as I passed by. It was my "professionals" table, full of well-dressed young men drinking fairly expensive wine. "Hey, we're throwing a party this spring. It's a blast. Totally for charity. You should be there."

"Do you have an email address?" another piped up.

They'd been one of my more mature-acting tables. "Oh yeah, let me get you my card." I found this was easier than handing out my number or email address on scraps of paper. I fished through my apron and found one of my Watters and Co. cards.

"Great, we'll send you the info. Oh, and we're ready for our tab."

They tipped me handsomely and I hoped they were serious about their party. In the meantime, the present party carried on a couple hours past closing time, when the last of our guests either left or were put into cabs. Dupont Circle was still a madhouse, and inside the Upscale was a disaster. Once we got all the dishes to the dish room, T.J. huddled us together for a meeting.

"Here's how we'll attack it," he said. "Get the brooms and start with the walls. Be careful of the paintings, but get all the other confetti and everything else off the walls and onto the floor. Next, clean all the tables, just knock everything onto the floor, and scrub the tabletops. And the chairs. Don't forget the chairs, they're disgusting. After that, we'll sweep and mop the floor and get the trash out of here. Sound good?"

Raul and I looked around at the mess. Every available space, be it floor, table leg, countertop, or light fixture, was covered with stuff that shouldn't be there. "Start from the top," Raul said, and I nodded along.

"Alright," T.J. said. "I'll join you as soon as I'm done scrubbing down the dessert area. Okay?"

"I know it's the end of the night, but you're Amy, right?" Raul asked me as he handed me a broom.

"Yeah, nice to meet you," we shook hands. "You started at the same time as me, right?" I asked. Up close I could see that Raul's shaved head was due to his receding hairline. He was a little older than the typical Upscale waiter. But when he smiled, his whole face lit up, especially his blue eyes, making him seem a lot younger.

"Yeah, I think we were hired the same day," Raul said, "but you were done with your training much faster than I was." We walked toward the corner of the room and started sweeping down the walls.

"Oh, that's because I worked at another Upscale before this."

"Oh!" Raul sounded relieved. "I thought maybe I was just slow at this," he confided. "It's been a while since I was a waiter."

"What do you do?" I asked the standard D.C. question.

"I worked in the IT field until about three months ago," he said, attacking something that moved on the wall with his broom. "I was laid off after September 11. What do you do?"

"Oh, I'm sorry," I said. "I work for lobbyists—but I don't lobby. I do their paperwork." Raul had a sweet, girly voice with a melodic quality. I liked listening to it.

"Do you like your job?" he asked.

"It's alright. Sometimes it can be a little dull, which is why I work here. I need the excitement."

"I hear *that*," he agreed.

"Did you like your job?"

"Yeah, I liked it a lot," he said. "I was sorry to go. But I was also working all hours and didn't really have a life. Now I'm broke but I have all the time in the world."

"That's awesome," I said, and Raul nodded.

"It's weird, though," he said, and I expected him to tell me about having suddenly finding himself with free time. Instead, he said, "In order to qualify for unemployment, I can only work here three days a week, or else, technically, I'm employed."

"Aren't you employed anyway?" I asked. "I mean, this is your job now, right?"

"Yeah, but the government doesn't see it that way. The rules allow for me to work, and I want to work, but I can't work as much as I'd like to. If I drop unemployment so I can work here full time, I won't be able to afford my house payments."

"That sucks," I said.

"Yeah. I made enough in IT that my unemployment checks are still more than I could ever make here. I like working. I want to be full-time, but the system is encouraging me not to. Isn't that the most screwed-up thing you've heard? Anyway, so how about tonight! Unbelievable, huh?"

When we finished up, we could see it was already getting light outside. "Is that the sunrise?" I asked.

"It's going to take days before I'm over this exhaustion," Raul said, and then he smiled. "And probably just as long to count all the money I made."

EIGHTEEN

66 I would sign up for the class," Chad said, "but I'd probably test into one of the higher levels. I'd hate to show you up, Amy."

I couldn't help myself. "Oh, and they have many more classes beyond the one I'm in. You could test into Italian II, or III, and then beyond that there's some kind of advanced class."

"That's probably where I'd land," he said.

"Probably," I agreed.

Soon Chad's excuses got more elaborate. "I would take a class myself, but I just don't have the time, what with my exercise schedule and all. Monday and Thursday I have kickboxing, Tuesday and Friday I go to cardio, Wednesdays and Saturdays I run, and I just started a Sunday aerobics class, but I know the moves better than the instructor already. I heard some of the others talking about making me the new instructor. I'd hate to oust the other guy, but I would do a better job. I'm making up a few of my own routines, just in case."

After that he went back to beating up the office plants. But between the Upscale, the Dupont Circle house, and now language classes, Chad was only one facet of my life, and a small one at that. I was busy.

On the first day of class, I stood in the cold rain with scores of other students waiting through the security process. Once inside the small lobby of the government's Agriculture building, we all had to show ID, have our names checked off of an official list, pass through metal detectors, and then sign in before gaining access to our classrooms.

Finally through security, I wound my way through the halls looking for my classroom. Hallway after hallway, the group of students I was with got smaller and smaller as the others found their rooms. Only one tall, dark haired girl stayed with me, turn for turn. We were the last two to arrive, and we sat in the back.

When we introduced ourselves, I found out that the girl's name was Kelly, she was 29, and planning a trip to Italy in the fall. During the break I asked her about the trip.

"Yeah, my boyfriend and I were planning to go together," Kelly said with her slight southern accent. "But then I found out over Christmas that he's an asshole," she assured me. "But I'm here anyway. I'll go without him."

"Good for you," I said.

"Yeah, well . . . Honestly? I'm really glad he's not here today. I think he dropped the class. So, why are you here? Are you planning a trip?"

"Oh, um, a friend told me to try it. Something different, you know?"

By the end of class, my head was swimming. The look on Kelly's face told me I wasn't alone.

"What are you doing this weekend?" she asked. "Do you want to meet up to go over this stuff?"

"Yeah," I said. "I work Saturday, but I'm off on Sunday. We could go to Starbucks? In the afternoon?"

"Great. Which one?"

We got our plans straight and quickly settled into a study routine. Sunday was fast becoming my favorite day of the week. It was hard to drag my aching self out of bed, but once I got moving the day was a lot of fun. In the evening, I'd drive to Beau and Peter's for Sunday dinner. Before that, my whole afternoon would be spent lounging at Starbucks. Kelly and I chose to meet at the Starbucks in Dupont Circle that had the triangular-shaped point to the building. Architecturally, it was a beautiful setting for discussing work and men, and daydreaming about Italy. And eventually getting around to learning some Italian.

"It's a wonder you're sane, with your schedule."

"I'm a normal person," I protested, "except that I work Thursday through Saturday at a restaurant."

"You don't need to fill every moment of your life with some activity."

"Then how would I get anything done?"

Kelly thought for a moment and smiled. "Delegate?"

"Delegate? What, to my secretary?" I laughed. "Yeah, let's call her Pandora. And she can type away on that little box of hers."

"You're a lot weirder on Sundays than you are in class."

"I'm just out of it. Three straight nights at Upscale is brutal. Things hurt that I didn't know I had. By late afternoon I'll feel fine again. It's kinda like a hangover. Not that I drink at work, but . . . I'm sorry, I'm not making sense. Actually, the bartender's been known to make up pitchers of this pink stuff, but I tried it once and it made me so stupid I could hardly remember what I was doing. No more of that, thank you very much. But today I'm feeling blah, like I'm dehydrated. Which makes sense because I don't get enough water on shift. That's how come the lemonade with my coffee.

"Our old manager Stuart was somehow able to keep everything in line. But, I don't know what happened. He left, and since then we can't seem to get any leadership in there that can handle it. Their management training programs don't teach them how to deal with real situations. We're averaging two to three a week."

"That quit?"

"That we lose, yeah. God forbid a customer ask to speak to the manager—that's how we'd lost the first two. For the most part, we're our own bosses. We run the place and shelter the manager who's usually holed up in the office." We kept the place together, and didn't abuse our privilege except in the way of food. We snagged whatever food we could—anything to keep us going. In Virginia, the servers shared food, but we usually used separate plates. That wasn't an option at Dupont. I learned quickly how to talk with my mouth full in a way that no one could figure out I was eating at all. It was a handy skill. The managers knew we did this—because we told them, much to their astonishment.

"It would be nice to know some more people," Kelly mused. "But I don't think I'll be applying any time soon. I've got enough on my plate with work and this class."

"But you have fun people at your work," I reminded her. "If Mr. Watters would have put some cool people in my office, I don't think I would've applied at Upscale. The money's awesome, don't get me wrong. But I was looking for people."

I loved my new coworkers just as much as at my old Upscale. Raul, T.J., Jessica, Katie, Patrick, and I were the faces seen most often at Upscale. We had plenty of others on staff, but most of them were in and out in less than a week. They'd either walk out mid-shift or they'd just stop showing up for work. The rest of us would handle the slack. Raul was still my favorite, but the rest of my coworkers were a close second. T.J. had been there the longest, and we deferred to him with any questions or problems we encountered. Jessica was a petite girl with short, blonde hair; a student at one of the area universities. She was one of those naturally beautiful girls who didn't need to wear makeup, didn't put up too much pretense over anything, and was always smiling and looking for the next party. She was dating a military guy who loved to be out at the bars as much as she did. Katie had short, jet-black hair, and looked more like a leggy model in a waitress outfit than someone who would serve you dinner. She was only twenty, and was enrolled in grad school for chemistry, having skipped two grades in high school. Patrick, the bartender, was tall and thin, with platinum hair and a bad attitude with customers. He believed in his job: he loved mixing drinks, and was a perfectionist at it. But having to serve his creations to "lowlife whiny customers" really set him off. He had no qualms about throwing handfuls of ice at people or yelling obscenities at them as they asked where their drinks were.

There were romances, and everybody was a fair target. This wasn't one predatory guy working his way through all the waitresses; this was constant flirting among everyone. Some of it was innocent, but even when it wasn't, no one worried that this was a job and that romance didn't belong in the workplace. The atmosphere of wall-to-wall people and constant movement left very little room, or desire, for secrets. And in that light, nothing was really taboo.

"Well, you found people alright," Kelly said. "Dupont Circle's got it all. Men dating men, women dating women . . . "

"And at some point, everyone visits the Upscale on a date."

"I don't want to know what goes on," Kelly laughed. "I don't think I'm old enough to handle it."

"You'd be surprised, actually," I said. "It's usually the thirty-something straight couples that act lewd," I told her. Kelly raised her eyebrows at me and I nodded. "Okay, down to business . . . What do you think the quiz will be on tomorrow?" I asked. "He said it's just a written quiz, right?"

"Yeah," Kelly said. "So we don't have to worry about the conversations. Let's go over the numbers and colors. Oh, and that little vocab list Renaldo gave us on Wednesday."

"This list?" I showed her.

She looked it over. "No, where'd you get that?"

"Renaldo gave it to us," I said as she dug through her papers.

"Here it is, I found it," she said, momentarily excited before dismay took over. "Shit, now we have two lists to study. This is gonna take a while. Look at all these words! Let's get some more coffee first."

"Good idea," I said. "And some cake, too."

In class we were barraged with material, so to keep it all straight I made flash cards that I brought with me everywhere. Any spare moment I got I'd take out the cards and thumb through them. I brought them to the restaurant, because occasionally there was some down time, and because having the cards meant we'd be busier than hell. It was like carrying an umbrella to guarantee a sunny day.

On warmer days, we propped the doors open to get some fresh air in the restaurant. One night a bouncer from the club down the street walked in with a group of other customers. He passed the host stand and walked around as if he owned the place.

"Dante!" Jessica ran up and hugged him. He had a military haircut, so I assumed he was the boyfriend she'd been talking about, and I continued on my way toward the coffee machines. A moment later I was face-to-face with the guy.

"Hi," he said to me, "What's your name?"

"I'm Amy."

"Nice to meet you, Amy, I'm Dante," he extended his hand.

I moved the tray of coffee to my left hand and shook his. "Nice to meet you. You're Jessica's boyfriend?"

He laughed. "No. I used to work here," he nodded slightly and then cocked his head toward the wall. "Now I work down at the Tumult. Oh, listen, the reason I'm here," he shifted his weight, "other than to snag a latte, is to warn you guys the purse-snatcher is back."

"Purse-snatcher?"

"Yeah, he's a wallflower-looking guy, usually in some leisure suit. We've been following him around Tumult watching for him to strike, and he caught on to us and left. But he's in the area somewhere." Dante had a lot of energy as he talked, but his eyes stayed locked on mine. "He carries a shopping bag with him where he puts the wallets and purses he snags. You'll know him when you see him. But watch out for him, okay?"

"Okay, thanks," I said as some of the other servers walked up to talk to him.

"Dante!" T.J. walked up to us. "What's going on?"

I excused myself and delivered the coffees. When I looked over again, I saw T.J. talking, and Dante nodding and watching me. I'd apparently left an impression. But the next time I looked over, Dante was gone.

That week at Watters and Company, a curious email popped up in my inbox. The guys from New Year's Eve somehow rented or otherwise secured the Slovak Embassy on the last Saturday night in April. I went to the Embassy's website directly and found the party listed on their Upcoming Events board. I emailed Andy and Kelly and told them they had to come with me.

"So, what are you up to now, Amy? Oh, emailing I see. An Embassy party? You can't just show up to those. You have to be invited."

"Then I guess I should print this invitation out, just in case."

Chad hid in his office for the rest of the afternoon, which gave me a chance to finish the newsletter uninterrupted. But work that night was altogether different. I'd be right in the middle of something and forget what I was doing.

"What do you want, Amy?" Patrick was in the middle of making drinks and his tone was rather annoyed.

"I want, I want . . . " I rubbed my eyes and forehead, trying to visualize the drinks I needed. "I want . . . " I slapped one hand down onto the bar, "God that's the story of my life," I said.

Patrick stopped what he was doing and seemed to be staring down at his shoes. Then I realized he was laughing. He put down the shaker cup, looked up at me, "God, that's awesome," he said, still laughing.

"It's cool." I laughed at myself. "I'll come back."

"So, where's our drinks?" the girl asked me when I got back to her table.

"They're not ready yet," I said. "But here's some water, and I'll bring your drinks as soon as they're ready."

"How long will that be?" the second girl at the table asked. She sounded annoyed, though they'd only been waiting a few minutes.

"Well, Patrick's got a bunch of drinks to make at the moment, but I rang them in right away so they should be near the front of his list. I'd say not more than another minute or two," I told her as she rolled her eyes at her friend. "The blender drinks take just a little longer," I assured her, finally remembering that they'd ordered strawberry daiquiris.

"Well, could you ask him to hurry?" the first girl demanded.

I smiled. "Certainly." I'd seen Patrick in action before, and when Jessica messed up his flow one night, he let the customers have it. "Pat?" I crossed the floor back to the bar again. "The girls at table twenty-three would like you to get your ass moving on their daiquiris."

Pat looked over my shoulder toward table twenty-three and hissed, literally, like a cat. "Their drinks just went to the back of the line," he announced, and went on with what he was doing. "Order goddamned blender drinks during the dinner rush and you expect them yesterday," he mumbled. "Tell 'em to fuck off."

"I'll let them know." I smiled, and went back to the girls, who had heard the whole loud conversation. "Uh, it will just be another minute or two. I'll get them out to you as soon as he's made them."

"Um . . . thanks," eventually came out of one girl's mouth. At least she dropped the attitude. Okay, so I could have been nice and made the drinks myself. I had time on my hands and I knew how to make daiquiris. But these were two snotty, tight-assed women who weren't going to tip me worth a damn anyway, so why bother? They could wait. "God, will you listen to my attitude?" I asked Jessica back in the dish room. "What's wrong with me?"

"You're just having an off night," she told me. "What you need is to come out with us tonight. We're going over to Tumult after this. Want to come?"

"Definitely." This was the first time the servers had asked me out with them, and I didn't want to turn it down. "Who's all going?" I asked.

"Oh, a bunch of us. Patrick, Raul, T.J., you, and me. My boyfriend is going to meet up. And Dante works there. So, seven of us."

So it was. We closed our place down by two-thirty, a record for us, but we were all on a mission to be drinking before Tumult did last call at three. I'd never been in the place before, and found it to be a gaming paradise. There were billiards tables, dartboards, an arcade room, and even a shelf of board games. There were two large bars, scores of cocktail tables, and waitresses in referee outfits.

Dante was there, drinking on the shift as was customary at Tumult. He offered to buy me a drink, and I accepted.

"How are things going over at Upscale?" he asked me.

"Oh, just fine. It's crazy busy, but not altogether a bad place to work. How are things here?"

"Never been better."

"Are you always busy like this?"

"Yep. People want to drink, and we keep them occupied with games while they do it. You wouldn't believe the money this place takes in. And the alcohol that flows through here. Amazing." Dante showed me around, introducing me to the staff as we went.

"Now, aren't you in the Army?" I asked.

"Yeah, and before you say anything, yes, even guys in the military can have second jobs so long as they don't interfere with the Army's schedule.

There aren't many jobs that don't, but this one works out right nice. Cheers." He touched his beer bottle to mine.

Patrick wandered up to us. "Oh, hey, how did those ladies treat you?"

I cracked up. "The daiquiri ladies? They left almost fifteen percent."

"That sucks," he said.

"Yeah, I'm worth twenty. But at least they dropped the snotty attitude after that. I can't stand people who assume all waitresses are idiots."

"We ought to unionize," Raul said.

"I'll drink to that," Jessica said.

"The Teamsters building is right over by Capitol Hill. We can march in and demand our own Teamster-backed union."

We laughed and drew up the terms of our union. The Server Union would first demand at least minimum wage for all servers. This was Raul's idea because, as this was his first waiter gig with us, he was appalled to find out he was only being paid three dollars an hour and that it was legal. Jessica insisted servers get medical benefits for tired feet and shin splints, and that there should be a minimum standard tip imposed, one that could be increased as the customer wished. And, of course, we could write off massages, pedicures, and physical therapy. And if you kept your receipts, you could write off your after-work drink tab. We were proud of the new benefits.

Most of Dupont's customers were students and businesspeople who would come in with laptops and would eat an entire meal while working. And though we were located in the middle of the city, we didn't get as many tourists as there had been Virginia. Though only a few Metro stops away, down on the National Mall, they were everywhere.

Probably half of our customers spoke more than one language. They'd speak English plain enough to me, but would delve back into their native language for each other. There was a group of five men who seemed to be regulars and they spoke French, two sisters who spoke German, and various others who spoke Farsi and would try to teach me how to say hello. But they always laughed so much that I was sure they were teaching me bad words. There was another group we called the "Persian Mafia," eight well-dressed young men who would drink coffee and smoke cigarettes like it was going out of style, and they wouldn't tip for anything. They were in at least once a week, if not more.

The tipping hierarchy for the city went as follows: Students were at the bottom, the lowest tippers of the bunch, along with the Persian Mafia. Above them, though just barely, were straight couples on dates.

Above them were the businesspeople and anyone for whom English was a second language, and still tipping higher were the gay couples on dates. Surprisingly, the best tippers of the bunch were the occasional families who would wander in to our restaurant. They'd hear the loud music, see the other customers wandering about the place in droves, and they would expect very lousy service. They were pleasantly surprised to find that, as a wait staff, we *did* know what we were doing, and they'd leave well over twenty percent.

"Dante," the other bouncer, a big guy named Dennis, walked up.

"What's up?" Dante asked him.

"Purse snatcher's back. John's moving in, let's go."

"Duty calls." Dante smiled at me and took off with Dennis.

Patrick sidled up next to me. "So, Amy, so what's with you and Dante?"

"Nothing," I said.

"Yeah, well, he seemed to be flirting with you."

"Oh stop."

"Well, you guys," Raul said, "They're about to close anyway, we can stick around and watch the purse snatcher or we can go get some breakfast," Raul said.

"Breakfast!" Jessica said.

"Yeah, I say breakfast," T.J. agreed.

We went to The Diner in Adam's Morgan, a well-lit greasy spoon that had great omelets and seemed to always be open. The waitress looked overworked and tired of waiting on the bar crowd, so we ate quickly, didn't complain when she brought two wrong orders, tipped her really well and got out of there. I got four hours' sleep, and with plenty of coffee, was ready for work the next day.

NINETEEN

In the few months that I'd lived in Francesca and Paolo's house, Gerry and I managed to set off the house alarm a couple times. Each time, the alarm automatically alerted the police, who would eventually arrive and ask me a bunch of questions.

Then in late April, we each set it off again, much to the dismay of the police department. I'd hit the wrong disable button on my way to the bathroom one morning, and though I called in the false alarm right away, I was told a squad car was already *in route*. So I sat on the front steps, waiting from 4 to 5 a.m., feeling more angry than guilty. Had this been an actual emergency, I could have been dead.

Gerry, for his part, came home drunk one Friday night and set off the alarm. The police arrived and pounded on the front door, but Gerry had already passed out. Luckily I got home from Upscale in time to talk them out of breaking the glass door. The next day, I brought it to Gerry's attention. Much good that did me.

"I didn't hear anything last night," was all he had to say as we stood in the doorway to his apartment. So I explained the whole police showing up, banging on the door and almost breaking it down part. "Oh, well, these things happen," he said, adjusting his towel. He apparently just got out of the shower. Or maybe he just sat around in the towel waiting for someone to knock on his door. "I drank a lot last night. I mean, a *lot*. My girl's out of town so I was out on the prowl."

I took a half step back. "Well, that's great and all, but . . . "

"You know, Sara's the only person I've ever considered marrying. I guess that's what true love does to ya. But I still go out when she's out of town. Do my own thing."

"You know, I've been wondering how true love worked. Thanks for the tip."

Gerry wasn't listening. "She doesn't keep tabs on me. Why would she? She trusts me. And she's doing grad work in English of all things, so she has no idea what the law says. But technically, if I were to marry her while I'm still in law school, she's entitled to half of everything I ever make my entire career. I love her to death, but I'm not about to support her. Now, you work hard. You know what I'm talking about."

Gerry was a real piece of work. "Sure," I said. "Listen, last night the police nearly . . . "

"Last night!" he interrupted. "Last night, I gave the bartender my credit card," he said, nodding.

"That's not a good idea," I said.

"My bill was in the hundreds."

"You didn't have any food?" I asked.

"Not that I remember."

"That's a lot of alcohol."

"You're telling me it is," he leaned on the doorframe.

"Where *were* you?" I asked. "The Ritz-Carlton?"

"No. But I think I was in Georgetown, though."

"Well, listen, about the door . . . "

"Why don't we stop using the alarm altogether? It would make our lives much easier."

"Forget it," I said.

"Alright, have it your way. But don't worry about the door. If it happens again, my parents will just send the money to fix it. Listen, I gotta get ready for a date," he said. He adjusted his towel with one hand. "You're welcome to come in."

"Uh, no. I have to get ready for a party myself. See ya later," I said. Just talking to him made me want to shower. But tonight was the party at the Slovak Embassy, and I wasn't going to let him ruin my night off. Once I heard him leave the house, though, I relaxed a lot more.

I curled my hair and stepped into a new and shimmery blue dress and checked my appearance in the mirror. The hem could have been a little longer, but then, it wasn't super short, either. With heels on I definitely looked leggy.

Andy arrived right on time, and we followed Kelly's directions to her place in Virginia, the whole time Andy instructing me to turn right, left, or "gaily forward" instead of "straight." We were giggling like little kids by the time we got to Kelly's. I introduced Andy and Kelly and they immediately liked each other. "I've never seen you with your hair down," I told her. You should wear it like that more often."

"Yeah, maybe. But it's such a pain. I like my ponytail," she said, and then starting fussing in the back seat.

"What are you doing?" I asked.

"Ah, well," she said, still struggling, "My dress is caught in my shoe strap. There, okay. It's a wonder I didn't kill myself."

"That dress is fabulous," Andy said, and I had to agree. Kelly's long black dress gave her a timeless elegance. She and Andy discussed the designer, and then the three of us went on complimenting one another until we arrived at the embassy. Andy wore a simple shirt and tie with dress pants, but the pants were dark blue and had a sheen to them, which contrasted well with the white of his shirt and the sheen of his black tie. And his hair, currently blonde, had that popular bed-head look to it. But Andy always looked like a million bucks. Since I'd met him, I'd never known him to look average.

I parked the car easily enough—this wasn't Dupont Circle, after all. Once inside the embassy, we didn't have to look long for the hosts, as they were at the welcome table.

"Amy, right? I'm glad you could make it," he said.

"Thank you for the invitation," I said, and introduced Kelly and Andy to him.

"It's so awesome of you to put together a charitable party," Kelly said. "I never would have thought of this. It's such a great idea."

"We thought since a lot of 9-11 charities are getting donations this year, some of the others that usually get contributions are hurting. We've chosen a couple of environmental charities for this party."

We paid our donations and entered the lavish party. The main floor of the embassy was ornate and shiny, like a museum. The main room had a stage set up for a swing band, a grand piano off to one side for the pianist who played when the band took breaks, a bar in the back corner, and a wide dance space in between.

The adjacent room was lined with chairs along the perimeter, and held large tables in the center for all the catered foods. This room opened to a large patio and courtyard.

"Wow, this is amazing," Andy said, in awe.

"Yeah . . . " was all I could say.

And there were literally hundreds of people there. "I can't believe the size of this place!" Kelly said.

Not swing dancers ourselves, we settled in with plates of food and glasses of wine until the lights went low. Then we stood at the edge of the main room, drinks in hand, watching the dancers. Some were good, others were just beginning, a few were in the corner teaching some moves, but the whole thing was a grand spectacle. Andy slipped out for a cigarette, and came back gushing about a cute guy he'd seen out there. We all watched the patio door to see him walk in. Within a few minutes, he did.

"That's him! That's the guy," Andy whispered to us as a tall, tan guy with dark hair walked in wearing Dockers and a white t-shirt.

"Wow," I said, noticing that the guy walked without any apparent attitude. "Do you think he's gay or straight?"

"Not sure yet," Andy said. "But I'll find out."

"You two are ridiculous," Kelly rolled her eyes.

"What?" I shrugged.

Kelly raised her eyebrows back at me and mirrored my innocent look. "I'll get us more drinks while you two stand here and plot."

"Okay," Andy agreed. "Does she ever remind you of Cher?" he asked me when Kelly was out of earshot. "Just the way she looks?"

"Yeah," I said. "Especially with her hair down like that, definitely."

"I told you I met Cher?"

"No, never!"

"Oh my God," he said. "What a great story! So I'm sitting in Subway, on Capitol Hill, and a woman comes up to me. I'm pretty much the only other person in there and she asks if someone's sitting in the chair across from me. I look up and it's Cher! I told her she could have the chair, and she sat down."

"She sat down with you? At your table?"

"Yeah. Just like that. And she thanked me. So, I'm all star-struck and trying not to be, and I asked her how it's going and she says she's doing pretty well. She said she was in town doing something for Mary Bono. She does it all the time, you know," he told me, "shows up to be the celebrity so that people can raise money for all sorts of causes. It's just amazing that she's so willing to help Sonny's widow."

"Is she as beautiful as she is on TV?"

"More so." He nodded. "It's hard to believe, but she's actually more beautiful in person than she looks on TV. That striking quality she has?"

I nodded.

"Yeah, more."

"Wow!" I said. "How could you not love Cher?"

"I know."

Kelly returned with wine for each of us and we told her how she reminded us of Cher, which she thought was funny and completely untrue. And I made Andy repeat his Cher story, which he was happy to do. After he finished he said, "Hey, look, Cute Guy is by the dance floor. Uh-oh."

"'Uh-oh' what?" I asked, turning to see what Cute Guy was doing.

"Well," Andy said, looking guilty. "He was just looking at you, Kelly, but I was looking at him. I think he got the wrong idea because he looked away pretty quickly."

"What wrong idea?"

"Well, I was staring at him, trying to figure out his deal and he looked straight over at you. Then he looked and saw me staring, and I must have been frowning, I'm sure I was, and . . . I think he assumed I'm your jealous boyfriend."

"Andy, you really could be more gay right now," I teased.

"Ah," he said, adopting a pose and brandishing his hand over his head, "Allow me to be flaming!"

Kelly and I cracked up and pulled him onto the dance floor. The Cute Guy never did look our way again. Not that we noticed, anyway. And we didn't really meet any new people for that matter. Most D.C. parties are about networking, but this one seemed more about dancing, relaxing, and just plain having fun. It was a great time. And for Kelly and me, it was our last big hurrah before buckling down for the Italian final.

Sunday found us again at Starbucks, making study sheets. We mapped out each day until the final, with next Sunday set aside as a total review. It was a lot of work putting together the study sheets, but by following them, I really only needed to set aside as much as an hour each day to review them. That seemed do-able.

On Monday, Chad walked in looking like he'd joined the Yankees. I knew he'd tell me all about the uniform, so I didn't ask.

"What do you think?" he asked.

"It's interesting," I said.

"I joined the softball team at my apartment complex. Tonight's our first game."

"So you thought you'd wear the uniform to work?"

"I wanted to get in the spirit," he said. "I'm really excited. This is going to be a new form of exercise for me. I don't know if you've noticed, but I get angry if I don't work out enough."

Of course he found an excuse. "Yeah, I've noticed it."

"You have?" he seemed surprised. "When? Amy, I think you take things a little too seriously."

By Friday, he wore the uniform again, and his time declared, "I'm cursed! Amy, I'm cursed!"

"Okay, I'll bite," I said, turning away from my computer screen. "Why are you cursed?"

He pulled up a chair opposite my desk and plopped down, laptop bag and all. "I don't know what to do. There's this girl, see?"

"Oh," I said, starting to understand.

"She's on my softball team and we've had two games so far and she just ignores me."

"Maybe she's concentrating on the game," I offered.

Chad shook his head. "We go out after the games. The whole lot of us, to our little local pub, and she ignores me even there. I talk to her and she just rolls her eyes."

"What are you saying to her?"

"The usual stuff, telling her that I work here, that I have a Masters from GW, that I do cardio classes three times a week . . . Just stuff so she could get to know me."

"I think that if people want to know you, they'll ask. Did she ask you anything about yourself?"

"No. Because I can never get close to her."

"Do you think maybe you just gave her a lot of unwanted information?" He looked at me blankly, so I tried another tactic. "I mean, when someone does that to you, what do you think?"

"I think they're indirectly asking about me, so I tell them about myself."

"That clears up a lot of things for me, actually," I said. "Okay, but it's not getting the reaction you wanted."

"No, she's acting like she's not interested. But I'm sure she would be if she knew me. Yes," he seemed to be convincing himself. "She'll like me once she knows me. I just need another plan, like finding out which apartment's hers. I'm a lobbyist after all, I can switch gears, adopt a new strategy. I'm flexible," he said.

Who was I to stop him?

That night at Upscale, a tray of glasses crashed somewhere in the back of the restaurant just as I was walking in.

Back in the dish room I found the cause. Someone had put a tray of clean glasses on top of a stack of dirty plates, getting enough mess and slime on the bottom of the tray that it slipped out of Jessica's hands when she tried to move it. I found her back there trying to clean it up by herself.

"What the hell have you done to my system?" boomed Jake, the dish guy, who burst onto the scene.

"I only tried to pick up this tray, but it slipped," Jessica explained.

"Who told you to come back here and mess with the system? Goddamned servers think they own the place!"

"We're out of glasses," Jessica explained.

"You could give us a hand here," I said. "Where's the trash can?"

"How the hell am I supposed to know? The goddamned servers probably ran off with it, right after little missy here trashed my dish room."

"It slipped!" Jessica yelled back. "Who the hell put it on top of the dirty dishes in the first place?"

"Are you accusing me?"

While they went back and forth, I found one intact glass and set it on the rack with the other dirty dishes. Jake was still yelling at Jessica, when he saw me set the glass down.

"That doesn't go there!" he shrieked. "You're messing up the system!" He was towering over Jessica but looking in my direction. "I do my job!"

"If your job is standing outside smoking, then yeah, you do it."

"Stacks of dirty plates will sit here for hours while the restaurant has none," Jessica fired at him. "The other dish guy cleans the dishes and isn't a jerk to everyone, so why can't you do your job? Amy, we're done in here."

"Yes, I think we are."

Jessica and I left the dish room, but Jake followed us out, yelling the whole way how we thought we were better than everyone else and how he's been doing his job longer than we have. At some point he left Jessica alone and decided to follow me, but I turned on him and said very calmly, "If you continue screaming, I'll find a few choice places to shove the dishes." I turned around again and ran straight into Dante.

"Wow, remind me not to make you mad," he said. I just stood there, not knowing whether to look embarrassed or fierce. He laughed, "Um, listen, I would like to know if you want to go out, with me, uh, this weekend. But if you're busy telling off the cooks or the management by then, I understand."

I smiled. "I'm not always like this," I said.

I heard Jake behind me. "You don't want to date her, she's a bitch."

"Would you shut up?" I said, without turning around. "Okay," I said to Dante. "Um, when?"

"I was hoping this weekend."

"This weekend? Well, I've got a final to study for. Next Tuesday or Wednesday would be better."

"I'll be in the field. We leave Monday and we're gone all week."

"Oh, okay," I said. "Let me think . . . Sunday night?"

"Works for me," Dante said. "I'll make sure to have all my military stuff done ahead of time. Not a problem."

"Okay. Um, let me give you my phone number."

"Jake! Amy! Can I see you in the office for a minute?" our newest manager, Anderson, yelled at us.

"I've got to go get in trouble right now," I said to Dante. "Call me Sunday, around eight?"

"Will do."

I wandered over to the office to join Jessica and Jake.

"Before you say anything," he said sternly, "Jessica just told me the whole story. I don't want to know your version. I just want you to bring these things to me from now on. *I* am the manager. Got that?"

I nodded, but it was a lie. Managers were never around when we needed them, never where the action was.

"It's not up to you, Amy, how the dishes get clean. You're excused. Let me talk to Jake about bullying the employees."

With that, Jessica and I were pushed out of the office.

"Hey, girls! Nice going!" Patrick said. "It's about time something was said about the dishes. Way to go."

"Just doing our part," Jessica said.

After work, I walked to my car thinking about the Italian final and Dante. As I approached the car I noticed someone had placed one of those annoying fliers under my windshield wiper. On closer inspection, I realized it wasn't an annoying flier but a parking ticket.

"What?" I looked around, taking note of the seven different parking signs closest to me, but saw none that I'd violated. I searched the ticket for more information and saw the fine of "one hundred dollars" staring at me.

"You're fucking kidding me," I said to the ticket, and then I crumpled it. "There's no way in hell I'm paying *that*."

TWENTY

The next night at the restaurant I had to run the cash register and basically stand in one spot all night—a spot that kept getting filled with dirty water as the bar drain overflowed. Anderson insisted he'd left a message to let me know of the change, but I never got one. And he still hadn't done anything about the dish situation. Tuesday marked his seventh day at our restaurant, and I couldn't wait for him to walk out.

At the very least I remembered to bring my flash cards, so when the night started to slow down, I was able to get some studying done.

"Kel, is it me, or is most of this stuff pretty easy?" I asked, halfway through our study session on Sunday.

"No," she said, "This stuff is easy. Either we know it or maybe we just haven't reached the hard stuff yet."

"But don't you think this older material would be harder to remember?"

"Yeah. Maybe we do know more than we thought. The study sheets did the trick. Do you want to keep going or do you have dinner at Beau and Peter's?"

"No, I called a couple days ago and cancelled. They didn't mind when I told them I have a date for once."

"You have a date? Why didn't you say anything? Who is he?"

"He's a bouncer at a club near the Upscale. Everybody just loves him. He's nice . . . attractive. I don't know. I'll have to tell you how it goes."

"I want more details. Come on," she said, putting her notebook down. "I tell you about my dates."

"I don't have any more details," I said, tossing her notebook back at her. "I haven't gone on the date yet. I'll tell you all about it tomorrow. Okay? Okay."

We switched to decaf and reviewed all the conversations we'd learned. Then we reviewed all our vocabulary sheets one last time before calling it a day. At seven-thirty I drove home to change clothes and wait for Dante to call.

I remembered when a normal first date involved taking a shower, picking out the perfect outfit, and perfume and hairspray and a curling iron, new lipstick . . . But I just didn't have that kind of time. Dante called from his car and arrived at the house a few minutes later. He wore all black, and looked great.

Since it was nice outside, we decided to walk to 17th Street for some sushi. We were both nervous, which made me quiet. But Dante seemed to talk a lot when he was nervous.

"So I grew up in Philly, and I love it there, but I got into some trouble, so I decided to go into the Army because I thought I could see the world that way. But they had these recruiters come in during Basic and talked about guarding our nation's capital, which sounded pretty cool to me. So here I am, stationed in one location only, with no real prospect of traveling or being a part of any of the fighting going on unless I re-enlist. Sucks. I don't know what I was thinking."

"So, you'd rather be fighting?" I asked after we'd sat down and ordered dinner.

"Hell yeah. I mean, we do our part here, but with everything that's gone down in the last year, I'd much rather be in the thick of things actually doing something. But I'm making the best of it. Got the job at Tumult to get me away from the jarheads. Don't get me wrong, I'm not talking about my friends here. My *friends* are awesome. I don't know what I'd do without them. But the Army's got some real freaks, you know, who don't have much upstairs. It's tough being around *those* guys all day and then just sit around playing video games with them at night. I'd much rather be out making money someplace. Thanks," he said as our waitress set down two trays of sushi rolls in front of us. "So what about you?" he asked me.

I told him about studying for the Italian final. "But I get two weeks off before Italian II starts up. Oh, and I got a parking ticket Friday night. For a hundred dollars."

"Shit! That's insane. Where were you parked?"

"Dupont Circle. And I got it about three minutes after I parked. Really made me mad. I went back last night and finally found the sign I violated—It's half a city block away, facing the other direction."

"Sounds like you can fight it."

"I hope so."

"Lemme ask you this: What kind of paper was it? The ticket."

"Some funky stuff. Alien paper. I was so mad I crumpled it up, but it flattened itself out again."

"Ugh," he said. "That would be from the parking police. D.C. has two ways of giving tickets: regular police and parking police."

"Sounds like you know a lot about this."

"Oh yeah, they've taken plenty of my money. But here's the thing, see, tickets from regular cops, on regular paper, you can fight and win because the police have better things to do than show up in traffic court. But the parking police, well, they're whole job is to annoy people, one parked car at a time. You can fight it, but they're tough to win."

"Well, I'm not paying a hundred dollars."

He shrugged. "Fight it." Then he brightened, "And the thing to do is take pictures. Then you have a chance."

We were quiet for a while and then I asked, "What do you plan to do when you get out of the Army?"

"I don't know," he said, poking at the last of his sushi and finally putting his chopsticks down. "I'm actually thinking I might re-enlist. I've got a year to figure it out yet."

After dinner we walked to a basement bar where Dante knew the bartender. (I would later find out that Dante knew pretty much every bartender in Dupont Circle.) For a basement, the place was nice, filled with young people wandering about—getting ready for some kind of show it seemed—and we settled in at a table and ordered rounds of half-price apple martinis. Dante washed his down with whiskey.

"Have you been here before?" he asked me. I shook my head. "Sunday nights they do 'Drag Bingo.' It's a blast! Wanna play?"

I laughed and took the bait. "Okay. What's 'Drag Bingo?'"

It was Dante's turn to laugh. "You'll see," he said. We took our drinks and left our table, opting for one in an adjacent room with a stage. This room was filled with long tables with chairs, a large movie screen on the left wall, a makeshift stage to our front and a switchboard for sound behind us. Pretty soon, people walked through handing out bingo cards and chips. Dante took two cards; I took one. "It should be starting soon," he said to me. "I'll get us another round of drinks. I'll be right back."

A few minutes passed where everyone was shuffling cards and chips, and people wandered in and out getting drinks from the bar. I looked from table to table and took account of the people around me. The other bingo players were a mix of gay and straight youngsters—mostly students I guessed.

The table of students beside me had about eight people sitting at it—the guy and girl on the end were obviously dating each other, and they had a couple of jock-looking guys with them, and a few homosexual guys, and one lesbian. I was happy to see all these sexual preferences sitting together at one table, drinking and cheering one another on as they got ready to play bingo.

Dante returned a short while later with two more martinis and set one in front of me. "Thanks," I said. "No whiskey this time?"

"No, I couldn't carry it all, so I drank it at the bar while I waited for these."

The stage lights suddenly went on and I noticed a doorway at the back of the stage. The music got loud and a spotlight was pointed on the doorway where one after another, three men dressed to the nines emerged onto the stage.

The first was probably forty-ish, wearing an elegant, black sequin gown, lots of face powder, and a silver wig. She called herself "The Countess." The second was about ten years younger, wearing a bright pink jumpsuit with plunging neckline accented with pink sequins. Her name was Michaela, and she wore a tall, brown wig. The third "hostess" for the evening, also dark-skinned like Michaela, was wearing a green sequin gown and blonde wig and went by the name "Honey." Honey and Michaela seemed to be about the same age. They welcomed all of us, in soft, feminine-sounding voices, exchanged greetings with one another, and they introduced their sound man, Ramone, as he wheeled a cart with the bingo balls out onto the stage. They teased and taunted him, and he did an interesting little dance for them that they, and the crowd, loved. After laughing at this display, I stopped being so journalistic about the details and instead sat back to enjoy the show. The Bingo game got underway and our hostesses called out numbers and made fun of each other's wigs and ages.

"We're thinking about expanding," Michaela said at one point.

"You'll pop that dress if you expand any more," Honey said.

"I'm not talking about my personal expansion. I'm talking about drag bingo two nights a week."

"You mean I have to sit next to you two twice a week now?" The Countess asked.

"No, we're replacing you with a younger and firmer model," Michaela said.

"Oh, you're so cruel to me!" The Countess wailed.

"Oh, she's such a queen," Michaela said to Honey beside her. "Okay!" she turned back to the Countess. "Okay, we're not replacing you! How could we?"

"Yeah, if we got anyone prettier they'd make us look bad," Honey said.

And once in a while they dropped into their masculine voices, which was hysterical. Giant Barbie dolls talking like men. The crowd went wild.

"Gays! The gays! They're to blame!" Michaela said, and the crowd laughed.

They gave out gay porn videos and bizarre sex toys along with other prizes like hair dryers, perfume, and clock radios.

"Well, of course, we can't just *give* away porn," Honey said.

"Right, we should make sure it's good first," Michaela agreed. "Roll it, Ramone!"

The movie screen to our left lit up with segments of the videos. I would have blushed except that I was laughing too hard. Our hostesses gave a running commentary throughout, things like "Whoops, where did I put that?" and, "Do you mind?" and "Whoa, would you look at that, boys and girls?"

During the intermission, they each came out among the crowd to sing and dance, and everyone watching became part of the show. The whole thing was mesmerizing, but not in that perverted staring-at-a-traffic-accident kind of way. There was a lot of camaraderie, a feeling of inclusiveness.

Even as the show wrapped up, the hostesses lined up to hug everyone as we made our exit. "Dante! So good to see you again," Michaela said as she hugged Dante. "And who is this?" she asked, seeing me and smiling like a proud mother.

"Michaela, this is Amy," Dante introduced us.

"Nice to meet you," she said, shaking my hand. Up close she was flawlessly beautiful. There was no masculinity to her, which made it all the more funny when she gave me her line about being "Michael by day" in her masculine voice. "So wonderful to meet you," she said again. "Take good care of Dante. Keep him out of trouble," she winked at me.

"I'll try," I said.

Back out on the street again, Dante asked me if I'd enjoyed it.

"Yes! I never laughed so hard in my life. Thank you for bringing me."

"I wasn't sure if you'd like it. My army friends would never set foot in there, or in Dupont Circle for that matter."

"Yeah, how is it that you don't have that same mentality?" I asked.

He shrugged. "My best friend back home is a lesbian. We were sort-of the outcasts of our school, because we were both dirt poor—our school was in a really affluent area. Anyway, I was the first person she came out to, and I thought it was an honor that she trusted me. It was a big deal for her to do that." Feeling the weight of what he'd just said and needed to lighten it, he said, "We used to go to the mall and girl-watch together."

"Oh stop!" I said.

"No, really! It helped to keep me out of trouble, at least. When I was around Lindsay I never tried to break any laws." He shrugged. "Never felt the need."

"What kind of laws?"

Here he realized himself. "Oh, well, you know. The usual."

"Stealing cars, knocking over convenience stores, high speed chases?"

He laughed. "Let's just say I'm not proud of some of the stuff I did. But I didn't get into as much trouble as I could have. I had *some* self-control, even then."

"Well," I said, wanting to steer the conversation to something else, "I haven't played bingo since my grandpa took me to the VFW. I think I was seven then."

He laughed again. "Tonight was probably a little different."

"No, not at all," I said with a straight face that soon vanished. "Okay, maybe it was a *little* different. How do you know Michaela?"

"She stops in over at Tumult at least once a week. Always says hey to me, tips well, never causes any problems . . . "

We stopped in front of my house. "Well, I've got to get back to the base pretty soon," he said nervously. "We're doing World Bank drills first thing in the morning and then I have to get my field paperwork in order."

"World Bank?" I asked. "No, not again! I didn't think they did meetings this late in the spring."

"They've got something going on next weekend. Nothing major, but they want us to be ready just in case."

"Not another weekend of sirens every thirty seconds! The protestors don't even bother me anymore; it's those damn sirens. I can't take the noise."

"This one should be smaller, though, so hopefully not so much fanfare. Not so many ass-clowns running around like last time. We're hoping it goes as unnoticed as possible." With that, he leaned over and kissed me goodnight. Not a knock-your-socks-off kiss, but pretty damn close.

The next day I got through work, keeping myself on task as best I could. With the Italian final looming over me, I barely had time to revel in the details of my date with Dante. Everything was a blur as I stepped off the Metro and walked toward the Ag Building.

"So, what did you think?" Kelly asked me as we walked out together.

"What did *you* think?" I asked her. "'Cause I thought it was, well, *easy*."

"Yeah! I can't believe he didn't test us on those new verbs!"

"And we studied our asses off!"

"And that essay," Kelly rolled her eyes.

"'Describe a typical day in your life.' Most of my essay is about work; that made it pretty easy."

"Don't tell me you just used *lavoro* through the whole thing."

"No," I defended. "Okay, there was a lot of 'I work,' but I threw in some other verbs for good measure. What did you do?"

"I talked about taking the Metro, work, and about choosing a place to eat dinner."

"Yes!" I agreed. "I can't remember the last time I ate at home."

"Me neither. So where are we going tonight? How about sushi?" she asked.

"I just had that last night. But I could eat it again."

"Oh yeah, how was your date?" she prodded.

"It was fine."

She raised her eyebrows.

"I don't know. It was a nice time. But I'm not sure that this is it, ya know? I mean, we just kinda squeezed the date in, right in the middle of all these other things. But really, it was fine. He was a gentleman. He took me to drag bingo."

"What? Okay, we're definitely talking about this at dinner. And I'll fill you in on the happenings in my weird love life: Dave called me."

"What?" I asked. "The asshole—I mean, your ex?"

She smiled, much to my relief. "Yes, my asshole ex-boyfriend. Says he made a mistake stomping on my heart."

"What did you say to him?"

"I agreed. He did make a mistake," she said, taking a deep breath and letting it out slowly. She smiled, a mixture of relief and pain. "I *did* get to tell him that I'm taking Italian lessons. He sounded surprised. Ha! That's right, I'm going without him." She sighed again, "But I wish I had a great boyfriend to tell him all about. I almost made one up. How ridiculous is that?"

"That's not ridiculous."

Kelly rolled her eyes at me. "Well, I decided not to be that girl."

"You are gonna meet an amazing guy in Italy. And he'll have the accent and everything," I told her and she laughed despite herself. "Come on. Let's go to Georgetown. We can get some pizza."

"And do some barhopping," Kelly said. "I think we've earned it."

TWENTY-ONE

T he office door opened one morning and it was Mr. Watters, back from his travels. "'Morning, Amy."

"You're back! Good to see you," I said.

"Thank you," he bowed slightly. "I'm in town for a little while, yes. I've been getting all of your progress reports on email, as well as the articles. You've been getting my edits?"

I nodded. When Mr. Watters liked to send email messages like, "Change the tone," "Punch it up," or "Set the pace," and he gave me creative freedom to interpret these "edits." Only on occasion did he rewrite an article and show me just why his name was on our front door. With a simple turn of phrase, some rewording, and the addition of his own ideas and experience, Mr. Watters could produce astute and solid articles that were well out of my league. He made genius look easy. "I got all the edits," I told him.

"Good," he said.

Chad came in, saw that our boss was in, and managed to behave himself all day. He offered to get coffee in the morning, quietly worked in his office all day long, and didn't call his mother once that I noticed.

"Oh, that reminds me," Chad said as we stepped into the elevator at the end of the day. "I've been meaning to tell you that I'm sorry. I'm sorry for sabotaging your work, for being a control freak, and all that stuff. I'm not trying to act like that. Anyway, I'm sorry."

"Oh," I said.

"I've got a secret," he said. "I've been taking these over-the-counter pills to mellow me out. I'm not addicted or anything, but as long as I take them, I feel much happier. See?" he showed me the bottle he took from his pocket.

"St. John's Wart?"

"Yeah, they're herbal, so you can't get addicted. My therapist told me about them. It's a secret."

Moments later we were in the parking garage and I was glad to see that Chad hadn't parked close to me. He went his way and I went mine.

"Bye, Amy!" he called.

"Bye, Chad."

Of course there'd been a reason that he apologized to me. I didn't trust the pills, but they did seem to be turning him into a human.

I drove to the Upscale and found myself scheduled five straight nights. Somebody must have told them that Italian II didn't start up until June. It certainly hadn't been me. I sighed. It was a lot of work, but I could handle it. I had to.

"Amy, we've got some new trainees for you."

I turned and saw our newest managers—a duo that replaced Anderson when he failed to show up for work—fast approaching. Clipboards in hand, these two thought and acted as one person.

"Whoa, who let them out of the office?" Patrick asked, without looking up from the taps. I tried not to smile.

"Amy, we've got some new trainees for you," they repeated.

"For me? Shouldn't T.J. train the new people?" I asked.

"Yeah, but he's not here today and we figure you know what you're doing," the duo told me. I referred to them as Fric and Frac, because no one told me their names and I figured they'd be gone soon, anyway.

"They tell us you've worked here for a few months in a row," Frac said, adjusting his glasses. "So you're certainly qualified in our book."

"You've got the seniority," Fric winked at me, or maybe he was Frac. "Today you've got Miraz, and tomorrow you'll train Serja."

I didn't mind training anyone, but these two had their facts wrong. I didn't have seniority. "What about Katie or Jess?"

"Nice try, we know Katie just started here."

She did, huh?

"And Jessica isn't allowed a trainee since," he made quotes with his fingers, "'the incident.'"

"Oh, right, the incident."

Jessica laughed when I found her in the dish room. "I told them I referred to my last trainee as my 'slave' in front of one of the corporate big wigs and that they refused to let me train anyone after that."

"You made that up," I said.

"Sure. Trainees slow me down. I didn't want to do it."

"What about Katie?"

"She told them she's new."

"Yeah, I heard that. You guys are screwing with their heads."

"Yeah, but it got us out of training," she shrugged.

"You guys suck," I said, and Jessica laughed.

"When does your slave get here?" she asked.

I shrugged. "Beats me. Soon I guess."

"What's his name?"

"Miraz?"

"Funky."

"And tomorrow I get Serge, or something."

"Oh la la," she said.

As it turned out, Miraz was pretty cool. He was polite, in his early twenties, and kept pace with me.

"I trained in Virginia for two weeks before this," he said, revealing a British accent.

"Down by the waterfront?" I asked. "I used to work there! Who trained you?"

"A young man named Jason," Miraz said.

"I love Jason! How's he doing?"

"I like Jason as well. He's doing fine."

"How are the girls? Sandy, Jenny, Gretchen . . . "

"Yes! Everyone is doing well. I really liked working there."

"So did I. But this place is a lot of fun. You're gonna love it."

Training wasn't so bad. I showed him around the restaurant, as T.J. had done for me, and then I talked a lot, explaining everything as I did it. After a couple hours, I let Miraz take the tables and I followed him. I helped him here and there, but really he'd done a good job on his own.

"You really seem to know what you're doing," I told him at the end of the night as we snacked on some of the kitchen's leftover French fries. "You remembered everything, you're good with the computer. I'm really impressed."

"Thank you," he said.

"You're welcome," I said between bites. "So, how do you feel? You seemed like you were comfortable out there. Do you have any questions?"

"I felt comfortable, except when we got busy. I'd like more practice for that." He was putting a lot of energy into using his fork and knife.

"Just use your fingers," I told him and he gave me an astonished look. "Or not," I offered. Miraz was a character. Definitely the most refined waiter I'd ever met. "When do you work again?"

"In two days."

"Okay, T.J. will be here then and he'll help you out with the pace of things. He trained me when I first got here. You'll like him. Listen," I said, "I was meaning to ask you. Your name?"

"It's my father's. I was named after him. It's an Indian name."

"And you're very well-spoken. Where did you go to school?"

"Bangladesh. My family is there, as well as my fiancée."

"You're getting married?"

"Yes, this December. She arrives here in November and we'll get married a month later."

"Wow, congratulations."

"Thank you."

I picked up our plates and his silverware. "I'll take this to the dish room and we're pretty much done. Do I have anything in my teeth?"

Miraz's eyes got big. "Pardon me?" he asked. "You want me to look in your teeth?"

Just then Patrick walked in, "Where's the fries?"

"There's more over there," I said. "Pat, do I have anything in my teeth?"

He gave me a glance. "Nope, you're good, Sweetie."

"Thanks." I looked back at my trainee. "Really, Miraz," I teased.

The next night I met Serja—not Serge, as I once thought. Serja was not French, but of Indian descent like Miraz. He was dark-complected like Miraz, and about the same age, but that's where the similarities ended.

Miraz was rather stocky, with a sincere wit and quiet way about him. I imagined his family back in Bangladesh probably had servants, and probably treated them well. Serja also seemed to come from money, but he seemed more spendthrift and reckless. Serja was openly gay, and clung to me like we were best girlfriends. Serja was a college student from Michigan who took some time off to work an internship on the Hill, and was hoping the Upscale would allow him to meet more people.

"I was on this first date the other day," he said, grabbing my hand to get my attention.

"Really? Me too," I said.

"With an older man . . . " he said.

"Oh, okay, tell me."

"Well, there'd been an attraction for weeks but our schedules didn't allow us to get together. So finally we met for dinner on Sunday, and we drank a bottle of wine."

"What did you get?"

"Chardonnay. Australian, delicious. My date was an artist, and he's somewhat older . . . "

"You said that twice now. How *old* is older?"

"Just older. Anyway . . . We were walking back, talking the whole time, really getting along, and we get to the crossroads where he has to go one way and I have to go another. You know where Connecticut hits, oh, what's that street? Anyway, it doesn't matter. Well, we got there wherever it is, and decided instead to go to my date's house."

"Just like that?" I asked.

"Well, yeah. I mean, he wanted to go to my place, but I told him that was out of the question. I have a roommate and all, you know. He said his place was messy, but I stood my ground. So we went to his place, and it turns out it's the most gorgeous place I've ever seen. Not only did he decorate it himself, but designed it all himself. From the outside, it's nearly half a city block, all row houses, but they're connected on the inside."

"You're kidding!"

"No, how amazing is that?"

"Wow," I said. "So, how old is he?" For all the information Serja was giving, I didn't understand why he was dancing around this issue.

"Uh," he blushed. "He's . . . Okay, he's in his thirties."

"That's not a big deal."

"It's a lot older than me.

"Why, how old are you?"

Serja skirted the question. "Well, I woke up in the morning, and he was drinking coffee and reading the paper. And he had on these cute little reading glasses, oh!" He smiled, rolled his eyes and put his hand over his heart. All the while his other hand was still holding mine. "So tell me about your date."

"Serja! How *old* are you?" I challenged, smiling.

He sighed. "I'm twenty," he said quietly. "So you see what I mean about the age difference. I mean, he's nearly twice my age. But anyway, what about you?" he asked me. "Tell me about your first date."

"It was fun," I said.

"Did you . . . ?" he raised an eyebrow.

"No."

"Honey, why not? You can do that, you know," he said and I laughed at him. Serja was so easy going about sex. Maybe that's because it happened so easily to him. "Are you going to go out again?"

"I think so," I said.

"Oh, well if you think it could go somewhere, then wait, definitely. If I think it could go somewhere I immediately instill the 'One Month' rule. But this, this wasn't going to go anywhere; it just felt wrong. I mean, he even made me some coffee the next morning, and passed over the Entertainment section."

"That's very nice!" I said. "Very masculine and grown up . . . You could wake up to that every morning and have a very good life."

"I know! So I had to get out of there. It just wasn't right."

"That's understandable," I said. "Think you'll go out again?"

"I don't know. Probably not."

TWENTY-TWO

M id-week, Chad called in sick to the office. An hour into the workday, the office door flew open in a hurry and I thought Chad changed his mind, but it was Beau.

"Amy, have you heard?" He looked around, startled. "Is Chad here?"

"No, he's out sick."

"We have to turn on his TV."

"What?"

"They found her."

My stomach fell. "Oh no," I said. I didn't need to be told who Beau was talking about. We rushed to Chad's office and turned on the TV.

" . . . jogging . . . Rock Creek Park . . . body . . . missing intern . . . Chandra Levy . . . "

"Oh my God," Beau and I said together, and he grabbed my arm for support.

"They don't know anything conclusive yet," Beau said. "It might not be her. Not that that makes finding a body any better." But we exchanged a look.

Everything had changed in an instant. I hadn't even known her, but I felt as if all the wounds from the previous fall were opened again.

At the restaurant that night, Andy and Kelly stopped in for coffee and to say hi to me. I sat with them at their little table.

"I stopped by the bookstore today," Kelly said. "It turns out we're using our same books for Italian II."

"Good," I said. "It was expensive. I'd hate to buy another one."

"How much was the first book?" Andy said.

"Like sixty dollars," I said.

"Yeah, that sounds right," Kelly said.

We were all quiet for a moment and Andy said quietly, "You heard the police reports today?" He said it as a statement.

Kelly and I nodded. "I don't want to talk about it," Kelly said.

"Me neither," I said.

As the night wore on, someone turned up the volume on the bar TV. Like all bad news, I remember exactly where I was when I heard it. Standing in the middle of the serving floor, tray in hand, I learned the body in Rock Creek Park did belong to Chandra Levy. The rest of the evening was pretty solemn, and even our upbeat restaurant seemed dingy. No one I knew was callous enough to discuss it beyond, "You've heard, right?"

I fell into bed that night sad and tired, and relieved that the day was over.

June arrived, and with it, hot, swampy weather, Italian classes, and I finally heard back from Dante.

"It started with a trip in the field, then I worked the World Bank weekend, and then they scheduled us for a few weeks of training up in Pennsylvania," he told me over the phone. "I'm sorry I haven't called."

"A likely story," I mused.

"No, really, I'm sorry. The Army can do this to you . . . "

"It's alright, I was just kidding. I stopped in to Tumult a week ago and Frank told me you were away doing the Army thing."

"Thank God for Frank. Really, you're not mad?"

"It's your job," I said.

"Can I see you?"

"I'm off on Tuesday."

"I'm working at Tumult," he said. "But I can switch with Dennis and get the early shift."

"Okay, I'll meet you there."

Before going to Tumult on Tuesday night, I stopped in at the Upscale. Jessica ran up to me.

"Amy! You heard about the party?"

"I'm here to get my paycheck," I said, spotting most of my coworkers drinking at the bar. "What party?"

"It's Katie's birthday in just over an hour. She turns twenty-one at midnight and we're all taking her out after the shift. You're in, right?"

A real reason to go out drinking and carousing? "Of course I'm in," I said. "Can Dante come?"

"Absolutely! The more the merrier," she said, so I walked over to Tumult to see if Dante liked the idea.

As I crossed the alley, it occurred to me that maybe Dante wouldn't want to go out with everyone. I really should have thought before I changed our plans. After spending time with Serja, I decided there was nothing wrong with relaxing and seeing where things might go with Dante. I didn't need to feel he was "the one," and I didn't need to stress or worry about any of it. Whatever happened, happened.

"Hey, welcome back," I said as I climbed the stairs to where he was sitting.

"Hey, good to see you," he said. "I should be getting out of here any time now. Why the look?" he asked.

"Uh, well, I kinda told the Upscale crowd that we'd hang out with them tonight. But if you don't want to, then I'll get us out of it. It's Katie's twenty-first at midnight, and I didn't want to pass it up."

"It's cool." He smiled. "For a second there, I thought you were canceling on me. But you know me, I love a good party. I'll come by when I'm done, unless you want to drink here with Frank. Well . . . " he reconsidered. "Maybe you should get a head start over at Upscale. We've been dead here for almost two hours now, so the bartenders are all hitting the sauce pretty hard."

"You're not drinking?" I asked.

He smiled and reached toward the shelf behind him, picking up two tall glasses of beer. "I'm double-fisting, actually. I gotta keep pace with the boys inside. Go back over there, and I'll meet you when I'm done."

I agreed and got back to the Upscale just as they were beginning clean up duties, and everyone was excited. T.J. and Miraz were already sitting at the bar drinking, so I joined them. Mike made me something strong that had tequila in it. He claimed it was a margarita but it wasn't. Mike was our backup bartender for Patrick, and he was used to doing everything by taste. But since the court system recently forced him into AA, his drinks were fairly lousy. Strong, but lousy. I sat down on the end of the bar next to Miraz, and Serja popped up behind me from somebody's table that he'd joined. He, T.J., and Miraz all passed their drinks over to me so I could taste them.

As I handed his "tequila surprise" back, Serja whispered to me, "Listen, I really like T.J."

Immediately coming to mind was the story I'd heard about Raul, T.J., and Serja going to a bathhouse together. I don't know much of the details, only something about Serja getting separated from the others for a while, and when Raul and T.J. surfaced, they were dating. Hearing the pouty sadness in Serja's voice, I said, "Come on, *everyone* likes T.J. If I were male, *I'd* have a crush on T.J."

Miraz, overhearing this and wanting to help Serja feel better, said, "Are you kidding? I *am* male and I have a crush on T.J." Upscale was definitely affecting Miraz.

Miraz, as it turned out, was getting his share of attention as well. He had a slight wave to his dark hair, smart looking little glasses, a nice smile, and of course, the accent. Something about that combination made him irresistible to women. The "German girls" in his building always asked him over for dinner, "Because they like to cook," he'd told me, innocently enough. But, working late hours at the Upscale, he wasn't able to accept their invitations. That wasn't a problem, however, since the German girls started making food for him and leaving it on his windowsill. Every night he arrived home in the wee hours to find homemade food ready for him. He'd leave his empty dishes on the windowsill and the next day the girls would wash them and fill them again.

"You don't even wash your own dishes!" I said.

"They like doing it," he defended.

It seemed none of his admirers knew he was engaged, and he'd come to have quite a cult following. Women were always asking to sit in his section, and when he wasn't there, they'd write him notes and leave them with the rest of us to deliver when we saw him.

We ordered another round from Mike as Dante showed up. By then, the Upscale closed down, and we were off, the lot of us. We went to a gay bar called DIK, which stood for Dupont Italian Kitchen, where it happened to be drag karaoke night. A man in a pink dress with a tall blonde wig sang sultry karaoke tunes on the small dance floor. He didn't have a piano to drape himself over, which really would have perfected the look.

There were two seating sections on either side of the dance floor. One side was a little more formal, obviously for dining customers during the day. The other seating area had cocktail tables, and was closer to the bar. This was where we congregated.

With closing time only an hour away, I could tell from the dismay on the bartender's face as we piled in that he wasn't happy to see us. That is, until he spotted Dante.

"Juan, how's it going, friend?" Dante shook hands with the tall, dark, and handsome bartender who must have missed his calling as an underwear model.

"Dante, good to see you!" Juan beamed. "I've been experimenting with a new drink this week, and I want you all to try it."

"Sure thing," Dante said. "Juan, I want to introduce you to someone. This is Amy."

Juan took my hand and looked me over. "Nice to meet you. So, you're Dante's girl, huh?" he said with more than a hint of hostility.

"Uh . . . " I stammered. Dante and I really hadn't talked about anything yet.

"Yes, she's my girl," Dante said, without missing a beat. "And Katie over there," he pointed, "It's her birthday tonight. She's twenty-one. We're here to celebrate, so I need you to make her something good."

"What do you have in mind?" Juan asked.

They carried on, talking drinks, and Juan insisted he didn't know how to make whatever Dante ordered for Katie. "I can't hear you," Juan said, so Dante leaned over the bar to shout the ingredients again, but Juan waived him quiet. Juan then opened the hatch door and invited Dante behind the bar to make the drinks himself. Dante jumped at the chance to mix the alcohol, and Juan hovered on his every word. He conveniently closed the hatch door to separate me from Dante, so I went back to our friends.

"Jessica, your underwear is showing!" came from someone beside me.

"I know," she said, not bothering to look down. "Until I find a belt I like, this is how I'm gonna look." She didn't mind her red underwear, so neither did we. "I'm starting a trend," she said, flicking her cigarette.

Once we all had something to drink we toasted to Katie. Even the men in drag stopped the karaoke machine long enough to sing Happy Birthday to Katie. The party was well under way.

By now the word was out that Dante and I were an item, and if anyone had any doubts, they were dispelled when Dante planted a kiss on me mid-dance floor. I wasn't sure how anyone would take the news. They'd all known Dante a lot longer than I had. But they toasted to us, and everyone seemed genuinely glad. Everyone except Juan, that is.

"He seems to have a crush on you," I told Dante.

"Yeah, I keep hearing about it," he said. "But he knows I'm straight and he's always nice to my friends."

"He was a little less than happy to see me," I said.

"He'll get over it," he said. "And we're getting free drinks, which reminds me, I'm due for another."

"Are you sure you want another?" I asked. "How many have you had?"

"I'm not sure. But just one more. I'll be back."

As Dante went back to the bar, Serja walked up to me. "Amy, you've got to come cheer Patrick up. One of his friends OD'd earlier today and is in the hospital. All he's talking about is doom and gloom. Come on, help me," he said, and grabbed my arm.

"Ay-Mee!" Patrick slurred as I sat down with him. "Dante adores you," he said.

"Uh, okay," I said. "How are you doing, Pat?"

He waived his hand, dismissing the question. "Everything's better . . . now that you're here." He spoke slowly, but fairly clearly. "My friend is in the hospital . . . It's a scare, but sit with me and I'll cheer up . . . It's good to see you and Dante together."

"Thanks," I said. "It's new, so I'm still getting used to it."

"Well, don't worry . . . He adores you," Patrick repeated. "I've known Dante a long time . . . and I've never seen him this happy. But you're beautiful . . . how could he not be happy?"

"How much have you had?" I asked.

"It's not the alcohol talking, Amy, really. You are . . . beautiful. If I were straight like Dante, I'd be in love with you, too."

"Now Dante's in love with me, is he?" I asked, completely amused.

Patrick nodded. "He is. And so am I. Really, you're beautiful," he said, reaching across the table for my hand. "And I am in love with you right now, I just can't do anything about it because it's not a straight kind of love."

It was the strangest, and most honest compliment I'd ever been given.

My friends drank heavily, and since Juan was drinking with us now, he closed the bar nearly an hour late. Juan didn't want to charge Dante, so our tab was much lower than it should have been. I did notice, however, that all of my drinks were on the tab, which Dante paid, so I don't know what Juan was trying to prove.

By the end of the night, a very drunk Dante had gone home in a cab, Jessica took Dante's car back to her place, I fell asleep in the back of Katie's car, Miraz had a bad tarot card reading by one of the drag queens and left halfway through the evening but not before doing an impressive tango with a gay man twice his age, and Serja got a nasty lecture from Raul on the importance of not whining all the time so he left and wound up smashing the side mirror off his car while backing it into his parking space.

All in all, it wasn't a bad evening. We have pictures. And Katie is smiling in all of them.

The next night, Dante showed up to get his car at the same time that I was just arriving for my shift. "Hey, honey. Have you seen Jess?"

"No, I just got here," I said, hurrying with my apron. "I stayed late at the office to finish what I was working on, and then I had to take the Metro up here 'cause there's no way I'd find parking now . . . " I took a deep breath. "Okay, how do I look? 'Cause I feel frazzled. I look like hell, don't I?"

He smiled. "You look great."

"Alright, I gotta get to work," I kissed him on the cheek and sprinted to my section.

Raul and I were on the main floor together, which was filling up fast.

"Amy!" Raul ran up to me. "I'm so glad to see you! I'm starting to freak out. It's ten after seven and you're never late. I thought you weren't coming. Mike's filling in for Pat, have you heard? No one's heard from him."

"I'm sorry! I took the Metro. I'm sorry I'm late!" I said as he talked.

"You're here, that's all I care about," Raul said. "I can't work this room alone. Anyone who has a menu, I haven't gotten to yet. Oh my God," he stared toward the corner. "Table Six has been waiting all this time for water and I never brought over their menus . . . They'll hate me."

"I'll take them. I'll take them. It's okay."

"They're pissed off."

"Not at me." I winked. "I just got here."

"I could slap you right now," he said, and managed a smile. "If you can take all the new people, then I can handle what I've started."

"I can do it," I said with determination, hoping to calm Raul down, but I had no idea what I'd agreed to. I counted eight tables waiting for service before I gave up counting. I could do this, somehow. I had to.

"Pat has my car, somehow from Jessica," Dante said as I typed in the orders for three tables. "This place is turning into a zoo, so I'll be out drinking in the Circle somewhere for a while. I'll be back later. If Pat shows, tell him to sit tight."

All I could manage was "uh-huh, uh-huh, okay," as he talked.

Miraz was given three trainees to work the deck. Raul and I worked the entire first floor alone and were busier than hell. The upstairs servers, two of them plus Miraz's entourage, couldn't seem to restock plates, pick up anything, or roll silverware. Raul and I did those things as we waited full sections.

"If I have to clean one more dish, I'm walking out!" I threatened.

"Not before me you're not," Raul said.

Two hours and countless tables later, Patrick showed up and sat at the bar. Nobody cared that he blew off his shift and then showed up to drink. We all went up to greet him, and to laugh with him at how he bucked the system. Mike didn't even mind, and he was the one pouring Patrick's drinks. The manager didn't so much care as he didn't seem to notice. It started raining outside, which slowed down our business a bit. All the upstairs servers were sent home, including Miraz and his trainees. Half an hour after that, Raul informed me that one of Miraz's customers was sitting out on the deck waiting for him.

"But the manager sent him home a while ago," I said.

"I know," Raul said with a smile. "But she thinks he's still here. I asked her to come in, but she says she's waiting for Miraz and doesn't want to leave his section."

"But it's raining outside," I said. "The girl is sitting in the rain, waiting for Miraz—who's engaged—and he went *home*?"

Raul nodded, smiling. Raul and I started laughing. "I can't believe how they love him," I said. "She's sitting in the rain. Unreal."

"Well, somebody has to go out there and tell her he's gone. I tried, but she won't listen. She thinks he's coming back. You do it, Amy. She's not listening to me."

"Me? This sucks," I said. "Alright, I'm going. But if she doesn't listen to me, either, then she can sit out there."

"Agreed," Raul said.

By the time Patrick started talking really loud, Dante came back in. Soon afterward we closed up for the night, and Dante drove me back to Watters and Co. to get my car.

Outside the building, we sat in his car and talked about our pasts. I told him about my run-ins with players that I thought were nice guys. He admitted to being a player himself, though that was behind him now. And just so I wouldn't hear it from anyone else, he told me which Upscale waitresses he'd dated in the past year. It was quite a list.

When I drove back to my house that night I was following a car whose license plate read *MadLove*. Exactly.

TWENTY-THREE

"Blitz-Italian," as Kelly and I soon called Italian II, started up the following week. We were learning a chapter a week, completing hours' worth of homework, and our lazy Sundays discussing life and love and maybe some Italian were replaced with multiple study sheets, verb conjugations, and intensive conversations. The conversations in our last class had been easy. It was all a bunch of "Hi, how are you?" stuff with some vocab words thrown in. But the conversations outlined in Blitz Italian were complex, and Kelly and I had to translate them before we could practice them. The pace was rigorous, especially with work and more work thrown in to the mix, but I knew that if I slowed down any I'd fall behind and never catch up.

Moving at a much slower pace was my relationship with Dante. True, he spent most of his off-time with me, but the relationship felt like a good friendship, comfortable and easy, and best of all, unstressed.

"Here, give me one," Dante sat opposite me in Francesca's living room as I rubbed my sore feet after a double shift. I stretched out and gave him a foot.

"Do you think I walk improperly and cause the circulation not to flow so well?" I asked as Dante's foot rub started to warm my toes.

"No," he said. "I think the body wasn't built for the abuse it's taking. It wasn't designed to do a ten-hour shift without sitting down."

"Are you talking about waiting or the Army?" I asked. He smiled, and glanced around the room, the golden lamplight brightening his dark features.

"This house is awesome," he said after a few minutes.

"Yeah, I can't believe I get to stay here."

"At some point in my life, I'm going to have a place like this."

"Really?" I thought about it. "Yeah, I could see that. I don't know. It's gorgeous and I love staying here, don't get me wrong. But, sometimes I walk around at night, touching the antiques, looking at all their pictures, and I just think, this isn't me. Or actually, I think *these memories aren't mine*. I can make up in my head where they got things, like that wooden elephant, over there by the fireplace. I love him. But look at all this stuff! It's a lifetime of memories and stories. The few things I have right now are in storage in Virginia, and I kinda like that. Maybe one day I'll have a house and I'll fill it with my own memories. Maybe one day. But right now . . . It's a comfort not having all that."

"I guess I can see that," he said. He set my foot down and tapped the other one, so I gave it to him. "Your buddy Raul told me you have a degree in writing."

I nodded.

"Well?"

"Well, what?"

"Well, what are you writing?"

"Nothing. Stuff at work. Nothing of my own."

"Well, if these aren't your memories and your antiques, write your own."

I smiled. "They say you should write what you know."

"Do that then."

"I know about working too much and about being surrounded by dysfunction and making it work, and about . . . about how to serve iced tea with a spoon . . . and purse-snatchers and, and 'ass clowns' as you call them. People don't want to read this shit."

"I'd read this shit. Are you kidding? You're talking about my whole life," he laughed, and I laughed with him.

"I don't know," I said. "I don't know . . . You used to work at Upscale, right?"

"You know it."

"When was that?"

"Well, let's see . . . I started there last spring and worked through the summer. And then September 11 hit and I was stationed as part of the Pentagon cleanup for a while."

"You were?" I interrupted, suddenly feeling a dread within me.

"Yeah," he said. "And with the aftermath, we were so busy that I stopped working at Upscale and only did the Army thing for a while. Then this spring I got the job at Tumult."

"Oh," I said seriously. "I didn't know you were at the Pentagon."

"We were the first of the military on the scene. We were eventually put in charge of setting up supports so that the Red Cross could go in and do their jobs. But I wasn't there the day they handed out security badges, so I wasn't allowed to go back after that."

"They wouldn't let you back?"

"No, see, when we first got there, nobody was in charge. Different groups were all just doing whatever needed done. Then after about a week the government came in and took charge, handing out security badges to the different teams and assigning tasks to everyone. That day the army had me teaching the new recruits back at the base, so I didn't get to the Pentagon until after noon. By then they wouldn't let me on the site."

"Oh, I'm sorry," I said, and then I thought about it. "Or maybe not."

"Yeah," he said. "I wish I could have helped out more, done more, anything. But, my friends who were there through the whole process are kinda messed up now."

"Messed up?" I repeated.

"Yeah, nightmares, they see shit, they get quiet sometimes, just space out, and they drink a hell of a lot. More than I do, which tells you something."

That it did. He pulled me close to him, and for a long time, we just didn't say anything.

~

Watters and Co. was closed on Friday for the long 4th of July weekend, so I went to traffic court, which was remarkably open, to fight the parking ticket I got in Dupont Circle. It was this, or take a day off to do it, so I sat there for hours, reading a book and watching people come and go until it was finally my turn.

For a moment, it looked pretty grim, because the court never received my denial of the ticket. Assuming I was trying to ignore it, they'd doubled the fine. But I pled my case, showed the judge a photocopy of my denied ticket and the pictures I'd taken of the scene. In the end he waived the penalty fee, and cancelled out the fine itself. Ruling for the defendant, $200 saved.

"But you have to understand, Miss," the judge said, "That you were issued this ticket because you parked there during rush hour. Normally it's a fifty-dollar fine, but at rush hour it's doubled. We do that because need to get the volumes of people, who work in the city, out of here. We can't have parked cars clogging the streets just because owners won't read the signs."

"Oh," I said, ignoring his tone. I'd waited tables and worked with Chad long enough to ignore condescension.

"This, young lady," he held up the photo I'd taken, "Is the entire reason you're winning your case today. This photo is your saving grace."

I left, only to find it was a beautiful day outside. It was sunny and warm, and there wasn't a cloud in the sky. How long had I been in there? It was summer all around me, and I was missing it.

For that matter, when did we begin opting to sit in offices all day long, only to lose out on feeling the sunlight on our faces? When did we, as a society, decide we'd rather be indoors for ninety-nine percent of our lives and only spend one or two weeks each year doing what we loved best?

How did I trade my freedom for this working existence? It was summer, and I was pale as a ghost, as usual. The only way I could get a tan was to sit in a tanning bed, because my daylight hours were completely taken up at the moment. But tanning sessions cost money, so if I picked up an extra restaurant shift, I'd have that money to put toward tanning sessions. But that still didn't clear up any free time to get to a tanning bed. Or, I could quit the restaurant, be broke, but have time in the late afternoon to sit on Francesca's back deck and sun myself. This is what my life had become. I needed to stop procrastinating and give Mr. Watters and the Upscale my notice so I could go out and live. At least until the money ran out.

Kelly's boss was out of town and she was house-sitting at his apartment, which happened to have a perfect view of the Fourth of July fireworks from the living room. It was also air conditioned, and the city temperatures hadn't been below ninety-five degrees in weeks. We threw a small, last-minute get-together at her boss' place, and watched the fireworks with Andy, Dante, Jessica, and Katie.

Dante invited me to come to something called a Twilight Tattoo the following week.

"Okay," I agreed. "What is it?"

"It's an Army performance in front of the White House, down on the Ellipse. It starts at dusk and it's free. There's a lot of marching, flags, drums . . . You'd like it."

"I'll be there."

"Great, and maybe we can get dinner after."

"Sounds good. I'll check my schedule, but we have some people at Upscale looking for extra shifts, so I should be able to get free."

I was looking forward to seeing him performing Army duties, but when I arrived on Wednesday, I found him without his uniform, just sitting in the stands.

It was a nice show, the Army band played while flags from every state were presented, rifles were tossed, which was Dante's favorite part, and a drum line played impressively fast and did drumstick tricks in unison, which was my favorite part.

"Why aren't you in uniform?" I asked him as we watched the show together.

"I am, technically," he said. "See?" he showed me the earpiece he was wearing. "I'm wired to the other plainclothes officers. We're posted two to every set of bleachers, about one to every fifty people."

"Just to keep people in line?"

"To look for terrorists and stop them before they blow anything up," he said soberly.

"Here?"

"Why not here? We're in front of the White House, there are families and children present, and a chunk of the Army is busy doing a performance."

I looked around warily, feeling shocked and a bit stupid for not realizing we could be in danger. "But . . . "

"It's okay," he said. "Relax and enjoy the show. It's the same as anything else since September 11th. Nothing happens in this town without the army being present—even if we're not seen. It's been this way for almost a year now."

"But I didn't know about it."

He smiled. "You're not supposed to. We're looking out for everyone. You see that obnoxious guy in the flowered shirt who looks like a tourist over there? The one letting his fat kids run all over the place?"

"Yeah," I said.

"We're even guarding that guy, and those bratty kids."

I laughed, feeling a large amount of respect for Dante's job.

"We're on a different level, you and me, but we're very similar," he said, and then explained, "The place can be falling apart behind the scenes, but we keep up appearances for the public."

"Even as we expect the roof to fall in an circus animals to take over," I said.

"We're well trained," he remarked.

"I've been meaning to ask you," I said, "Is the Upscale the same as when you worked there? People showing up when they wanted to, or not at all, complete disorganization, managers without a clue . . . "

"Yes and no," he said. "We were always disorganized, that's pretty constant. But we had Stuart, who was an awesome manager, and did a kick-ass job."

"Yeah, I remember him. Stuart's the one who hired me. But he left soon after that."

"Yeah, I heard they screwed him out of six months of overtime pay, so he finally walked. But he was our steady leadership, which made a big difference. Lately it seems even the atmosphere has toned down. Dupont Circle's changed. It's more subdued . . . "

"You're kidding," I said.

"Oh no, I mean, just look at the dress code. You used to get away with a lot worse until one of the owners told the servers they were dressed entirely too flashy for their own good. The tight or see-through shirts and the girls in their short skirts, leather chokers, half-shirts, spiked hair . . . The managers said we were scaring the customers off, and they were probably right."

"So even though it's so calm now, you came back to work there?"

He nodded. "Having only one job just feels kinda slow-paced. There's a lot of time to fill."

This, he could not have been more right about. I could hardly remember what I used to do before the Upscale, even before Italian class. Like the summer before this, my life was again back to work and partying, only this time, it was serious. I assumed I'd be out after work the same way most people assumed they'd show up for work five days a week.

It only made sense to know the bartenders around town so that we didn't have to pay for our drinks. We could arrive fifteen minutes before closing at any bar and can be drunk by last call, all while maintaining day jobs and normal waking lives. It was only natural to get breakfast at a local greasy spoon around 3 a.m. before calling it a night. We woke up at two or three in the afternoon on weekends, and went back to work again. Sunlight wasn't seen very often. We forgot the days of the week as they blended one into another. I didn't have time to watch TV or relax. We were awake so much that "two days ago" seemed like two weeks ago, because we'd been to the moon and back since then.

The same way they looked out for us, our fellow Dupont workers didn't pay for their food when they popped in at the Upscale. And we all lived on Upscale's food. That is, everyone who didn't have Miraz's "German arrangement." A sit-down meal was seen as a luxury, and we were excellent tippers when we were out. We didn't complain when the food was late or cold or not quite what we'd ordered.

Caffeine was a life force. Everyone smoked, except for me. Everyone drank, except for those in AA, whose numbers were steadily growing. Raul had invited Serja to his own AA meeting, and Serja'd had such a good time that he was planning to go back. (Serja got a handful of phone numbers at that first meeting, and wanted to make this a weekly thing for himself and Raul to do so that he could find more people to date.)

We dealt with the politics, with the drugs, with the outsiders—of which most of us were since none of us, or anyone we knew, was actually born in D.C. And we dealt with our steady stream of managers sent to us by our Corporate office.

Corporate was a far off place where everything could easily be done according to some applied rule, but even they got a rude awakening when it came to our establishment. We were their "special" restaurant, the one that had to be handled with kid gloves. Yet we were pulling in enough money that Corporate did its part to supply us with managers, and let the rest of us run the ship.

At the restaurant, I was learning to expect the unexpected, because on any given night the police would be in two or three times, someone would wander in bleeding on the floor at one end of the restaurant while the purse-snatcher was running out the opposite door, a few men in drag would parade through the restaurant, businessmen would skate in on roller blades for cappuccino to go, and the bums would climb the lattice to panhandle on our deck. Upscale usually hired only the weirdest or most open-minded of the people who applied. Our staff currently included flamboyant gay waiters, a few sassy lesbians, alcoholic college students, down-and-out partiers, and a couple of fresh-faced workaholics. I was in that last category because of my day job. And I knew I'd been hired based on my experience and a glowing recommendation from my old manager in Virginia. But the fact that I was hired into Dupont at all made me accepted into the ranks. Everyone was welcome in Dupont Circle, but being a jerk wasn't tolerated. Being imperfect, however, certainly was.

I was working as many hours as I could around my study schedule, but still some of the managers insisted I could do more. They didn't seem to be bugging anyone else, so for weeks at a time I felt like I was about to be cut at any moment. It was a powerful feeling. At first I was afraid to step out of line. But there was only so afraid I could be, and for so long, before that fear turned into apathy. "Go ahead and fire me," was my attitude. "It will save me the trouble of quitting." It was just a job after all.

Our new girl, Laney, was in some financial trouble, so I offered her some of my hours. Our restaurant had done record-breaking sales the week before, and I'd worked four of those shifts. I was exhausted, and felt that was contribution enough on my part. "You're going to burn out and hate this place," I warned her as I agreed to give her two of my shifts.

"I already do," she said. "I'm goddamned sick of the food, the shitty-ass customers, the lazy-ass managers, but I need the money so fuck it. As soon as I get what I need I'm outta here."

Laney was a short, brown-skinned girl with an enormous chest and what she called her "ghetto booty." She had come to us around the time of Katie's birthday. She liked to keep her money in her bra, liked to dish out sass, and had a mouth on her that would make a drunken sailor blush. We loved her immediately.

That night we were short staffed at the restaurant, which was becoming the norm. I had so many tables I could hardly keep up even though I was literally running at times. And since all I had time for was taking orders, delivering food, and then delivering the check, I made very little in tips because people thought they were being ignored. Miraz worked next to me and admitted to having a leisurely night, calling his dad a couple times to discuss his upcoming wedding plans, and taking frequent smoke breaks. He made $160. I made half that.

TWENTY-FOUR

M y tonsils had swollen on and off for most of the summer, and each time I debated seeing a doctor and getting an antibiotic. I was getting tired out of nowhere and wasn't sure if I were just being a bum or if I were legitimately sick and should rest, so I tried to take it easy as much as I could. I even took a day off, at one point staying in bed all day and watching TV as they pulled nine coal miners out of a flooded mine shaft in Pennsylvania.

The weeks dragged on, and I again threw myself into my work. I wasn't one hundred percent, but being sick was getting boring. Something had to give, and I had work to do.

By mid-August my tonsils had swollen beyond toleration, and I finally made an appointment at the Georgetown medical clinic. I had rested as much as I could stand, and was now forcing down liquids and ice cream. I'd taken my recovery as far as I could without help.

"I believe I have tonsillitis, or possibly a sinus infection that is irritating my tonsils," I told the nurse as she took my temperature and checked my blood pressure.

"Temp's a little high, blood pressure's normal," she said.

"That's because I'm not at work."

"Well, we're going to give you a throat swab and see if you don't have strep throat. It's going around."

Twenty minutes later she returned and announced that I didn't have strep throat, and that I could go.

"Right. I know that. Would you please look at my tonsils?"

She conceded, and I waited for her astonishment at finding the two giant orbs hanging at the sides of my throat.

"They look fine to me."

This girl obviously slipped through the nursing school cracks. "The pain in my throat is pretty severe," I said, "And I really don't think my tonsils are supposed to be swollen like this. Usually I can't see them at all when I open my mouth. Please, is there a doctor who could see me? Something's wrong."

"There's no doctor who can see you. She's busy with a patient and has a backlog of others to see. Ms. Ashe, you don't have strep. You can go."

So I went to wait in the check-out line to hand over my ten-dollar co-payment. When it was my turn at the cashier, a nice woman who was probably my grandma's age asked me if everything was alright with my care.

"No," I said. "But thank you for asking." I explained how my swollen tonsils weren't strep throat, so nobody believed I was sick. "Tonsillitis is just pain, really, and I can deal with it because it has to stop sometime."

"I'm sorry about that, Miss," she said. "Two of our doctors are sick with strep throat, so we're down to one doctor to handle the patient load. Half the city has come down with strep, that's the problem."

"I totally get it," I nodded, understanding what it was to be short staffed while the customers just keep coming. But she saw my discomfort as I swallowed, and could see that I wasn't faking it.

She thumbed through the book in front of her. "There are very few scheduled patients tomorrow. That doesn't mean that there won't be a crowd of walk-in patients like today, but today's schedule is full of appointments on top of the walk ins. Tomorrow you might have to wait a bit, but you can probably see the doctor then."

"It's okay," I assured her, beginning to think that by using positive thoughts, I could talk my body into healing itself. "Thank you for your help," I said, making eye contact with her as I thanked her so that she knew I meant it.

I went home and immediately fell asleep. But when I woke up, I realized I hadn't tried medicine yet. There was a twenty-four-hour drug store in the Circle, and I decided to try some over-the-counter medicine. From there, I could walk over to the restaurant where I could get a glass of water and wait for the pills to take effect. Then if I'd bought the wrong medicine, I could always go back for a different one before coming home. I could also ask Upscale's most recent manager for Saturday night off, because once they saw how awful I looked, they'd know I wasn't faking it.

I got to the drug store well after midnight, stunned to find the place full of people. They all stared at me as I entered, in jeans and a ruddy t-shirt, and blue zip hoodie that looked like a ratty bathrobe. I looked at them, and they at me, and we all knew I was the only sick person in the place.

I found the bracket on the wall listing the names of the pharmacists on duty. Only one name: Lopez. To my left behind the half wall of drugs, I saw Ms. Lopez arguing in Spanglish to someone over the phone. How I'd gone my whole life without learning Spanish was beyond me. I was so behind the times.

I was getting dizzy again, so I made my way to the sick people's aisle and sat down to stare at all the choices in front of me. Finally, I picked two different boxes in the hopes that they would cure me, and when I felt safe enough to stand up again, I went to the cashier.

Trying not to sway, I took my place in one of the long lines. To occupy my mind away from my throat and aching body, I studied the people in line around me. Well-dressed guys with red eyes were stumbling around with Cheetos in their hands. Cheetos and Gatorade. Some were talking loudly and laughing at each other. To my left were a number of well-dressed couples, the guys saying cheesy lines to impress the girls, and again, much to my surprise, the lines were working. The girls looked impressed.

Alcohol—I was finally figuring it out. Alcohol brought people to the CVS in the middle of the night. The drunk guys who struck out for the night standing in the left line, buying munchies to help sober them up, and over to my right, the hook-up line where each couple was buying a box of condoms.

Interesting dynamic, I thought. *Somebody ought to write a book about this place. These CVS workers must see it all.*

I paid the cashier when it was finally my turn and stumbled past the security guard and out the automatic door, realizing that I looked just as messed up as all the partiers, only in worse clothing. I made my way over to the restaurant, which was booming.

Everyone said hi, and asked what I had. Some told me not to give it to them, others said they could use a day off and embraced me. Patrick gave me some water, and I squeezed the first batch of pills past my swollen tonsils. He was swamped with customers, so I went over to the manager's office.

Gary let me in and I was glad to sit down. "You look like something the cat dragged in."

"Thanks."

"What do you have?"

"Tonsillitis."

He made a face.

"It hurts," I agreed with his face. "Listen, I'm supposed to work tomorrow at five, but I don't think I'm going to make it. I can hardly stand up. Are you working tomorrow?"

"No. But you'll be alright by tomorrow."

I shook my head. "It's been days of this."

"But you're taking something. You'll be fine by tomorrow."

Why was he arguing with me? I swallowed some more water and winced. *No more water*, I thought.

"Okay, I'll write a note here that you're not feeling well, that you're going to be here unless you call tomorrow."

Call in on a Saturday expecting to talk to the manager? I was delirious, and maybe a little slow-witted, but not born yesterday. I knew what he was up to, but suddenly felt more loyalty to my aching body than to this job, and least of all to this manager who could clearly see I was sick and still wouldn't be troubled to call in a replacement for me. *What an ass*, I thought. And I nodded at him and let him think I would follow along with his stupid plan.

"Thanks, Gary," I said as grateful as if he'd given me Saturday off, and headed back home to my sick chamber and hopefully some rest.

Saturday found me much worse, though I wouldn't have believed that possible. I called the restaurant mid-morning and left a message for Gary that now I was too dizzy to even stand and had taken to crawling around the house on all fours. I was sorry, but there was no way I could wait tables, nor was it a good idea to have me breathing germs in the restaurant. That had to be against a health code.

I went back to bed to lie there and stare at the ceiling. My mom called a while later, just as I was hoping to finally fall asleep.

"Go back to the pharmacy! And this time, don't leave until you've talked with the pharmacist," my mom insisted.

"Okay," I said. "I'll go now." We hung up, I turned off my phone, and rolled back over. I didn't come-to again until Sunday, and remarkably, I felt much better. The swelling in my throat had gone down considerably, and the left side was almost normal.

I got up and managed to get a shower, which made me feel almost new. Since cleaning the disease out of my room would help pull me further into my recovery, I started collecting everything I'd touched in the last few days from off the floor and scraped them into a laundry pile. Midday I found my cell phone lying in a heap of bed sheets and covers that I was about to load into the washing machine. I turned it back on and found four messages. The first was from Dante, wishing me good health and asking me to call. Andy left a similar message. There was a message from Gary, telling me they needed me for last night's shift after all, and that he figured I could work at the cash register and could lean on the counter since I couldn't stand up. He was serious. And finally, a concerned message from Kelly insisting I may be a victim of biological warfare and to call the Health Department. She, too, was serious.

I went back to my room and remade my bed so I could lay down. It seemed I was always running just to fit everything in, but if I stopped running, it would all happen just the same. I felt like my life was about hurrying to put out the little fires, but if I just stood still to battle the big blaze the little fires would stop occurring. There had to be a way to live and feel like I was getting somewhere. And then it was obvious.

"I need to give you my notice," I told Mr. Watters as I sat in his office Monday afternoon.

"Amy, what are you talking about?"

"I like working for you, but I think I need to make a change."

"Why not continue to work here while you figure it out?"

"I thought of that. But I've been trying to figure myself out for a long time." This must have sounded insane. And it was certainly no easy decision for me. I didn't take it lightly. But I'd been searching for months, and asking myself again and again what it was all about for me, how I could feel really alive. "Mr. Watters, I'm not taking big enough steps, not taking enough of a risk. This job is great, but . . . "

"But it's not a career," Mr. Watters pointed out. "If you don't jump out of bed in the morning, excited to get to your day and feel fulfilled in what you do . . . I've known for some time that this is not as creative as you need."

Yes, exactly! I couldn't have put it better. "It's almost become a safety net for me. I think if I'm out there fending for myself without this job to take care of me, things will change in my life."

"Are you financially able to do this?"

"I think so. I've been saving up for a long time. For what, I don't know. But the money's there. My debts are paid; I don't owe anybody anything . . . " I sighed. "I've been working so much for so long, and I think it's time."

Mr. Watters was quiet, but then he said, "Let's find somebody else who can handle Chad," he said. "Of course I don't want you to go. But if you're going to go, let's do it with some style. I'll take you to lunch on your last day." I was going to miss him.

TWENTY-FIVE

"   his is madness!" the new register girl complained. "If the phone would stop ringing for one second I could get through all the customers in my line."

"Here's the cure for that," Patrick said as he walked by. He picked up the phone as if to make a call and then let the receiver slip from his hand. "Oh, oops!" he said, and walked away, leaving the receiver dangling.

The girl's jaw dropped, making her look a lot younger than she probably was. She bent to pick up the phone but I stopped her.

"I think he's serious," I told her. "And I think it's a good idea."

She thought about that for a moment. "Alright with me," she shrugged.

"Amy, come over here," Patrick said as he went back to making drinks.

"What's up?" I asked.

He turned so we were out of earshot from the new girl. "Know why we got that little blue-eyed thing over there?" he asked. "She's from one of the Maryland Upscales. The old register guy was fired."

"They fired Jonesy?"

"Yeah, while you were out sick, he and that asshole from the kitchen, Emery, got into a down and out brawl."

Jessica showed up to get her drinks. "Are you talking about the fight?" she asked. "Amy, you should have seen it! They'd been bitching at each other all night, and then after closing Emery got right up in Jonesy's face, and the next thing we knew, Emery had him in a headlock so he grabbed a Snapple bottle and *slammed* it over Emery's head."

Patrick's turn again, "And that made Emery *really* mad, so he started body slamming Jonesy into the coffee machines. They broke a bunch of shit, the cops were called, and both were fired. I don't think either of them were really hurt. But the next day they sent us Jamie, that mild–mannered little thing over there."

"I don't believe it," I said.

"Believe it," Patrick said. "It was quite a show."

The phone started ringing again, and Patrick reached for the bar extension. "Who the hell put the phone back on the hook?" He picked up the receiver, "Java Junction, what's your dysfunction??"

This would soon be my one and only form of employment.

It took a few weeks, but Mr. Watters finally spread the word that our office was looking for somebody new. It seemed he waited to allow me time to change my mind. I liked him for that, especially since this new idea of mine was making me nervous. But it was time for me to move on. I could feel it.

Chad, conveniently, was scheduled to work from home when the interview process was taking place, and so he was left out of the whole procedure. Not the kind of treatment you give to your Right Hand Man, but then Mr. Watters did things his own way.

"I've decided not to involve Chad because it's not up to him," Mr. Watters said simply. "And I'd like you to find someone who can handle him if necessary. Someone with a backbone and a sense of self. You know, someone who has your qualities," he said. I wasn't sure I had all those qualities, but I wasn't going to correct him. "At the same time," he said, "I'm going to have a talk with Chad to set some things straight just in case they aren't."

We received hundreds of applications, half of which had way too much experience and would probably leave the job after a few months. Of those remaining, I had to throw most away because their cover letters had misspellings and other errors. This was an editing position. From the remaining applications, I decided on a mere ten to call back.

I filled the following week with interviews, setting up the most promising applicant for Friday. I was new to conducting interviews, so I figured this way I'd have something to look forward to if the week started out depressing. But I'd done well; by Friday afternoon I was hoping the final interview would go badly so that at least I could cross somebody out of contention. And that's when Ms. Price walked in.

"Amy? I don't believe it! Are you interviewing me?"

"Haley? Oh my gosh! You look great!" I jumped up and gave her a big hug. She traded in her blue miniskirt and pigtails for a gray suit and had cut her hair, but she was the same girl who talked her way in to free admission one bizarre night at a gay strip club.

I put my top four applications on Mr. Watters' desk, and handed him Haley's application.

"This is the one," I said. "You can call all five for follow-up interviews, but she's the one you want. She's qualified, energetic, just graduated with a Bachelor's in English, and she put herself through college."

"Really?" he looked up. Mr. Watters liked self-made people.

"And she's got the right personality," I said. "I worked with her, waiting tables in Virginia. She'll like this job, and she'll be able to handle Chad."

He smiled. "In that case," he said, "Call *two* of the others. Any two. Set up interviews for me next week, just so I can compare. And I'll call . . . " he read the application in my hand, "Ms. Price, is it? I'll call her myself."

It's not what you know, it's who you know. And Haley was as good as hired.

At the restaurant that night, I was still smiling to myself about it when I saw Raul slip out the door. It was strange that he went out in such a hurry, without even saying hello to me, so I set down the salt and pepper shakers and started to go after him.

"Amy, we need to talk," New Manager Jim stopped me. "Now."

Thinking it was about the length of my tiny skirt, I reluctantly followed. Once inside the office, Jim said, "I need you to cover extra tables tonight."

"What's going on?" I asked.

"Raul's no longer with us. I'll explain it to everybody later, when the whole staff gets here. Right now, I need you to cover his section until Laney gets here to help you."

About two hours later when all the servers finally showed up we had a meeting where Jim told us Raul had been fired for changing his credit card tips. "It's serious, guys," Jim said as we gathered around him in the kitchen. "Altering anything on a credit card is a federal offense. Raul's lucky no charges were pressed. He only lost his job."

I couldn't believe it—not that Raul had changed some credit card tips but that he'd been fired. It was obvious to me that a handful of servers were changing their credit card tips, but why Raul was fired and no one else, I didn't know. Of everyone, Raul worked the hardest. And I didn't doubt that he deserved more than the tips he was given. He was the only one willing to haul ass with me, the one I could count on to really work when we got busy. Now I'd have to do it all alone. I loved my fellow servers, but sometimes they were slackers. Especially some of the new people.

But Raul wasn't being greedy. Since he'd lost his computer job he was on the verge of losing his house. To me, that was a good enough reason. I also knew it was a felony. I wondered what that said about me, because if I had been the manager, Raul would still have a job, someway . . . Somehow.

Jim said, "If there are others among you doing the same thing, this is a good time to turn over a new leaf." Everybody looked stone-faced.

I was always honest about my tips, for good or ill, so I wasn't worried about myself. I was relieved, at least, that the others would have to be honest for a little while. Soon it would blow over and they'd start doing it again, but for tonight we'd all walk out with earned money at the end of the shift. For tonight, the playing field would be level.

As the night progressed, there was a lot of complaining going on. Suddenly, customers were rude, demanding, and tipped ten per cent regardless of how hard the server was working for them. Money was just the half of it. The frustrating part was that the customers ran you all night, and then you mentally beat yourself up when they left you a lousy tip for it.

That night as we finished up, Jim told us that customers and people, by their nature, don't notice things. We had all gathered in the office to count our money as he told his story.

"I worked for years at a country club, and in that atmosphere, the clientele had money to burn. But separating them from it for a job well done was next to impossible. Then one day my manager told me something that changed my life, something I never forgot." We stopped counting money hearing this, and gave him our quiet attention. Any piece of inspirational genius that would help us understand our zoo of a restaurant was welcome sentiment.

Jim said, "What she told me I'll never forget. What she said is this: People do not see the things going on around them. People see usually about three feet in front of their faces only, and that's it. You want them to notice that you're busy, that you're trying hard, that you're remembering all the special things they asked for, but they don't . . . " He paused here for effect. "And there's nothing wrong with them, because they are the norm. *They* are normal. *You* are not."

Everyone began discussing at once this new-found information. To further prove the validity of what he was saying, Jim said, "Do you normally walk into a restaurant and sit down at a dirty table? No, you wouldn't. But people do it. You need to lead them by the hand; they won't think on their own." He repeated, "*They* are normal, you are not."

But this was no tidbit of genius if you asked me. In fact, it was downright depressing. Were people really this blind? Experience would say yes, but I couldn't believe the human condition was such that we just didn't notice things anymore, didn't pay attention to the details. Were we that busy in life that we just needed to get in, get it done, and get out? I walked around all weekend wondering if what he said could be true, and what the implications of its truth would mean for me.

It was also strange teaching someone all that I'd been doing for the last three years and watching her pick it up easily and even improve upon my methods. Whenever I'd show Haley anything, she'd say, "Why don't we just do it like this?" And I'd have to say, "Oh, yeah, that *would* work better, wouldn't it?" And I'd wonder why I hadn't seen her way sooner. Despite my slight jealousy, I remembered the way Chad refused to give up control when I'd first started, and how useless that had made me feel, so I tried to hold back and let Haley do things her way. She had great ideas and fresh energy, and was going to be a real find for Mr. Watters. I wondered if I'd become too complacent all this time.

Chad, for his part, was trying to be friends with Haley. It was amazing how nice he could be when his job was on the line. He was cordial, chuckled at all the right times when she described for him the new book she was reading, and he even invited her to a kickboxing class.

"It's a great workout, isn't it?" she asked. "I do it in conjunction with karate to keep up my fitness level."

"Oh, you do karate?" Chad asked. "I was thinking of taking a class, but how different is it, really, from the cardio workouts I've been doing? I mean, I know the kicks and punches."

"There's a little more to it," Haley said. "You should try it. My class meets three times a week, and we're always glad to have new faces. Some of the white belts can get a little rowdy, but they calm down once they understand the teachings."

"Maybe I'll come out, show everyone what years of kickboxing have done for me," Chad said. "What color belt are you?" he asked, not masking his condescension too well.

"I'm a brown belt," Haley said.

Chad looked pale.

CHAPTER
TWENTY-SIX

W alking to the Upscale on the weekend, I noticed that the trees had started changing color. I only noticed because I was scanning the rooftops for a masked person with a gun. Feeling reasonably secure that anyone attempting a sniper attack in Dupont Circle would have a hell of a time getting away in traffic, I convinced myself I was safe. As safe as anyone was in Dupont Circle, anyway.

But this was the first time I'd looked up in a while. Some of the buildings around me I'd never even seen before. It reminded me of what Manager Jim had talked about with his "They are normal, you are not" speech, though I was still hoping to prove him wrong.

I could agree that sometimes it took a really awful occurrence to make us wake up and take note of our surroundings. But I still didn't think it was *human nature* to only see what was immediately around us. That was more of a programmed reaction, a protection against all the hoards of people in this town and their problems and our stupid logic-defying solutions. To think that it was normal to focus only on ourselves and our own climb up the success ladder, that we didn't look out for each other anymore or notice when our waitress has done a good job, that left no hope of making a decent living in a restaurant. As my days as Watters and Co. wound down, I needed to believe that I could make it on my Upscale shifts alone. I had to believe that my customers weren't entirely self-centered.

Despite having steady management—Jim had been with us for just over two weeks now—the weekend at the Upscale was a complete disaster. One lousy thing happened after another, and it all conspired to make me miserable. At one point, a new girl exploded a container of whipped cream, the contents of which went on my entire section of tables and all over me. Covered in the stuff and looking like an idiot, I had to sop up the mess from off of my customers' tabletops, purses, and other belongings, and I had to have their dinners remade since they'd all been ruined. All the work I'd done for the last hour was in vain. Everyone was upset enough at the stickiness that I knew they would take it out on my tip, even though I wasn't to blame. Worst of all, the girl who did it laughed her ass off when it happened, which added too much insult to the injury. When my shift finally ended, I walked over to Tumult to wait for Dante to get out.

He finished about twenty minutes later, and made about eighty dollars in tip outs from the servers. I made sixty, I was exhausted, and my feet were killing me. Dante had sat in a chair, checked ID's, and got to read a book. And to top it all off, Tumult did a "shift drink" for the employees, so he got a free beer when his shift ended, not that he hadn't been drinking before that. He really lucked out with his job. I was seriously starting to question why I waited tables.

When Dante finished his drink, we walked to the Circle to catch a cab. I was too tired to walk back to the house. But when we got to the Circle, we saw a man running through the traffic.

"It's three in the morning, and there's still traffic," I said.

"There's always traffic," Dante reminded.

We watched the running man as he jumped onto and around cars, and one car even nipped him before it came to a stop. Chasing him were three other people who nearly caught him as he separated himself from the bumper of the car. He took off again, amid the honking and the light change and headed straight into the park in the Circle's center. His pursuers followed, two men and two women, this time catching him, and knocking him down. The men grabbed him, punching his face and head. He fell again, and his attackers kicked him in the stomach and head. Dante and I stood frozen with others on the street, seeing this unfold as if it were a beating scene on TV.

The two women, dressed in their party clothes with hair and make-up done, watched. The men finished and went back to their women and the four of them started to walk away. The man on the ground didn't get up. Suddenly we were running, Dante and myself, and a slew of other people from all directions, toward the guy on the ground. We crossed the street and could see swarms of people coming from seemingly all over to help. The closest man approached rapidly, talking on his cell phone. "I've got the police on the line!" he yelled. "They're a block from here. They're on their way!"

One of the women chasing the hurt man was still standing nearby as we approached. She was like nothing I'd ever seen. Dressed up, shiny hair in place, she had no remorse for the damage her boyfriend had done to this man on the ground. She walked away cold and unaffected, as if her boyfriend had just emerged from making a phone call. Good Samaritans were approaching as the man's attackers walked away.

"Are you alright?" people were asking. The man was moving. "What hurts?"

"Help is on the way."

"Stay still. Can you feel your toes? Can you wiggle them for me?" One of the Samaritans was a nurse. The rest of us gave her space to take charge. The man responded to questions about what hurt, and he could wiggle his toes. Once the police and the ambulance showed up, Dante and I left, knowing we weren't going to be of any help.

"I'm going home," I told Dante. "Alone." I was miserable, angry, and frustrated, and I knew he'd just try to comfort me. "What's wrong with people lately?" I asked quietly. "And with life in general? Does everything have to be so fucking disturbing?"

"It's okay. Shit happens," he said. "You're sure you want to be alone?"

"Yeah, I'll see you tomorrow." I flagged down a cab and got inside. When the cab stopped at a stoplight a block from the Circle, I heard shouting coming from the van next to us. My nerves were pretty shot at this point and I was sure something was about to explode. Then I saw that they were just part of the loud party crowd. I was quickly annoyed, but the cabbie laughed.

"Sounds like they had a good night."

I didn't care. But I told myself to stop being a jerk just because I'd had a bad night. It could have been a lot worse. I could be lying on the ground in Dupont Circle. "You sound happy," I managed to say to the cabbie. "Are you having a good night?"

"Who, me? I am happy."

"How is that?"

"Well, I drive my car, pick people up when I feel like it, drive around this city, make enough to pay my bills . . . I'm a right happy fellow."

I never knew happiness could be so simple. I was always looking for the next hundred-dollar mark in my savings account, the next "A" on an Italian test. My life had become a series of mile markers, one after the other, with no real time for enjoyment. We stopped in front of my house and I paid the cab driver, giving him a hefty tip.

A few days later, I was stationed to work on the patio, but the sniper had managed to escape capture and was still shooting people, now on a daily basis. Needless to say, the patio was practically empty. Inside, the restaurant was booming. To keep myself occupied, I took out my Italian flash cards and tried to memorize a new verb tense. I'd just about gotten the hang of it when the flower man came in.

He smiled at me and said, "Do you want to send one to a certain someone down the street?"

I nodded. Dante and I had been sending a single flower to each other for a couple weeks. It didn't mean anything, really. But it was fun, and Moab, the flower guy, loved embarrassing us. The last time, he'd interrupted me while I was taking a table's order and very ceremoniously delivered a flower from someone who "very much admires" me. My table thought it was from a stranger, so they spent their meal trying to figure out what customer did it.

It was payback time for Dante. Plus I felt bad for the solitary mood I'd been in lately. Moab and I agreed to a price and he went off toward Tumult to deliver it.

"That's so sweet!" Kelly gushed as we sat down to dinner after class. "So are you two in love yet?"

"No," I laughed. "We spend time together, but it's not really serious. It's hard to explain."

"Not Mr. Right, but Mr. Right Now?" she asked, checking the pockets of her book bag.

"Not quite that casual," I said. "He's a sweetheart. But we're taking things slowly, which is weird for restaurant people. What are you looking for?"

"This," she handed me a colorful brochure.

"Cute little bungalows," I said. "Where is this?"

"Rome," she said. "They rent these places out, but some people keep them for a year, unless I misunderstood what the lady was telling me. That's why it has that 'neighborhood' look to it. That's where I'm spending my vacation."

"Awesome!" I said. "So it's official, you're booked and everything?"

"Yep," she said triumphantly.

"Listen, I know this is crazy, but, if you want to come with me . . . I know you've got your whole work schedule and everything, but you're leaving your day job anyway." She changed her tone slightly, "The only thing is, you'd probably have to quit your restaurant job, too, unless they'd give you two weeks off at the last minute."

"It would be awesome to go to Italy," I said. "But the restaurant's never going to give me that kind of time. It'll be weird enough having only one job. I'm putting myself on the line by giving up my steady day job. I don't know that I'm ready for complete unemployment."

"I figured as much," she said. "But I had to ask. You can keep the brochure, though, just in case."

"Thanks. It looks awesome. You're going to have a blast."

"I can't wait," she said. "Listen, I've been thinking to invite Andy, too. Same thing, no pressure, but just extend the invitation. What do you think?"

"Definitely! I don't know if he can get away from work, but he'd love to be invited. I think it would mean a lot to him."

"Really? Good," she said.

After dinner we stopped in to the Upscale so I could pick up my paycheck, and we stopped to have a drink at the bar. The girl on the barstool beside us was talking away to the guy beside her when she abruptly stopped. "Oh my God," she whispered.

Judging by her serious tone, I hazarded a glance to see what she was looking at. Our mouthy and wonderful server, Laney, had approached the bar to pick up her drink orders, and had a black eye, scratches and claw marks on her neck, a bruise in the shape of a large hand around her bicep, and numerous red marks all over. She didn't look good.

"Patrick, what the fuck?" she said. "Where's my Jack and Coke?"

"What are you talking about?" Patrick asked.

"It's right fucking here on the ticket," she pointed out. "I'll come back."

When she left I called Patrick over. "What happened to Laney?" I asked.

"Oh, I have no idea," he said. "Rumor has it she was mugged. But she's not in good spirits, so I haven't asked her for details."

"She doesn't look so good," Kelly said.

"I don't think she should be working," I said.

"That girl is lucky to be alive," said the girl beside me. "I'm in my last semester of Forensic Science. That girl has marks on her like we see on cadavers." She was slurring her speech somewhat, so I wasn't sure if she were just trying to be dramatic or not. "Those aren't bruises that people walk away with."

"That girl's my friend," I defended. "I think they just lost her drink order so I'm not going over there right now, but before I leave here I'm going to make sure she's alright."

"How are you going to do that?" the girl asked. "It's not like you can just walk up and ask. I mean, how do you *ask* something like that?"

"Directly, how else?" I asked. "We serve in this zoo together, side by side. She'll talk to me. She'll talk to me because I asked." We hid pain from our customers, not each other. Every table could look right through us, but to each other we were solid.

When I approached Laney, she assured me she was all right. She had been mugged, on her way home from work the night before. Her boyfriend had found her outside. "I was near the house," she told me. "I was walking alone—I know, I shouldn't do that. But I was. Steve ran out to get me when he heard me screaming. There were two guys, and Steve chased them off and carried me into the house."

"Laney, I'm so sorry," I said. "Are you sure you're alright?"

"I'm fine. I'm too stubborn to die. They gave me some good meds at the hospital, which is the only way I'm able to work today. This morning I felt pretty shitty, but now I'm feeling pretty good."

"There were two guys?"

"Yeah, they called to me, like they didn't know me. Like they just wanted a handout or something, so I turned and one of them jumped me. Then the second one jumped out from the bushes, there are bushes lining the street where I live. I just started kicking and screaming and punching as hard as I could. Steve heard me and ran out. He described one of the guys, and his description of him is what I remember, too."

"Did you fill out a police report?"

"Yeah, eventually. Steve brought me home and let me black out. And when I came to," she swallowed hard, "I thought I was still being attacked, so I woke up kicking and screaming. I flipped out on him until I really gained consciousness, and then I recognized him and stopped. And he was like, 'Do you want to go to the hospital?' and I said yes because I was having trouble breathing, like one of my ribs was broken or something. But he thought the hospital would blame him for doing this to me, so we argued for a while about whether to go or not. I really just couldn't breathe and I was starting to freak out over it, so finally he drove me to the hospital. And they had me file a police report."

"My God, Laney, do you realize what could have happened to you? I'm glad you're okay," I said, and hugged her carefully.

"Thank you, Amy. It's really nice to hear," she said, and she hugged me back.

I wasn't sure how okay Laney was. But the hospital released her, and she told me she'd take a cab home from now on.

When I got home, I found Dante sitting on my front steps. "What are you doing? Sleeping?" I asked, seeing how he'd snapped his head up.

"Hi," he said. "I was out making my rounds," at the bars, he meant, "And thought you might be back from your class."

"I'm just getting back now. Kelly and I had dinner. And then we stopped at Upscale and you wouldn't believe what happened to Laney. She says she was mugged, and she's pretty beat up."

"Is she alright?"

"She said so. But those weren't the kind of marks you allow to pass out. She said her boyfriend found her, ran off the two attackers, and then brought her inside so she could pass out. But you just don't argue about going to the hospital over something like that. Why the hesitation? It doesn't make any sense."

"She's in bad shape?" he asked, and I realized how out-of-it he was.

"How much did you drink tonight?" I asked. When he shrugged, I said, "Listen, I'm beat. I've got to go to bed," I helped him up. "You're welcome to stay. I don't think you should drive anywhere."

In the middle of the night, I heard the front door open and close. I bolted awake, fearing that someone was in the house. I woke Dante and the two of us crept out to the landing to listen. We could hear keys jingling, meaning that it was Gerry, or someone who had Gerry's keys. A few seconds later we heard a small crash as the person tripped over something. "Damn!" we heard, and I recognized Gerry's voice.

"It's just Gerry," I told Dante, and we went back to bed. I woke up later, to see Dante standing in the doorway of my room. "What are you doing?" I asked.

"Gerry came in," he said.

"I know," I said, rolling over. "Why are you standing at the door?"

"Because Gerry came in, to your room."

"Okay," I said, but after a few seconds, I woke up a little more. "Did you say Gerry came into my room?"

"Yes."

"That doesn't make any sense. Why would Gerry come in my room?" I rolled back to face him again.

"You tell me."

"I don't know," I closed my eyes. Dante wasn't making any sense. "I'll think about it tomorrow."

The next day, Dante clarified his story. He said he woke up when Gerry stumbled in the front door, just like I had. But after realizing it was just Gerry, he hadn't fallen back to sleep right away. "After a little while, I heard the handle on your bedroom door turn," Dante said, "and the door opened a bit, and I could see Gerry's head poking in. Then suddenly he stepped in to the room. He was only wearing boxers, and he was staring at the bed, and then he left. A few seconds later he returned, opened the door again, and pushed his cell phone through the opening."

"His cell phone?" I asked. This was unreal.

"Yes, his cell phone. He held it out, like he was trying to shine the green light around to get a better view. He stepped into your room again, and this time I couldn't stand much more, so I said, 'Something I can help you with?' and Gerry closed his hand over the cell phone to hide the light and he left the room and closed the door."

"I just, I can't . . . Are you sure you weren't dreaming? Or still drunk?" I asked.

"No, Amy. I slept for a couple hours, and then I woke up and couldn't get back to sleep. So I got up for some water, and a few minutes after that, this happened. I gotta tell ya, I'm really unnerved at this point. I mean, does Gerry do this all the time? Do you two have something going on that you're not telling me about? And I'm trying to convince myself that he just wanted to talk, but the psycho behavior doesn't quite fit."

"This is really disturbing," I said.

"You're telling me!" he said. "So I got up to stand at the door where Gerry was," Dante stood on the spot, just inside my doorway, "I wanted to see from his vantage point, and from here, I could see you clearly."

"Could you see that I was wearing a t-shirt?" I asked, wondering if Gerry had thought he'd seen something he hadn't.

"Yeah. I could see pretty clearly. And that's when you asked me what I was doing."

"I didn't hear or see anything," I said, not sure what to believe. "I only remember Gerry coming home late, and we figured out it was him in the entryway. How he got in my part of the house I don't know. Why he was in my room shining a light around, I have no idea. I just don't know what to think at this point."

"I don't know either," Dante said.

"Well, I want you to know, this is not welcomed behavior as far as I'm concerned. I don't have anything going on with that jerk, and I'm just as shocked and sickened by the whole event as you are."

"I believe you," he said. "I just don't know where this puts us."

I was floored. I didn't know how to defend my character to Dante any better than simply denying any involvement. But the fact that I was in this defensive position at all was ridiculous. And the fact that Gerry was in my portion of the house . . .

Gerry was nowhere to be found that morning, not that I really went looking. The first chance I got, which was a harrowing few days later, I drove all the way down into Arlington to buy door wedges at Home Depot. Hopefully these would bar Gerry from entering my room if he were stupid enough to try it again. I wanted to buy something more sturdy, but I was hesitant to drill into the wood doorframe to put in a lock being that it wasn't my house.

Home Depot was really close to Beau and Peter's place, so I stopped in to see how they were doing and stayed for a home cooked dinner. I didn't mention Gerry. Beau and Peter's place was a safe haven, a place where I could put Gerry out of my mind.

TWENTY-SEVEN

When I got back to the house that night, I switched on Francesca's TV, and the news coverage came up immediately. The sniper had claimed another victim, and the story was on all the channels. I watched in horror as they gave the details and showed the Home Depot that was, indeed, right by Beau and Peter's house. The one I'd been to earlier that day for door wedges.

"Well, I haven't been to Home Depot in months," I lied to my mom when she called. I mentally went over my Home Depot visit for anything that seemed out of place. "I'm safe."

"Yeah, but for how long?" she said. "Okay, I mean, you have to live your life. You can't just stop because of this madman . . . Can you believe this?" she asked. "Look at that, they've blocked all the roads."

"I see it. Looks like everyone has to clear through a police checkpoint. It's all backed up. It'll be hours before anyone gets home. The guy's probably long gone anyway. That poor woman."

"They said she survived breast cancer, or something."

We hung up and I paced around the room a little, trying to avoid the windows just in case. Finally I sat down on the bed, frozen. It was sinking in that we just weren't safe anywhere. At any moment, anything could happen. And really, it was astonishing that I'd survived this long. The odds were completely against it. I thought about all the dangers I must encounter in a single day, things that could take life away in an instant. Yet here I was, alive and breathing, and sitting on my bed, unwilling to move a muscle out of fear that it would all come crashing down.

I woke up in the morning stiff from the strange position I'd slept in. My door wedges were still in place, but I knew they wouldn't protect me forever. It was my own safety at stake and I had to stop being lax about it. I crept around in the house as I got ready for work, checking every room expecting to find Gerry hiding and ready to spring. I found no one, but I did find his school ID near the couch.

I'd heard somewhere that tenants have more rights than landlords. And technically, I wasn't the landlord, anyway. At least I hadn't signed anything. What I needed was a lawyer to tell me what I could do. Good thing I was in a town full of lawyers. As soon as I got to the office, I made a phone call.

"Andy! I'm glad you're in your office. I need some legal advice . . . "

Once Andy made sure I was alright and said a few choice words about Gerry, he gave me the grim news. "Sweetie, you cannot change the locks on his place. And you really can't make him leave, either. He's on the lease. Breaking those things can take months. You're better off letting Francesca and Paolo deal with it when they return."

"That won't be until Thanksgiving! Andy, I can't live like this. He broke the law by breaking in, didn't he? I mean, that was wrong, wasn't it?"

"Yes, but you can fill out a police report and it's still going to take a few months. That's how the system works. The best thing I can tell you is to change the locks on your part of the house only. That's really all you can do. Maybe they can get you in today. If not, it might take a couple days. You're welcome to stay with me for however long it takes."

"Well, I was going to ask Dante to stay, but he's not too happy with me at the moment. I really don't think I should be in the house anyway. But what if something happens and I'm not there?"

"Count your blessings. I'm sure Francesca and Paolo would rather have you alive than not. And the chances of something happening to the house are slim."

"Andy, I keep really odd hours."

"Honey, I don't care. But you're not staying in the house alone. Come and stay with me. I insist, really."

After that, I called a few locksmiths, none of which could give me an appointment to change my locks until Friday. I made an appointment anyway.

"Is everything alright?" Haley asked.

I sighed. "It will be. I don't want to think about it. Let's go get some coffee and I'll walk you through the newsletters."

That night at the Upscale there was a river of sewage backing up from a drain in the kitchen floor. Cute little Jamie was trying in vain to mop it up.

"Why are we even open?" I asked. "This has to be against some health regulation."

"Close the restaurant?" Laney asked, feigning astonishment. "Why the fuck would they do that? Especially since it's behind the counter where the customers can't see to complain about it."

Once the restaurant got busy, the servers had to rush in and out of that area, ultimately stepping in it. We carried it on our pant legs and on our shoes for the remainder of the shift. Jamie's mopping did no good; it just overflowed again. Manager Jim had sent Patrick home early to avoid paying him overtime. Jamie was on her own behind the counter to take care of the bakery, bar, and sewage.

"Miss, I need another iced tea," one woman kept telling me every time I passed her table. She'd already had six of them.

"Right away," I told her, and had to fit the trek to the iced tea machine into my mental list. In a rush, I stepped in the sewage without thinking, and was horrified at my clumsiness. I still had to go back out on the floor to deliver food and drinks, smiling as if my toes weren't curling inside my shoes. Somehow no one seemed to notice the smell or the spots on the calves of my pants. No matter how many times I washed my hands with sanitizer, it did nothing to make my feet feel any cleaner. Finally, the end of the shift came. The people eventually left, the lights came up, and we were busy cleaning and putting everything away. As I cleaned up the dessert counter I heard a frustrated sigh from behind me.

Jamie was calling her boyfriend to pick her up, but he wasn't answering his cell phone. "I've called the house phone, too, but no one ever picks that up really. Maybe I should just take a cab home. But it's thirty dollars—that's what it cost last time."

"You took a thirty-dollar cab ride?" I asked, thinking she'd been had.

"Yeah, I live out in Hyattsville."

"Oh, yeah, I guess that makes sense," I said.

"Last time Upscale paid for it because I was supposed to get out in time to take the Metro home. They did it to me again tonight, kept me here longer than I was scheduled, but Jim says he's not paying for a cab. I've been calling my boyfriend's cell phone, but I just get the voicemail. I don't understand it."

I'd put off a hot shower this long, what was a little longer? I did the math in my head. Half an hour to Hyattsville, half an hour back . . . Andy told me to show up whenever I wanted. I'm sure that didn't mean 3 a.m., but Jamie needed a way home. "Listen, I'll take you home," I said. I needed to pack a bag anyway, and I'd rather not do that alone.

Jamie debated. "Well, think about it," I said. "We'll be done cleaning up here in the next half hour, so if you don't get through to your boyfriend, the offer stands. Okay?"

"Ooh, where are we going?" Serja asked.

"Maryland," I said. "To take Jamie home. Wanna come?"

"Absolutely!"

We invited Laney and now we were four.

But just before we left, Laney backed out. She said she needed to get home to see if Steve had moved out or not. "We have to be out by the end of the day tomorrow, but I think Steve might be gone when I get back there. It's this whole fucked up situation with the landlady," she said. I raised my eyebrows at her so she explained, "I needed to bail my brother out of jail," she said, "So I used the rent money for that. But I made all that money back when I worked all those extra shifts, so we would have been fine if I hadn't been attacked."

In my experience, there were those who sought drama, whose lives didn't provide enough fodder so they wound up crazed over the lives of their friends or families. And then there were those select few who were sought out by Drama itself. Laney was one of these. Since she'd first joined our staff, Laney had been through one awful ordeal after another, first with her brother, then with her boyfriend, then the brutal mugging, and now this.

"So the ER wouldn't release me until I paid part of the bill, so Steve had to leave me there and go back to the house to get the rent money we had stashed. So I set it up with my landlady that I could get her the money, just a little bit late, and she agreed to an extension, which was fine because I should have been able to cash my paycheck. And it should be a good check because of all those extra shifts I worked. But Jim wouldn't give it to me, the fucker, and now I'm up a shit creek."

"He wouldn't give you your paycheck? Why not?"

"How the hell should I know? He's an ass, that's why. He said he was too busy when I came for it and wouldn't unlock the office so I could get it."

"I got my check just fine," I said. "A couple of others were here then, too, and he gave them theirs."

"Yeah," she said. "I don't know what Jim's deal was, but I couldn't have my check. So I had to go back and tell the landlady and she wouldn't let us stay any longer without the check, so . . . " she took a breath, "We have to be out."

"If it's a matter of money, Laney, I can help you out. The others will be willing to chip in, too, and you can hand cash to your landlady. Money's better than a check anyway . . . "

Serja overheard us talking and handed Laney his apron. "You can have all this. I don't want it."

"Thanks, guys, but I don't want your money," Laney said. "I got my check now, and I can pay the rent. But the landlady doesn't care; it's too late. I promised her the check by last night and couldn't make good on that, and she wants us out."

I didn't ask, but I was wondering where Steve's part of the rent was. The guy must have had a job, but where was his money? I was hoping Laney wasn't paying for everything, especially since there had been some stories circulating—actually by Laney—that Steve was sleeping with another girl, an ex-girlfriend of his.

Laney went on, "So Steve's supposed to move out today and move into his mother's place a few blocks away. I wrote him a long note before I came to work. I basically begged the jerk not to leave but to wait for me. But to go home and see that his things are gone," she said with sudden tears in her eyes, "It wouldn't feel like home anymore." She composed herself, toughening up right in front of Serja and me, back to the Laney we were all accustomed to. "I wanted to put off going home that much longer, so your road trip sounded like a good idea. But now I just think I need to go home and see if the bastard's moved out yet. I need to face it."

There were things missing from her story, things she held back. If they had to be out the next day anyway, what would it matter if he were already gone or not? And if Steve had gone to his mother's as planned, why would that be hard for her to face? It was getting late after a long shift, and I assumed she wasn't talking in straight lines because it hurt her to think about the truth. I also figured I wasn't listening in straight lines—my brain was downshifting into sleep mode and nothing was getting in or out very clearly.

She bailed on us, for her strange reason, and I didn't try to change her mind. Nobody should live with a feeling of dread for too long.

So our road trip was down to three. We went to my house so I could pack a bag and change clothes. I put my sewer clothes, shoes and all, into a plastic bag and tied it shut.

When I came back down to the kitchen a moment later, I found Serja and Jamie whispering because they didn't know if psycho Gerry were home or not. They asked me questions about "that" night, so I took them up to my room reenacted Gerry's bizarre actions based on what Dante had said.

Serja dismissed it. "It sounds strange," he said, "but Gerry was drunk and probably wanted to talk."

But Jamie had the same sickening feeling that I did that Gerry was up to much worse that night. "Had Dante not been here to startle him, who's to say what would have happened? Who's to say what he had in mind?"

"You're both crazy," Serja said, and for a moment I almost went with his logic. But I shook my head.

"He isn't supposed to have the keys to get in here," I pointed out. "As a female, you need to be protective of yourself. It's a sense you grow up with, unless you want to get hurt. You look out for yourself." Jamie was nodding as I said this. "In a way, I feel like I've been given a warning already, and that there might not be another. I have to listen to those things." I picked up my overnight bag. "Okay, I've got work clothes for both jobs . . . I think I've got everything. Let's get out of here."

We closed up the house and got on our way. We got out of D.C. and into Hyattsville with no problems, as it was the middle of the night and there was actually little traffic. "Okay, this is the start of Hyattsville. Jamie, where's your house?"

"Well . . . " she said. Turns out, she didn't know. This was her boyfriend's mother's house we were looking for. She and her boyfriend had taken the semester off from school to live with his mom for some reason. She'd only lived in the house a couple of weeks.

We got to East-West highway, and I wanted to turn left, based on Jamie's description of the neighborhood, but Jamie thought she lived to the right, so we went right. After a few miles, nothing seemed familiar to her, so we turned around. Serja was complaining from the backseat the whole time that he shouldn't have drunk two coffees while we did our side work. I stopped at a gas station, but Serja refused to get out of the car.

"I'm not going to the bathroom at a gas station," he said. "Besides, we could get shot just being here. The sniper just shot a kid the other day, and he's been targeting gas stations."

"We're gonna have to use *the force*, you guys," I said. "Because we don't have any directions and my Maryland maps only have the state highways."

"Let's head back the way we came," Serja said.

"I'm so sorry, guys," Jamie said.

"Why?" I asked. "We don't have anything else going on. How about you, Serja?" I said to the rearview mirror.

"No plans to speak of. Oh, how depressing," came the answer from the back seat.

We backtracked, made some U-turns, and scanned neighborhood after neighborhood as Jamie complained that her boyfriend wasn't very thoughtful.

"I'm fat," Serja complained out of nowhere.

"You are not," Jamie said.

"You are almost drug-addict thin," I said.

"Really?" he brightened. "You think so?"

We assured him and he calmed down. Then he checked his cell phone messages to give him something to do. "My ex-boyfriend called me!" he said, sounding excited. Then he quieted for a moment to listen to the message. "Ugh! He wants me back. That just pisses me off." He tossed the phone onto the seat beside him.

"Oh, this looks like it!" Jamie said suddenly. "Turn at this next road."

We made a few more turns and found her house. She hopped out and Serja got in the front seat. Jamie waved us on, but we wanted to wait until she was inside the house. She knocked on the door and waited, then knocked again after a minute with no response. "Everyone's probably asleep," Serja said.

"Shouldn't her boyfriend be awake?" I asked. "He was supposed to pick her up tonight. Is he even home?"

"Maryland looks spooky," he said. "I don't think we should leave Jamie here." This was Serja's first trip to Maryland. But the door to the house finally opened and Jamie's boyfriend let her in.

"I can't believe this guy left Jamie stranded in the city. So what if she could get a cab, it's 3 a.m.!" I said. "What a jerk." I wondered what Jamie was thinking, dating this guy.

"He looks pretty built," Serja said. That summed it up.

"Speaking of jerk boyfriends," Serja said, "I think Laney's 'mugging' was really her boyfriend Steve beating her up." He said it very matter-of-factly.

The bottom dropped out of my stomach. And I thought, *What if this is life? What if, while I'm waiting for life to begin, it's already started? What if this is it?*

"You really think Steve did it?" I asked. "How can you be so calm about it?"

"Well, she's getting out of there, or at least *he* is. She said he'd be moving out tonight. But I think the way she describes things and leaves the details out, it just sounds like he did it. But I think she'll be fine now—now that he's gone."

We drove back to D.C., neither of us saying much. I got to Andy's pretty late, but he opened the door for me and didn't complain. He showed me to the bathroom, so I could take a shower. And he'd made up the couch for himself, insisting I was staying in his room. It was the best night's sleep I'd had in a long time.

The next day, Andy was stuck in a late meeting, so I went to Francesca's by myself to check the mail and pick up a few things. Of course I ran into Gerry. I'd hoped to avoid him a little longer—like forever—but here he was and I couldn't walk away and say nothing. As expected, he said he drank so much that night that he didn't remember coming into my room. So I filled him in, calmly using words like "disturbing," "psychotic," and "sickening." Gerry said nothing as I presented my case. "Where did you even get a key?" I asked.

"Francesca must have left it lying around, how should I know?" he dismissed. "Well, don't worry," he said. "I won't do it again."

"I know you won't," I said. "Because under no circumstances are you welcome in my section of the house. I don't care if you're on fire and the only water is in my area. You burn, sorry. In the meantime, pack your things. You're no longer welcome in the apartment, either."

"You're kidding!" he laughed.

"You have until the end of the week to get out. I don't think what you did was very legal, seeing as how you shouldn't be in my part of the house. And I have a witness."

"Renters have a lot more rights, and you don't have much of a case."

"Well," I said, "I'm sure I can find your girlfriend's number if I need to. I'm sure she'd like to hear what kind of person she's dating."

Gerry glared at me, and I met his eyes and didn't look away. "You have until the end of the week. Start packing."

Gerry turned his back on me and went in, slamming the door.

I was pretty much screwed once Francesca and Paolo came back. I'd been unable to reach them in Italy, but I knew they'd be looking for Gerry's rent when they returned. I could pay it myself, and would probably have to. Gerry was pissed, and capable of doing just about anything. Yeah, I was in trouble. But I wasn't going to change my mind. I'd finally said what I meant.

TWENTY-EIGHT

I threw away my tennis shoes and went to Georgetown for a new pair. The new shoes I got were cute and expensive, but had no real support in them, so I was going to have to run out to Target to find little footpads. The Target parking lot was usually crammed, and could make a regular trip take up to three hours. Half an hour to find a space, fifteen minutes to find what you're looking for, an hour and a half standing in line at the register, and another forty-five minutes or so waiting to get out of the parking lot. Dante lived on the way there, so I called him to see if he wanted to waste time with me. There was dinner in it for him.

"Sounds good," he said. "Where are you now?" he asked.

"I'm in Georgetown. Oh, wait, shit . . . "

"What?" he asked.

With a large open field next to the Route 1 Target, I didn't want to go there any time soon with the sniper still on the loose.

"No problem," he said. "The Franconia Mall has a Target, and a parking garage. We'll be perfectly safe. It'll be a hell of a lot quicker than Route 1 anyway."

I picked him up and we got down to Franconia in record time. "What if the sniper's down here today?" I asked, pulling into the parking garage.

"He won't see us in the garage," Dante assured me.

"But he already shot somebody who was in a covered parking area."

"That was at night," Dante said. "But the sun's out now. He can't see us because he'll be out where it's light looking into the dark garage."

"What if he's parked in here with us?" I asked, parking the car.

"He wouldn't be. He can't get away so easily from here, he'd be trapped."

"I'm glad you've thought this through," I said, and gritted my teeth until we were safely in the mall.

"Are you really this scared?" Dante asked.

"I don't know," I said. "Sometimes I am, and other times I'm just mad about it. I got a frantic call from my mom after the last shooting. It's stuff like that: that my mom has to call, panic-stricken, from three hundred miles away because some asshole is lurking around here with a gun. Sometimes I'm scared stiff, but other times, and lately, I'm just pissed off."

We did some shopping and tried to decide on a place to eat. "Anything's good with me," Dante said.

"How about pizza? We could go to that little place on P Street again."

"Sounds good," he agreed.

A while later we arrived at the restaurant where smiling, friendly servers greeted us as we walked in. I couldn't remember the last time I had smiled while at work. The hostess approached and promised to clean the table by the window for us if we waited.

Table by the window? Nice. A server came up to us while we were waiting and tried to seat us at another table, and Dante was agreeable to it. "But we're waiting for that table over there," I pointed out. "By the window."

"Oh, sure thing," the server told us, eyeing what the hostess was doing. "Looks like it'll just be a minute until it's ready," he said.

Dante flashed me a look of embarrassment. "We just became those people I hate," he said.

"Get over yourself," I rolled my eyes. The fact was, it was my money and my night off and since I'd come by both the hard way I wanted to spend both my way. And really, when I thought about it, I could have given my money and my night to any restaurant in D.C., and I chose this one, really *chose* it, on purpose for their thin-crust pizza. And since I didn't have a night off for another few days, I needed this night to make my whole week. They owed it to me.

I was sure that some of the people who came in to Upscale just came for the hell of it to have someplace to hang out. But there were probably just as many, or more, who came to our restaurant looking to spend their money on a good experience because in this town, they needed it. I promised myself I'd do better by them.

During dinner, Dante announced that he just wanted us to be friends. The whole Gerry situation wasn't sitting right with him. I was tired of thinking about it, so I'll let Dante back off.

"I'm really starting to fall for you, Amy," he said, "And I don't want us to stop spending time together, but . . . I'm not sure what I'm saying. I believe what you said about Gerry, and I don't want things to change, but . . . I don't know. You're leaving your job, not sure what you're going to do next . . . What if you decide you want to leave D.C. altogether? I mean, what's keeping you here? And I'm just not ready for a relationship. I thought I was, but after this and worrying about you, it's just a lot."

"It's okay," I said. "If I were you, I wouldn't know what to think either." I didn't tell him about my conversation with Gerry. Dante sounded as overwhelmed by me as I felt about my own situation, and I didn't want to add any more twists to his state of mind. Besides that, I had the impression that he'd be upset to know I confronted Gerry alone. And, I suppose, he was right. I had no idea what was coming next for me.

What I wanted was to rise above all the bullshit in life, to get beyond it to a place of happiness, of free time, of feeling complete. And every time I thought I was nearly there, something would trip me up.

Sometimes I just felt hollow, a shell with an echoing drip, drip sound inside, and always, there was the wanting, the clawing desire for something I'd never seen nor heard, but lack of definition didn't stop the want. To chase down this shapeless thing, I was sinking further and further into my beaten path with every step, a caged animal dreaming of freedom, dreaming of the world.

But maybe all the freedom one needed was to sit at the open doorway of the cage and look out to a view absent of iron bars. Maybe freedom didn't have to mean seeing the world, but rather seeing one's own smaller version clear of obstruction.

Over the next two weeks, two more people were shot and killed by the Beltway Sniper. Gerry moved out of the apartment—I told Dante Francesca made that happen—and the locksmith had come through so I could stay there again. In the meantime, I wasn't sleeping much in order to get in my studying for the upcoming Italian final.

And then one day in Richmond, police had surrounded a white van in broad daylight. As we watched the broadcast from Chad's office, Beau and Haley and I held our breath for the final word. When they announced it was a false alarm, our hearts sank. Beau went back to his office, and Haley and I went back to the payroll.

"I was really hoping it was over," Haley admitted.

"I was trying not to get too excited," I said, "just in case. But now . . . " I felt the dam had been about to burst—which in this case would have been a good thing. We were so ready to have relief, but there wasn't any. And a madman was still out there. "I was really counting on that being it today; it being over." Hours later the news channels said the van had been full of illegal immigrants, so, they reported, the effort had not been a total loss. But no one I knew cared.

By the time the Italian final was over, Kelly and I heard the news that they'd caught the sniper. It was a more subdued broadcast this time, and we knew no one wanted to put us through another false alarm. But the news turned out to be true: a man and a minor were arrested, and we were once again free to roam the streets in relative safety.

The day after the arrests was my last day at Watters and Company. Mr. Watters took me to lunch at the Willard Room and reminded me I could change my mind about leaving.

"But Haley's great," I pointed out.

"Yes," he agreed. "She's a bright girl with a great future. But if you want your job back, all you have to do is say the word." It was really nice to hear. And again he brought up, "What are you going to do instead?"

"Well, my class just ended," I said, "And I've got to decide what class to take next." I explained, "Once you get past Italian II, you get the choice of taking Italian III, literature, or writing. Or maybe I'll just do my own writing for a while."

"I'm a big fan of the school of life," he said. "A lot of people don't know that about me because my job is here. If I could do what I do anywhere in the world, do you think I'd still be living in this swamp?" Mr. Watters never laughed at his own jokes, but he did smile a lot. "There's a lot to be learned out there, and you don't have to sit in a classroom to do it, and you don't have to stay in one place, either. But whatever you do, I wish you luck." He smiled. "You'll do well, Amy, I know it."

After lunch I packed up the last of my things from my desk and took the small box to my car. When I returned, Haley and Chad surprised me with a farewell cake, more Haley's idea than Chad's I knew, but we turned it into a party. And Mr. Watters, who'd been out "running an errand" while I went to my car, returned and handed me a gift: Stephen King's book, "*On Writing*."

"I thought it would come in handy," he said. "My wife is crazy about this book."

"Thank you," I stammered. "Really, thank you! I don't know what to say."

"You don't have to say anything," he said. "Put it in your arsenal. Maybe you'll need it."

When we'd finished our cake, everyone lined up at the door to say goodbye. I hugged Haley and handed her my office keys. Chad was next in line. I'd pictured saying goodbye to Chad a thousand times in the last two years, and never did the daydream involve embracing him. But I was not the same person I used to be. I hugged him. And then I hugged Mr. Watters.

"Thank you again for the book, and for everything," I said. "Are you going to be okay?"

"No, I'm not," Mr. Watters complained rather loudly, and I felt tears welling up in my eyes. He was like family to me, and I would forever miss him.

But I willed my emotions to stay down, and managed to barely say, "Thank you for believing in me."

"Amy," he said, looking at me squarely, "I wouldn't let you go if I didn't."

I thanked everybody again, and, book in hand, made my brave exit. I got about three feet before I started to cry.

But I kept walking, head held high, so that, if they were watching me from the door, they wouldn't notice. I had no clear plan for my life to cling to at this moment. A plan might have made leaving easier. All I knew was that I had to go, I felt it, and I really didn't know why. When I got to my car, I let myself really fall apart. When I remembered that there were cameras in the parking garage, I straightened up, started my car, and drove out onto the streets of Washington, thankful to take my chances with the evening traffic. I'd have to stop crying and pay attention if I wanted to get to Dupont Circle in one piece.

When I arrived at the Upscale, in one piece, I found the place short-staffed. Again. Serja and I were working the entire upper floor together, including the deck, upstairs bar tables, and the Perimeter, while Laney and Jessica split the main level.

Suddenly Serja and I heard a commotion on the main floor. Laney was throwing a fit about some food that was made wrong, and the fit hit had hit the shan.

"Welcome to D.C.! Southern service with Northern hospitality," I heard her shout.

Most of her section, that is, half of the main floor, wanted to speak to the manager. So Laney did the only thing she really knew how to do: she yelled some more.

Serja and I stopped running long enough to look over the railing to survey the scene. Laney was in the middle of her section, staring down a table of college kids. "You want your mother-fucking shit? I'll get you your mother-fucking shit."

"She's gone crazy," I said in monotone.

Serja shrugged. "She was crazy before."

The college kids seemed impressed with her language. She left them and went over to the bar. "Patrick? I need a chocolate *fucking* milkshake for that last order."

"One chocolate fucking milkshake coming up," was the answer from the bar.

"Why the hell didn't you give it to me in the first place?"

"Don't start, Laney," Patrick warned. "I made the damn thing—one of the To Go fuckers took it."

"Mother fuckers!" Laney complained, and looked around for the culprit. She got the drink and walked it back over to the college table. Her other customers moved out of her way as she passed. Her entire section seemed to be scared of her. Some people were just putting money on their tables and leaving. So Laney scooped up the money.

So Manager Jim, who was helping out on the register, decided to lecture Laney. It turned into a screaming battle in the middle of the restaurant. By now, Serja and I were going to have to really run to catch up. Besides that, we were getting bored with the scene. Seeing it drag on seemed to take the humor out of it. We looked at each other and shrugged, and went back to our customers.

I had a table of men out on the deck who were waving me over to them. "Is everything alright?" I asked.

"We're wondering something," one of the men said in a low voice. "Is this a gay neighborhood?"

"You're not from around here, are you?" I asked, and smiled. "Welcome to the gay capital of the nation."

"Well, is there a bar we could go to after this, a non-gay bar?" the second man said, in a near-whisper.

"Um, well, you can always go over to Tumult," I said. "They have a lot of pool tables and games and things there. Good music, two bars, usually a nice crowd in there. I'd say."

"Are there gay people in there?" the first man asked. "Because we're here on business, and we don't want anyone to think . . . "

"You're serious? Listen, when I said you were in the gay capital of the nation, what I meant was people accept each other here. Gay or straight, just be yourself. That's the way of life here. It's really nice when you think about it." The men looked at me like I'd grown a second head, which prompted me to say, "Everyone will know you're not gay. It's pretty obvious."

The men looked relieved. "We're not like these people."

Look around you. You are *these people,* I protested in my head.

"Amy, I saw your men looking over at me," Serja observed in a playful voice back at the wait station.

Serja had better perception than that. "They're freaks," I said.

"No way."

"If you must, then," I said, hoping it wouldn't get ugly. "But I thought you didn't like the businessman-type."

"What?" he asked, looking around. "Honey, I don't want to hit on your tourists. They're way too hostile. I'm talking about *that* table over *there*."

"Oh!" I breathed, finally getting a clue. "Yeah, go for it."

Serja and I made decent money for the night, considering that we got mostly out-of-towners. The regulars who tipped well were all sitting downstairs where they had front row seats for the Laney-Manager Jim feud. For a while, it seemed Manager Jim was winning because he fired Laney. But when she pointed out how short-staffed we were and that she was scheduled the next seven straight nights, Jim wavered.

An hour into cleanup that night, Jim and Laney were still grumbling. Instead of setting himself to the task of finding a replacement for her, or even calling other Upscales for a temporary and less volatile replacement for her, Jim finally settled on writing her up and letting her keep her job, much to the detriment of her future customers. Not that any of us cared that much, mind you; we liked having Laney around. But it would have been nice if the two of them had stopped arguing and helped with cleanup.

The weekend passed, and Monday was my first day to sleep in without needing to be at the office. It was a different sort of day. I was free to do whatever I wanted, but I kept panicking that I was supposed to be at the office. I don't know how many times I'd check the clock in a panic before suddenly realizing I didn't work at the office anymore. For two days this happened over and over again, and the panic was never less intense. Tuesday night I met up with Andy for the Drag Race, and told him of these new mental lapses.

"This is the first time I've gotten a full night's sleep in a really long time, and it's messing with me," I said. "Really, I don't think I'm supposed to get this much sleep."

"You do sound a little crazy," Andy agreed. "But it should wear off."

"I don't know. Last night at the Upscale I actually looked around and couldn't believe I'd opted to keep that job. What a zoo."

"Hey, at least you escaped Chad."

"Yeah," I said. "I got out without turning into him. Years from now, he'll probably die in that office, still under the impression that he owns the place."

Andy and I left Starbucks, drinks in hand, and headed back out into the rain to watch the race.

I'd heard about D.C.'s Annual High Heel Drag Queen Race, but this was the first Halloween I'd attended. The police had blocked off a Dupont street and men from everywhere in high heels and dresses were getting ready to run the race. Thousands of cheering spectators showed up to stand in the cold rain.

"Too bad Kelly's missing this," I said.

"She would have hated this rain," he said. "Hell, I hate this rain. I'll bet it's warm and sunny in Italy right now."

"I think their weather's a lot like ours, which means it's cold, at least. But your way sounds better. Let's pretend it's warm."

"Done," he said. "You should have gone with her, you know."

"I know," I said, and sipped at my hot chocolate.

"Yeah, well, I'm just as bad," Andy said. "She asked me to go, too," he admitted.

"We're idiots," I said.

"Yeah we are. I told her I already used up all my vacation days this year."

"You can get more vacation days, especially to do some traveling. This is D.C."

He shrugged, warming his hands on his coffee cup. "She's there for two weeks; I've got time to change my mind." Just then we heard someone on a loudspeaker at the far end of the street. "Looks like the race is about to start," Andy said. "We've got to get closer."

The crowd pressed forward, and Andy and I went with it. We could hear cheering toward the starting line, to our left, and the noise traveled closer and closer toward us until finally we saw the runners. Men in ball gowns and heels sprinted past as if they were in tennis shoes and jogging pants. Following them were dozens of costumed men, prancing by, waving and blowing kisses as they passed. One man wore a wooden lattice with roses growing from it over his evening gown. Another was dressed as Princess Diana and had an entourage of bodyguards walking with him. Many others were wearing sexy cop costumes, and some men were hardly dressed at all.

"There's always a group that shows off recent surgeries," Andy told me.

A few runners actually sprinted the whole race, taking it very seriously. Most, however, used the event to show off their costumes like in a fashion show. There was a lot of pomp and fanfare, and a lot of cheering. It was difficult to find a good place to stand, usually when Andy and I found a good location, others crowded around us and we were on our tiptoes again. The race itself lasted only minutes, but contestants continued parading in the street for most of the night.

Finally, the wet weather got the better of us, and we decided on dinner. "So what are you going to be for Halloween?" Andy asked me as we were seated in a warm, dry booth.

"I don't know," I said, peeling myself out of my wet coat. "Maybe a lobbyist," I teased him. "I can just wear a suit."

"In that case," he said, "I'll be a waitress."

"You'd look good in a skirt," I said.

"Why thank you. I just hope the weather clears up. This cold rain sucks."

"I heard the rain's supposed to stop, but it's going to get colder."

"Marvelous," Andy said in monotone. "'Hey everyone, you don't have to worry about being sniped anymore, but don't rule out freezing to death.'"

"At least we can all dress up and not have to look over our shoulder . . . "

"Yeah, but who has time to get a costume? Halloween's two days away."

Our waiter came by and we ordered drinks. "I'll be right back with that," he said.

Andy opened his menu. "I'm starving."

"Me, too. And dinner's on me tonight."

"Sweetheart, no," he protested.

"Yes, you helped me out with Gerry, and I want to say thank you for letting me stay with you. That was just awesome of you. At the time, I didn't realize just how unsafe I felt there. But now I have a completely different feeling being in the house. I can't imagine if I hadn't gone to stay with you."

"Let's not think about that. I'm happy to help. And I'm glad he's gone."

"Yeah. I kinda threatened to tell his girlfriend what he'd been up to if he didn't leave."

"I was wondering how you got him out," he said. "You're unbelievable. So did you tell Francesca and Paolo yet?"

I shook my head. "We've been playing phone tag. I'm going to call them when I get back tonight, which should be morning where they are."

"Think they're going to freak out?"

"I don't see why not. On the one hand, they're better off without someone like Gerry living there. On the other, they're out his rent money until they find a new tenant. I hope they're not too disappointed, but I can always pay them his part of the rent since I'm the one who kicked him out. So there went my Italy money, not to mention the restaurant would never let me have all that time off. I'm lucky I could switch to get tonight off."

Our waiter returned and we ordered dinner. We toasted to Gerry's departure and to Kelly's vacation. "May the world find out the real Gerry, and may Kelly find the man of her dreams in Italy," Andy said.

"Here, here," I chimed in, and we drank.

"Speaking of men, how's your love life?"

I laughed. "Dante thinks he loves me, but we're not dating anymore."

"Good! We can compare. Something similar just happened to me . . . "

When I got home from dinner, I called Francesca again. This time I got through. And I got a different reaction than I expected.

"What matters is that you are safe," she said.

"What about the money?" I asked, taking the line I expected her to say.

"Please! I don't care about the rent money and Paolo won't either. Amy, I am so sorry that you had to deal with this situation! Paolo has another week or more here to do, but I will come home right away. Let me get a flight and I will call you back." Amazing.

The next day the rain stopped, and I walked to the Upscale, dodging puddles as I went. When I walked in, the first thing I heard was from Laney. "No one tipped out the dishwasher last night, the assholes, so the floor didn't get mopped. Now Jim says we have to mop the damn thing ourselves from now on."

"I don't believe this," I complained. "Who the hell worked last night? Is it really that expensive to give five dollars to the mop fund?"

"Don't look at *me*," Laney said. "I gave Larry my money. That man busts his ass every night. He's a hell of a lot better than that bastard they had before him. I paid him. It's these new servers they keep hiring. They suck."

"We'll get this corrected," I vowed, and I went off toward my first table of the night, gritting my teeth. I introduced myself to the table of college girls and they said hi and asked the standard *how are you?* But instead of lying and saying my usual, "Alright," I stopped and looked at them.

"Man, you know, I'm really pissed off right now." And somehow, they were interested. So I told them about the cheap jerks I was working with and about their inability to wrench a couple dollars from their take for Larry.

"You're kidding!" the first girl said. "I worked in a restaurant all summer and it was mandatory to tip out. And our dishwasher wasn't even doing our floors."

"Well, I have no restaurant experience," the second girl said, "But when we came in here I looked around and thought about how cool everyone seemed. I guess they're not so cool after all.

The three of us talked about it, and restaurants in general, for quite a while before we got back to what they wanted to eat for dinner. Turned out they weren't ready yet anyway, so I needed to come back. But by now, I knew them enough to like them, and them me.

As the night progressed, it became more and more interesting. The electricity kept cutting out, which messed up the computer system. We were down to writing orders by hand, which wasn't so bad, really. The bad part was that we had to figure out which orders the kitchen had received and which it hadn't, and the bar, and the dessert counter.

Two guys got into a fight in the upstairs bar and one had his wallet stolen off the table during the scuffle. I let him sit in my section while he waited for the police to come. An hour later, someone stole our newspaper rack and went running out the east door, so the police, who'd come in for iced tea, ran out after him. At the same time, someone walked out the west door not only without paying their check, but they took money from another table on their way out. That's when Dante wandered in to snag lattes for Tumult and to alert us that the purse-snatcher was back in the area.

"Two of our guys were following him around, but he was on to them and slipped out. Anyway, he might be showing up here soon. How's your night going?"

"Ah, the usual," I said.

He looked around, nodding. "Yeah. Sometimes I miss this place," he said.

Dante went back to work, and I went to my next table. "Hi, I'm sorry for your wait, but this place is in chaos."

"We waited a long time," the man of the table said.

"And there was no place to sit," his wife informed me. "We had to stand outside."

I nodded. "That's because a fight broke out an hour ago upstairs, and a couple chairs got broken. So they took the extra chairs from the bar and hauled them upstairs for the tables." They started looking around themselves.

"Really?" their teenage girls asked.

I nodded. "And the electricity keeps cutting out, so we're writing orders by hand. It takes an extra minute for me to write legibly for the cooks, so bear with me. I'm used to my scribble, but they're not. If you look to your left, you'll see the guy who got beat up—and also had his wallet stolen during the process," I said with the back of my hand to my mouth as if to whisper. "He's sitting with a bike messenger who played chicken with a car and lost. Over here to your right, you'll see our fearless leader trying desperately to fix the computer system, though he doesn't know what he's doing. That's management for ya. Well, that's just the beginning of our tour here this evening. I'm sure you'll notice many more things along the way. I'm Amy, I'll be your tour guide. Can I start you off with something to drink?"

In the past, I would tell them a little about me so they'd think of me as a person and not just a waitress when paying their check. Sometimes that worked, but I'd get bored talking about myself to table after table.

Then I thought, if I did a good enough job with each table, they'd oblige when paying their check. But even the best service didn't warrant tipping. It always seemed The Upscale was like an unequipped stage, and we were trying our best to entertain the audience without them noticing the stage was falling apart. Today I gave up the act. After all, insanity was our selling point.

Once I dropped the professionalism and admitted how screwed up our workplace was, the customers found themselves suddenly on the inside track. And they liked it. And I found that I liked them. Less of "The Show Must Go On," and more of "On With the Show." Customers actually thanked me for opening their eyes to the weird things around them. They'd gone out for a good time and found our drama suited them perfectly. The madness was a show, and one they tipped well for. It was like I'd reached into that thin layer of fog that separates our two worlds, mine that has to notice all the details and theirs that is able to shut them out, and we saw eye-to-eye.

And then, one by one, all my cool tables paid their checks and left, and I suddenly had a section full of high-maintenance people. Everyone needed so many things to make them happy, and even when I brought everything, they weren't satisfied. I was trying to like them, but they were making it impossible for me.

Then the two girls from the beginning of my shift showed up again for a cup of coffee. It was really nice to see some familiar faces.

"We wanted to see how you're doing," one said.

"We couldn't stay away," the other remarked.

"I'm glad you're back," I said. "Everything was going fine for a while, but I've got a few tables now that are just nasty. Some people think you can actually be an idiot and work this job. It's amazing. But I'll get some coffee for you, and you can sit back and enjoy the show."

Patrick and Jamie were both swamped, so I got the coffee myself. The machine went nuts, spraying hot coffee on the counter and the floor. I jumped back, getting out of the way almost in time, and turned the machine off. It coughed out a cloud of steam before it gave up.

"I'll clean that up," Laney said behind me. "The damn thing just did it to me, but I was able to fill some water pitchers with coffee. They're sitting over there,"

"Thanks," I said, pouring two cups. "You don't have to clean that up. Don't you have customers now?"

"Yeah, but fuck 'em. Everyone's asking for the moon and I only have two hands. So I'll take five and do this, and when I get back there, they'll appreciate me or I'll kick their sorry asses out of here."

"Think that'll work?"

"What the hell do I care?" was her answer.

I laughed and headed back to the girls. "Here we are ladies. Sorry for the delay. Don't ask."

"So how are you doing?" they asked.

"I'm alright. This place is a zoo, but it's been like this for months. Every hour is something different, but I've just been rolling with the punches. I'm pretty good at it, really. But, I'll tell you I've got half a mind to just walk out the door."

"So what's stopping you?"

"I don't know. I guess money?"

"There are other jobs out there," one of the girls pointed out. "Unless you're in dire straights."

"No, I'm not. Actually, I'm doing pretty well. But . . . "

"You're coworkers would be mad?"

I laughed. "No. They'd completely understand," I assured them. "But I can't leave you two high and dry. As for the rest of these people . . . " I looked around at my section.

"Don't stay on our account," one said. "We don't mind."

"The door's open," the other pointed out.

I looked over and saw one of our new servers using a brick to prop open the door. I braced myself for the cool night air to hit me. But the breeze that blew in felt warm and the air smelled sweet. That breeze didn't belong here. It was out of place, out of season. And suddenly everything changed. Upscale's heavy glass door, illuminated by the Exit sign and some outside coppery-colored lights, stood wide open. It was my turn to have my eyes opened, and by my customers no less. I could either jump at this opportunity, or stay still and always wonder why I let it pass me by.

"So it is," I said, setting down my tray. "Thanks, ladies."

"Good luck!" they called after me, but I knew I wouldn't need it.

TWENTY-NINE

I leaned against the fountain in the center of the circle and stared up at the hazy rust-orange sky, thinking I could make out some stars. I was waiting to regret leaving the restaurant, but so far so good. My life was my own, one big, blank page waiting for me to fill it up.

In fact, everything was beginning to make sense to me. Francesca would be back on Friday, and I would be done babysitting the house. I had no job to worry about, some money in savings, and I still had time to meet up with Kelly in Italy. Maybe I'd even to stay an extra week. For travel, things wouldn't line up better than this.

Francesca had offered to let me rent the apartment, and I had been prepared to decline the offer, but . . .

"There you are," Dante said as he approached. "Sorry it took so long. A brawl broke out just as I was supposed to get my break. I had to wait 'til my shift ended to get out of there."

"So you're done? Or do you have to go back?" I asked.

"Done," he said. "Are you cold?."

"Not really," I said. "I was so overheated from running around the restaurant; I only put my coat on a little bit ago. It's dry right here if you want to sit down."

"You shouldn't be out here with an apron full of money," he said, sitting beside me.

"I'm sitting in the park, with people all around, lights everywhere . . . " I defended. "If something's going to happen, it's going to happen. Anyway, most of the thieves are prowling around the Upscale tonight."

He looked up at the sky. "Want to tell me about it?" he asked.

"Eh," I shrugged. "I worked too much. I stayed busy and I didn't have to think about what was next for me. Today I found the readiness—finally—to leave it all behind. The thing is," I said, "the door's been open for me all along. I've been feeling like a caged animal, but I put myself there. And I could take myself back out. She was right the whole time: I had the key."

"I don't follow," he said.

"Sorry, Francesca's thesis. I know you don't know what I'm talking about, but it makes sense in my head . . . The key was *trust*. I saw that open door and I felt a pull, and I trusted it. I'm right about this. I know exactly what I have to do—I think I've always known. I just didn't trust it. I was standing in my own way."

"Amy!" called a familiar voice. We looked up and saw T.J. trotting toward us. "I thought you'd be here," he said. "So you *have* walked. Hey, Dante."

"T.J., I've been gone for a while," I said. "Don't tell me Upscale's just figuring this out."

"It's a madhouse, are you kidding? Anyway, Laney said she saw you walk out the door. So we looked around and, sure enough, you're not there . . . "

"Nope, I'm here."

"You're alright?" T.J. asked.

"I'm amazingly alright," I said.

"Well, I'm gonna get back there. Jim's working your section now. It's quite the show, I don't want to miss out. I take it you're not coming?"

I stood up and hugged T.J. "Nope," I said.

"Good for you," he said as he embraced me. "I'll let the servers know."

"Here, will you take this back there for me?" I untied my apron which was full of money and receipts and held it out to him.

"No problem," he smiled at me, and took it with him.

Dante and I watched him cross out of the circle and out of sight. "All this time," I said, "I thought I had to have it all figured out. But, life can change on a whim, and you have to be able to change with it. I do that. I thought I had to have all the answers," I looked at him, "But the answers themselves change."

At that moment, we were distracted by people cheering and a car honking and watched as a convertible drove around the circle with a carload of helium balloons. It did a victory lap around the full circle and turned south down Connecticut. Dante smiled. "Man, I love this place," he said. "What a trip."

I couldn't agree with him more. Once the initial culture shock wore off, Dupont Circle's energy and excitement felt like home. I was welcome here, despite having arrived with no direction, hiding out as a workaholic. In Dupont, nobody judged you. They just asked the same of you in return. I was allowed to figure out my life for myself. It was the last place to expect to find peace, and yet the perfect place to find it.

"I'd been thinking about getting out of D.C.," I said, sitting down beside him. "Away from the Circle . . . But I don't think I'll fit in anywhere else the way I do here. I'll be looking for traits of the Circle everywhere, and won't find them . . . This place has given me exactly what I needed. And I should be here to get it right . . . "

"You might stay in town, then?" He sat back to relax against the fountain, and looked at me with a slight smile on his face.

"Looks that way," I smiled. "I need to write this, and see if I can get others to see the Circle through my eyes. That's exactly what I have to do: Explain it. Explain how crazy it is, and how it's really not crazy."

"I told you!" he said, triumphant. "I told you to write this."

"I know you did. I just didn't know what the story was until now." I looked him in the eye, so he would know I meant it, and I said, "I'm about to do the thing that scares me the most. Putting my heart out there and believing in it, not just for a grade in college, but really putting it out there . . . will be the truest thing I've ever done. I'm staring down my own truth. It's frightening." And then I smiled and closed my eyes. "And liberating."

"This," he said, "Is what you know."

We were quiet for a few moments, and I tried to let it all sink in, but my mind was racing. I looked toward the north side of the Circle. "Too bad Kramer's is closed. I could use a kick-ass notebook or a journal or something. I need to get these initial thoughts down."

"Hard to believe anything closes anymore," Dante said as he checked his cell phone for the time. "I have a buddy who works there. Come on, I bet he's still there."

We stood up and he put his arm around me as we headed out of the Circle toward Kramerbooks.

"We'll get you a notebook," he said. "Sorry, a 'kick-ass' notebook."

As we walked, he turned us around and waved his free arm, displaying Dupont Circle to me. "You can write this all down," he said. We surveyed it all, walking backwards for a step or two, and then spun north again.

"Think anybody will believe it?" I asked.

"All of us? In his insane place?" he shrugged. "Call it fiction."

"Fiction, you say?"